SPLENDID

ISOLATION

A Mystery Suspense Novel

Lucinda O'Neill

Splendid Isolation

Lucinda O'Neill

v. 1.2

ISBN 979-8-218-18117-8

For Dean

Prologue

I thought I'd miss the ocean when Andy and I moved to California. I'd grown up in a suburb just north of Boston and spent my childhood summers at one Massachusetts beach or another—Nahant, Crane, Good Harbor. In the arid country east of Sacramento, where Andy and I bought our first house, where spring was a burst of green on dun-colored hillsides at the beginning of April and by June the leaves were brown and rattling on the trees, I pined for the blue Atlantic, the fog banks and moisture-laden breezes, the humid summer days spent splashing in saltwater followed by the slow ride home on dappled back roads, happy and relaxed.

But that was before I discovered that the Central Valley of California has its own ocean—the grasslands that flow down the center of the state between the Sierra Nevadas to the east and the coastal range to the west. In our first months of living there, Andy and I would take our bikes out on the county roads south of Folsom and ride through oceans of prairie grass that shimmered from silver to gold and every shade in-between. The whispering of the grass in the early evening breezes was calming in a way the restless Atlantic wasn't, and I suppose I grew to love it just as much, maybe even more.

So I told myself it was fitting that was where Andy died, alone in his car in the early hours of a Saturday morning in June for no reason that anyone could say. If Andy had to die, at least he'd died in a place that was beautiful, a place we both loved.

But I was wrong. Because Andy was thirty-four years old, too young to die anywhere. Not even in the most beautiful place in the world.

Part I:

The Widow's Checklist

Chapter 1

A shutter banging in a windstorm. That's the last thing I heard before I opened my eyes. But there were no shutters on the house, and this wasn't New England, not anymore. A wind was rare in the desert east of Sacramento in summer. We often prayed for the relief of a delta breeze.

The blue digits of the bedside clock swam into focus. Two forty-seven. Claws pricked my arm through the thin cotton blanket—our Siamese, Juju, going on high alert. I reached past him to the other side of the bed. Empty.

"Andy?" I called.

Bang, bang, bang. A soft growl issued from Juju's throat. My husband hadn't come home last night and now, an hour before dawn, someone was at the front door. Maybe he lost his car keys, I told myself as I groped for my robe, slipped on a pair of flip-flops. Maybe he took a taxi home. The bedroom air was icy. The June day preceding the night had reached 113, the central air sending out a steady blast.

I crossed the hallway to the front door, my flip-flops slapping against the cold tiles. It was an act of faith to switch on the porch light. Brightness filled the window panels on either side of the door.

But it wasn't Andy standing there, looking exhausted and apologetic. It was two men in uniform. A badge glinted on desert khaki. I wondered if it was too late to crawl back into my dream of New England, the innocence of sleep. But I'm a practical person who believes in meeting the worst head on, so I opened the door to face them.

The older officer took off his hat. "Mrs. Stevenson? Mrs. Andrew Stevenson?"

The two California Highway Patrol officers sat across from me in the living room, high-crowned hats in hand, elbows on knees, their eyes shifting away from me with every word they spoke. Shortly after one o'clock that morning, on a routine patrol, a fellow officer had spotted Andy's Honda Accord parked thirty feet off the road. In long prairie grass on a lonely stretch of Route 16 east of Sacramento.

"The patrolman found your husband sitting behind the wheel with his seat belt on," the younger officer said, his blue eyes kind under his buzz cut. "His body appeared uninjured, but he was . . . unresponsive."

"Evidence collected at the scene so far is inconclusive," the older officer said.

I wrapped my robe more tightly around me, but my shivering wouldn't stop. "That's wrong," I said, my voice barely a whisper. "There must be some mistake." My teeth began to chatter.

"Ma'am?"

"I don't understand. What was he doing on a back road at one in the morning? He would have taken the freeway."

The grandfather clock, an antique from Andy's family, ticked faintly in the hallway. I'm not cooperating, I thought, I'm being difficult.

The younger officer spoke again. "We're very sorry, ma'am. We understand what a shock this is for you."

"Are you sure it's Andrew?"

"You know of no reason your husband would have been on Route 16 at that hour?" his partner asked.

"No. None."

They both waited.

"He was coming home from a client dinner. He would have taken the freeway." My stubbornness sounded pathetic under the circumstances.

The older officer leaned closer, too close, the Queen Anne chair he was sitting in—another Stevenson family antique— creaking under his weight. "When was the last time you spoke to your husband?"

"Last night around seven. He was just leaving the office."

"How did he seem to you?"

"Fine," I said. Fine at seven, dead four hours later. "What happened?"

A glance exchanged. I saw how uncomfortable they were with the whole conversation, and how tired they looked too. The older officer informed me that because Andy's death was unattended, there would be a complete investigation into the circumstances. He said an investigator would be contacting me soon, probably later that morning.

Morning, I thought. The morning of the day Andy died. My chest constricted under a crushing weight. "Can I see him?"

The younger officer nodded, looking happy that at last there was something positive to say. "Yes, of course you can." Then, after a heartbeat of hesitation, "As soon as the coroner completes his examination. It should only take a day or two. The coroner's office will call you when they're ready to release the body."

The body. Andy's body.

"But . . . I don't understand. Don't they need me to identify . . . him?" *The body.*

The Queen Anne chair creaked again. "That won't be necessary, ma'am," the older officer said. "The patrolman on the scene was able to get a positive ID using your husband's driver's license photo."

I sat on the sofa saying nothing, as if I hadn't even loved him, while inside me another woman ran screaming down empty corridors, flinging herself at concrete walls, desperate to get out of the reality she was suddenly trapped in.

"Ma'am? Mrs. Stevenson?"

I came back to the living room of our house in El Dorado Hills, our house with its four-thousand-dollar-a-month mortgage that we'd bought less than a year ago, trading up from our beloved bungalow in nearby Folsom. Our bow to conformity, the affluence you embrace when your husband is a rising attorney in a prestigious downtown firm. What did any of it matter now?

Something grazed my calf, a friendly pressure. Juju, the cat, gazed up at me, his intelligent eyes asking a question. I scooped him up and pressed his long, purring body against mine.

The younger officer extended two fingers to scratch his head. "Hey, kitty."

And then the two men were on their feet. "Is there anything we can do for you now? Anyone you'd like us to call?" the older one asked.

I thought of Jacey, my neighbor a few doors down, my one close friend on the cul-de-sac. Soon enough she'd be scrambling to get the kids off to school, hustling to get herself ready for her almost 24/7 job as an event planner. It wouldn't be fair to cheat her out of her last precious hour or two of sleep, even if my husband was dead. I shook my head.

Out in the front hall, the younger officer pressed a card into my hand in case I had "questions." I stuffed it into my bathrobe pocket without even looking at it, still hugging Juju. The two men stepped back out onto the porch and walked down the terraced steps to their patrol car. I watched them go, afraid to move.

In the waning night the cul-de-sac slept on, but dawn was paling the sky over the Sierra Nevadas. Beyond the mountains, another ocean stretched—an ocean of desert and high country flowing eastward a thousand miles to the Rockies. As empty as my life would be going forward.

Chapter 2

*H*is body. Andy's body.

October. Twelve years ago.

I was cruising along the Esplanade, just getting the feel for the rollerblades under my feet, when some asshole masquerading as an expert blader cruised past me and clipped my shoulder, knocking me off balance. I skated off the pavement into the grass and stumbled, falling on my hands and knees. Exactly the reason I'd never been much of a sports person—I hated being embarrassed in public.

"Hey, are you all right?"

Still on all fours, I barely glanced up at my would-be rescuer. "I'm fine. Just give me a second."

He looked down the path at my rapidly receding assailant. "You want me to go after him and take him down?"

"What? No, let him go. He's a jerk. Just ignore him."

A ragged smile crossed his face. "Good. Probably not the best idea to have an assault and battery on my record."

"Your record?"

He reached out a hand and I wobbled to my feet. "Law school," he said.

Grass stains smeared both knees and my wrist hurt, but I wasn't too banged up to miss the spark of interest in his eyes. For my part, on my way to a vertical position, I'd already noted the graceful, athletic build only partially concealed by his "Life is Good" T-shirt and cargo shorts.

"Oh, I see," I said.

Our eyes met again, his gaze a warm blue under a thatch of fair hair that was more ash-colored than blond. His cheeks had an odd sunken quality that made him look older than what I guessed his actual age to be. It gave him a brooding movie star look. And then he flashed another boyish smile.

"I'm Andy. Stevenson."

"Hi. I'm Melissa. McLaren."

His eyes flicked over the logo on my T-shirt. "Mass Art, huh? You're an artist?" It was encouraging that his gaze didn't linger on my chest, the way it did with so many guys I met. Not that my breasts were anything to ogle, really—just nice in a perky sort of way. Or so I'd been told.

His gaze was open, friendly, but confident too—a disarming combination that made me want to look away. A slow smile curled his upper lip.

"I should be in the studio now," I muttered, on the verge of blushing. "I'm working on this . . . bust. But it was such a beautiful day." *Shut up, you ditz.*

The truth was, I was making a concerted effort to turn over a new leaf. No more partying with my friends until dawn, staggering down Boylston Street holding onto each other, crashing into bed back at the dorm and sleeping until noon. No, instead I was up early, eating healthy, yoga and exercise in the morning, sunlight and fresh air while the beautiful fall weather lasted. Hence, my aborted attempt at roller-blading. Afternoons were reserved for the studio, because that's when my biorhythms were at their peak and I was most creative.

I took a wobbly step back onto the path and staggered forward a little. "Oh, f—." I stopped myself from dropping the f-bomb, but couldn't help another mortified glance in his direction. "I'm not very good at this. It's a lot harder than it looks."

"You'll get the hang of it. You just have to find your center." He shifted on his skates, an effortless, fluid movement that was almost breathtaking, and offered me his hand again. "Come on. I'll show you."

He skated me back to the rental shop, where I left my skates without a backward glance, and then skated alongside me as I walked back to the dorm, even though I told him it wasn't necessary. On the way, when I wasn't mesmerized by how easily he moved around the pedestrians crowding the sidewalks, how gracefully he jumped the curb when necessary, I listened as he told me about himself. He'd grown up in southern Connecticut, near Greenwich, had been in Boston for five years, was graduating from law school the following spring. He appreciated art and went often to the MFA when he wanted to relax. He had an older sister who was a lawyer, and a younger brother who wasn't. "Theo's on his own path," he said, with a laugh that didn't quite make it to his eyes.

We went out the next night for pizza and craft beer, even though he wasn't much of a drinker, and the night after that to a late showing of "Mystic River" because we'd both loved the book. The weekend came and I was sitting on his single bed in his studio apartment on Gainsborough Street sketching him with charcoal on drawing paper as he studied for the case he was arguing that Monday in class.

My fingers worked rapidly on the thick paper, limning the outline of his body hunched over his law books, then smudging the charcoal to create the ditches in his cheeks, the places where his dimples hid. Until at last—as it got so late I wondered if I should just say good-bye and go home—my drawing came off the page and hovered over me in the flesh and I knew without a doubt, as he lowered his lips to mine, that this time I had found someone real.

Chapter 3

I f I didn't tell anyone, then it wouldn't be true. Andy could
still walk into the house and tell me it was a mistake, that
he'd had a flat tire, that his cell phone needed charging, that he'd
walked twenty miles on back roads to get home. Or my phone
would ring and I'd hear his voice, apologetic, contrite,
explaining he'd been stuck at work and had fallen asleep on the
couch in his office.

But the sky was growing lighter by the minute and the
nighttime coolness was already vanishing in the building heat of
another day. I sat unmoving in a chair by the pool and clutched
my phone, watching the minutes advance.

Four a.m. came and then four-thirty—seven-thirty Eastern
Time—and I knew I couldn't wait any longer. My finger scrolled
clumsily down my list of contacts and stopped at Dorrie, Andy's
mother. My heart squeezed and my finger kept scrolling, on
down to Liz, his older sister—wise, energetic, capable Liz, who
always knew what to do in an emergency. I tapped the screen and
the phone began to ring in Connecticut.

I caught her coming in from a jog, out of breath and
sounding pleased to hear my voice until it hit her. "Melissa, it's
awfully early out there." A pause. "Has something happened?"

I heard kitchen noises in the background, the kids' voices, a
burst of happy barking from the dog. I imagined her husband
Henry, her laidback opposite, making pancakes, a peaceful
Saturday morning breakfast scene that I was about to hurl a

bomb into. I opened my mouth to speak, but my eyes welled up and my throat closed over the words. And that was how Liz learned that her younger brother was dead.

It was terrible to hear her first startled cry—and almost as terrible to hear Henry's concerned voice low in the background and the kids' "Mom! Mom? What happened? What's wrong, Mom?" We talked for only a minute before we both cut the call short, too devastated to go on.

Another human being besides police officers now knew that Andy was dead, and I'd never felt more alone. "Andy," I whispered, "please come home. This is too hard. I can't do this, I can't do this."

My phone vibrated in my hand. Andy, I thought for a wild few seconds. But no, it was Liz again. Who else would it be? Blowing her nose, her voice shaky but back in control, at least a semblance of it. "Please," she said. "Tell me everything you know."

She listened silently until I told her there would be an investigation into the circumstances of Andy's death. "Do you know what they're looking for?"

The officer's phrase came back to me. *In cases of unattended death.* "I think it's routine. Because Andy di—. Because he was alone when it happened."

"Routine. A thirty-four-year old man dies for no reason? How can that be routine?" The sudden prosecutorial edge in her voice startled me. Like Andy, she was a lawyer. She couldn't help herself. "When will you be talking to the investigator?" she asked.

"Today, I think. Later this morning."

"Can you put them off? I'd like to be there, too. I'll need a day to clear my schedule, but I can be out there on Tuesday."

The childish part of me wanted to blurt, *He's my husband and I can handle this*. Instead I told myself I should be grateful for the offer of support. Normal families were there for each other—something I knew very little about first-hand. I was an only child and hadn't grown up in that kind of family. "Thanks," I said, "but I need answers now. I can't wait until Tuesday."

"Right," she said after a strained silence. "Of course you do."

"Please come when you can. If you think you can leave Dorrie, that is." It was enough of a reminder to jog our conversation back to my cowardly reason for calling. Who was going to tell Andy's mother?

"Mom," my sister-in-law murmured, almost to herself. "Poor dear Mom."

"I know it's my place to tell her," I said, hating my weakness, "but I just can't right now. I'm sorry."

"No, you did the right thing. She needs to be told in person. Someone needs to be with her when she hears."

"Thank you," I said, truly grateful. "Thank you for understanding."

"I'll call you when I have my flight information," she said, because of course she was coming, whether or not she'd be there for the investigator's visit. "I—" Her voice caught. "I just want to see him."

I saw it then—Andy's lifeless body on a cold slab in some basement room, his blue-tinged skin. His face, more familiar than my own, a death mask. "I do, too," I said, even as I wondered how I'd find the strength to bear it.

A goldfinch flitted from the branches of the yucca tree above my head, the morning so still I could hear its wings flap. I said good-bye and dropped the phone in my lap, the tears crowding behind my eyes but not yet ready to fall.

I dreaded the next call, dreaded inflicting the inevitable shock even more than I'd dreaded telling Liz—but right now my need for my mother, the mother I'd always wished I had, was greater than my distaste for how the whole conversation would probably play out.

She answered on the first ring, surprising me.

"Mom?" my voice croaked.

"Melissa! My goodness. You must be clairvoyant. I've been up most of the night with this awful back—"

I listened for almost a full minute to her rambling tale of nighttime discomfort before I said it again. "Mom."

Something in my tone made her stop. For a full few seconds neither one of us spoke.

Then her voice came on the line again. "What, dear, what is it? And why—"

"It's Andy."

"What about Andy?"

"It's—really bad news, I'm afraid." And then I told her, and listened to her break down and weep inconsolably for the rest of us who couldn't get past our shock to shed more than a few painful tears. Because she loved Andy almost as much as I did—a fact I often resented, given the reason. She had always been absurdly grateful to him for "rescuing" me, her loose cannon of a daughter, from my flaky artistic self.

"But what will happen to you?" she cried, her despair taking another tack. "Do you have enough money? Are you working at all?"

"Mom."

"Can you even get a job? A real job?"

Ridiculous questions, all, irrelevant and pathetic, considering Andy's more than ample salary as a fourth-year associate.

"Mom, I can't do this right now. You have to stop."

She blew her nose noisily. "Should I come to you?"

It was the one saving grace in our relationship—that she lived in southern New Hampshire, on the other side of the country.

"No, I'll come to you."

"When?" she sniffed.

"I don't know, Mom. Soon. When it's over."

As if it ever would be.

Chapter 4

Friday morning, just twenty-four hours earlier. The alarm clock going off at five-thirty. Andy rolling on top of me and resting for a minute, his chin against the top of my head, the beginning of an erection pressing my thigh. A brief kiss before rolling off to begin his day. A quick jog on the treadmill in our basement exercise room, the muffled thump thump of his feet reaching me in the master bedroom above. Shower. The morning smell of soap and hot water. Cereal in the kitchen. The clink of the spoon against the dish. The low murmur of the TV news, then quiet. Back in the bedroom. Tie knotted. Suit jacket on. Another kiss. The lovemaking that didn't happen. Out the door. Good-bye forever.

Now, a day later, back in bed because I didn't know where else to go, didn't know how to escape the awful stillness, I buried my face in his pillow and inhaled his scent, my hot tears mingling with the salty tang of his scalp. Four paws landed softly on my back, four sets of claws kneaded me through the cotton blanket. Juju, attracted by my cries, his feline attempt to comfort me. I pulled his purring body to me again, soaking his fur with my tears.

The landline rang in the kitchen, startling me out of an exhausted stupor at ten o'clock. It was the Sacramento County Sheriff's Department calling to tell me that the investigator on Andy's case, Detective Darla Roussekoff, was on her way over to ask me some questions.

Fueled by coffee and dressed but unshowered, I ushered Detective Roussekoff into the living room, where she took a seat in the creaky Queen Anne chair the death notification officer had vacated just hours before.

"I'm sorry for your loss," she said without visible sympathy, then flipped opened her notebook. She rested it on her plump, polyester clad thigh and clicked her ballpoint pen.

The room was dim and cool, the bright chinks of light coming through the blinds the only hint of the June inferno outdoors. In the filtered light the detective's complexion looked pasty, her dull brown hair pulled back in a severe ponytail. Her face was taut with fatigue, or some other unreadable emotion, causing me to wonder what private misery she might be contending with.

She apologized again for intruding on my grief, reminded me of the obligation to conduct an investigation in cases of unattended death, assured me that the questions she was about to ask were mostly routine. She promised that the objective was to wrap things up as quickly as possible so that I could get on with my arrangements to usher Andy's remains into the ground or the next world or whatever I believed.

I nodded, my head pounding dully. How long had it been since I'd drunk any water?

"We'll start with some background questions. Who was your husband's employer?"

"Wolders Palmer in Sacramento. The law firm."

She jotted it in her notebook, apparently familiar with it. "And what was his position there?"

"Associate lawyer. Corporate law division."

"How long was he employed there?"

"Four years. Four years and a few months." Her questions seemed utterly pointless, but still it felt good to be talking about Andy, anything to ease the searing hurt throughout my body.

"And who did he report to?"

"Reg Wolders, the senior partner."

She scribbled it down. "How would you characterize your husband's relationship with his employer?"

"Good. Respectful. Reg has a high opinion of Andy."

"Did your husband have any friends at the firm?"

"Yes, of course."

She waited without looking up from her notebook.

"Warren Cheung is his closest friend there."

"Could you spell that?"

"C-H-E-U-N-G," I said.

"Anyone else?" she asked.

I gave her a couple of more names.

"What were your husband's habits?"

"Very busy with his career, lots of long hours. He doesn't . . . didn't spend much time at home." The truth of the statement sank in with a sad jolt.

"How was his health?"

"Fine. He's very . . . athletic. He trains practically every weekend. Eats right . . ."

"Was he under the regular care of a physician?"

"No."

"When was his last physical or doctor's visit?"

"In February, I think."

"And who was the doctor?"

I told her. Another scribble.

"Any mental health issues? Depression, bi—"

I shook my head.

She glanced at me. "Nothing you're aware of?"

"No."

"When was the last time you talked to your husband?"

"Last night around seven. He was leaving the office to go to a client dinner at the Hyatt."

"How would you describe his mental state?"

"Fine. Not looking forward to the dinner."

"Why not?"

"They drag on. They're a chore."

"Anything bothering him? Besides the boring dinner?"

"No."

"No problems at work weighing on him?"

I hesitated. In the last few months Andy had frequently seemed tense, even distant, had often been in a bad mood when he got home, but I'd attributed it to the usual culprit, a seventy-hour work week.

"Ma'am?" Detective Roussekoff said, still waiting.

"No problems," I said carefully, "but he did seem stressed out sometimes."

"Because?"

"I don't know. The nature of the job. It's a high-stress environment."

"So would you call it ordinary job stress or out of the ordinary?"

I paused again before answering. "I'm not sure."

"So your husband didn't confide in you?"

The insinuation annoyed me. "He didn't believe in bringing his work problems home with him. Besides, he couldn't discuss the details of his cases with me. It's . . . unethical."

Her eyes rested on me for several seconds. "Tell me about the dinner he attended last night. Who was there?"

"The lawyers from his department. And his boss, of course —Reg. I don't know who else. You'd have to ask them."

"Yes, we'll be talking to them next." She flipped back to an earlier page of notes. "He was found at one a.m. this morning. Did he usually stay out so late?"

"No."

"You weren't worried?"

I ignored the suspicious tone of the question, determined not to let her get under my skin again. "I wait up sometimes, but I was tired last night. I fell asleep."

"Did you speak to your husband at any other time during the evening?"

I stared at her. "No, I told you—"

She lifted two fingers as if to say, "Forget I asked that," then flipped a page in the notebook and poised her pen over a fresh line. "And you're sure nothing was bothering him? Besides the boring dinner and the stressful job?"

So she wasn't buying that nothing was bothering Andy. I could have told her that Andy's father had suffered a stroke six months earlier and that his mother, as primary caregiver, was wondering how she could cope, that Andy felt guilty for not being there to share the burden, guilty to the point of considering leaving his job and moving us to Connecticut to help with his father's care. His younger brother, Theo, of course, was no help at all in a situation like this. The family was reluctant to place any adult demands on him for fear he'd relapse.

"Some family stuff," I said with a lame little shrug.

Her colorless eyes bored into me for a moment.

"His father is sick," I admitted. "But it's a close-knit family, so everyone is managing." My hands turned icy in my lap. I had no idea why I had just lied, unless over the years I'd absorbed by osmosis the Stevenson family's pride, their inability to admit weakness under any circumstances.

She scribbled again and went on. "Tell me about your husband's drug use."

The faint spinning sensation I'd been experiencing since we started talking stilled. "Excuse me?"

She met my look but stayed silent.

"My husband doesn't—didn't—use drugs," I said at last. "That's—crazy. He was a health nut. He didn't even like to take over-the-counter meds."

"Your husband was found with a quantity of cocaine in his possession at the accident scene."

"No." I shook my head. "No. That's impossible. He wouldn't—"

The detective's eyebrows lifted fractionally.

"No! He hated drugs." And despised drug users, I could have added.

"Because?"

Oh, shit, here we go. "His brother," I murmured, "became addicted to heroin as a teenager. He's clean now, but it caused Andy's parents a lot of misery."

"And that leads you to conclude your husband would never use drugs?"

"No! I mean, yes."

Another scribble on the pad. This time, I read her upside-down handwriting clearly. "Wife unaware??"

My mind sifted rapidly through all the office parties and other functions Andy and I had attended during the years he'd been employed at Wolders Palmer, the friendships he made there, the late nights, whether he'd ever seemed high when he arrived home, any evidence that would point to illicit drug use. Drug use he'd concealed from me for God only knew how long. And then the awful implication of what she was saying dawned on me. "Did this have something to do with the accident?"

"Undetermined. We'll have to wait for the coroner's report."

"I mean," I said, starting to lose it. "If he really *was* doing drugs, then you need to be talking to the people who were at that dinner with him—"

"Don't worry, Mrs. Stevenson. We intend to. Just two more questions and we'll be done here. Again, this is purely routine."

"Go on."

"Did your husband have any reason to take his own life?"

"Oh, Jesus," I blurted, but that clearly wasn't the answer Detective Roussekoff was looking for. "No," I said after a grudging pause, and waited for the other question.

She fingered her pen before making eye contact again. "Did your husband have any enemies?"

Chapter 5

My entire body hurt, even my skin, as I closed the door on Detective Roussekoff. *Cocaine? Enemies?*

One conversation in particular came back to me. Just a few days earlier, I'd come out on the patio while Andy was grilling and surprised him talking on his cell phone. The furtive way he spoke made me wonder briefly if he was having an affair. But his tone didn't sound like a lover's. He sounded almost afraid. "You don't know what you're asking," he muttered, then ended the call quickly when he saw me listening.

"What's going on?" I asked, feigning innocence.

He mumbled something about a client and went back to flipping steaks.

"Some client," I said. "You look upset."

He eyed me vacantly, then surprised me by putting down the spatula and pulling me close. "Meliss," he whispered in my hair.

His unexpected embrace gave me hope that the strange barrier I'd sensed between us in recent months might dissolve, that we'd be able to talk again the way we always had, but after a few seconds, he dropped his arms and sadness crept into his face.

"Andy?" I asked.

"It's nothing. Nothing I can talk about, anyway."

I wanted to confront him, I planned to do it when he wasn't so upset, but the timing was never right. His strange behavior had been on my mind yesterday morning, in fact, when he rolled on top of me, his first amorous gesture in weeks. If only I'd held onto him, forced him to say something. Put my arms around him and not let him go until we'd made love one last time. Instead, "Late," he'd whispered and slipped out of bed. And I'd allowed myself to be lulled almost back to sleep by the thump thump of the treadmill coming up through the floor. The weekend was coming and I wasn't worried yet. Maybe we'd go to that new restaurant at the Town Square, that French bistro knock-off that was getting so much buzz. I could bring it up there, as we sipped red wine at our outdoor table and people-watched. He'd be relaxed, unguarded. He'd tell me the truth then, I was sure of it.

Now, twenty-four hours later, it was too late.

"Mel? I don't want to pry, but is everything all right? Nosy Mrs. Alvarez next door just told me she saw a patrol car outside your house in the middle of the night."

At last, someone I could talk to. Jacey, my closest friend, home early for a change. It was just after six.

I choked back a sob.

"Oh, God, Mel, what is it?"

She came over right away, of course, leaving her two children eating a microwaved dinner at home, and sat listening as I poured it all out, everything—even the fact that Andy had been in possession of cocaine when he died.

"Jesus," she whispered. "Andy?" Her expression said it all. *I thought he was one of the good ones.*

I wanted to say, *He is one of the good ones. He is!* Because who was I going to mourn if not the Andy I knew?

And that's when it hit me, as Jacey sat next to me on the sofa and held my hand and listened, that my husband wouldn't be coming home that night, that in fact he would never walk through the door again, weary from a long day at work, never stand in the kitchen cracking open a club soda and telling me about his day. That I'd never again have the comfort of crawling into bed next to him at night, never even brush our teeth together at the bathroom sink and take turns spitting into the water swirling down the drain.

Chapter 6

The first of the condolences arrived the next day, even though I'd told no one except Jacey, Liz, and my mother. It was all over the local news stations: *Sacramento lawyer, 34, found dead in his car*. Early on Sunday morning I looked out the bedroom window to see a news van parked at the curb in front of the house, a reporter and a cameraman leaning against it. They waited with ghoulish patience until my next-door neighbor, a middle-aged engineer with whom Andy had often shared man time over the back fence, strode down to the van and shouted at them to leave me in peace.

My email inbox began filling up with messages from clients conveying their sympathy. In this age of texting, few people called, but it was understood that a text wasn't right either, so some sent cards, a few sent gift baskets or flowers with a personal note. Casseroles, banana bread, and other food items arrived at the front door from the neighbors on the cul-de-sac. By Sunday night there were too many covered dishes to fit in the refrigerator, so I gave most of it to Jacey to feed herself and her always ravenous kids. I couldn't imagine eating any of it, couldn't imagine the day would ever arrive when I'd eat for pleasure again.

The coroner called on Monday morning, his voice crisp, almost impersonal as he reported the findings of the autopsy. Cause of death, heart failure brought on by an episode of ventricular tachycardia. Time of death, between ten p.m. and midnight. Toxicology testing showed that the decedent had ingested a large amount of cocaine earlier in the evening. This was in keeping with a quantity of cocaine found in the decedent's possession at the scene.

I refused to go there. "But he was thirty-four-years old. He was in peak condition. How could this happen? He had no history of heart problems."

"Actually it's not that uncommon. Athletes collapse and die from heart seizures with depressing frequency. We've all seen the news stories. Your husband's heart actually showed some scarring."

"Scarring?"

"Again, not unusual, even in someone your husband's age. Even in someone fit. Could have been due to illness—a bad case of flu, an untreated strep infection—or overtraining at too young an age. The heart gets strained—" He paused, and I sensed it coming. "And if he was regularly abusing drugs—"

I swallowed my angry response. "Is that what killed him?"

"Impossible to say with one-hundred-percent certainty, but it's likely it was a contributing factor. Depending on the quantity consumed and the severity of the underlying heart damage—"

"But people use drugs all the time . . . " I stopped myself, realizing how damning that sounded.

He went on, ignoring the avenue my comment opened up. "Look, I understand your shock and your frustration, I do. The good news, if good news is possible in a tragic situation like this, is that the investigation is over. I'm releasing your husband's body to the mortuary, so you can proceed with funeral arrangements."

I muttered my thanks.

"Did your husband have life insurance?"

"He had a policy through work." For five hundred thousand, if I recalled correctly. No one could accuse Wolders Palmer of being stingy with their employee benefits.

The coroner's voice became quieter, more sympathetic. "You'd better have a talk with the insurance company. I hate to have to tell you this, but typically, death by drug overdose voids the policy."

Cocaine. The word reared up like a snake again.

Shit, Andy, how could you? No, that's wrong. Why would you?

I'd never been a drug user in college, or at any other time in my life. Sure, I'd take a hit off a joint at a party if one was being passed around, and once my roommate and I popped Ecstasy on a dare. We'd ended up wandering around the Public Garden at three in the morning professing our undying love for each other. But alcohol was always my drug of choice. I discovered early on my high tolerance for booze, the "hollow leg" I'd inherited from my father. Not a fact I was proud of. He was a-case-a-weekend kind of guy, nursing one beer after another from morning to night, every weekend for forty years, a habit that made my mother miserable. But my drinking just about stopped when I met Andy. Exercise was his addiction. And love addiction became mine. Andy and I had that rare chemistry. Our bodies fit together as if made for each other. A cliché, I know, but a mind-blowing one.

But cocaine. *Jesus, Andy, how could you?*

A large part of me still refused to believe it, but tell that to the half-crazed zombie standing in front of her dead husband's clothes closet wondering where to start looking. A long row of suits and dress shirts confronted me, their empty sleeves and blank fronts accusing. *I dare you to find me*, they seemed to taunt. The wool suits were holdovers from the Boston days, too warm for California weather, too formal for the borderline casual attire most Californians sported when conducting business, even lawyers at top firms. But other, lighter garments he'd been walking around in just days or weeks ago. I grabbed the first suit, a summer beige, off the hanger. My hands went through both pockets feeling for powder, grit, a plastic baggie, whatever cocaine felt like. I turned both pockets inside out. Nothing except some lint. I pulled a blue dress shirt off its hanger and felt inside the breast pocket. Nothing again. Seersucker suit. Nada. Navy blue chalk stripe, my favorite of the bunch. Nothing. Charcoal gray mid-weight. Nope.

Come on, Andy, not even a receipt or a movie stub? Who *were* you, anyway? Of course, the one suit that mattered was with the coroner.

I abandoned his clothes and grabbed his gym bag from the floor of the closet, my heart beginning a slow pounding against my breastbone. Somehow the gym bag felt more personal, a more likely hiding place. I dumped its contents on the bed and clawed through the items. Gym shorts, extra pair of socks, T-shirt—all clean and smelling of laundry soap. Who didn't keep at least one dirty item of clothing in their gym bag? I wondered. Running shoes, almost new. I knew he kept one pair for the gym and another pair for running outdoors. Front pouch. Comb, stick deodorant, truss. Truss? Huh. Swimming goggles. Hershey bar wrapper. Busted, Andy! So much for your purist rep.

The dresser was next. I combed quickly through socks, briefs, a stack of T-shirts. My fingers grazed something under the T-shirts—a dog-eared magazine at the bottom of the drawer. I pulled it out. *Penthouse*. It fell open to a nubile woman with her legs spread wide. A straight crotch shot framed by a tight mini-skirt. I swallowed hard. Okay, so this was new information, a new wrinkle on our lack of sex in recent months. I sat down on the bed, my bravado collapsing. It's a magazine, I told myself. A magazine. So what if he was masturbating? You think you're the first wife to have a husband who sometimes preferred jerking off to sex with you?

Christ, Melissa, get a grip. It could be a lot worse.

The surge of energy that had carried me through the first acts of privacy invasion ebbed away. I left the open drawers and mess of gym articles on the bed and went upstairs, past the guest room and the north-facing bedroom I used as my studio, to Andy's home office. It seemed silly to have a four-bedroom house with no children in the picture, but Andy and I had decided quite early in our relationship that we didn't want any.

My parents had made child-rearing look like a distinctly unattractive proposition. If that wasn't convincing enough, there was Theo, Andy's younger brother, to consider, whose teenage addiction to heroin still haunted the family. Who would want to pass *that* gene on to our defenseless offspring?

So no children for us, and no chance to change our mind now. Ever.

I stopped on the threshold of Andy's office and stared across the room at his desk. The laptop he used at home sat there, the cover closed. I knew the password, or thought I did. And then I caved. I just couldn't go there. I suppose I was too afraid of what I might find.

Instead I went to my studio next door and switched on my iMac, opened a browser window, and navigated to our joint bank account online. I scrolled through the recent transactions, looking for any suspicious activity, unexplained withdrawals. Nothing.

Nothing, nothing, nothing.

Chapter 7

I picked up Liz at the Sacramento airport late on Tuesday afternoon. Andy and I had always taken the nonstop to and from Oakland when traveling to our families on the East Coast, but my sister-in-law insisted on flying the extra leg to Sacramento to save me the two-hour drive to the Oakland airport.

I watched her emerge from security into the main terminal, struck by how much she looked like her brother—an older, female version, and a worn out and bedraggled one today. Her linen pantsuit was creased from her eight or nine hours on planes, and strands of ash blonde hair escaped from the hairclip at the nape of her neck. The deep lines of fatigue around her eyes and mouth told me she wasn't sleeping any better than I was.

The Stevensons were not a hugging family, but we hugged awkwardly as the other passengers parted around us on their way to baggage claim and the exit.

"How terrible for you," she murmured when we pulled away from each other. "How terrible for all of us."

I nodded, determined not to cry—at least not until we'd had a few minutes together. We turned and followed the stream of exiting passengers, Liz wheeling her carry-on suitcase, her purse and laptop case slung across her shoulder.

For the moment she'd dropped her lawyer's stance, I noticed with relief. When I'd called her the day before with the coroner's verdict that Andy had died of a heart attack, she'd been shocked into silence. I couldn't bring myself to admit the likely cause of the heart attack—cocaine overdose.

"It's good to see you," I said, a bit belatedly. "Thank you for coming."

"You know the whole family would have come if we could have managed it."

"Of course," I said, giving silent thanks that it had not been possible. Without Andy as a buffer, one Stevenson at a time was enough. "Well, you survived the trip," I added, attempting a smile. "What can I get for you?"

"Some food and a stiff drink. The only thing I've had since this morning is a power bar, and I'm ashamed to say my stomach hasn't stopped working even though . . ." she stopped herself. *Even though my brother is dead.* "The last few days I've been ravenous."

"It's the ghrelin," I said, relieved to latch onto a neutral subject.

"God," she muttered. "What is it? Am I being attacked by aliens?"

"The hunger hormone. It kicks in when you're under stress. Or not sleeping."

"Right. Well, I'll blame it on the ghrelin then."

My plans for the evening meal were simple. A lasagna left by one of the neighbors and boxed salad greens. My own stomach felt like a bottomless pit, but I still couldn't look at food without wanting to gag.

"You look like you're holding up, at least," my sister-in-law said.

"What choice do I have?" In truth, I'd had to pull myself together because of her visit. Today was the first day I'd put on make-up and earrings and at least made an effort to eat breakfast.

We walked out the main door into a blaze of light and heat.

"How's Dorrie?" I asked, as we waited on the curb to cross.

"Oh, you know, as well as can be expected."

"Was it terrible? Telling her, I mean."

"She went up to her bedroom, closed the door, and didn't come down for the rest of the day. But the next morning she got up, got dressed, and went back to nursing my father. It was frightening, that steely determination to take it in stride."

"I'm sure she must be devastated," I said, not knowing what else to say.

"We haven't told the kids yet," Liz said, after a pause. "They barely remember their uncle Andy as it is."

We crossed through a break in the traffic and entered the parking lot. I remembered the last and only time they'd visited us in the El Dorado Hills house, Andy and Henry in the back yard grilling, the kids doing cannonballs into the pool, their whoops of delight echoing off the surrounding houses. Tears blurred my eyes and I stopped walking. Liz led me to an empty bench and we both sat down. Kindly, she held my hand and let me cry while, across the street, arriving travelers got out of idling cars, hugged loved ones good-bye, hurried into the terminal with their luggage.

"I'm sorry," I blurted. "I wasn't going to do this."

"Please," she said, dabbing her own tears away. "I think it's fair to say the past several days have been the most difficult of my life. How much more so for you."

Her kindness undid me. More tears gushed down my face. The truth, apart from missing Andy intensely, was that I was afraid. I hadn't been alone, without a partner, since I was twenty, and I had no idea how I was going to move forward from here. I rested my elbows on my knees and hid my face from her. "What am I going to do?" I practically whimpered.

"You'll get through it," she said.

She was seven years older than me and successful in a way I'd never be. Her plum job as in-house legal counsel for a pharmaceutical giant in Stamford, Connecticut, paid the bills many times over, dwarfing her husband's salary as a public school teacher. Alongside her, I'd always felt like a lightweight, an adult wannabe, with my unfulfilled artistic aspirations, my catch-as-catch-can graphic design jobs, my pet portraits.

I blew my nose and wiped my tears away. "I'm sorry we didn't visit you and Henry as much as we should have. Andy was just so busy with work."

My sister-in-law gazed past me, squinting in the harsh sunshine. "Work. It seems foolish, doesn't it? All that industriousness. And for what?"

It was a decidedly un-Stevenson-like remark. I glanced at her laptop, resting on the bench next to us.

She raised an eyebrow. "You know how it is in corporate America. You're indispensible, until you're not."

Outside the kitchen windows, the evening coolness had descended, the high desert air beckoning us outdoors. Numb to its appeal, we remained inside. The designer kitchen was what had sold me on the house—the glass-fronted cabinets, the acres of granite countertop, the many windows looking out on the lushly landscaped back yard—a much more inviting space for entertaining than our small galley kitchen in the Folsom house. But we'd had few dinner guests since buying the house, and tonight it was just Liz and me. My sister-in-law poured three fingers of scotch into a juice glass while I served up the lasagna and tossed the salad greens with oil and vinegar.

"Want some?" she asked, nodding at the bottle of J & B.

"If I started, I probably wouldn't stop."

"No one would blame you," she muttered through the bottom of her glass.

The liquor fumes hit me full force, making me queasy. I was thankful that scotch had never been my poison. I wasn't even sure how the bottle had turned up in our liquor cabinet. The lasagna turned my stomach too, the tomato sauce and cheese glistening red and yellow over the thick noodles. I tried not to think of blood over a skin wound as I lifted a forkful to my mouth.

We sat side by side on barstools at the kitchen island, chewing silently.

"Lasagna and scotch," Liz mused. "A disgusting combination." She poured another slug into her glass. "I'm turning into my father in my old age."

I glanced at her, surprised. Andy's parents, as far as I knew, had always been teetotalers.

She caught my quizzical look. "Dad joined AA late in life." It was a night for revelations, apparently.

"I had no idea." It explained Andy's disapproval of alcohol and the mystery that was Theo. Not a genetic aberration after all. I'd always wondered how two upright people like John and Dorothy Stevenson could have an addict for a son. It was only very lately that I'd faced the fact of my own father's alcoholism. As a child I'd assumed that all fathers came with a beer can grafted to their dominant hand.

The weight of the secret I was carrying settled over me again. Now would be the time to tell Liz about the cocaine, but still I held back. It just seemed too cruel a blow. If only the police had spared my feelings too. Another emotion lurked inside me, too. Shame. As if Andy's alleged secret drug use was somehow a reflection on our marriage.

"So," Liz said casually as we finished eating. "Funeral home tomorrow."

"Yes." It would be our only chance to see Andy before he was cremated, the main reason for her visit. I got up to clear our dinner plates.

Liz slid off her stool, too. "Let me clean up."

"No, please—just relax. You've had a long day."

I ran the plates under cold water, picking up the sponge to scrub off stuck-on cheese. The remains of the tomato sauce ran red down the drain. I stacked the plates in the dishwasher. When I turned again to clear the rest of the dishes, Liz was standing at the refrigerator, drink in hand, perusing the photos of Andy and me attached to the double doors with an array of magnets. Her eyes roved over Andy in his biking clothes, his face streaked with dust after a big race at Prairie City, a group of us skiing at Lake Tahoe, a selfie of Andy and me kissing in the Gulf of Mexico on a vacation at Playa del Carmen. "You had a wonderful life together," she mused. She ran her thumb over one of the fridge magnets, a ceramic black-and-white tuxedo cat playing a baby grand piano. "How cute," she murmured.

I spoke over the lump in my throat. "It was a game we had. Andy would hide these little cat curios around the house and wait for me to find them."

Except the game had stopped some months back, about the time Andy began keeping secrets from me. Just like I was doing with his sister now.

"Liz," I began.

She turned at the catch in my voice. "What is it?"

"There's something I have to tell you. It's terrible, but I think you need to know."

She smiled, a defensive gesture, as if to say, what could be worse than learning that my brother is dead?

My hands were wet from rinsing the dishes. I let them drip. "Andy had cocaine on him the night he died. The coroner is saying that's what caused his heart attack."

Her head jerked a little, like she'd been hit from behind. Her smile froze in place and then faded. She seemed to will herself to stand up straighter, to wipe all evidence of shock off her face.

"I'm sorry," I said. "I still can't believe it myself."

She finished her scotch and placed the glass deliberately on the island. Her eyes stayed fixed on her fingers around the glass. "I think I'd better go up now."

There. I'd told her. But I didn't feel better. I felt much worse. She walked out of the room like an old person. I stood there, lost, my nerve-endings smarting from the cruelty of it. I wanted to cry—for both of us—but I was past crying now. All I could do was load the dishwasher numbly and try not to break anything else.

A little while later I summoned the courage to go upstairs and check on her, to make sure she had everything she needed, to talk if she wanted to. But the guest room was empty. I found her sitting in the dark in Andy's office.

Tears glistened on her cheeks in the muted light from the hall. "I thought maybe I could feel his presence here," she said.

"Do you?"

"No."

It was something I'd noticed too. Wherever Andy had gone, he'd left nothing of his spirit behind. Not even a vague essence to comfort the rest of us in our grief.

Chapter 8

Liz appeared downstairs the next morning looking shattered but composed. I remembered what she'd said earlier about Dorrie, her steely determination to take Andy's death in stride. Like mother, like daughter, it seemed. We barely spoke at breakfast, our interactions made tenser by the knowledge that we would soon be leaving for the funeral home.

On the short trip down the freeway, Liz leaned back against the passenger seat headrest, her eyes closed as commuters whizzed past us on either side. Despite another horrible night's sleep, I didn't mind the rush-hour traffic. It was a relief to focus on something besides the elephant in the car.

"How unhappy he must have been," she mused.

Was that a criticism of me? I didn't think so. "He was unhappy at work."

She opened her eyes. *Why?* her look said. As if it weren't possible to be unhappy at one's job.

"I don't know. He wouldn't tell me."

The traffic slowed suddenly, the morning sun flashing off the cars ahead of us.

"Was it recreational? Was it something you did together?"

My foot slipped off the gas pedal at the unfairness of the question. "No! Of course not." In the right side mirror, I watched an SUV glide up behind us and then fall back. Luckily for us, California commuters were more polite than their irritable Boston counterparts. In Beantown, we would have been treated to an angry driver laying on his horn, maybe even rear-ending us. I turned my eyes back to the road. "You think because I'm a ditsy artist that I use drugs?"

"I'm sorry," she said. "I'm just trying to make sense of something that makes no sense at all." A pause. "And I *don't* think you're a ditsy artist."

I stewed for a minute before offering her a bone. "The coroner said that with Andy's underlying heart condition, using cocaine even once could have been fatal."

"God help us," she muttered.

I flicked the turn signal to exit the freeway.

The Grace Funeral Chapel was a new stucco building in an immaculately verdant setting, far enough off the road for the traffic noises to be muted. The place was part of a chain that was springing up all over the state, tasteful purveyors of bereavement for upscale consumers, the bland images on the company web site implying that death was nothing more than a trip to the country club for a round of golf. It repelled me, all of it, but I'd called them anyway. What difference did it make, really, who ushered Andy's remains into the next world?

The assistant funeral director met us in the foyer, a clean-shaven twenty-something man with an open face and a soft, almost feminine voice. He led us into a little anteroom and closed the door. Not a single extraneous sound penetrated the room's plush appointments as he prepared us for viewing Andy's body. "Take as much as time as you need," he told us. "You'll have a full half-hour to say your good-byes." He went on to remind us, tactfully, that Andy had been dead for more than four days now, so we might see some bloating and discoloration around the face.

I recalled my conversation with the funeral director, his pitch for having Andy embalmed, even though he was going to be cremated. I'd said no.

"Can we touch him?" Liz asked.

"Y-es," he said, "but we advise leaving the sheet in place. There's a Y-incision in his chest from the autopsy. Some loved ones find it upsetting." His voice was soothing even as he laid out the ghastly details, so soothing I stifled a yawn.

"More questions?" he asked, carefully making eye contact with each of us.

We shook our heads.

"Then come this way, please." He opened a door on the other side of the room and held out his hand to shepherd us through.

My sleepiness vanished as we entered the room where Andy lay. A cold sweat sprang out on my forehead even though the room was noticeably colder than the anteroom. His corpse was arranged in a white box, apparently meant to simulate an open casket. The light was subdued, artificial, designed to soften the ravages of death. His eyes were closed, of course, the familiar ditches in his cheeks, the mouth so often quirked in humor, now an expressionless mask. Surprisingly, no tears came. A psychic wall, hastily erected, separated me from my feelings about the body on the table. In what world was there any connection between this gray, ruined form and my lithe, graceful, caring husband? The door closed softly behind us as the assistant funeral director withdrew.

Beside me, Liz stifled a sob. Hesitantly, I slipped my arm around her shoulder. We leaned against each other and then separated. Liz bowed her head, praying to her Episcopal God, I guessed, while I waited, not praying. In respect to my sister-in-law, I let a couple of minutes pass, then reached out and touched Andy's shoulder. She took it as my signal that I was ready to be alone with my husband and wordlessly left the room.

I brushed my fingers across his cheek, let one finger trace his jaw. His skin felt surprisingly rough, unnaturally so. I looked closer in the dimness and saw what looked like scrape marks, as if they'd shaved him for the viewing. I pulled back my hand. Then, like a child told not to touch, I let my fingers lift a corner of the sheet that covered his chest up to his neck.

I gasped.

Just below his collarbone, a welter of purple, almost black bruises covered his upper torso. I wanted to look away but couldn't. A hideous secret revealed, the indecencies of death on shocking display.

Oh Andy.

I covered his chest and sought the comfort of his hand under the sheet, the familiar feel of bones and sinew. The sheet fell away from his wrist. More black bruises, this time in a striated pattern. Almost like finger marks. The grip of a strong hand.

Jesus. Whatever words I planned to say in my last moments with Andy's earthly remains were sucked away. Instead, I groped in my purse and pulled out my cell phone. I snapped a photo of his wrist. I had to snap at least half a dozen before I got one that wasn't blurred. Then I folded the sheet back from his chin and took a photo of his chest.

I replaced the sheet and smoothed it out, feeling the solidity of his inert body underneath. Almost as an afterthought, I pressed my lips to his forehead and whispered the only thing I could think to say, that I would always love him.

Back in the anteroom, after Liz had entered the viewing room, I turned to the assistant funeral director.

"Those marks on his collarbone. The bruises. What caused those?"

He covered his surprise quickly with a bland half-smile. "Seatbelt abrasion, most likely."

"Seatbelt abrasion?"

"From the force of the crash? The blood pools under the skin." He went on as if he could read my mind. "Sometimes the pattern is unpredictable."

But there was no crash. "What about his wrist? Why would the blood pool there?"

Now he made no attempt to cover his discomfort. "He put his hand forward to brace himself?"

"Even with his seatbelt on?"

His eyes bulged a little. I realized I'd seen that look before. Recently. The younger of the two officers in my living room, wanting so much to help me, to tell me what I wanted to hear, but being unable to.

"Ma'am," the assistant funeral director said gently. "You should talk to the coroner about this. You shouldn't have to live with unanswered questions."

There was the crunch of tortilla chips in my mouth, the murmur of people eating at nearby tables on the patio where Liz and I sat. It wasn't yet noon and the restaurant was still half-empty, but it was easier to be there with other people than alone at home, just the two of us. It was the last time I would ever eat Mexican food.

I had a sudden thirst for alcohol. Gallons of it. But it seemed wrong to get drunk today of all days. When the waiter returned to the table with the margaritas we'd ordered, I shook my head. "I'm sorry. I've changed my mind. Take it away, please."

Liz gave me a surprised look, but didn't comment.

I wanted to ask her if she'd lifted the sheet too, if she'd seen the bruises, but I was afraid of what new pain I might be inflicting. We had only a few hours to repair our fragile relationship before she flew home to Connecticut. So I kept silent, screaming inside, while Liz sipped her margarita.

A hot breeze shivered through the leaves of the mimosa tree shading our table, the sky a hard, deep blue overhead. I thought of Andy lying in the muffled chill of the mortuary a few miles away. Out in the car, his personal effects—the suit he'd been wearing when he died, his cordovan wingtips and billfold, the braided wristband he'd worn for as long as I'd known him—lay in a plastic bag on the back seat. Oddly, his briefcase and cell phone weren't among them. The assistant funeral director, clearly embarrassed, had promised to call the police and track down their whereabouts.

Our plates came, enchiladas, refried beans and rice, the rising steam redolent with the mingled flavors. More food that I had no appetite for. I asked for a glass of water. The waiter glanced at Liz and she nodded. Water, too.

We ate without speaking until the waiter brought the water, two sweating glasses garnished with lime. Then Liz broached the subject of the memorial service. The plan was for me to fly to Connecticut with Andy's ashes for the interment. The church was already booked for the Saturday after next. The Stevensons were prominent in their community and an overflow crowd was expected. It was unlikely that Andy's dad would be well enough to attend, but everyone was hoping.

"What about here in California?" my sister-in-law asked. "Will you have a memorial for him here?"

The question caught me off balance. "I—haven't really thought about it."

"But I think you must."

It startled me a bit. Did anyone even say "must" anymore? The Stevensons did, apparently.

"But the way he died—"

"Do you think anyone knew about it?"

The cocaine, she meant. Neither of us could even say the word.

I took a sip of water, wishing I hadn't sent my margarita back. "Those guys he worked with? What do you think?" After all, he'd spent far more time with them than he had with me.

"Melissa, suppose it was *one* tragic mistake. Do you really want to let that prevent us from honoring Andy as a person?"

I pushed some refried beans around with my fork.

"Regardless of how he died," she went on, unstoppably, "he was a good man and a respected member of his firm. I think we have an obligation to give his colleagues a chance to say good-bye."

We. I shook my head. "To be honest, I'm just not sure I'm up to it."

There was kindness in her face, but something else too—the desire to salvage Andy's reputation, to maintain appearances at all cost. She swung into helpful mode. "You could have it at the funeral home. They would take care of everything for you."

"I don't want to have it there. They'd want to embalm him —just for the viewing. I don't want to see him like that." Lying there waxlike, wearing makeup, pumped full of artificial vitality. God, how it repelled me—the obligations of death and doing the right thing. I preferred his corpse the way it was, ugly bruises and all.

"You wouldn't have to. His urn would be enough," Liz said, unwilling to let it go.

Of course, I thought, feeling stupid. Only Catholics insisted on the ghoulish rite of the open casket. But I was no longer a practicing Catholic and Andy had been raised Episcopalian.

Still, I wasn't ready to be coerced. "If I have any kind of memorial, I'll have it at the house," I said, hoping to close the subject. "Andy would have wanted it that way. He was a simple guy. He didn't like a fuss."

She looked away, and we didn't speak of it again.

I called the coroner's office the next day, and after a couple of failed attempts, got the coroner himself on the line. I asked him about the bruising I'd seen on Andy's body, what possibly could have caused it.

"It's consistent with seatbelt abrasion," he said.

"Can a seatbelt cause that much damage?"

A slight pause. "The pattern of bruising is a bit atypical, I admit. More localized to the neck area than we usually see."

"What about his wrist?" I asked.

No hesitation this time. "Wrist injuries are very common in car accidents. The driver instinctively puts out an arm to brace for impact."

"Except there was no impact. Didn't his car roll to a stop?"

Another pause. "Yes. I believe that's right."

"Could anything else have caused the bruises?"

"Mrs. Stevenson, please don't upset yourself. Bruising, especially post-mortem, can be . . . vivid and form unusual patterns. Unless your husband was in an altercation before he died—"

"Was he?"

A prickly note crept into his voice. "As I've stated in my report, it's my opinion the bruises were a result of injuries sustained during the acci—after the car left the road and before it came to a stop. If you have a reason to doubt those findings, you're free to take it up with the police."

When I didn't respond, he went on more gently. "It's natural to want to know what the loved one went through in the moments leading up to death. But your husband bruises didn't cause his death, did they?"

Chapter 9

Everywhere I looked, amidst the flowers on every available table top, Andy's face looked back at me—Andy as a skinny twelve-year-old landing a fish, Andy posing with the commencement speaker at his law school graduation, Andy and me hiking the Mont Blanc circuit on our honeymoon, the sugar-coated Alps in the background. I wanted to run, but there was nowhere I could go, no way to escape my weary, aching heart.

My sister-in-law's guilt trip had worked its poison on me. My husband's co-workers were having their chance to pay their respects after all. The downstairs rooms of our house were packed with friends, neighbors, and business associates and more were arriving every minute. After a week of silence in the house, the noise of so many people, even their muted conversations, felt crushing to me, but I kept my mask firmly in place, doing my bit to make sure none of them pitied me more than was necessary.

Warren Cheung came through the front door in his dark suit, his fiancée, Bernice, at his side. Their sad smiles vanished as they saw me—I'd lost at least ten pounds since Andy's death and even with the sleeping pills my doctor had prescribed, I was still lying awake for hours every night—but Warren stepped forward bravely and put his arms around me. "Melissa, I'm so sorry. How are you holding up?"

I rested against his shoulder, thinking how good it felt to be supported. When I pulled away, Bernice stepped forward and hugged me too, her sweet expression bringing me close to tears. Andy and I hadn't known her well, but with the announcement of Warren's engagement a few months back, we'd hoped she'd become as close a friend to us as Warren.

"If there's anything we can do," Warren said, his eyes searching mine.

I felt a twinge of guilt for not returning any of his calls since Andy's death. "Thanks, Warren. You've been great. I really appreciate it."

"I don't have to tell you what a loss it is . . . for both of us."

"I know," I murmured.

A black Porsche pulled up at the curb far down the cul-de-sac while I stood with Warren and Bernice at the door. I watched with sidelong glances as Ralph Gutierrez, an associate who'd joined the firm the same year as Warren and Andy, got out and made his way past all the other cars lining the street. Ralph was legendary at the firm for his punishing exercise routines. It was hard not to read a latent threat in the way he carried his sculpted body. Whether it was that or the sullen edge to his dark good looks, I couldn't help feeling uncomfortable around him, the way I had in high school around the most popular jocks.

I screwed up my courage as Warren and Bernice left my side and Ralph took their place, his face as much a mask as mine. "Tough break, Melissa, very tough break," he muttered, with only the lamest attempt at eye contact.

Not very eloquent for a rising trial lawyer, but apparently he was just one of those people who didn't know how to deal with another person's grief.

"Andy was . . ." he began, but his voice trailed off and his glance shifted to the crowd in the living room.

I waited. "Andy was what?"

"It's a shitty break, that's all."

It was no secret that Andy and Ralph had been rivals at the firm—Andy, the Eastern WASP, and Ralph, the first-generation son of a Mexican farmer in Fresno and a product of the state university system. It was not a rivalry that Andy relished, but typical of law firm culture—pitting associate against associate to sharpen their competitiveness.

Ralph tagged my arm and moved past me, leaving me alone at the front door for the first time in many minutes. I took the opportunity to step into the living room and lift another cosmopolitan from the tray Jacey was circulating, her day job as an event planner put to good use. I told myself how lucky I was to have her as a friend and made a mental note to do something incredibly generous in return when this whole nightmare was over.

Drink in hand, I drifted past the knotted groups of co-workers, Ralph standing awkwardly among them. How many of them knew about the circumstances of Andy's death, I wondered. How many of them pitied me?

In the dining room, the guests spilled out onto the back terrace despite the punishing five o'clock heat and the brush-fire haze from the surrounding hills. Reg Wolders, Andy's boss, looking every inch the senior partner, held court in front of the French doors, his profile chiseled by the smoky light. His tan was impeccable, as if painted on, his suit poured over his tall, fit body. But even Reg was not immune to time's relentless march. His once handsome face had coarsened with age and the many leisure hours he spent golfing under the punishing California sun.

We'd known each other for four years in the context of holiday dinners and firm outings. At one time, I'd even felt a certain affection for the man. The fact that he'd singled me out among the wives for his special brand of courtly attention—gentle flirting leavened with fatherly advice—was hard to resist. Now I approached him warily, vaguely resentful that he managed to look so perfect on such a sad occasion.

His craggy features arranged themselves in a paternal expression as he caught sight of me. "Melissa," he said, and opened his arms. His wife of thirty-five years, Karen, was talking to one of the paralegals nearby, but that didn't prevent him from holding me longer and closer than was appropriate, even on the day of my husband's funeral.

I pulled back with the scent of his aftershave in my nostrils, the vodka starting to kick in. "Reg, I don't get it. Cocaine? What was going on at that party?"

His blue eyes stilled, lizardlike. "We need to talk, Melissa."

"Okay," I said.

His eyes flicked away. "Not here. Come by the office on Monday. Any time. I'll make myself available."

Anger rose up in me like bile, startling in its intensity. Did I blame him for Andy's death? Maybe. Was I being unfair? Probably. Still, I found it repugnant—his arrogant self-assurance that all he had to do was snap his fingers and the world would remake itself in the order he decreed. I wanted to shout for the whole room to hear that my husband, *his employee*, had been found dead in his car from a drug overdose after a company event. But I didn't, of course. I held it in. "The thing is," I said, "I'm not sure I am. Available."

My combative tone surprised him, that much was obvious. "Melissa, believe me. It's as much of a shock to us as it is to you."

Us.

"I bet."

He laid a placating hand on my forearm. Right, calm the distraught widow. Clearly she's had too much to drink. I pulled my arm away.

"Melissa, please. We're all on the same side. Aren't we?"

I left him standing there and headed to the kitchen, where Jacey and a server she'd hired for the afternoon were getting the trays of food ready. Convention dictated serving the deceased's favorite foods at events like this, so Jacey had ordered massive takeout from the rib joint down at the Town Square. It was going to be messy to eat, but hey, I wasn't paying the dry-cleaning bills.

Another tray of cosmopolitans sat on the counter, waiting to be carried out. I put down my empty glass and took one, bringing it to my lips.

"Have you eaten anything?" asked Jacey, glancing up.

"Not yet."

She gave me *the look*, as in *What are you doing?*

I gave her *the look* back, as in *I appreciate your concern, but it's not your problem.*

The aroma of roasted meat, sweet and smoky, filled the kitchen, as she dumped the big tinfoil tray of glistening ribs into a chafing dish. Normally my mouth would have watered, but today I just let the vodka slide down my throat.

"That Ralph is a hottie," Jacey said, poking the ribs into greasy formation in the dish.

"Cabana boy Ralph," I said, suppressing a hiccup.

"What?"

"Just a joke Andy and I had." In a teasing moment that now seemed like a million years ago, I'd dubbed Ralph, Warren, and Andy "the cabana boys" in tribute to their combined attractiveness.

Jacey, whose memory for chance romantic encounters was encyclopedic, sent me a knowing look. "Wasn't he the one flirting with you at that Napa weekend?"

"Right, if that's what you'd call it." A doubles game of badminton at a company event thrown to showcase Reg's new weekend house, almost a year ago. Warren and me against Ralph and one of the paralegals. Andy, who'd just been promoted, was inside talking to Reg. He'd been inside for a long time. Ralph, flying solo at the event despite his active dating life, kept swatting the shuttlecock over the net directly at me, like a bullet or maybe a hunting kill laid at its master's feet.

"Hey," I protested, after the second or third direct hit.

Totally out of character, he'd flashed a mischievous smile. Later, during cocktail hour, he'd hovered close by, fetching me another glass of wine when my glass was empty, offering me speared canapés from his own plate. Until Andy emerged from Reg's study to claim me, sweeping me off with a territorial look that said, "Thanks, bud, I've got her now" and a whispered apology in my ear, "Sorry, I didn't know this was going to be a working weekend." I'd felt almost sorry for Ralph as we walked away.

"Maybe I'll go introduce myself," Jacey mused, rinsing the utensils in the sink. She stiffened suddenly and sent a guilty look my way. "Whoa. Sorry. I shouldn't—"

What? Dare to look at a man and feel desire while my husband, or what remained of him, sat in a canister in the bedroom? "Don't," I said, "Please. It's okay. Really. You're fine."

But it wasn't okay. Cosmopolitan still in hand, I returned to the crowded living room feeling lost. In the couple of minutes I'd been away the noise level seemed to have gone up many decibels. Too many people talking, too many faces glancing at me and looking away. Laughter escaped here and there, quickly squelched. A clutch of neighbors, adrift in a sea of lawyers, watched me with sympathy in their eyes, but didn't approach. They'd conveyed their condolences at the door, and beyond that, it was becoming clear that no one really knew what to say to me.

Stranded in my own house, I suddenly felt the lack of food, the loss of many nights' sleep. The room tipped. I moved to the nearest wall and braced myself against it, attempting a casual pose. Warren chose that moment to leave Bernice's side and come to me. "Want to sit down? You look a little rough."

I let him steer me to a quiet corner, where we sat across from each other, our knees almost touching.

"Oh, Warren," I said, my voice close to a sob.

His brown eyes sought mine, earnest, kind. "I can't believe this happened. I mean, a heart attack. Shit. Andy was such a *physical* guy. How is that possible?"

I shook my head. Did he know about Andy's cocaine use? At some point in my many sleepless nights, I'd arrived at the bitter assumption that he must have known, being Andy's closest friend. If so, he was doing a very good job of pretending not to.

"I just feel bad I never had a chance to say good-bye to him," he was saying.

"Of course not. How could you have known?"

"No, I mean at the dinner."

"What?" My alcohol buzz receded a little. "What do you mean?"

"He just got up and left. I figured he was going to the men's room, but he never came back."

"What time was that?"

"Nine-thirty? Quarter to ten, maybe. We made plans to meet at Prairie City the next morning to do a practice run on the course. He wanted to get there early." It was a passion Andy and Warren shared—trail biking, the rougher the terrain the better. "When he didn't come back, I figured he'd gone home to get some sleep."

Just for a moment we were talking about the Andy I knew, my husband of eight years. Not the new Andy, the stranger I found myself widowed by.

"Did he leave with anybody?"

Warren looked at me oddly. Maybe it was the urgency in my voice.

"No, I don't think so. Why?"

"Because he died with cocaine in his system."

Warren blanched. "What? Melissa! That's crazy! Andy never—" His shock seemed genuine.

"So you didn't know," I said.

"Huh? No way! I don't even believe it."

"That's what the police are telling me."

"Wait a minute," he muttered, his brown eyes darting around. "*Shit*. Is that what caused the heart attack?"

"It looks that way."

"Oh, Melissa. No."

"Was he . . . impaired when you were with him?"

"He was drinking a club soda. You know Andy."

"Do I? I don't know anything anymore."

A movement in the hallway caught my eye. Ralph Gutierrez

coming down the stairs. Odd, I thought, but maybe the downstairs bathroom was occupied. He rejoined one of the Wolders Palmer groups, but kept looking our way. "What's Ralph's problem? He keeps checking us out."

Warren glanced over his shoulder. "You know Ralph. He and Andy were never exactly best buds. He probably feels weird about being here."

But we lowered our voices, anyway. "Did you tell Darla Roussekoff about any of this?" I whispered.

"Who?" Warren asked.

"The investigator on Andy's case. Didn't you talk to her?"

He frowned and shook his head. "No. I didn't."

"Unbelievable." The room did a sickening slow motion spin. I closed my eyes against it.

Warren squeezed my hand, then stood. "I'll get you some water."

But the tumbler of water he brought from the kitchen remained untouched on the coffee table, while it flashed on me like some waking PTSD nightmare—the bruises on Andy's collarbone, the weird striations on his wrist. I was about to tell Warren when a hush fell over the room. Reg stood in front of the guests, his glass raised for some ghastly toast in Andy's memory. Warren turned to listen respectfully, but I couldn't get away fast enough. I slipped out into the hallway and back to the kitchen, where a few cosmopolitans remained untouched on the tray of drinks. Against all sense of self-preservation, I helped myself to another one.

Jacey came in from the dining room with an empty serving dish and shot me a look on her way to the sink. A few seconds later she was leaning over, her forehead almost touching mine.

"Mel, sweetie, don't you think you've had enough?"

A belligerent voice reached my ears. Mine. "No, I haven't had nearly enough." A couple of heads turned in my direction.

"Come on," Jacey whispered, "let's go have some food."

I pulled away from her and walked in the other direction, away from Reg holding forth in his honeyed tones, away from my guests, and down the hall to the bedroom. The floor pitched like the deck of a ship in a storm as the first wave of nausea hit the back of my throat. I shut the bedroom door and deposited my empty glass on the dresser next to Andy's ashes, then staggered on into the bathroom.

The vast quantity of vodka I'd consumed in the past hour or so came up neatly in the toilet bowl. I flushed the toilet and moved determinedly toward the bed, stripping off dress, bra, and underpants as I went. I crawled in naked and pulled up the top sheet, my head already starting to pound. Unconsciousness lapped over me like a dark river and carried me away.

Chapter 10

Light filtered through the bedroom blinds as I opened my eyes. Morning light. My body ached all over, as if I'd been running a marathon in my dreams. The glass of water on the nightstand had been sitting there for two days, but I drained it anyway. The bedside clock said 7:21.

Another morning, another day to get through.

Juju lay stretched out next to me, his spine pressed against my thigh, his toes pointing up in a gesture of pure bliss. I ran my hand absently down the length of his body, then reached for my phone. No calls.

I pulled on a T-shirt and a pair of Andy's boxers and stumbled barefoot into the living room. The house was immaculate, with no sign of the fifty guests who had crammed the downstairs rooms the day before. Jacey had left a note on the kitchen counter. "I'm home all day tomorrow," her loopy, generous handwriting read. "Come over any time."

Clearly I owed her big-time, and I was grateful, immensely so, but I couldn't face being with her this morning. Not yet, at least. I couldn't face anybody. I drank another full glass of water, popped three aspirin, and went back to bed.

When I woke again, it was ten-thirty and Juju was perched on Andy's pillow, his blue-eyed gaze in his chocolate face conveying feline love. I kissed his nose and stroked his silky coat, the first sincere attention I'd bestowed on him in many days. "What's the matter, Jujie? Are you hungry?" His head tilted. "Yeah, I bet you are."

In the kitchen, I poured food into his dish and filled his almost empty water bowl, then left the coffee percolating and went to shower. Getting dressed, I checked the phone again. One call from Jacey and another from Reg Wolders' private line at work. I ignored Reg's call and quickly texted Jacey: "Thank you SO MUCH for yesterday. Going out for a while. Talk later. XO."

It hit me as soon as I opened the garage door—the much-loved delta breeze that brought with it a temperature drop of about fifteen degrees. Coming from New England, the home of the nor'easter, I still hadn't gotten used to cool weather coming from the southwest or the sun setting over the ocean. The mirror-image quality of life on the West Coast felt unreal to me, even after four years.

I groped for my sunglasses and put them on as I drove out of the garage into the cul-de-sac, the bright air stabbing my aching eyes. My stomach growled, but not with a healthy hunger. It was the sick, gnawing hunger that comes after a night of binge drinking. A sudden overpowering craving hit me, for grease and salt, ketchup and sugar. I made the ten-minute drive to the In-N-Out Burger on Placerville Road and got in line for the drive-through. It was barely lunchtime, but I ordered a burger with everything, fries with extra salt, and a large Coke. "No, make that a Diet Coke," I told the disembodied voice taking my order. Thanks to Andy's lectures, I'd given up my guilty attachment to diet soda years before. A purist, he regarded artificial sweetener as the equivalent of strychnine. For one perverse moment, it almost pleased me to think how horrified he would be.

"You don't like it, Andy, too bad," I said out loud. "In fact, screw you."

But then it hit me all over again. Andy's opinion of my unhealthy habits didn't matter anymore. It was never going to matter ever again. And without warning I was crying in the drive-thru, hot tears scalding my cheeks, at all the things Andy would never say to me again. Through the blur of tears, I grabbed the paper bag being thrust at me from the take-out window and stepped on the gas.

I turned out into traffic, blindly. A car honked and swerved around me. Two blocks down Placerville Road, I pulled over to the curb and wept. But crying couldn't begin to get to the bottom of what I was feeling. Suddenly I was beating my fists on the steering wheel.

"You hear me, Andy, wherever you are? Screw you, I said. Screw you! I hate you, do you hear me? I hate you! How could you do this to me?" Anguished sobs exploded from my chest. I stopped, embarrassed and ashamed, pushing the tears away. How could he do this to me? How could I do this to *him*?

Wilted and panting, I slumped against the seat. Eventually, I shifted into drive and eased back into traffic, heading for the freeway. As I drove, I tore open the bag and began eating, surrendering to a hunger that felt unappeasable. Ketchup and grease dripped off my chin onto my lap as big mouthfuls of burger and fries slid down my throat, and I didn't care at all. The only thing that mattered was the tingling sensation of the Diet Coke washing it all down.

Still eating, I turned onto Route 50 and drove east into the white-hot sun. It was Sunday morning and the traffic was light, the surrounding countryside scorched and empty. I'd finished eating by the time I reached the El Dorado Hills exit, but I kept driving, the shimmering road unspooling in front of me. The roofs and clock tower of the Town Square loomed and then receded on the right, a Potemkin village on the prairie, so different from the organic sprawl of New England. The developers had built it all—movie theaters, restaurants, gym, big box stores—in the space of a few months, a ready-made suburbia etched against the sun-baked hills. I'd often poked fun at the Hollywood set quality of our surroundings, but Andy had just laughed, not bothered by it at all.

Route 50 climbed as I drove east toward Placerville—an authentic town, at least, dating back to the Gold Rush. We'd visited there a few times when we first moved to California, on sightseeing trips to Sutter's Mill. Today, I blew past the Placerville exit and kept my eyes on the horizon, blue and cloudless in the rising terrain.

Somewhere past the cut-off for Grizzly Flats, the road entered the piney shade of the Eldorado National Forest. I lost reception and shut off my phone. A fleeting lightness came over me, as if I'd cut the cord that bound me to everything that remained behind on the valley floor. Ten miles on, I pulled over at the trailhead of a hiking spot Andy and I had frequented in the cooler months. It was a quarter-mile walk over stepped boulders and pine needles to a waterfall, beyond which a series of rolling vistas opened out into gold prospecting country.

I remembered the trail as peaceful, refreshing. But today, in the noontime sun, the heat coming off the rocks was solid and withering. No sign of the delta breeze here. I'd only gone a few hundred feet when the ground lurched and my stomach with it. I crawled off the path into a copse of scrub pine and sank down on the nearest boulder, my head whirling into blackness. I leaned forward and hugged my knees to my chest, willing myself not to be sick for the second time in twenty-four hours.

When the nausea subsided and it felt safe to stand up, I scrambled down the path back to the car. Common sense told me to turn west and just return home, but instead I continued east on Route 50, opening the car windows to the cooling air. A half-hour later I reached the summit and began the winding descent to Lake Tahoe and Nevada beyond it. A two-lane road meandered its way down to another valley floor. I remembered how surprised I'd been the first time Andy and I had traveled this road —that desert brown Nevada could actually have green, gentle valleys too.

At two o'clock I rolled into Genoa, a town Andy and I had loved from the moment we discovered it, perhaps because of its quaint, almost New England feel. I parked in a shaded parking lot next to a playground and walked down the tree-lined main street toward the two-story brick courthouse. It was Sunday afternoon and very quiet, the leaves shivering in the mild desert breeze. Beyond the courthouse, on the side terrace of a white-clapboarded inn, a few people sat at tables under umbrellas enjoying lunch and drinks. I strolled past them and turned down a side street.

It was still there, unchanged, the cottage we both loved—raspberry-colored with white shutters and gingerbread fretwork all along the roofline, like a cottage in the campground on Martha's Vineyard. The lush green of the back yard gave over to the vast prairie beyond it, separated only by a modest picket fence. I knew then why I'd come. I was looking for Andy. I wanted to feel him somewhere, anywhere, and this was the best place I knew.

The last time we'd visited Genoa we'd talked about moving there over sandwiches at the inn. We could buy the cottage, we said, have a giant backyard garden, keep a goat or two. Andy could trade his high-pressure job at Wolders Palmer for country lawyering in nearby Carson City. For a few hours, we'd both wanted it so much we could almost believe it was ours to have. But the sun had dipped behind the mountains and we'd returned home, just as I'd have to do today.

But for now I found a bench across from the courthouse and sat without moving until I felt it, Andy's spirit distinctly beside me. I closed my eyes and let the tears run down my cheeks. "Why did you leave me?" I whispered.

"I didn't," he said. "I'm here."

My breathing slowed and the aching in my chest eased. I became calm, even peaceful. We sat together, Andy and I, in the dappled shade of the cooling afternoon.

Awhile later, I went back to the car, reclined the driver's seat, and shut my eyes. The sound of car doors thunking closed and kids' excited voices as they ran ahead of their parents to the playground brought me awake. I'd slept for more than an hour, the first dreamless, untroubled sleep I'd had in a week.

Deep, lovely shadows cloaked the Sierra Nevadas as I headed up the eastern slope toward home, still sleepy and relaxed. I was back in the sun on the western descent into the Central Valley before I remembered that my phone had been switched off all afternoon. I powered it on and glanced at the screen.

While I was on walkabout, three calls had come in—all from Reg Wolders' private line.

Chapter 11

I showed up at Wolders Palmer a day late and half a million short, if you counted Andy's voided insurance payout. Ignoring Reg's invitation to drop by like I was still part of the "WP family," I'd called his secretary and made an appointment.

Glass and mahogany greeted me as I walked off the elevator into reception, a vast space that seemed designed more to intimidate clients than to welcome them. My footsteps echoed on the cold marble floor as I approached the desk.

A twenty-something receptionist whom I'd never seen before gave me a bored look that vanished quickly when I told her my name. My stomach tightened as her obligatory expression of sympathy switched on. "Oh, Mrs. Stevenson, we were all so sorry—"

I murmured my thanks and turned away.

"I'll tell Mr. Wolders you're here," she called after me, unnecessarily.

I walked over to the seating area, with its floor-to-ceiling windows framing a panoramic view of downtown Sacramento. Not that impressive, if you were used to the skyline of, say, New York or San Francisco, but impressive enough from the seventeenth floor. What it lacked in the "wow" factor was made up for by the towering, twisted metal sculpture that dominated one corner of the space. Was it intentional that it resembled a giant bird of prey, I wondered, as I took a seat within striking distance of its jagged metal beak. A plaque near the talon-like feet announced that the sculpture was on loan from the collection of Reg and Karen Wolders.

A door clicked open in the paneled mahogany wall and Reg himself came over to greet me. "Melissa," he said, "it's good of you to make the time to come in."

If a barb lurked in his words, he hid it well behind his cordial smile. I let him steer me back through the door down a short, private corridor to his corner office, where he waved me toward a pair of leather couches facing each other on a richly hued Persian rug.

"Please. Sit."

I sat.

The glass-topped coffee table in front of me held a carton of items. A younger version of myself, dark blonde hair streaked lighter by the sun, smile wide and trusting, gazed at me from a framed five-by-seven photo on top of the pile. The stuff from Andy's office.

"Can I get you something? Coffee?"

"No, thanks. I'm good."

"Bottled water?"

I gave in with a nod, my eyes drawn to the painting on the wall behind me—gouts of discordant color like blood splatter. Another reminder of Reg and Karen Wolders' peculiar taste as local art patrons.

Reg pulled a Fiji water out of a recessed fridge and passed it to me, his fingertips grazing mine in the hand-off. A small shudder went through me. He sat down across from me, his workmanlike hands resting on his pin-stripe-clad knees. A few seconds ticked by as we sized each other up.

I drew in a breath and forced myself to say it. "Reg, I'm really sorry about the other day. Obviously, I wasn't myself."

"No apology necessary. I understand that you're angry. You've had a terrible shock and you're looking for someone to blame."

His conciliatory tone surprised me. Comforted me, almost. My body relaxed into the soft leather of the couch. "Thank you for understanding."

"Not at all. You want answers. I get that. Believe me, we want answers, too. Andy was like a son to me. You know that."

"I do," I conceded.

His fingers toyed with an onyx cufflink. "If I'd known he had a drug problem—"

The surrounding hush, so soothing a moment ago, felt suffocating. Alleged, I wanted to blurt out. Alleged drug problem.

"—I would have done anything in my power to help him. As it was, we were on the verge of firing him."

I pushed away from the enfolding leather of the couch. "What?"

He shrugged. "It was the last thing I ever expected to have to do. But his job performance declined sharply in the last few months."

"Declined," I repeated stupidly. All those nights Andy had arrived home, his face ashen with fatigue, no sign of being high, only to work long into the night at his desk upstairs.

"I talked to him about it, and the situation improved for a while, but then his performance got so bad, I worried he'd compromise the integrity of the firm." His gaze left mine for a moment and seemed to get lost in the painting behind my head. "It's painful to have to tell you this, but there's even some evidence he . . . mishandled funds in an escrow account of one of our biggest clients."

I stared at him. "You're kidding, right? *Andy?*" I remembered Andy's letter of recommendation from the judge he'd clerked for in Boston, the one he'd submitted with his job application for associate attorney at Wolders Palmer. *Highest moral character, unimpeachable honesty.* "That's crazy, Reg. Andy wouldn't do that."

"Andy wouldn't do that," he repeated. "That's exactly what I told myself."

His tone was kind, scrupulously so, but I thought, *You bastard. You son of a bitch.* I opened my mouth to respond and then closed it. My mother's voice came at me loud and clear, words she'd flung at me often during my teens. *Don't be a hothead like your father. Where did his anger ever get him?*

As if reading my churning thoughts, Reg raised a placating hand. "Melissa, please, I know how hard it must be for you to hear these things. And it's hard for me to have to say them. But we're not the bad guys here. Your life has been turned upside down, and we want to do whatever we can to help. But it's possible we're going to need your help, too."

"My help?" I asked, startled.

"You see, it gets worse. For us, at least. Our IT department tells me that Andy uploaded a large number of confidential documents to a USB drive before he died. Granted, they pertained to cases he was working on, but still it's a clear violation of company policy. I was about to confront him on it, but then . . ."

He died of a drug overdose. How convenient.

"Let's just say this data breach could prove embarrassing to a major client if the information fell into the wrong hands. We could be facing millions in malpractice."

Gosh, I feel for you, Reg.

"I didn't mention it to the authorities for the obvious reasons. Andy is deceased and there's no point in tarnishing his memory. But it's imperative that we recover that thumb drive. I'd appreciate it if you'd check Andy's home office to see if it's there."

My frenzied ransacking of his possessions a couple of nights ago in search of telltale traces of white powder came back to me in lurid flashes. True, something as small as a thumb drive could be hidden anywhere, but at that moment I wanted to see Reg sweat. "It's not."

"How can you be so sure?"

"Maybe," I said, "it's in his briefcase. But the funny thing is that's gone missing too. It wasn't in his car the night he died."

He fingered his cufflink almost as if he hadn't heard me. "Melissa, please, I'm trying to be patient here. You have a lot on your plate right now, and the last thing I want to do is give you more to worry about. If you feel unable to help us, I'd be happy to send Ralph over to help you look."

"Ralph?" It shocked me more than anything he'd said or insinuated up to this moment.

"With your permission, of course."

"I'll look again," I said evenly.

For just for a second or two, the veneer cracked—the smooth, in-control persona Reg showed to the world. Then slowly, like a shadow passing over water, the paternal smile returned—a chilly version of it. "Melissa, don't do this to yourself," he said softly. "Don't make yourself an accessory—"

"An accessory? To what exactly?"

"Isn't it obvious? Andy had a reason for taking those files."

"Why, Reg? Why would he do that?"

"As insurance against getting fired, I'm afraid."

I was on my feet before I even realized it. "What are we talking about here?"

The word hung unspoken between us. His silence infuriated me.

"Reg," I said, my voice shaking, "I don't know what was going on the night of that dinner, but I do know my husband suffered a fatal drug overdose on his way home. If I find out that you, or anybody else at this firm, is even remotely to blame, you can bet I'll be filing a civil suit—"

He stood, too, and laid a hand on my arm. "Be careful, Melissa. You're among friends here."

I glared at him with restrained fury. "Was Andy among friends?"

He held my look but released his grip.

I grabbed Andy's carton of possessions and left his office, not looking back. Cold sweat sprang out on my neck, under my arms. I smelled it coming off me, the rank smell of fear. What had I done? I'd threatened the senior partner with a wrongful death suit, and Andy's last paycheck hadn't even hit our joint account yet.

Hothead hothead. Shit shit shit.

Somehow in my blind haste to get away, I took a wrong turn, and instead of heading straight back to reception, emerged into a maze of cubicles. Small offices with glass doors lined the exterior walls of the space. I kept my head down, avoiding eye contact. In one office I passed, I glimpsed Warren standing behind his desk talking on the phone. Our eyes met as I hurried by. A few doors down, I passed an office that I was sure was Andy's the last time I visited, but there were photos of someone else's family on the desk now.

I turned a corner and ran full tilt into Ralph, Andy's carton of stuff ramming him in the stomach. I caught a whiff of his aftershave, his olive-scented skin.

"Melissa," he said. "Are you—?"

"I'm fine."

An odd look crossed his face—very odd for Ralph. The sympathy he'd failed to show at Andy's memorial gathering. Or was it pity? Then I understood. He knew about Andy, the whole sordid mess. Of course he did. If Andy sat at Reg's right hand, Ralph sat at his left.

"Excuse me," I muttered, and pushed past him.

I reached the elevators and jabbed the down button, willing myself not to look behind me. My phone chirped suddenly, an incoming text from Warren. "Meet me downstairs in 5. South entrance."

I closed my eyes, breathing hard. Where was the damn elevator? The light blinked on and the doors glided open. I stepped inside and held my thumb on the button to close the doors. An agonizing second or two later, the elevator began its smooth drop.

I texted Warren back with shaking fingers. "Not a good time."

His reply was instantaneous. "Please."

I walked out of the lobby into the bright sun of the south entrance and crossed the courtyard to a granite bench in partial shade. I sat on it, feeling light-headed. A minute or two later Warren appeared, glancing around as he approached, the noontime sun flashing off his white, short-sleeved shirt. He caught sight of my expression and stopped. "Wow. What happened up there?"

I shook my head. "I just can't . . . talk about it right now."

"So it wasn't about death benefits?"

"Not even close."

"Do you want to get a coffee?"

"No more caffeine. I already feel like I'm flying apart."

"Where are you going from here?"

"I don't know."

"Well, you look like you shouldn't be driving." He glanced across the street at Starbucks. "Come across with me. I'll get you a hot tea. Or a yogurt smoothie or something."

I bent over Andy's carton on my lap, making an effort to catch my breath. "Yeah, okay."

He took my arm as we crossed the street, but I barely felt his touch. The heat of the pavement under my sandals, the lanes of city traffic stopped at the crosswalk, the other pedestrians pushing past us to get to where they were going felt about as real as the lunchtime rush on Planet X in a parallel universe. I let Warren pull me along, locked in my own private nightmare.

The coffee shop was like a cave after the intense sunlight of the street, its tinted windows blocking all solar heat and most of the light. I sat at a table near the back while Warren stood in line. My teeth were chattering, but not because the place was over-air-conditioned. When he placed the hot tea in front of me, I wrapped my fingers around it and let the steam hit my face.

He sat down across from me and waited. I wanted to blurt it all out to him, every horrible moment of my confrontation with Reg. But something stopped me. Warren was Andy's best friend. I had no reason to distrust him. And yet. I gulped in more air and pulled myself together. "What did you want to talk to me about?"

The guy sitting next to us was engrossed in his laptop, but Warren glanced at him before leaning forward. "Look, Melissa, the more I think about it, the more I think this cocaine thing is a bullshit rap. Let's face it, I probably spent as much time with Andy as you did. Don't you think I would have *known* if he had a coke habit?"

Cocaine. Coke habit. I'd had enough.

"So, what, Warren? What? The coroner *lied*? It was in his *bloodstream*."

His expression darkened. "Or somebody . . ."

"What, Warren? Somebody hurt him? Who would do that? *Tell me*."

He pulled back, stunned. "I don't know."

"I'm sorry," I said immediately. "I shouldn't be yelling at you. Of all people."

"Hey, it's chill. I understand."

"It's just—"

It gets worse. For us, at least, Reg had said. *The data breach.*

"Did you know Andy was about to get fired?"

His eyes went wide. "What?"

"Did you know he took some documents off the server without permission?"

"Melissa, you're really freaking me out here. What documents? Why?"

"Reg called it a data breach. Some documents for a case Andy was working on."

"So? We download documents from the Corp Div all the time. Technically we're supposed to go through channels, but—"

"What case was Andy working on when he died?"

Warren popped the plastic lid off his iced coffee and took a swallow. "Some real estate deal with the American River Group. They're a big client of Reg's. That's confidential, of course."

I nodded. "How did Andy come to be working on the case?"

A flash of good-natured envy crossed his face. "Because Reg *wanted* him. Andy was the anointed one. You knew that, right?"

My reflection wavered in my milky tea. "So Andy wasn't in any kind of . . . trouble at the firm?"

Warren's phone started buzzing on the table between us. He palmed it and brought it to his ear. "Hey, bro', what's up?"

An annoyed voice reached me from the receiver. Male. *Where the hell are you?*

Warren glanced down at his watch. "I just stepped out for an iced coffee. I'll be back in five." He glanced over at me and mouthed the word, "Ralph."

I started shivering again.

A couple of terse exchanges later, he clicked off the call and slid the phone back into his pocket. "Sorry, my bad. Lunch meeting. My absence has been noted."

He got up to leave. I stood too. He gave me a brief good-bye hug. "We'll talk later, okay? This whole thing is crazy insane, but there's got to be an explanation."

He walked away, threading his way through the line of the customers at the counter. He was almost at the door when I called after him.

He turned and looked back across the room at me.

I wanted to say *Be careful*, but I could see I didn't have to. Our eyes held each other's for a long second. Then he slipped on his sunglasses and stepped out onto the sun-dazzled street.

I carried Andy's carton to the parking garage and stowed it in the car, but I still felt too shaky to drive, so I returned to the street and started walking, grateful to be back outside in the warmth and light. The objective part of my mind, the part that seemed to function no matter how terrible I felt, noticed that it was a beautiful afternoon, breezy and almost comfortable, but I was much too appalled at the day's turn of events to feel anything besides horror and a growing sense of dread. Like a sick loop playing repeatedly in my head, Reg's words came back to me.

Mishandled funds in an escrow account.

Millions in malpractice.

Insurance against getting fired.

And then another word inserted itself, from out of nowhere, an ugly word that harked back to the financial meltdown at the end of the last decade. *Clawback.* If Reg's accusations were founded, what exactly was Andy's liability in this situation, and mine by extension? Could Wolders Palmer sue me for damages? Or worse, being the all-powerful law firm that they were, suck the money out of our bank account right back into theirs without me being able to do a thing to stop them? Okay, I told myself, now you're being paranoid. This is your poverty programming talking (hey, thanks, Mom) and your distrust of authority figures (you, too, Dad, thanks a bunch).

Just the same, I couldn't help appreciating the grim irony when I looked up and found myself standing in front of the main branch of the bank where Andy and I had our checking account. On impulse, I pushed through the heavy revolving doors into the lobby. Thanks to electronic banking, the place was almost empty of customers. I claimed a chair near the entrance and checked the balance in our joint account on my phone. Fifteen thousand and change. Then I did a quick calculation of the monthly expenses that would be hitting in the next week or so.

A teller at one of the two open windows looked across at me, a brief look—of curiosity and not suspicion, I hoped. I wondered if I looked as wild-eyed and disheveled as I felt.

I imagined myself approaching her window and asking to withdraw ten thousand dollars in cash. Would she act surprised or take it in stride, tapping my account number into her computer before asking, pleasantly enough, to see my identification. I saw myself nodding and pulling out my wallet, sliding my driver's license through the opening to her.

A drop of sweat started at my hairline and trickled down the side of my face as if I were actually standing in front of her watching her eyes go back and forth from my license to my face. At which point I would reflect, resentfully, that even though

Andy and I had had our business at this bank for the past four years, including the mortgage on our house, I was being made to feel like a criminal for wanting to withdraw my own money.

Ridiculous, of course—my assumption that there was anything I could do to make myself safe. If I truly wanted to be safe, I'd have to make good on my threat to bring a lawsuit against Wolders Palmer. Lawyers suing lawyers. It made my blood run cold.

A bank officer came out from behind his glass enclosure. "Ma'am? Is everything all right?" He had that wide-open, Scandinavian kind of face I'd seen often since coming to California. The great-grandson of Okies, I imagined.

I sat up straight and brushed a strand of hair back in place. "Yes. I'm sorry. I just needed to get in out of the heat for a minute."

"Is there anything I can help you with?"

I stood up quickly. "No. I'm good. Thank you."

He smiled, looking relieved. "You have yourself a fine day, then."

I was out on the street hurrying back to the parking garage when it came to me. What I had to do.

Chapter 12

"I need to see Darla Roussekoff."

The middle-aged receptionist regarded me through bulletproof glass. "She's not in right now. She's on her way back from Petaluma."

"When do you expect her?"

"Not until two."

I glanced at my watch. It was just after twelve-thirty. "I'll wait."

"And you are?"

"Melissa Stevenson. My husband died in his car on June fifth, an unattended death. Detective Roussekoff was the investigator on the case."

Unmoved, the receptionist nodded at the chairs behind me. "Take a seat."

The detective came through the double doors a little before two, looking hot and harried, hungry too. She carried a bulging briefcase in one hand and a fast food meal in the other. The smell of hamburger and fries filled the tiny waiting area.

I stood to greet her.

"This is Mrs. Stevenson," the receptionist called through the glass.

For just a second Darla's face was blank. Then it clicked—who I was.

"I'm sorry—I don't mean to interrupt your lunch," I said.

Her eyes grazed the paper bag in her hand, the large soda tinkling with ice. "No worries. Come this way."

The receptionist buzzed us through to the interior of the building. Halfway down the cinderblock hallway, Darla opened a door on the left and went inside to drop off her lunch and her briefcase. She emerged with a case file, note pad, and pen, and ushered me into the small, windowless room directly opposite. I recognized it as an interview room—the kind featured in those gritty inner-city crime dramas on TV. The stale air smelled of body odor overlaid with disinfectant. I could well imagine what went on inside this room under other circumstances. Suspects being thrown against the wall, questions sneered. But maybe not. It was just the county sheriff's office, after all.

We faced each other across a wooden table tattooed with coffee rings. I watched her flip open her notepad and click on her ballpoint pen—gestures I was intimately familiar with from our last encounter.

"I'm sorry," I said again, "I don't want to be a thorn in anyone's side, but I still have a lot of questions about my husband's death."

"I'm listening."

I gulped, wondering what it was about this woman that intimidated me so. "I went to view my husband's body at the funeral home. Those bruises on his neck and his wrist—I don't understand what caused them. He was wearing his seatbelt."

No emotion penetrated her face, but her fingers began twirling her ballpoint pen. "Mrs. Stevenson, have you studied crash forensics?"

"But he didn't crash, did he? His car rolled to a stop. At least that was my understanding."

"That's not quite accurate. The terrain was pretty rough where your husband's car went off the road. Even at a low rate of speed, even wearing a seatbelt, he could have been bounced around quite a lot before the vehicle stopped. Even more so if he was unconscious. You'd be surprised."

"The coroner said it was possible, based on his injuries, that he was in a—" my throat was suddenly bone dry "—an altercation before he died."

The pen stopped twirling. Her eyes flicked toward the door. I imagined she was thinking about her takeout lunch growing cold across the hall, her soda getting watery. "Ken raised that possibility before he wrote his report," she said at last. "But he came to the conclusion, based on the evidence, that your husband's injuries were sustained in the manner I've just described."

"But if there was any doubt—couldn't you at least have followed up on it?"

If Detective Roussekoff had a tell, it was that she became even more stone-faced when she was annoyed. "Mrs. Stevenson, I wish I had unlimited resources to investigate your husband's movements in the hours leading up to his death. But—as I'm sure you're aware—the same taxpayers who demand these kinds of services also vote against having their taxes raised."

I supposed she was taking a shot at the affluent residents of El Dorado Hills, a fair number of whom were rabidly anti-property-tax conservatives.

She went on. "But even if I did have the resources to conduct an exhaustive investigation, how would that change the facts? Your husband died of a heart attack in his car, he was in possession of cocaine at the scene, and he had cocaine in his system when he died."

The countless frustrations of the day, my helplessness against Reg's accusations, the sensation of beating my fists against an immovable wall of denial, crashed down on me all at once. "I'm sorry," I said yet again, my voice rising, "but I was Andy's wife. If he was using cocaine, don't you think I would have known? His behavior was *normal*. No unexplained withdrawals from our checking account, nothing to suggest he had a drug habit. And his closest friend, Warren Cheung, would say the same—but you know that, right? Because you interviewed him."

A very faint blush crept into her pasty features. She opened the case file in front of her and glanced down at the cover page. "Mr. Cheung was in court the day I was at Wolders Palmer."

"And you didn't bother to follow up?"

"Mrs. Stevenson, with all due respect, I've investigated hundreds of these cases. Allow me to speak from experience. The people closest to the drug user are often the last to know."

"That's it? That's all you can say?" For the second time that day, I found myself shaking with anger. "Who—if you don't mind me asking *as a taxpayer—did* you interview about my husband's death?"

She consulted the case file again. Clumsily she turned one sheet over and then the next. My burst of anger must have rattled her. If the stakes weren't so high, I might even have felt sorry for my outburst. The third sheet was a photocopy of her handwritten notes. I recognized her handwriting. She read what was on the page. "Mr. Wolders and Mr. Gutierrez."

Ralph! I shook my head in disgust.

Detective Roussekoff rose from her chair, a signal that her patience and our time together were at an end. "Mrs. Stevenson, if you have a problem with the way this case was handled, you're free to take it up with my superior."

"Fine," I said, standing too. "Who would that be?"

"The receptionist will be happy to direct you."

During our entire conversation, her tone had not altered by even half an octave. The consummate professional. It took every last ounce of self-restraint not to slam the door on my way out, entitled El Dorado Hills bitch that I was.

But I didn't follow up with her superior, the credibility of the sheriff's office blown, as far as I was concerned. Trembling with exhaustion and unspent rage, I drove straight home and got into the shower, as if mere water could wash off the indignities of the day—the stink of fear I'd carried with me out of Reg's office, the body odor bouquet that clung to my hair and clothing from the sheriff's office interview room. I let the steaming water drum down on my head and shoulders until my skin burned pink. Then I flipped the faucet to cold for as long as I could stand. The object, almost achieved, was to stop the churning in my brain, the pumping adrenaline. Afterwards, wrapped in my robe even though there were many hours of daylight left, I curled up on the sofa with my laptop. I opened a browser window and searched on the phrase that had been nagging at me since leaving the sheriff's office.

Crash forensics.

My search returned a definition (the study of the accident scene by a police officer or private investigator) and a list of firms claiming to be experts at it. Another term, almost synonymous, started cropping up as I clicked through the sites: *accident reconstruction.* Since Andy hadn't crashed at all, except maybe with some very long prairie grass, I decided that what I was really looking for was an expert is accident reconstruction. On my next search a couple of names bubbled to the top of the list. Some guy in Redding, California—much too far away—and a firm that was actually local. By a strange coincidence, the offices of Haydon Investigations were in historic downtown Folsom, just a few blocks from where Andy and I lived before moving to El Dorado Hills.

I clicked on the link to the website. Unlike the competition, Haydon Investigations didn't blare its qualifications. Its website was quiet, tasteful, aesthetically pleasing in its minimalism.

There was a short bio of Tom Haydon, the principal of the firm, and shorter bios of two associates. They advertised themselves as a "full-service firm" with expertise in a relatively short list of areas. Accident reconstruction, civil matters, and insurance investigations jumped out at me. At last, maybe there was someone who could help me, someone whose offices were in the next town over. For the first time that day, I was able to take a deep breath.

Chapter 13

"**Y**ou need a signature on that?" a male voice called through the half-open door to an inner office.

"Uh—." I let the dog-eared *People* magazine I'd just picked up drop back onto the pile on the waiting room coffee table.

A tall, lanky man appeared in the doorway, his gray hair combed back from a high forehead. He was dressed almost shabbily, in a faded short-sleeved shirt that was somewhere between green and gray and pants of the same nondescript color. I wondered if all the investigators were out on cases and I was speaking with the office cleaner.

"Oh," he said, "I thought you were the UPS guy."

"I'm sorry. I—don't have an appointment."

"Guess you'll have to take a number."

Maybe it was his long Irish face—a familiar sight back in Boston—or the merest suggestion of humor lurking in his gray eyes, but I felt myself relax a little. A foreign sensation since Andy died.

He extended his hand. "I'm Tom Haydon. And no, in case you're wondering, I was never married to Jane Fonda."

"Excuse me?"

"Tom Hayden? Peace activist back in the seventies? Politician?" He sighed. "Forget it. You probably don't even know who Jane Fonda is."

Out of all the private investigators in the area, I had to pick a comedian. Still, I couldn't help smiling. No one had dared to joke with me in so long.

"Actually I do," I said.

He raised an eyebrow.

"She played the grandmother in *Georgia Rule*."

"Millennials!" He shook his head in mock bewilderment. "I assume you're here to see me on a 'matter'?"

I nodded.

"Come on in."

He swept the papers on his desk into a pile and moved them to one side. Then he spun his office chair to his computer to close an open document. A desktop picture of black sand and palm trees came up. Hawaii, probably—maybe even Punalu'u Beach, where Andy and I had once vacationed. The computer itself was an iMac with a 27-inch screen, the same as mine at home. I supposed that said something in Tom Haydon's favor.

"You're a Mac user," I said.

"Graphics are king in this profession."

The office was cool, dimly lit, the blinds half closed, the walls a soothing pale green. It felt like an oasis after the turmoil of the day before. I sank gratefully into the visitor's chair and let my eyes wander to the framed credentials on the wall to my right. There were a couple of photographs too, one of a much younger Tom Haydon in police uniform, accepting an award.

He sat across from me, waiting expectantly.

"I'm not sure where to start," I said.

"How about your name and contact info?" he said pleasantly.

I flushed, realizing I hadn't introduced myself. Not that he'd given me a chance.

He recorded my information in neat block letters at the top of a yellow legal pad. Left-handed, I noted, like Andy. "So, Mrs. Stevenson, what brings you to our fair abode?"

"Your website says you specialize in accident reconstruction."

"My associate handles most of that work. My background is more in criminal investigations." He read my disappointed look. "But of course, I'd consult with him if you decided to hire me. What accident are we talking about?"

By now it had become almost rote, the story of how Andy had died alone in his car on the night of June fifth on the way home from a work-related dinner, on a road he never would have taken at that hour, how he'd been wearing his seatbelt but had unexplained injuries. How the coroner had ruled the cause of death a heart attack, but that cocaine had been found in the car and in his system.

Tom Haydon listened intently, recognition flitting across his face. "Is this the lawyer who was found out on County Road?"

I glanced up, surprised. "Yes."

"It got a lot of buzz on the local news for a few days."

"Right. I wasn't really paying attention."

"Of course not," he said gently. "I'm sorry for your loss." When I didn't respond, he went on just as gently. "I assume, since you're here, that you're disputing the Highway Patrol's version of the accident. May I ask why?"

My hand closed over my phone in my purse. I pulled it out and scrolled to the first photo of Andy lying in his cardboard coffin at the funeral home. "This." I slid the phone across the desk to him.

He studied the photo for several long seconds.

"Does that look like seatbelt abrasion to you?" I asked.

Haydon spun his chair to his computer and opened a browser screen. His long fingers tapped a few keys and a page of densely packed entries appeared. "Police accident reports," he explained. "June fifth, you said? Here it is." He read silently, scrolling down the page. "Evidence at the scene indicates that the car slowed before leaving the road. It was found about twenty feet in, no skid marks. Which would indicate that the driver pulled off the road on purpose." He glanced back at my phone. "Hard to square with bruises like that."

I reached over and scrolled to the next photo, the weird striations on Andy's wrist. "What about this?"

He glanced up sharply from the phone screen. Maybe he saw the same thing I saw. Finger marks. "What does the coroner say?"

"That he put out his hand to brace for impact.'"

"Curiouser and curioser." He rubbed his jaw for a moment, lost in thought. Then his gaze cleared. "Let me ask you this. What do you think happened? Something must have brought you here."

The silence in the room was thick, broken only by a random gurgle from the water cooler out in the waiting room. I drew in my breath and said the thing I'd been thinking ever since leaving Reg's office. The thing I hadn't had the nerve to say to Darla Roussekoff in that depressing interview room. "I have this awful feeling my husband was murdered."

Chapter 14

Tom Haydon leaned back in his chair with a wordless stare.

My cheeks started to burn. "But you probably hear that all the time."

"Not as often as you might think." The humor on his mobile Irish features was a memory.

The street door opened, startling us both, and footsteps crossed the waiting room. Something heavy hit the floor. Tom stood up. "Excuse me. That's the package I've been expecting."

He disappeared into the outer office, but was back behind his desk in less than a minute, his pen poised over his legal pad as the street door closed behind the UPS guy.

"Go on. By whom?"

I stared blankly for a second.

He spoke quietly. "Who do you think murdered your husband?"

"His boss? The people he worked for?"

"This is Wolders Palmer you're talking about?" He studied me intently. "So what motive would the good folks at Wolders Palmer have for murder?"

"His boss is saying Andy downloaded some documents—sensitive documents—without permission. He called it a data breach." Spoken aloud it sounded flimsy, ridiculous, but Tom Haydon's gaze didn't waver.

"Why would your husband do that?"

"I don't know. As insurance against getting fired, his boss claims."

"So you've talked to the boss."

"Yesterday. It didn't go well."

"What would be their reason for firing him?"

"They said his coke habit was affecting his job performance. "

"Fair enough."

"But—"

"But?"

"My husband—at least the man I *thought* I knew—wouldn't have done that. Any of it. He wasn't like that."

"So he picked up a bad habit. He was in with a fast crowd."

"No," I said. "No! He was completely against drugs."

"Really? Say more."

I twisted my fingers in my lap. "He has a brother who—well, he got into heroin as a teenager. It tore the family apart."

"So, basically, what you're saying is that your husband was behaving completely out of character in the hours leading up to his death."

"Yes."

"Who was the last person to see him alive?"

"Maybe Warren Cheung, his closest friend. He was at the dinner too. He said Andy got up and left the table at nine-thirty and never came back. He didn't even say good-bye."

"Nine-thirty," he mused. "And the time of death was . . ." He spun to his computer again and read off the screen. "They're saying between eleven and midnight. So that leaves, what, an hour, maybe a little more unaccounted for."

"The coroner admitted that the injuries could have been caused by an altercation. He told me to take it up with the police."

"Altercation, huh? Any idea who your husband might have been altercating with?"

"No. None."

"So did you? Take it up with the police?"

I nodded. "I talked to Detective Roussekoff yesterday. I kind of ambushed her. She wasn't expecting me."

"Darla," he said with a faint smile. "We've worked together before. She's a good cop. Does things by the book." A judicious pause. "That can cut both ways."

"Honestly, it was like talking to the wall. She couldn't wait to get rid of me."

"Unfortunate. But in all fairness, the SaCo sheriff's office is under incredible pressure to clear cases. They've been short-staffed since the budget crisis."

"Which one?" For as long as Andy and I had lived in California, the state government had been teetering on the brink of collapse.

He gave a mirthless chuckle. "Right."

My eyes were drawn back to the wall of framed credentials. "It was almost like she was . . . paid off."

"Darla? Not a chance. That's not to say someone further up the food chain hasn't been applying pressure."

"What do you mean?"

"Think about it. Wolders Palmer is the premier law firm in Sacramento. They do a lot of work at the state level. They're not gonna be happy when one of their bright young Turks dies of a drug overdose right after a company event. They're going to want that investigation to be over quickly. Doesn't necessarily mean the firm bears any blame. It could just mean they don't want their name in the news."

We're not the bad guys here. Had I antagonized Reg for no good reason? "So you think I overreacted? That there's nothing to be concerned about?"

"I didn't say that. I just think it's important to look at a situation from as many angles as possible." His eyes narrowed thoughtfully. "Let's go back over this a little. This malfeasance your husband is accused of. That's a harsh thing to unload on a grieving wife. Why would Wolders say that?"

"It's a ridiculous accusation anyway. Like Andy would ever . . . *blackmail* anyone. He's the most honest person I know."

"Maybe the boss wants something from you. Does he?"

We'll do whatever we can to help you. But we're going to need your help, too.

"Permission to send someone over to search Andy's home office."

He let out a low whistle. "For?"

"The thumb drive with the documents Andy allegedly downloaded."

"Huh. Whatever's on it must be pretty important. Do you know where it is, the thumb drive?"

"No idea."

"So your husband didn't clue you in?"

I stiffened, remembering Darla's surprise that Andy hadn't confided in me about his work troubles. Except her question had had an insinuating edge, while Tom Haydon just regarded me with his clear, nonjudgmental gaze.

I shrugged. "Maybe he was trying to protect me."

"Point taken." A thoughtful frown kept him silent for a few seconds. "Has Wolders offered you anything in return? In exchange for your cooperation?"

"I think he was about to, but I got mad and threatened him with a civil suit over Andy's death."

"Gutsy move," he said with a hint of admiration. "But maybe not the smartest move you could make." He studied me for a long moment, his long fingers tented. "Well, I agree, there's something here that doesn't pass the sniff test. But murder—that's a big leap. Why would you even suspect that?"

Why indeed? "It was just a feeling I had, for like thirty seconds, when I was talking to Reg yesterday."

"A feeling that was strong enough to prompt you to seek out a private investigator?"

I nodded, thinking how much I was beginning to like this man.

"Your husband's employer—are you dependent on these stiffs for anything? Health insurance? 401K rollover? Life insurance?"

Life insurance. Right. Still, I almost smiled. "Yes. All of the above."

"Okay. *If* you decide to hire me, I'll do some nosing around . . . discreetly. Typically I work in conjunction with the authorities, but I'd like to get my own read on the situation before consulting with the sheriff's office. No point in ruffling Detective Roussekoff's tail feathers just yet."

"No, we wouldn't want that." This time I couldn't help smiling, if only because he wasn't laughing me out of his office.

He glanced at his watch. "I have another appointment in a few minutes, so if you want to go home and think about it—"

"No, I don't need to think about it. You're hired."

Chapter 15

*L**ie low.*

That was what Tom Haydon advised me to do just before I left his office, after I'd signed the paperwork to hire him. *Go home and relax. Don't tangle with the boss again. There's no point in making an enemy of him. Just lie low until you hear from me. Watch a Jane Fonda movie.*

His words were still in my head the next morning when a silver BMW pulled up at the curb in front of the house and a twenty-something woman got out. Through a slit in the living room blinds, I watched her saunter up the path toward the front door, her workout clothes skintight over a lithe, athletic body. She tossed her shoulder-length brown hair as she went, the bright sun catching its reddish highlights. Not a Jehovah's witness, that much was clear. Normally I didn't open the door to strangers, but the morning was quiet, too quiet, and my curiosity was aroused.

She passed out of view onto the front steps. The door knocker thudded, the first time I'd heard that sound since the highway patrol came calling. My stomach lurched a little, the beginning of dread. But something compelled me to answer it.

She was gazing off into the crepe myrtle when I opened the door. Her eyes, a clear hazel, turned to meet mine. "Melissa?"

My name, from a stranger's lips, shocked me. "Do I know you?"

"No," she said. "But I knew Andy."

"Andy? How?"

Her eyes held mine through the grudging two inches of space between the front door and the jamb. "We were friends."

"Friends?"

"He was going to tell you," she said.

"I don't know what you're talking about." The dread pooled in the pit of my stomach. I stepped back to shut the door.

She put out a hand to stop me. Her face crumpled and a tear trickled down one cheek. "I know it was wrong of me to come here, but you're the only other person in the world who could possibly know what I'm going through—"

I couldn't breathe. "You'd better go."

"The truth is we loved each other—"

"Right. And how do you know Andy again?"

She flicked her tear away with her fingertips in that delicate way attractive women being interviewed on TV did. "We met in New Orleans."

"That's impossible," I said. "Andy has never been to—"

Then I remembered. A business trip last fall. He'd traveled to Metairie, just north of New Orleans, to take a deposition. And then I remembered more. After the deposition he'd called to tell me he was spending another night there.

"Get off my property," I said, my voice shaking. "Leave now, or I'll call the police."

The tears vanished as quickly as they'd come. Her voice turned hard, resentful. "All right, I'm going. But you know what? Your marriage was a lie. Andy loved me, not you."

"Sure. Whatever." I slammed the door and waited, helpless, until the viselike grip on my chest eased enough for me to take a complete breath. Then I walked slowly down the hall to the master bedroom.

My suitcase lay open on the bed. I'd just started packing for the trip to Connecticut for Andy's memorial service. I'd booked a ticket on the red-eye to Boston for the following night. The plan was to spend a night at my mother's condo in southern New Hampshire, before making the four-hour drive to Connecticut on Saturday morning, Mom and me, to join the Stevenson clan in laying Andy's ashes to rest. A command performance I wasn't looking forward to.

My surprise visitor was acting, of course. She had to be. The whole thing had felt staged, fake, like a bad play. But why? Whatever the reason, I wasn't going to fall for it. At least one part of me wasn't. The other part picked up the phone and scrolled to Warren's number.

His voice came on the line, instantly sympathetic. "Hey, Melissa, I was going to call you today."

"Yeah?"

His voice dropped lower. "About what we talked about last time." *The data breach. The case Andy was working on when he died.*

"That's great, Warren," I said. "But that's not why I'm calling."

"No? What's up?"

"You remember when Andy went to Louisiana last fall for that deposition?"

"Yeah."

"Do you remember who the opposing counsel was?"

He chuckled. "Dickie Grosvenor. Kind of hard to forget. He's a real character."

"How so?"

"White suits, long goatee, waist like a beach ball. The Hollywood version of a Southern lawyer."

"Where is his office?"

"Metairie."

I opened my laptop and typed "Richard Grosvenor Attorney Metairie" into the browser window. "Um, did he have a partner or an associate? A woman?"

"You mean Marlene?"

"Could be. An attractive brunette?"

He snorted, an extreme reaction from decorous Warren. "No one has ever called Marlene attractive before. Super nice lady, don't get me wrong, but . . ."

I'd just pulled her up on Dickie Grosvenor's website. A bull-dog-faced blonde glared at me from the screen. Marlene Standish, associate attorney. "Yeah, I see that." I closed my laptop, my throat suddenly dry. "Warren, I'm going to ask you something and I want you to tell me the truth."

"Okay," he said, a wary note creeping in.

"Was Andy cheating on me?"

I waited for a passionate denial, the way he'd denied Andy's cocaine use. Instead, there was stunned silence on his end.

Oh, I thought. *Oh, shit.*

"Warren?"

He sighed. "Melissa, I don't want to have this conversation with you."

"Oh my god," I breathed. "Warren, do you know something?"

"Melissa."

"Warren, tell me the truth. Tell me the god-damned truth!" I winced, remembering too late that, as an evangelical Christian, he never took the Lord's name in vain. "Warren. Please."

"Look, all I know is what Andy told me. There was this woman who kept calling him, wouldn't leave him alone."

"When was this?"

"I'm not sure. A few months ago. February, maybe March."

"Who was she?"

"Somebody he met somewhere. Out of town. We only talked about it once."

"And what did he say?"

"He said he'd done something really stupid, something he really regretted."

"Where did he meet her?" I waited.

"I think he said New Orleans."

It was my turn to be silent.

"Look," Warren said, "Andy was a good-looking guy. You go on the road, it's not unusual to have women throwing—"

"Oh, and that makes it okay?"

"No. No! That's not what I meant. It's just—Andy's dead. Don't let this come between you and your memory of him. Whatever happened in New Orleans, he was really unhappy about it."

"Right. I bet he was."

I ended the call and stood frozen at the foot of the bed, my body numb except for a single node of unbearable pain. So this was what it felt like to be stabbed in the heart.

How long had it been since I lived with the Andy I actually knew? How long had I been cohabiting with this stranger? For a moment he stood in front of me, his tie unknotted, his eyes shifting away from mine, another woman's scent coming off him, her perfume, her sweat.

I threw open his closet doors and began pulling out his clothes—his suits, sport coats, pants, dress shirts, ties, everything. I took his shoes and hurled them one after the other against the wall on the opposite side of the room. But my ice-cold fury kept swamping me. Wave after wave. I collapsed on the bed and beat the mattress with my fists. When I was emptier and more hollowed out than I'd ever felt in my life, I found my phone buried under Andy's clothes and jabbed the screen on Liz's number.

It was a workday, but she answered almost immediately. "Melissa?"

"Yeah, it's me."

"Has something happened? Is there a problem?"

"I can't come to the memorial service."

There was a pause on her end. "What?" Her voice had gone flat, as if she sensed I was about to say something horrible.

"I'm sorry," I said, feeling like a shit-heel despite my righteous anger. "It's awful, I know. But I just can't come."

"If you're sick, we can postpone—"

"I'm not sick."

There was another, longer pause. "I'm sorry, Melissa, I'm just not understanding this. You're Andy's wife. You *have* to come."

Right. What a scandal it would be for the Stevensons if the widow didn't show up at her husband's memorial service. "No, Liz, I don't *have* to," I said quietly.

"But—why? I don't—"

As sisters-in-law, Liz and I had always maintained a cordial relationship, even in our recent messy sharing of grief together. But I had a feeling that was about to change. "Because your perfect brother has been cheating on me. I just found out. Not only was he doing coke the night he died but he's been cheating on me. For months."

Her shocked, ragged breath came at me through the phone. The same way I'd been breathing when that woman showed up on my doorstep. Finally she spoke, her voice shaking with what? Anger? Hurt? Denial? Everything I'd been experiencing in the last couple of weeks.

"Melissa, are you *out* of your *mind*?"

"Not yet, but I might be before this is over."

"I don't even know what you're saying," she stammered. "You're acting cr—"

Crazy? Yes, quite possibly. "I'll FedEx his ashes. You'll have them tomorrow."

There was no response to that. As the silence lengthened, I took my phone away from my ear and looked at the screen. She'd hung up on me.

I set the phone down carefully on my dresser, as if it might explode. Whether or not Andy had actually been murdered was an open question. But right at that moment, I felt like a murderer myself.

Chapter 16

Something leapt onto my back and sprang away. I lurched into consciousness on my stomach, my face mashed into a sofa cushion, the cushion wet with drool. Late-night TV images flickered at me in a silent barrage. I felt panicked, the way I sometimes did when I woke from an unexpectedly deep sleep in the afternoon, not knowing where I was or how I'd gotten there. On the floor next to my head was Liz's bottle of scotch, almost empty. That explained the headache and my desert dry mouth.

Juju sat in the doorway, his tail twitching, not looking the least bit guilty. "Did you jump on me, sweetie?" Trying to wake me up because I'd forgotten to feed him.

I crawled off the sofa, the evening coming back to me in jagged pieces. Andy's ashes disappearing into a Fed Ex box. My crazed, in-pain call to Jacey as the Federal Express truck drove away down the cul-de-sac. I'd interrupted her making her children's dinner, not a great time to talk, but somehow she'd been gracious enough to invite me over for spaghetti and meatballs. The three of them were just sitting down to eat when I arrived, but that didn't stop me from blurting it all out, the cruel disclosure of my husband's infidelity, my horrible behavior to Liz, the surreal nightmare of sending Andy's ashes off in a shipping box. Jacey's two kids—her daughter, frighteningly wise for her eleven years, her eight-year-old son round-eyed, a smear of spaghetti sauce on his chin—watched and listened as I forced my friend to bear witness to the latest disaster in my life.

I remembered returning home around ten o'clock and going straight for the cabinet over the refrigerator, where Liz had left the half-empty fifth of J & B. The taste of it made me want to puke up the little dinner I'd eaten, but I drank down half a tumbler anyway, not knowing how else I would ever get calm enough to sleep.

Now, three hours later, I turned off the TV and staggered into the kitchen. The under-cabinet lighting glowed softly, an oasis against the night. I filled a glass of water under the faucet and drank it down, my reflection staring back at me from the window over the sink. In truth I didn't feel drunk at all, just temporarily insulated from the horrors of the past twenty-four hours.

I filled the glass again and headed for the bedroom. The alarm box caught my eye as I passed the front hall. No reassuring blink emitted from it. I'd forgotten or been too upset to set the alarm when I returned from Jacey's. Even worse, the front door was unlocked. Anybody could have walked into the house while I lay passed out on the sofa.

Being alone in the house at night sometimes spooked me, but the possibility that an intruder could be lurking in the shadows of any one of its nine rooms barely registered. All I could think about was crashing into bed. I set the glass of water down on the hall table and punched in the alarm code. A second later the control box began to blink.

The view from the bedroom doorway brought the full weight of my emotional state down on me. Andy's clothes were heaped on the bed, his shoes strewn across the floor. When had I become such a maniac? I splashed warm water on my face in the bathroom, brushed my teeth quickly, and peed the long pee of excessive alcohol consumption. Then I pushed Andy's clothes to the floor on his side of the bed and slipped under the covers.

Jacey, I thought, the minute I opened my eyes the next morning. God, what had I done? Whatever else happened, I could not afford to lose her friendship. Not hungry at all, I breakfasted on a piece of toast with almond butter, a few spoonfuls of yogurt, and two Excedrin, then texted her at work. "Can you talk?"

Her reply came quickly. "Call you in a few."

Somewhat reassured, I waited. Her call came at ten-fifteen. "Did I do something last night I should apologize for?" I asked, bracing myself.

"You were pretty upset." She sounded a little distant, but I told myself it was because she was at work.

"I feel horrible that I said all those things in front of your kids."

"It's okay. They'll live."

No, there was definite distance in her voice. She was fed up with me, disgusted by my out-of-control behavior. And who could blame her?

"That doesn't make it excusable," I said.

"Mel, it's okay. They've been through a messy divorce, remember?"

Of course I remembered. I'd been there the whole time for Jacey, holding her hand during her nasty custody battle with her abusive, self-righteous husband. In a just universe I supposed I'd earned the right to dump my grief and rage on my best friend, to fall apart and ask her to pick up the pieces. Still . . . "Well, it doesn't *sound* okay. You don't sound okay."

She was silent for a second or two, as if weighing her words. "It's just frustrating, you know? You're going through the worst time in your life and there's *nothing* I can do to help you."

My hand, holding the phone, was suddenly wet with my tears. "You are helping me. Just by being there. I'm just sorry I had to put you through all the drama, *again*."

"Melissa," Jacey said firmly. "Please. Will you stop? Your husband just died. What kind of friend would I be if I deserted you now?"

Relief and gratitude overwhelmed me. I held my phone against my ear and just let myself breathe. Outside the kitchen windows, the sky was a relentless blue, the pool shimmering in the heat. Too hot to go swimming, too hot to even step outdoors. I snuffed back my tears and voiced the one coherent thought I'd been thinking since waking that morning. "I have to get away from here."

"What do you mean, away?" Jacey asked, suddenly curious.

"You know, geographically distant. *Away*. Somewhere else."

"Where would you go?"

She'll be glad to get rid of you, a nasty little voice in my head said.

"Somewhere it rains once in a while."

"Look," Jacey said gently. "Hold that thought. We'll talk tonight."

Upstairs in my studio, I unearthed the March issue of *Artist* magazine from the stack of back issues in the bookcase next to my worktable. A fogbound J. W. M. Turner oceanscape graced its cover, just the kind of weather I craved. I flipped to the classified section at the back, where the magazine cleaved to the quaint habit of advertising artist's retreats and summer rentals. My eyes went immediately to the ad because I'd circled it, faintly, in pencil.

"Island cottage. Private beach. Few amenities. Ferry to town. Splendid isolation."

I'd been looking at the ad less than a month ago—daydreaming about an artist's holiday without my husband in the place (give or take a few hundred miles) where I'd grown up. A month in Maine, just Juju and me. An odd thing, that fantasy, for a happily married woman who already spent too much of her time alone.

On impulse, I placed a call to the number in Connecticut. A woman answered—elderly, by the sound of it. I learned quickly that I was talking to the owner, that her name was Catherine Sutton, and that she was a watercolor artist who was simply getting too old to make the yearly trip to Maine. The cottage was located off Southwest Harbor on Mizzen Island, a tiny community that jealously guarded its privacy, letting few renters in. "Don't expect the neighbors to welcome you," the woman warned in her thin, aristocratic voice.

"*Are* there neighbors?" I asked, surprised.

"Oh, they're there. They're not close, but they're close enough."

We talked price and availability and briefly about the logistics of island living. A couple who had decided to rent the cottage for the summer had bowed out unexpectedly, deciding the amenities were indeed too few.

"Is it ready now?" I asked.

"It could be ready in a couple of days."

"I'll take it."

"Goodness, you are decisive."

"Yes," I said, "I guess I am." Far from scaring me off, the fierce independence I detected in the woman's tone told me I was making the right choice.

"May I inquire about your circumstances?" she asked.

I told her briefly that I lived in California, was recently widowed, and needed to get away from the memories of my own home for a while.

"Oh," she replied, "well, I'm sorry to hear that. I'll need personal references, of course. Two should suffice. You can fax them to me." The ad, I noted, included a fax number.

"That won't be a problem," I said, even as I was wondering whom I could get to vouch for me. Tom Haydon, the detective on my husband's murder investigation? My newly estranged sister-in-law?

As I was mulling this over, Catherine Sutton spoke again. "Are you a reader?"

"Yes, I love to read."

"You'll find the house has a well-stocked library. If you like British naval history, that is." A soft chuckle.

"Um."

"My late husband's collection. I couldn't bring myself to dispose of it."

"I'm sure it will be . . ." *Riveting.* "It sounds very interesting," I said.

"Very well, Melissa. I'll expect your references."

Silky fur brushed my calf, Juju sashaying past my leg, as if to say, "Remember me." He leapt onto the worktable and crouched there, his blue eyes searching mine. "Oh, no," I blurted.

"Is something wrong?"

"It's just that I forgot about my cat. I have a Siamese, a two-year-old male. Do you allow cats?" I steeled myself for the flat-out rejection that usually greeted the disclosure of an animal companion.

"Is he well-behaved?" she asked, her serene tone restored.

"Yes."

"Then bring him along, by all means. You'll find we're a cat-loving island." Another enigmatic chuckle.

I said good-bye quickly, not pressing my luck.

Chapter 17

❝Postponed? But why?" my mother asked, bewildered.

"They're waiting until Andy's father is well enough to attend." A lie. Time to hit her with the rest of the news: that after my visit to her, I would be spending the summer on an island off the coast of Maine.

She was too flummoxed to speak, but only for a few seconds. "Are you bringing that cat?" she asked, changing tack.

"Yes, Mom. I can't very well leave him home for the summer."

"But your father—"

"I know, Mom. Dad was allergic. But Dad's not alive anymore." *Remember?*

"But his hair. And the litterbox—"

"If it's really such a big deal, I won't stay with you. I'll stay in a hotel."

"Melissa, no hotel is going to take a cat and a litterbox."

Mentally I went over my list of friends in the Boston area, wondering if there were any I could cadge a bed from for a few days. None that I felt comfortable asking. It had been ten years since I'd graduated from Mass Art and four years since I'd left the Boston area with Andy. Staying in touch had never been my strong suit. I would have failed miserably as class secretary.

"Okay, fine," I told her, my discomfort making me cruel. "I'll stay here until the cottage is ready and then I'll fly direct to

Portland and not bother to visit you at all. Is that what you want?"

"No, dear, of course not," she said, wounded now. She sighed. "Bring the cat if you insist. He can stay in the garage."

"Mom."

"What, dear?"

How did I manage to escape from you with my sanity even partially intact? "Nothing," I said. "I'll text you with my flight info."

Tom Haydon had said to lie low, not leave town. I wondered what he'd think of my decision. If I'd had my wits about me, I would have seen my impulsiveness for what it was— just another manifestation of a grief too overwhelming to face. But at that moment all I could feel was relief bordering on elation at the prospect of escape.

I called the airline and canceled my reservation for that evening, not giving the two-hundred dollar rebooking fee a second thought. I'd rebook as soon as Catherine Sutton approved my references.

It was only later, as I threw myself into the task of rehanging Andy's clothes in the bedroom closet, that all the things I'd been putting off started pressing on me. "The Newly Widowed Checklist," one website called it. I had yet to call Wolders Palmers HR about Andy's 401K payout or the Social Security office to file for death benefits. I wasn't sure how much longer I'd even have health insurance through Andy's plan. I would have to transfer joint bank and credit card accounts to my name only, but I needed copies of Andy's death certificate to do those things—another task I was unwilling to face.

I was hanging Andy's summer weight beige suit next to his charcoal pinstripe when my phone rang. I expected to see "Mom" lighting up the screen—calling me back for a serious round of second-guessing my decision to leave town for two months—but I was wrong. The number was unfamiliar, but the area code was a California one, so I answered it.

"Mrs. Stevenson?" a man's voice said.

"Oh," I said. "Detective Haydon."

"Are you free to talk?"

"Um, sure."

"Good. Are you at home?"

"I am. Lying low."

"Can you come to the office? There's something I'd like to show you."

"When?"

"As soon as possible."

"I wish I could," I said slowly. "But I'm leaving on a trip and I don't think I'll have time—" Just two days ago I was so relieved to finally have an ally. Now I was blowing him off.

"You've changed your mind," he said.

"No. It's just that—"

"Has something happened? You sound upset."

I sighed. "A woman came to the door yesterday. She said she was having an affair with my husband."

"In that case, you're remarkably calm."

I laughed out loud. "Right. I don't think the bedroom wall would agree with you."

"I'll have to take your word on that. Go on. Did you get into specifics with her?"

"You mean like how many times and in what positions?" God, I was really losing it.

"Not exactly," he said, unfazed. "Although in cases of infidelity, those are understandable questions. No, what I meant was specifics that would verify that she's telling the *truth*. Where they met. How long they've known each other. Anything that would substantiate her claim."

"I don't need *her* to substantiate her claim. My husband's friend Warren already has. He didn't want to, but I forced it out of him."

"Really." His voice sounded more skeptical than surprised.

"You don't think I should believe him?"

"I don't think you should jump to conclusions. There's always the possibility your husband was set up."

Geez, these guys stick together. I squelched the thought, realizing he was throwing me a lifeline. I pushed the dwindling pile of Andy's suits aside and sat down on the bed. "Set up? How do you mean?"

"Think about it. Your husband has something on those bozos he works for. They sense he's about to blow the whistle on them, so they throw a woman in his path. Now they have leverage on him. It's the oldest trick in the book."

"Jesus. Do you really think . . .?"

"It's a theory. Not yet proven. But there's one thing I am sure of."

"What?"

"Your husband would have to be douchebag of the year to cheat on a stellar woman like you. So maybe something else was going on."

A suitable response escaped me.

"Look, Mrs. Stevenson," Tom said, "if you want this investigation to continue, I'm going to need your help."

"My help?" I swallowed a bitter laugh. "My husband seems to have arranged a whole secret life without any help from me."

"Yes, I know it looks that way. But we don't have all the facts yet."

"Okay," I said at last. "What have you found out?"

"I got lucky with some CCTV footage. But you're going to have to come in to see it. When are you available?"

Chapter 18

"The Hyatt was having problems with their security cameras that night," Tom said as I followed him into his office. "The camera outside the function room wasn't working. Ditto for the ones in the parking garage. Read into that what you will. But the camera at the garage exit was working fine." He pulled a visitor's chair around to his side of the desk and placed it in front of his computer. "Here, have a seat."

We sat down next to each other, our shoulders almost touching. He tapped some keys on the keyboard, and a grainy image moved across the screen. "Your husband's Honda Accord leaving the garage," he explained, his eyes on the unrolling footage.

I'd dreaded seeing Andy's face, captured impersonally by a security camera in the last hour or so of his life, but now I just squinted at the screen. "It's so blurry. How do you know it's him?"

"Time stamp matches up with his ticket validation."

As soon as Andy's car disappeared from view, a black SUV rolled into the picture.

Tom clicked his mouse to rewind. "Let's watch it again. Tell me if you notice anything."

I studied the Honda's murky image, the driver's face in profile partially hidden by a baseball cap. Was that really Andy? I looked at Tom. "A baseball cap? He was wearing a baseball cap."

"So?"

The only two pieces of headgear I'd ever seen Andy wear were his bike helmet and the Mets cap he wore hiking, which at that moment was hanging on a peg in his closet. I should know —I'd rifled through his clothes enough times in the past few days.

"Andy wasn't really a baseball cap kind of guy. It's not like he was going bald or—" My eyes went to Tom's receding hairline. "Besides," I went on quickly, "he was coming from a business event. Why would he be wearing a baseball cap?"

"Good question."

The footage advanced to the SUV again. A beefy-looking driver was just visible behind the closed car window, despite the glare picked up from a nearby light source.

Tom froze the frame. "Do you recognize this vehicle?"

"No."

"How about the driver?"

I shook my head. "But I can't really see him."

"Look closely."

"Huh."

"What?"

"He's wearing a baseball cap, too."

"Right."

The unknown driver's cap was pulled down almost comically low, begging the question of how he could even see to drive.

I looked at Tom, surprised. "Do you think there's a connection? Between this car and Andy's?"

"Could be. It's a Nevada plate. Vehicle was reported stolen from a parking garage in Reno. Okay, let's watch it one more time." When Andy's car came into view, he tapped the keyboard to freeze the frame.

"Note the time," he said. "Ten-twenty-one. Your husband's friend—"

"Warren?"

"—said your husband left the dinner at nine-forty-five or thereabouts. Correct?"

"Yes."

"That leaves about thirty-five minutes unaccounted for. Looks like he spent those missing minutes in the Hyatt—unless he left the hotel on foot and came back later for his car. So what was happening during that time? Any ideas?"

"No. Sorry."

"Maybe he ducked into the bathroom to do a couple of lines of coke," he offered matter-of-factly. "But that would have taken less than a minute, max." His eyes fixed again on the image of Andy's car, as if willing it to give up the secret of the missing thirty-five minutes. "Or," he went on, "maybe he did something completely innocent, like sit on the can for half an hour."

"He wasn't much of a bathroom sitter," I said. "Not his style."

"So maybe he had the runs. The point is, without that security camera footage from the corridor outside the function room and inside the garage, we just don't know what was going on. Yet." His fingers moved rapidly over the keyboard again. "But fortunately there's more. This is where we really got lucky."

I waited, almost forgetting to breathe, while he navigated through a series of screens.

"You're probably not aware," he said, "that a lot of ranches in these parts have video surveillance systems. The ranchers install them," click, click, "at strategic points along their property lines to deter illegal dumping and other criminal activity on their land." His right thumb banged the space bar. "And it just so happens that the sheriff's office has a nifty program that encourages these folks to register their surveillance systems with the county, so we can all, you know," another click, "fight crime together."

"Okay," I said.

"One of the ranches your husband passed on Route 16 on the night in question has a surveillance cam installed on the northeast corner of the property, just one-point-two miles west of where your husband's car left the road." He clicked Play. "Watch this."

The footage was completely black for a few seconds and then a car slid into view, moving from left to right, white glare bouncing off it.

"That's the infrared light from the surveillance cam getting reflected," Tom said. "But if you look closely, you can see that it's your husband's Accord. So we know this is the road he took.

And the time is about twenty-five minutes after his car left the garage, just about the right amount of time for a trip of that distance."

"So?" I asked, not following. "What does that tell you?"

"For one thing, that he didn't make any stops after leaving the Hyatt," he said, but I had the feeling there was more.

"I was watching this on my lunch break," he went on. "I let the video run while I was eating. It was a quiet night on the prairie, just a couple of cars and a bobcat passing by for the next twenty minutes." He clicked fast forward and then Play. "Then I saw this."

A bigger patch of white glare appeared on the right side of the screen, heading in the opposite direction of Andy's car. As Tom stopped the frame, the glare took on the outline of an SUV. "Looks like the same vehicle, doesn't it? The one that followed your husband's car out of the garage."

The infrared light bounced off the driver's side door and window. Even so, it was just possible to see the driver, a beefy-looking guy with a dark smudge covering the upper half of his head.

"Yeah," I said, "it does."

"As it happens, it *is* the same vehicle. Same license plate." He zoomed in on the back end of the SUV as it was sliding out of view.

"But it's going in the other direction," I pointed out.

"Yes, it is. It's going west. And there's no evidence on the video that it followed your husband *east* towards home."

"So what does it mean?"

He turned to face me. "Think about it. What are the chances of that stolen SUV leaving the Hyatt parking garage right behind your husband's car and ending up on the *same* lonely county road an hour later? Is it a coincidence? Maybe. But if there's one thing my profession has taught me, it's to be very skeptical of coincidences."

"So what are you saying? You think these guys killed Andy?"

He stood up abruptly and went over to a map of Sacramento County on the wall across the room. "One scenario keeps going through my head."

I waited.

"Let's assume, for argument's sake, that the SUV *did* follow your husband's car out of the parking garage and that it *was* involved in some way in the events that happened later. But instead of following your husband's car down Route 16 out of Sacramento, it traveled northeast up Route 50 and then took Latrobe south to Route 16." He traced the proposed route with the eraser end of a pencil, his arm sweeping up Route 50 towards Folsom and El Dorado Hills and then slashing down along the narrow county road known as Latrobe. Then, a final sweep left to indicate a turn west on Route 16. "That would put the SUV at the accident scene at about eleven-ten or so."

"But why would anyone do that?"

He glanced at me. "To avoid getting caught on a surveillance camera following your husband's car down Route 16."

I leaned forward in my visitor's chair.

"But then," he went on, "after leaving the scene, the driver appears to have gotten lazy. He decided not to repeat the out-of-the-way loop back up Latrobe and down Route 50," another sweeping gesture with his arm, this time in the reverse, "but took the shortest way back to Sacramento—Route 16—thus enabling us to pick him up on the surveillance cam at the ranch down the road."

"But again," I muttered, "why? I don't get it."

He hesitated. "Are you sure you want to hear this? It could be upsetting."

I nodded yes.

His expression turned grim. "Without witnesses or a confession, we can't be absolutely sure *what* happened. But, if . . . *if* your suspicions are correct and we are talking about foul play here, I'd bet that someone else was driving your husband's car when it left the parking garage that night. That whoever was at the wheel drove your husband's car to a predetermined location and drove it off the road to make it look like an accident. And that, by arrangement, the SUV came along a little later, from the opposite direction, to pick up the perpetrator."

"But what about Andy? Where was he during this whole thing?"

His expression changed again, a tenderness creeping in over the grim matter-of-factness. I didn't need him to spell that out. Andy was most likely dead before he left the Hyatt.

The tears gushed down my face and for once I did nothing to stop them. Tom left his office and came back with a paper cup of water from the cooler in the waiting room. He sat down facing me with his elbows on his knees, the doctor who has just delivered bad news.

"I'm sorry," I choked, swiping at my wet face. "When I think of him lying in the back of the car—dead."

"It's a tough image, but like I said, it's only one scenario. The worst one possible."

"He's dead. What could be worse than that?" Was getting murdered really worse than throwing his life away on cocaine?

Tom handed the water to me. "Here, take a sip." To his credit, he didn't shrink from my emotional display.

I drank and blew my nose. "I'm so tired of crying."

"Understood. There *is* some good news in all of this."

"Really? What?"

"If I'm right, we've got one thing on our side. These guys think they're so smart, but they're rank amateurs. They made some really dumb mistakes."

"Like what?"

"The baseball cap your husband was supposedly wearing when he left the garage. Where is it? Did it turn up with his personal effects?"

"No, it didn't." I drank the rest of my water. "So what happens next? How can you prove any of this?"

"As a PI, I'm constrained a bit by not having access to the same information as the authorities, but there's an upside too. I'm not under the time and resource constraints of the SaCo sheriff's office and I don't have to deal with the hidebound hierarchy there. And there are plenty of ways to get access to information, believe me. So on balance it's a win for us."

Us. A comforting word. "Good to know," I said. Not for the first time since we'd sat down together, I noticed that he'd dressed with care today— a crisp plaid short-sleeved shirt, even a hint of aftershave. Maybe Andy's case was giving him a new lease on life, I told myself. Or maybe yesterday was laundry day. All I really knew was that I felt calmer, saner, around him than I did around anyone else.

"So in answer to your question," Tom went on, "I'm going to be taking a hard look at Wolders' background to find out if there's anything incriminating your husband might have discovered. I'll also be paying a visit to the Hyatt, see if anybody on duty that night remembers seeing him that night. Then there are the people who were leaving the parking garage around the same time as his car. Maybe *they* saw something. I can go over the security video again and run down some of those plates. Do you have a photo of your husband you could text me?"

I scrolled through the photos on my phone, past the ones of Andy lying on the mortuary table to the last one I'd taken while he was still alive—enjoying a rare afternoon nap on the sofa with

Juju draped across his chest. Probably not what the detective needed. I scrolled further back, to one I'd snapped across the table at our favorite Sacramento restaurant back in January. There he was, my handsome husband, happy and whole, regarding me with that familiar look of affection, admiration even. I stared at it for a moment before handing the phone to Tom.

"That'll do," he said.

In the silence that followed, I became conscious of the hum of traffic outside the windows, a horn honking in the distance, the sounds of downtown Folsom on an ordinary weekday. I stood up to leave, our conversation at an end.

He escorted me out to the waiting room. "So where are you going?"

"Excuse me?"

"You said on the phone you were going away."

"Oh, right." It felt like a century had passed since our phone conversation that morning. "I'm going to visit my mother in Boston. Well, Boston area. Southern New Hampshire."

"No kidding? I have a sister in Boston. Well, Jamaica Plain."

"Wait. You're from Boston?"

"Actually I am. I came out here for college and never went back. Not to live, anyway."

"What happened to your Boston accent?"

"My first girlfriend out here was an elocutionist. Worked mostly with actors, but she made an exception for me."

I laughed, but my thoughts were already jumping past this thing we had in common, that we were both from the same city on the East Coast. "There's more," I plunged on, before I lost my nerve. "After I visit my mother, I'm going up to Maine to, um, spend a couple of months. On an island off Acadia."

I tried to read his look. Disapproval or just surprise?

"It was a sudden decision," I said, as if that could explain away the guilt I felt, as if I was giving up on the investigation instead of turning it over to a capable professional. My mother's criticisms were alive and well in me—flighty, undependable, hothead.

"Hey," he said pleasantly. "I'm sure you could use the time away. You'll be reachable by phone, I assume."

"I think so."

He thought for a moment. "This island. What's it like?"

"Small, accessible only by ferry. No cars allowed. The lady I'm renting from says there are neighbors but I probably won't see them."

"Huh. Well, do me a favor. Don't go posting your whereabouts on social media."

It took a moment to absorb the implication behind his words. "Do you think I'm in danger?"

"No, probably not. But I'm in law enforcement. It's my job to see threats everywhere. Do you own a firearm?"

"Shit. Now you are scaring me."

"I take it that's a no."

"I wouldn't feel safe with one in the house."

"Do you know how to fire one?"

I nodded reluctantly, remembering the summer I turned fifteen. My father—alarmed at my sudden metamorphosis from awkward gosling to long-legged jailbait—took me to the local firing range a few times, thinking to teach me how to protect myself. But, like most everything else in his life, he'd abandoned that version of father-daughter time quickly. An impractical idea, anyway. We never got around to discussing just when and under what circumstances I would pack heat. On the few dates I went on in high school? To a football away game?

"What kind of gun?" asked Tom.

"Handgun—the usual kind. Semi-automatic. Nine millimeter."

"Good choice. When you get to New Hampshire, buy yourself one."

"What about on the plane coming home?"

"Not a problem. Stow it in a locked case, unloaded, and put it in your checked baggage. Make sure you tell them at the baggage counter."

"I'll think about it. But do you really think it's necessary?"

He shrugged, a deliberately casual gesture that looked wrong somehow on his tall, spare frame. "Better safe than sorry is a motto that's always worked for me. As it stands now, your husband died under suspicious circumstances, and his boss is pressuring you to hand over a missing thumb drive. It's not clear how those two things are related—or even if they are related, but —"

"If you don't think I should go, just say so. Please."

"Melissa," he said, startling me. It was the first time he hadn't called me Mrs. Stevenson.

"Yes?"

"It's not my job to control your life. You're an intelligent, thinking woman. I'm just trying to keep you informed of the risks. You're free to make your own decisions."

I looked away, undone by the compliment, or was it just his simple faith in me? "Thank you for that."

He touched my shoulder lightly. "Not at all. Just keep your eyes open and call me if anything suspicious happens. Anything."

I nodded dutifully. "Of course."

The plane began to shake as soon as it dropped into the heavy cloud cover over Boston. Tray tables rattled and an overhead compartment flew open. The fasten seatbelt sign came on with a soft ding. A flight attendant hurried up the aisle to get the beverage cart stowed.

Another typical landing in Boston, I thought, but I gripped my armrests despite my attempt at self-soothing. There was a loud bang followed by a jolt, like a truck breaking its tie-rod on a road studded with rocks. Juju, tucked under the seat in front of me in his soft-sided carrier, let out a mournful howl that somehow carried over the din. My grandmotherly seatmate and I exchanged nervous smiles.

"Maybe your cat knows something we don't," she said.

Five minutes later we were on the ground. Several passengers applauded as the wheels touched the runway and the plane settled back onto terra firma.

Stepping out of the terminal with my suitcase, cat carrier, purse, and laptop, I walked into a wall of humid air. It felt welcome for about a minute, until I realized how stiflingly hot it was. Boston, it seemed, was in the middle of a heat wave. I crossed the pavement in a soup of exhaust fumes to the nearest bus stop to wait for the New Hampshire-bound shuttle. My mother, a borderline agoraphobic and terrified of driving in the city, would be picking me up in Portsmouth.

California was already a sun-parched mirage sin the rearview mirror.

Home. A complicated word.

Chapter 19

I fiddled with the thermostat in my mother's living room, my face damp with perspiration. "Jesus, it's hot in here," I muttered. So much for central air, New Hampshire style.

"It's going to break tomorrow," my mother said, setting our dinner on the little table in the dining area at the other end of the room. "Melissa, don't mess with that. I won't know how to reset it."

We sat across from each other over chicken breasts my mother had cooked on the gas grill on the back deck. I helped myself to potato salad, her specialty, and pushed some sliced tomatoes and cucumbers onto my plate.

My mother nudged the bottle of ranch dressing in my direction.

I shook my head.

"It wouldn't hurt you to have something fattening, dear. You look—"

"I know. I look terrible. You told me." I forked a piece of chicken into my mouth and chewed it slowly, my body tensed for the next onslaught of *Andy was such a great husband, I don't know what you're going to do without him.* I wished I'd snagged a bottle of wine off the shelf in the grocery story when we stopped to pick up a bag of cat litter and a litter box on the ride from Portsmouth. Instead I took a sip of water, the ice cubes making faint music against the blare and chatter of the TV news in the background.

"What are you going to do when you get back?" my mother asked.

"I don't know."

"You'll have to do something."

"Will I?"

"You won't have Andy to make plans for both of you anymore."

My knife screeched on my plate. I put down my cutlery and took another slug of water. "No," I said, "that's very true."

"Will you go back to work?"

"Mom, you *know* I already have a job."

"But that's not—"

A real job, she meant. The kind where you go to work in an office, get coffee for the boss, and wear pantyhose. Like the last job she had before she married my father back in the late seventies. She had always considered my freelancing a whim, further proof of my artist's frivolous nature.

A sliver of self-pity penetrated my defenses and bloomed like a drop of blood in water. "Look, I know I'm going to have to *earn money*. I can't very well afford to live on my own without a job."

"You'll have Andy life insurance to tide you over for awhile, won't you?"

Andy's life insurance. "No, actually I won't."

My mother stopped eating. "Why not?"

The ugly truth hovered somewhere behind my mother's head, begging to be told. I lost my nerve. "The insurance company has refused to pay. They're saying Andy lied on the application, that he knew he had a heart condition and concealed it from them."

I watched her face turn from alarm to something hard. "You're going to have to hire a lawyer, Melissa."

A lawyer. I almost laughed in her face.

She stared at me. "You can't let them get away with that."

"Maybe not. But it's a lot to deal with right now."

"You've always been so quick to give up," she pronounced, recalling some shadowy version of my younger self that I fervently hoped I'd left behind. "There must be a lawyer at Andy's firm who can help you."

I laughed, bitterly. "No, Mom. I don't think so."

Now she looked afraid. "Why not?"

I pushed my plate away. "Because Andy isn't the person you thought he was, Mom. He was in trouble at work before he died. He was about to get fired."

It was a twisted version of the truth, I knew that by now. I don't know why I said it, except to put my mother on notice that my widowhood was a complicated affair, and yes, to hurt her, to knock her vision of Andy as the perfect husband off its pedestal once and for all.

But the person I was really hurting was myself. I watched my mother struggle with my assassin's words, knowing that all I'd done was open the floodgates for more questions. And more questions after that. Questions that would just keep coming until the day I left—or smothered her with a pillow in the night.

I left the clatter of the dinner dishes being scraped and rinsed and escaped to the garage to console Juju in his forced imprisonment. He hadn't touched the food or water I'd put down earlier, even though he'd spent thirteen hours in his carrier without either. He was nowhere in sight, so I guessed he was hiding under the vehicle that occupied most of the space in the garage: my father's lovingly restored 1969 Corvette Stingray convertible. It was the best thing he'd done in his disappointing, Budweiser-lubricated life, the only project he'd ever really finished—restoring the car that reminded him of a brighter youth than the one he'd spent in a drab, blue-collar north-of-Boston suburb.

It surprised me that my mother hadn't sold the Corvette when she moved, considering how much she used to grumble about the expense of restoring it and the time it took away from their silences and bickering. Even more surprising that it commanded pride-of-place in the garage while her Ford Escort stayed in the driveway, exposed to New England's changeable elements.

I crouched on the immaculate concrete next to the Corvette and rested my back against the garage wall, waiting for Juju to make an appearance. My mother spent her life cleaning, so of course the garage floor was clean enough to eat bacon and eggs off of. A couple of minutes later Juju slunk out from behind a rear wheel, his guttural purr doing a fair imitation of a racecar rumbling to life. I pulled him onto my lap and rubbed the soft fur behind his ears, letting him knead my thighs with his claws. I kissed the spot between his shoulder blades, feeling some of the edginess that always possessed me when I visited my mother drain away.

"That's some snazzy car, huh, Juje? What do you think? Time to blow this joint?"

A typical morose teenager, I'd made a practice of turning a deaf ear to my father's ramblings about his beloved 'Vette, but I couldn't have taken myself seriously as an artist if I hadn't secretly admired its ultra-cool styling. I knew the car was still roadworthy because there was an inspection sticker in the lower right-hand corner of the windshield. I pictured myself sneaking the keys out of the kitchen drawer, loading my luggage into the trunk after my mother had gone to bed, and rocketing off with Juju into the hot summer night. Driving to Maine now. Catherine Sutton had already called to say my references were accepted and the cottage was ready.

And taking the Corvette sure beat the alternative: renting a subcompact for the next eight weeks to the tune of a couple of thousand dollars just to sit in a parking lot while I vacationed on a remote island.

I deposited Juju back on the concrete with a goodnight kiss and slid my hand along the Corvette's gleaming flank as I left the garage. Back inside, I caught my mother disappearing out onto the back deck with a pack of cigarettes and lighter in her hand.

"You're smoking again? I thought you quit."

"Well, I have to have something to look forward to, don't I?" she said and closed the slider behind her.

It was nine o'clock, too early to go to bed, especially since it was only six California time, but I left the dishwasher humming and went upstairs to the single-bedded guest room, cringing yet again as I crossed the threshold into an eerily exact replica of my teenage bedroom. My mother, alive and well in her bizarro world, had seen fit to transport all of it—bedspread, curtains, books, even the posters—from the house in Medford I'd grown up in, as if I'd never left my childhood home, as if my entire life from age eighteen to thirty-two was just some burst of REM sleep. I flopped down on the bed beneath a poster of John Cusack, my favorite actor ever since I'd seen him in "The Sure Thing," his dark eyes and ironic smile covered with fading love notes scrawled by high school friends I'd long since lost touch with. Those outpourings of teenage lust, liberally punctuated with smiley faces and trains of exclamation points, made me feel sad in some desperate and unaccountable way.

Within minutes I was climbing the walls, counting the hours until I could escape to Maine—anything that would connect me to the real Melissa Stevenson, the adult who had married her college boyfriend and moved to California, instead of this newly widowed stranger washed up on the shores of her childhood bedroom, as if in some nasty game of Chutes and Ladders. I picked up my phone and pressed Jacey's number, even though it was probably too early for her to be home from work.

"Hey! Mel!" her voice said in my ear, surprising me.

"Wow, I didn't expect you to answer. Where are you?"

"Just walked in the door. Is everything okay? Your mother driving you bonkers already?"

"Ya think?"

"I'm sure she appreciates your visit."

"Trust you to find the bright side."

"So what are you doing now?"

"Ogling John Cusack."

She laughed. "Your first love."

"Yup. What are *you* doing?"

"Pouring myself a large glass of red. Long day in stiletto heels."

"What about the kids?"

"Doing their homework. Maybe. At least they're not fighting."

We kept talking for a while, about everything and nothing, the way we always did. And then I heard Jacey yawn. "Well, sleep tight," I said.

"Can't wait. It's been a long day. You too, okay? Don't let the bed bugs bite."

At ten my mother climb the stairs to go to bed and said good night to me through my closed bedroom door.

"G'night," I answered, not bothering to get up. At that moment I was cruising Instagram, Tom Haydon's killjoy warning to stay away from social media doing battle with my scrolling index finger.

I pressed my thumb firmly on the power-off button on the side of the phone and watched the screen go black, then went to brush my teeth. I doubted sleep would come, but I turned off the bedside lamp and lay in the dark listening to the rural New Hampshire night sounds of frogs in the patch of wetland behind the condo building. The weariness of the long travel day must have claimed me quickly because a loud crash tore through my sleep and I bolted up in bed, my heart thumping against my ribs, before I even remembered where I was. I strained my ears in the darkness, wondering if the crash was the tail end of a nightmare. Whatever it was, real or imagined, the night was quiet again. The clock next to the bed said one-thirty.

Then I heard it. A furtive, scuffling noise, like something being dragged, coming from the back deck below my bedroom window. An animal looking for food, I told myself. I turned my pillow over to the cool side and lay down again.

Tom's voice, soft in the darkness, brought me bolt upright again.

Do you own a firearm?

His thin-lipped Irish mouth set in a mirthless line.

Shit, I thought. This is what I get for ignoring the advice of my private investigator, for not borrowing my mother's Escort to sneak over to Manchester and buy a handgun. Some deranged intruder was out on the deck ready to smash his way in through the slider.

It's an animal, I told myself. *Just go back to sleep.*

But a soft thump made me sit up again. Without thinking, I slipped out of bed and eased open the bedroom door. Down the hall, past the bathroom, my mother slept her drugged Ambien sleep, dead to the world. I could just make out her muted snoring coming through the closed bedroom door.

The stairs were directly across from the guest room, the stairwell a black void against the lighter blackness of the upstairs. There seemed no point in waiting for the murderer to come to me, so I plunged into the blackness, the silence of the house roaring in my ears. I inched down the carpeted stairs one step at a time until my bare feet made contact with the cold tiles by the condo's front door.

Random scraping noises came from the direction of the kitchen. I stood frozen in place, waiting for anything—the crunch of broken glass, a breeze caressing my skin—that would tell me an intruder had gained entry. Nothing.

I strode through the living room to the kitchen and flipped the light switch next to the slider. Bright light flooded the deck and I stepped back quickly, prepared for the outline of a human form. A pair of beady eyes stared up at me from ringed eye sockets, startled but unmoving. The creature's dainty snout was buried in the tinfoil that held the greasy remains of our chicken dinner.

A raccoon. What else would it be on a hot summer night in the wilds of New Hampshire? Behind the hunched mound of fur the gas grill was tipped over, the grate lying a few inches away. So much for the crash that woke me up.

I snapped off the outside light and left the raccoon there to finish his feast.

Back in bed I thought sleep would return quickly, but I tossed and turned in the closeness of the bedroom, exhausted but wired. The bedside clock advanced to two, then two-thirty, and then crawled towards three. Adrenaline-primed, a weird energy invaded my body—edgy, itchy, focusing itself as a warm, teasing pressure between my legs. It was so long since I'd felt any tug in that direction that I almost didn't recognize it for what it was.

Maybe my body was simply begging for release from the irritation of too many hours with my mother. Or maybe, surrounded by the detritus of my teen years, I was channeling my perpetually horny teenaged self. It was the first glimmer of sexual interest I'd felt since Andy's death. Like it or not, I'd just passed into that dreaded single state of not knowing where my next screw was coming from.

I fought it at first, too exhausted for the laborious build-up, building a wall brick by brick to the crashing release that would leave me . . . where? Alone without my partner, a husk of my former self. But the teasing pressure wouldn't go away.

In less than an hour it would be dawn. I could go out for a jog on the lonely country road outside the condo, or . . . My fingers slipped inside the loose waistband of Andy's boxer shorts, the pair I always wore to bed, and found the soft, wet, yielding place. Still the loyal wife, I willed myself to imagine my husband embracing me from behind, his muscular forearms tight around my middle, his hot breath teasing the back of my neck as he whispered my name. I saw us falling into bed together, his body sliding on top of mine, the weight of him on top of me, our eyes locking with desire as he slipped inside me.

Then I saw him dead on a stainless steel mortuary table, his face blue and still. Slipping inside a hotel room with that woman, burying his face in that brown mane of hers.

I groaned and kicked back the covers.

My thoughts went guiltily to my mother, asleep down the hall, floating through the night on her enviable pharmaceutical high. My anger at her welled up, along with my anger at my perfect husband, her hero.

And just like that, Andy faded back into the darkness and someone else took his place.

That Ralph is a real hottie. Jacey's voice, whispered in the dark. I was back in the kitchen of our El Dorado Hills house, swaying drunkenly on the bar stool next to the island as Jacey, in caterer mode, dumped ribs onto a platter.

My heartbeat quickened as my body found its groove at last. Yeah, Ralph, you are. Very hot indeed. That look you gave me during Andy's wake. So sullen, so smoldering. What do you say, Ralphie? Can you do it for me? Can you make it happen?

Guilt and shame tore at me, then flittered away as I pushed all other thoughts aside. It was Ralph's face hovering over mine, dark-eyed, heavy-jawed, intent. Ralph's body pressing against mine, methodical and cruel. Ralph's darkness swallowing me whole until my body clenched and I cried out, and then again, into the pillow I only managed to reach just in time.

Chapter 20

W e blasted off, Juju and I, into the bright, cool summer morning, the Corvette purring under us as my mother receded in the rearview mirror. For all her emotional clinging, she wasn't much of a hugger, but my last view of her, wringing her hands in front of the open garage door, brought the previous evening's confrontation back in vivid detail.

"The Corvette? You want to take *the Corvette*?"

As if I'd suggested using the Shroud of Turin as a cleaning rag.

"Why not? It's just sitting in the garage. It's not good for the engine to have it just sit there—"

"But your father—"

"Mom, don't you think Dad would have wanted us to actually *drive* it once in a while? Get some enjoyment out of it?"

"What enjoyment? You're a widow! Your husband just died!"

"Okay, I'm going to ignore that low blow."

"Besides, what if you have an accident? What if it gets stolen?"

"It's insured, isn't it? And anyway, it won't get stolen and I *won't* have an accident. Stop assuming something *bad* is going to happ—" The words were out of my mouth before the irony hit me full force.

Maybe she would have come to accept the logic of my argument, grudgingly, if I hadn't compounded my offense by suggesting that she take a bus trip with her friends instead of coming to Maine with me for the summer.

No matter. My cat and I were on our way now, thrumming along the back roads of southern New Hampshire as I got used to the low bucket seat, the way the skinny steering wheel slipped effortlessly through my fingers when I made a turn, the raw power of the engine each time I shifted. By the time we crossed the Kittery bridge into Maine on Route 95, I was starting to get the hang of it. I was even getting pretty good at ignoring the admiring stares of passing motorists.

Anticipating the unwelcome attention, I'd tied my hair back in a ponytail and pulled a baseball cap low on my forehead—another irony that wasn't lost on me—but my attempt at incognito proved pathetically lame as a carload of college boys pulled up alongside me just past Kennebunkport. The guy in the passenger seat stuck out his tongue and let it hang there canine-style while his buddy in the backseat made some very lewd hand motions before I hit the gas and left their shitty little Corolla in the dust.

I hadn't put the top down because I didn't want to terrorize Juju unnecessarily, but a scouring blast of summer air filled the car through the wide-open windows and I laughed out loud, my ever-present sadness loosening its grip for just an instant. What did it matter, really, that I was the biggest Tuesday morning show on the Maine Turnpike? I turned the dial on the radio and floored the accelerator, relishing the responding surge of V-8 power.

What would Andy think of me now, I wondered, shockingly close to enjoying myself less than a month after his death. I hoped he'd be grinning. He'd always had a sneaking admiration for my defiant spirit, maybe because he'd spent so much of his life hemmed in by his family's outsized expectations.

But Andy wasn't my only co-pilot as the 'Vette ate up the road and I kept a weather eye out for the state police. My father's ghost was riding shotgun, too. What a disappointment I must have been to him, never showing the slightest interest in his one consuming hobby. I missed him suddenly, even wished him back, though I'd barely mourned his passing two years ago. My grief over Andy's death must have been making me more charitable, for I suddenly saw my father in a different light—married too young, no opportunity to go to college, parents who thought small and didn't know any better. A dreamer and latent adventurer stuck in a box of a life.

Just like me.

Whoa. Where had that come from?

A brooder by nature, I chewed on that rogue insight for many miles: the box my perfect marriage had become—and whose fault was that, anyway?—until, outside Bangor, I turned south toward the coast and watched the lovely summer day dissolve into wet mist, the leading edge of a fog bank moving in from the ocean.

But wasn't that why I'd come back to New England? For rain and fog?

I flicked on the wipers and kept going.

The line of people waiting to board the ferry was already long when I pulled into the parking lot, even though I was twenty minutes early. I guessed that earlier ferries out of Southwest Harbor had been canceled because of the dense fog and wondered, with a blip of anxiety, if this one would be, too.

I wrestled the big cooler I'd bought for the trip out of the trunk, its soft sides bulging as if a body was stowed inside. According to Catherine Sutton, it was a must-have for transporting groceries from the mainland, and right now it was packed to the gills with the food and staples I'd quickly grabbed from the aisles of the upscale market in town. After dragging the cooler to the end of the line, I returned to the car for the rest of my stuff.

Juju shifted like a bowling ball in his carrier as I lifted him from the passenger seat and slung him over my shoulder, his plaintive meow registering his disapproval of this latest turn of events. "We're going for a boat ride, Juje," I said in my most reassuring voice. "Won't that be fun?"

I locked the Corvette, wondering if it would be there when I came back. *Of course it won't!* my mother's voice hectored me, but it was a fear I was going to have to get used to. If somebody wanted to steal a classic car, they had a lot to choose from in Southwest Harbor. I'd passed a Porsche Boxster and a Morris Minor on the way into town. Still, I made a furtive sign of the cross over the Corvette's LeMans blue hood before I walked away pushing my bag lady ensemble of suitcase on wheels, assorted canvas bags, and cat carrier.

Deep in my shoulder bag my cell phone began to ring. I unearthed it and glanced at the screen. Tom's office number. It was the first time I'd heard from him since leaving California.

"Mrs. Stevenson?" His voice, so familiar to me already, was a welcome sound.

I stepped out of line, leaving my luggage and Juju to hold my place. "Hey, Tom."

"Is this a bad time? How's life in Live Free or Die land?"

"Mostly okay. Survivable."

He chuckled. "No place like home."

"But I'm not, er, in New Hampshire anymore."

A gull swooped near my head with a raucous screech, waves slapped the pilings, and a fishing boat rumbled to life at the next dock over. All at once, the seaside noises seemed magnified a hundredfold. *Flaky woman escapes husband's murder case*, they screamed in tabloid unison.

"I can hear that," he said, without missing a beat. "You must be in Vacationland. How's life there?"

I relaxed, gratitude bordering on affection at his understanding of my need to get away. "Just got here. Waiting to board the ferry."

"So I'll keep this short. I just wanted to update you on a couple of things, if that's okay."

"Of course. Shoot. I mean, not literally."

His chuckle was pro forma. "In the interest of saving you money, I decided to go to Detective Roussekoff with the Hyatt garage footage straight off. If the sheriff's office is willing to do the leg work, there's no point in me continuing the investigation."

"And?"

"I laid out my theory for her and she's not buying it. As far as she's concerned, the coroner's report stands. Your husband died of a heart attack brought on by a cocaine overdose."

My anger at Darla Roussekoff flared up all over again. "I don't get it. What you said made so much sense. How could she be so—stubborn?" I wanted to say *stupid*.

"Ego, not wanting to be wrong, budgetary constraints, who knows? But that's why you hired a private investigator."

"So we're back to square one?"

"I wouldn't say that. At this point it's all about turning over as many stones as possible. I showed your husband's photo to the Hyatt staff who were working that night. No joy there, I'm afraid. No one remembers seeing him."

"That's disappointing."

"Again, it's easy to get discouraged, but it's not surprising considering the night in question was almost a month ago. I've also been tracking down the folks who were exiting the garage at about the same time as your husband. I've got a decent-sized list but I haven't had much luck reaching anybody by phone. People go around with their phones glued to their hands, but no one bothers to answer actual calls anymore."

So far I hadn't heard anything that made me remotely hopeful. "So what will you do?"

"Looks like I may have to go door to door."

A slash of sun had broken through the fog while we were talking. Its warmth on my face and hands was enough to make me want to shed my fleece. Now a low thrum announced the approach of the ferry. A subtle shift in energy rippled through the line of waiting people.

"But there *is* some good news," Tom went on. "Before I became a PI, I spent a lot of years in a white-collar crime unit. You'd be surprised how much information is out there if you know where to look for it. I've spent the last couple of days trawling my contacts. Let's just say that boss of your husband's has made some interesting friends over the years. I'm not going to lack for bedtime reading."

Reg a crook? That was rich, after he'd made such a point of impugning Andy's honesty. Still, I wasn't entirely surprised.

Tom's voice grew faint in the din of the arriving ferry. I pressed a finger to my free ear. "It would be great if I could access your husband's phone records, find out who he was talking to in the last weeks of his life."

"Damn. I don't have them. The law firm paid Andy's cell bill."

"I was afraid of that. We can't subpoena the records until we have enough grounds to open a formal investigation. So there goes that avenue. There *is* something else that could really help though. If I could talk to someone inside the law firm."

"Like who?"

"Your husband's friend, Mr. Cheung, for one. How much do you trust him?"

It would be hard not to trust Warren, despite my recent moments of doubt. With his guileless face, his gentle manner, he was the unlikeliest lawyer I'd ever known. "I'd trust him with my life," I said.

"You think he'll talk to me?"

"I know he wants to help. I'm just not sure how much he'd be willing to say. I wouldn't want him to get fired for talking to you." *Or worse.*

"Right," Tom said. "We'll have to proceed carefully."

The ferry bumped up alongside the dock, and a deeply tanned teenaged mate jumped out to tie up. The passengers pressed forward to disembark, the more elderly among them stepping gingerly over the gunwales onto a waiting step stool.

"Look, I have to go," I said to Tom. "We're about to board."

"This island you're going to. Who knows you'll be there?"

"Nobody."

"Not even your mother?"

"I told her I was renting a cottage on an island near Acadia, but I didn't tell her which island. She didn't ask."

"Good. Let's keep it that way."

"Tom, you're scaring me again."

"I just want you to be safe."

A breeze freshened the air, bringing with it more blue sky. The adventure of the island was upon me and I wanted to feel hopeful, not afraid. "You mean, like, lie low?" I teased.

He didn't laugh. "Yeah. Lie low."

We said good-bye and I stepped back in line, pushing my suitcase and cooler with my foot as we inched forward. Danger or not, it was too late to change my mind now. As Andy once said, at the beginning of our romance all those years ago, *In for a penny, in for a pound.*

Part II:
Splendid Isolation

Chapter 21

"**M**y man will be waiting for you at the dock," Catherine Sutton said the last time I spoke to her.

Maybe so, but her "man" was nowhere to be seen as I stepped off the ferry. Then again, I was too busy trying to reach dry land to scan the surroundings. I struggled forward, Juju's carrier, my shoulder bag, and canvas totes slung on either arm as I wheeled my suitcase with one hand and dragged the cooler with the other. Several disembarking passengers eyed me pityingly, but none stepped forward to help. A fishing boat departing a neighboring dock seemed to dawdle, the scruffy pilot in rubber overalls taking in the spectacle from a distance of twenty yards or so.

Ahead, a metal ramp rose at a steep pitch to a collection of gray-shingled buildings on a bluff, one building bearing the weathered sign "Mizzen Island." At least I knew I was in the right place.

"Here, let me get that for you." A silver-haired tourist came alongside me and bent to hoist up the cooler. A younger passenger stepped forward quickly to help him, both clearly of the opinion that none of us were going to get to the top of the ramp without a team effort.

Mission accomplished, I thanked them profusely and took in the milling arrival scene. A dozen or so Rubbermaid handcarts were parked helter-skelter near the ramp, some bearing last names in neat white letters on their sides—*Allerton*, *MacGilvray*

—while others the names of cottages—*Sunset Reach*, *Kestrel Haven*. No sign, though, of Edgar Hunt, the caretaker Catherine Sutton possessively called her man.

Then I spotted a likely candidate—a gnomish sixtyish man standing next to a golf cart about ten feet away. His Tattersall shirt, canvas shoes, and canvas hat screamed "Maine man"—or maybe I'd just been away from New England too long. I left my belongings in a heap on the ground and walked over to him. "Edgar?"

He took me in with a suspicious nod. "Friends call me Gar."

"Nice to meet you, Gar. I'm Melissa Stevenson." I extended my hand, but he was already walking past me to collect my luggage. I held onto Juju, straining mightily in his vinyl and mesh prison, as Gar loaded my stuff into the back of the golf cart.

Huffing a little, he climbed behind the wheel and I got in beside him. He eyed the shape-shifting pet carrier in my lap. "What's that you have in there?"

"My cat."

His colorless eyes narrowed under his canvas hat.

"Mrs. Sutton gave me permission to bring him," I said quickly.

He threw the golf cart into drive. "Thought it might be a whippet."

We bumped away from the dock area, Gar steering around the horde of tourists spreading out in a long line, like ants on the march with cameras and backpacks. A single narrow paved road led away from the harbor toward the interior of the island. The sky was a deep azure now, all traces of fog gone, with big puffs of clouds moving slowly across it. A southeasterly breeze brought the salt-tinged coolness of open water, a delicious change from the scorching summer breezes of Sacramento. I relaxed against my seat and watched the island unfold on either side of us.

Tall Victorian houses with gabled roofs and wide verandas slid past, their front yards thick with grass. Mature hardwood trees provided dense shade and sturdy boughs for tire swings. A side lane that was more a grass track than a road presented a beguiling vista of sapphire ocean. Too distracted to even research the island before coming here, I'd pictured rock and scrub pine, cottages hunkered down against the elements, not this.

"It's gorgeous," I murmured.

"Yuh," said Gar. Not quite an *aye-uh*, but a little close for comfort.

"Do you live here year round?" I asked pleasantly.

"That we do."

We. So there was a Mrs. Gar.

"Does it get lonely?"

He slid me a look as if I'd just asked the dumbest question going, which I suppose I had. His eyes went back to the road. "Missus and me are used to it. Lonely in the summer, too, come to that. Not like the mainland."

There was a warning in there somewhere. I reached into my bag and palmed my cell phone, a nervous tic.

Gar nodded at the phone. "That won't work here."

"What?" *You're kidding me.*

"And you can just about get a cup of coffee down to the general store."

Okay, city slicker, that's you slapped down good and proper.

We passed a modest white-clapboard church on the left, its green-shingled spire rising against the brilliant July sky. A little farther down on the right, a combination post office and general store looked calendar quaint in a derelict way.

Gar nodded in that direction. "Been closed for a while."

"Which one? The post office or the store?"

"Both. Postmistress ran the store, too. Left town last fall."

"But you said I could get a cup of coffee at the general store."

"Sibley's Bait and Tackle, down to the dock," he clarified.

I turned my attention back to the sights rolling past us in slow motion. A few side yards featured cars and pickup trucks from a bygone era, their flat tires and rusting bodies evidence that they hadn't been driven in years. In one front yard, two neighborhood kids hawked pink lemonade from a folding table while a third blew foghorn notes on a tuba that dwarfed his skinny seven-year-old's body.

"I'll be back later," I called to them and held up my wallet, determined not to let a grump just this side of geezerdom ruin my first experience of the island.

The road forked, and Gar veered right. The area grew more remote, the houses further apart and not as well kept. Lobster traps were stacked high in several yards, along with tangled piles of colorful nylon warp. A dense pine forest on either side of the track sent a swarm of mosquitos at us. I was still slapping at them when a modest Victorian hove into view, the last house on the road and a good distance from the nearest neighbor. Beyond it the ocean glinted. Gar pulled the golf cart onto the grass next to the sagging porch steps. A varnished board above the green-painted front door bore a simple epigraph. *Splendid Isolation.*

I turned to Gar. "So that's the name of the house?" I'd assumed when I read the ad that Catherine Sutton was riffing on solitude.

"That it is." He climbed out of the cart and hefted my suitcase from the back. I lugged it up the spongy porch steps while he wrestled with the mammoth cooler.

Puffing in earnest now, he fished a key from the front pocket of his khakis and inserted it in the lock. The front door opened onto an old house smell, but a friendly one—furniture polish and clean linens and salt air. I stepped over the threshold into a small central hallway. A staircase, somewhat steep, rose to the second floor.

To the right was a small book-lined study—Catherine Sutton's husband's naval history collection?—and to the left, a living room, comfortably furnished in chintz and wicker. The far side of the living room opened onto a glassed-in porch with a small wood stove on a tiled platform.

I put Juju down, still in his carrier, and followed Gar down the narrow hallway to the kitchen, which ran along the back of the house. Sunlight poured in through a large window over the sink and a sliding door leading to a back deck. A pair of wooden Adirondack chairs sat on the deck facing the ocean.

"It's lovely," I said to Gar, but his only response was a grunt. He made a show of turning the kitchen faucet on and off to prove that I had water and flipping a stove burner on with a whoosh to prove that I had propane. I ignored him, gazing instead out the window at the back lawn descending to a pebbled beach—a private beach for my use alone. Waves creamed toward the shore, slapping lazily at the pebbles before receding. The kitchen walls and ceiling danced with light off the sun-dazzled ocean.

Gar nodded toward the window. "Trash cans are in the shed."

"Oh, right," I said, spotting the small shingled structure on the edge of property. "So . . . is there a dump here?"

"Trash day is Tuesday," he said, sounding offended.

My bad for assuming the island was too primitive for trash collection. I followed him back to the living room, where he sent a terse nod in the direction of the wood stove.

"Am I allowed to use that?" I asked.

He gave a dismissive snort. "Might have to. Gets pretty cool 'long about mid-August."

"Where's the wood?" I asked. *Or do I have to chop my own?*

"Pile out back, under the tarp next to the shed."

"But the house has a heating system?"

He sniffed. "Furnace needs work. Scheduled for September."

"Ah." I glanced at the small flat-screen TV next to a bookshelf stocked with DVDs and, yikes, old VHS tapes. "Cable?" I asked.

"Out of Bangor."

"Wi-Fi?"

A narrow-eyed glance. "Included." Another city slicker question, apparently.

I said good-bye to Gar and shut the front door firmly behind him, thrilled to be alone with the house at last. Taking another turn around the downstairs rooms, I hugged myself with gratitude that I'd landed here, more or less on my feet, after everything horrible that had happened in the past month.

Eager to see the rest of the house, I climbed the stairs to the second floor. The master bedroom had wallpaper in a rose-and-trellis pattern, a four-poster double bed with a comforter, a pale blue carpet over a wide-plank floor, and white muslin curtains framing views of the sea on two sides of the house. I stood on the threshold and just looked. It's perfect, I thought. I hadn't been in the house ten minutes and already I loved it.

The other two bedrooms were smaller, but ready to accommodate an army of summer visitors, one with twin beds and the other with a double. Perfect for Jacey and her two kids if only I could persuade her to take time off. What could be better than a New England seaside vacation in August?

I was using the bathroom—turn-of-the century wainscoting painted sage green, a clawfoot tub and pedestal sink—when a baleful meow carried up the stairs, reminding me that Juju was still trapped in his carrier on the living room floor where I'd left him. I flushed and ran down to set him free, scolding myself for being a bad mother. He stretched luxuriously after his long hours of captivity and then stalked off in the direction of the kitchen, sniffing everything as he went. Not for my brave, regal feline to wedge himself under the sofa for three days, as a lesser cat might. It was clear that Juju meant to own the place.

And I did, too.

It came to me as I was unpacking the cooler, excavating my first week's supplies in search of the cat food. Gar's sour words: *That won't work here.* When I picked up my phone, a mere sliver of a bar of reception showed up in the top right-hand corner of the screen.

Another time, I might have welcomed being cut off from the world—to paint, or take photos, or loll in an Adirondack chair reading all day. But I was too fragile for that right now. I wanted solitude, not isolation.

Phone in hand, I walked through the downstairs rooms, hoping I'd stumble onto the one magical spot where the signal would leap to two or three bars. Nada. I climbed to the second floor, still watching the screen. Reception in the master bedroom jumped to a solid half bar. Better than nothing, even if I had some dropped calls.

Then a closed door caught my eye—out on the landing next to the bathroom. I pulled it open expecting a linen closet, but instead discovered the stairs to the attic. The steep steps led to an open space under the eaves, swept clean and swelteringly hot, with windows on either end. The window on the ocean side gave onto a narrow balcony, just visible through the salt-crusted panes. The bottom sash was swollen shut but yielded to a shoulder-wrenching yank.

A gust of cool sea air flooded in, beating back the trapped attic heat. I climbed onto the balcony to an amazing view, the horizon rimmed by ocean in every direction. Off to the west, where the harbor lay, masts of boats poked up above the treetops. If I clung to the peeling window frame and cantilevered my body out over the railing, I could almost see the dock where the ferry came in. Even better, my phone reception shot up to a solid three bars. I pocketed my phone, relieved.

Dinner that night was a simple affair—a haddock filet cooked in a frying pan with butter, lemon juice, garlic, and a handful of spinach, served over rice. Even without the addition of spices or condiments, it was quite possibly the most delectable meal I'd ever eaten, maybe because I was actually hungry for once. Since Andy's death the act of eating had been nothing more than a robotic feeding of my numb body. But not tonight. Maybe, I thought with a glimmer of hope, my gamble in coming to the island would pay off. Maybe, just maybe, I'd begin to feel the solace I craved. At any rate, something had shifted.

Gulls coasted in and landed on the lawn in shameless beggar mode, as I ate on the deck in one of the Adirondack chairs while the surf washed the pebble beach a few yards away. Back in the kitchen, I scraped the remaining fish crumbs from my plate into Juju's bowl. He'd disappeared into the far reaches of the house, still exploring.

It was just after six o'clock, the sun still strong in the western sky, and I paused at the sink, wondering how I'd fill the remaining evening hours. I pulled a bag of Oreos from the freezer and poured myself a tumbler of milk, offering up brief thanks to the gods that my desire to eat healthy hadn't driven me to deny myself the next the best thing to wine. I tore open the bag and surrendered completely to the crunch of crème-filled cookies collapsing in a gush in my mouth. I ate them the way I'd eaten them as a kid, placing each cookie vertically between my teeth before biting down. One after another, I washed the macerated cookies down with giant slugs of milk, until I saw that I'd mindlessly consumed a third of the package. So much for a healthy dinner.

Sated at last, I dragged the Adirondack chair down to the beach and sat there contemplating the water and the all-encompassing quiet. The rose hues along the horizon faded to pearl and the sky darkened. When a chill rose from the water and worked its clammy fingers under my thin fleece, I dragged the chair back to the deck and went inside.

Bedtime—the witching hour—had arrived.

I slipped between the soft, much-washed sheets wondering who had made up the bed for me. Gar? Not likely. Mrs. Gar, probably. The soft mattress yielded to my weight with random pings. Juju had not yet made an appearance, but now I sensed him in the room with me. His dark form landed softly on the bed, then leapt to the dresser, the armchair next to it, and finally the windowsill, where he stayed for a very long time, a black silhouette against gray. Then, obeying the mysterious rhythms that only cats are attuned to, he jumped down and slipped like a blade through a patch of moonlight and out of the room.

A loud crack split the quiet and jerked me back from the precipice of sleep. My heart tripped against my breastbone and then slowed again. Just the old house settling, I told myself, the heat of the day leaving and the cool of the night coming in. As if on cue, a damp breeze puffed back the curtain next to the bed.

The heat and glare and tragedy of my life in California seemed very far away. I closed my eyes and, minutes later, drifted off to sleep.

Chapter 22

In my first days on the island, I waited for grief to swamp me again, made worse by boredom—but the two demons kept a respectful distance, allowing me to commune with my surroundings in peace. I'd sit in my Adirondack chair at the water's edge with my morning coffee while the sun-warmed surf washed over my ankles, just the right degree of cool, and the wet pebbles massaged the soles of my feet. Mid-morning around eleven, I'd enter the ocean and swim out beyond the breaking waves to where the water turned icy, to float and gaze up at the sky. After lunch, I'd crawl into bed for a nap, and then rise to sit and swim some more. The paperbacks I'd bought at the airport lay unread on my nightstand, the TV seldom turned on. When the coolness of evening approached, or a fog bank or stiff easterly breeze drove me inside, I'd swaddle myself in the afghan from the back of the living room sofa and return to the beach until it was time to call it a day. I ate simply and went to bed early, sleep itself a kind of food that I was starved for after all my weeks of grief and disorientation.

Juju adjusted slowly to his new digs, settling at last after a restless few days. One morning I woke to find him perched on the dresser, watching me with his blue steadfast gaze. A patch of sunlight fell across the rug where moonlight had been the night before. I smiled, sleepily remembering the day I'd brought our gangly new kitten home from the breeder. It was a Saturday, and Andy and I had planned to go together, but as often happened, he'd been called in to work at the last minute, so I made the trip to the breeder's ranch alone. That afternoon, a rare beer in hand after his weekend stint at the office, Andy grinned as I picked up Juju to introduce him. "So who's this little guy?" he asked, reaching out to stroke the kitten's beige head, his chocolate face.

"This is Juan," I said, "Juan Hamilton, to be exact," because I'd already decided on his name on the drive home.

Andy's smile turned quizzical. "Somebody we know?"

I held Juan to my chest and stroked his purring side. "Juan Hamilton was the young potter whom Georgia O'Keefe fell in love with when she was, like, eighty-six."

He looked intrigued now. "So who's Georgia in this scenario? You?"

I laughed. "Right. I'm two-hundred and ten in cat years and Juan is about three."

"That's some age difference." He planted a gentle kiss on Juan's head and then pulled me close. "But you know what? You're one sexy super-centenarian."

But Juan Hamilton didn't stay Juan for long. Goofily, Andy insisted on calling him "Joo-an Joo-an," which quickly got corrupted by both his doting parents to "Juju."

I lay very still attempting to prolong the memory. It was the first I'd had since Andy's death that didn't hurt.

But the magic of the house was not a permanent shield. Eventually my grief found me there. At first it was a subtle feeling, like lead in my veins. Then a day came when I had trouble getting out of bed. The awareness of everything I'd lost with Andy's death grew sharper the more I made contact with something essential and life affirming in myself.

July fourth passed without fanfare, followed by a stretch of humid, thundery weather. One afternoon, a sudden cloudburst drove me indoors and I roamed the house feeling the ache of a new emotion—loneliness. Panicking, I sought a distraction, my attention latching onto the framed watercolors adorning the walls of the downstairs rooms. I'd given them a bemused glance here and there, but now the artist lying dormant inside me perked up. The paintings were a series of depictions of the same two cats— one black and white, the other ginger—their elongated bodies reclining in sensuous poses as in a Japanese woodcut. I moved from one to the next, studying them closely.

Each watercolor bore a cryptic code at the bottom, all in the same calligraphic hand—"C.S. 89," "C.S., 04," and so on. The name of the artist and the year. *Catherine Sutton, 1989.* I recalled her enigmatic chuckle on the phone, her elderly voice a kind of purr itself. "You'll find we're a cat-loving island." The most recent watercolor was dated five years ago—perhaps her last year on the island. I wondered what had happened to the cats.

Thunder rumbled overhead and the rain intensified, and I drifted into the study with all its books. An entire set of volumes bound in sky-blue cloth with gold lettering occupied the top three shelves. I pulled one volume down at random and leafed through the pages, scanning the maps and illustrations, the dense paragraphs of historical detail. The words jumped out at me, *splendid isolation.* I read the relevant paragraph—about Britain's mid-nineteenth century policy of avoiding foreign entanglements and alliances, a luxury the country could afford because it was an island.

Well, huh. So maybe Catherine Sutton, the solitude-loving artist, hadn't named the house after all. Perhaps her husband, the British naval historian, had done the honors. Or had they named it together—a neat double entendre speaking to the closeness of their relationship? I placed the book back on the shelf, feeling strangely let down. Did I begrudge an elderly woman the intimacy she'd had with her now deceased husband? Yes, I suppose I did. Andy and I would never name a house together, would never grow old side by side.

And just like that, the memory of FedExing Andy's ashes to the Stevensons came back in lacerating detail, making me burn with shame. What had I been thinking? What kind of wife would do that, no matter what sins her husband had committed? Obviously I owed Liz an apology. I could write the letter now. *It was a difficult time for me. I was half out of my mind with grief.* But the only paper I could find in the house was the magnetized kitchen pad attached to the refrigerator. Texting my amends was out of the question. Even email felt inadequate. I told myself I'd buy a note card suitable for the task the next time I was in town.

But if I owed my sister-in-law an apology, didn't I also owe her an honest accounting of my suspicions—that there was at least a chance her brother had been murdered and that the cocaine and the alleged affair were somehow part of a set-up?

And how would she respond to that? Hire the flashiest lawyer in the country? Get the FBI involved? The truth was, I just wasn't ready to fight Liz for control of Andy's murder investigation, raw nerve-ending though it was. So I gave up the idea of writing to her.

My phone was ringing. Faintly, through the open bedroom window.

I waded out of the ocean, grabbed my towel, and ran dripping toward the house, toward the promise of a human voice. Jacey's name lit up the screen as I grabbed the phone off the bedroom dresser and kept running, up to the attic to answer her call. "Hey," I said, lifting the attic window with my free hand to climb out onto the balcony. Three stories above the world, it was a perfect summer day, even if the ocean was still as icy as winter.

"Mel? You okay? You sound out of breath."

Not so long ago, out of breath might have meant answering the phone during foreplay. "I'm fine. I had to run upstairs. The phone reception here sucks."

"Oh." Her voice sounded oddly flat.

"What's up? Everything okay out there?"

"I'm not sure," she said slowly. "Mel, I think someone has been in your house."

I stopped breathing, mid-pant. "What do you mean?"

"The alarm was off when I came in to water the plants. And —you know what a neat freak I am—a couple of the kitchen drawers were open, and I *know* I wouldn't have left them like that, even if I opened any drawers the last time I was here. Which I didn't."

I heard the click of her heels on tile as she talked, a cabinet door closing. My breath was frozen in my chest. "Jacey, are you in my house right now?"

"Yeah. I am."

My stomach dropped. I thought of Tom. *Call me if anything suspicious happens.* Did this qualify as suspicious? Yeah, it did. Still, it didn't account entirely for the panic gripping me. "Jacey? Listen to me. Leave the house. Now."

"What about the plants?"

"Screw the plants! Just go."

"Mel—Jesus, why are you yelling? You're scaring me."

"I'm hanging up and calling the police." I clicked off the call and tapped on the phone's microphone. "El Dorado Hills, California," I blurted. "Police emergency number."

The number came up on the screen and I tapped Call with shaking fingers. Seconds later I was talking to a woman's voice at the police station, telling her my address and stating my emergency. "I'm away from home, but my neighbor is in my house *right now* and she just surprised an intruder."

"Slow down, ma'am. Address again?"

I pressed my forehead against the peeling window frame. "1-5-2-3-3 Ledgewood Circle."

I could hear her keying the address into her computer. "Okay, we're sending a patrol car over now."

I hung up and dragged the phone down the front of my bathing suit to wipe the sweat off the screen. It came away smeared with salt water instead. The peaceful summer afternoon below me—the ocean blue and serene, the sun-warmed breeze rippling innocently through the treetops—seemed as real as a photo in a glossy travel magazine. My chest was tight with fear for Jacey. "Please, please," I prayed out loud. "Please let everything be okay."

Two minutes later my phone rang again. "Jacey. Thank God. Are you outside?"

"Yeah," she said, sounding stunned.

There were voices in the background, the sound of car doors closing, someone barking an order.

"Mel, what the hell is going on? There are *three* police cruisers here. There are guys in *Kevlar vests* going into your house."

"You said the alarm was off and the kitchen drawers were open. I was afraid there might be somebody in the house. *With you.*"

I heard it then, how wildly dramatic I sounded. Jacey must have heard it too, because she wasn't saying anything. The silence stretched out between us.

"Right," she said at last. "Well, they're coming out now." She went back and forth with the police in muffled bursts, the words undetectable. Her voice came back on the phone. "They didn't find anyone. No signs of forced entry either."

Stupid, overreacting El Dorado Hills police. Trust them to send a SWAT team. "I'm sorry," I said. "I'm sorry if I scared you. I just—lost it."

More silence.

"Jacey—"

"Mel," she cut me off, her voice angrier than I'd ever heard it. "I don't know what the *hell* is going on with you, but obviously something is. You need to tell me *now*. No more lies."

Chapter 23

*Y*ou want the truth? Well, here it is. I suspect Andy was murdered. I don't think I fully believed it until now. When you said the alarm was off and you thought someone had been in the house, I was suddenly terrified that you were there with the murderer. And I couldn't bear to imagine what would happen if you were.*

"You're right," I said. "There is something I haven't told you. And I'm really sorry about it. Andy was in trouble at work before he died. He was about to get fired."

"That's what this is about?" The anger was still in her voice, but dialed down a notch, I was relieved to hear. "Was it because of the coke?"

"Yeah, but it's worse than that. The day I went to see Andy's boss, he accused Andy of downloading some documents he wasn't supposed to have access to. He claimed that Andy was planning to use the documents as insurance against getting fired."

"You mean like *blackmail*? This is *Andy* we're talking about?"

"Insane, right? I almost told the boss to go fuck himself."

"Too bad you didn't," she said. "But what does this have to do with—"

"I told him I didn't know anything about any documents, but he didn't believe me. He actually suggested sending Ralph over to search Andy's home office."

"So wait a minute. Are you saying you think it was *Ralph* who broke into your house? Jesus, what kind of lawyers are they?"

"The usual kind? News flash—lawyers aren't very nice people. Most of them."

"But still, what did you think *Ralph* was gonna *do*? Off the neighborhood lady who comes in to water the plants?"

I wanted to yell, S*top saying his name!* But obviously that wasn't going to improve the situation. "It sounds ridiculous, I know," I said. "But it might not have been Ralph. It could have been . . . somebody else."

"Like who?"

Some hired thug. "I don't know! Did you really want to hang around and find out?"

My tone must have told her I wasn't kidding around, because she got very quiet, taking it in.

"So what *exactly* are you saying?" she asked slowly. "I was in danger and you didn't tell me?"

This conversation was going south fast. I stammered, groping for the right words.

"Mel, I'm a *mother*!" she burst out. "I have two kids! Didn't you think I had a right to know?"

"Jacey, please. It never occurred to me you might be in danger. You have to believe me."

"Is that why you left town? Because you were afraid to stay here?" The anger was back in her voice, but something even worse. Distrust.

"What? No! That wasn't why. I told you—"

"Yeah, you told me you wanted to go somewhere it rains once in a while."

"You know that's not why," I said, my voice unsteady now, "I was upset because of Andy's—"

Infidelity.

I couldn't even say the word.

"Mel, I want to believe you, but . . . God, how can I trust you if you won't even be truthful with me?"

I rested my forehead against the peeling window frame and banged it softly, once, twice. "Look, Jacey, I overreacted and I frightened you. I'm sorry. I truly am. Can you forgive me?"

But it was too late to put the toothpaste back in the tube. My friend's stone-cold silence confirmed that.

"Jacey? Say something. Please."

She sighed. "Forgive, yeah. Forget, I don't know. I have to think about this."

"Okay," I said at last. "I understand."

I paced the house after we said good-bye, too wired to think straight. What the hell had just happened? The only thing that was clear was that I'd made another costly withdrawal from my emotional bank account with a friend I couldn't afford to lose. How much longer would it be before I was overdrawn? And what would I do if she cut off credit?

I palmed my phone numbly and scrolled to Tom's number. Dump it all on him. *Tom, guess what? Somebody broke into my house*. Except there was no concrete evidence that somebody had. No sign of forced entry, the police said. Besides, I could only guess what Tom's response would be. *Come home. If you're in danger, that remote island is the last place you want to be.*

I put the phone down without calling him. Then I threw myself on the couch and did the only thing that felt right under the circumstances. I wept tears of frustration and regret that I might possibly have jeopardized the closest friendship of my adult life.

A half-hour later, spent and still sniffling, I put on my running shoes and left the house.

The courtyard had a European flair—a wrought iron table and chairs sat in dappled shade, inviting tourists to rest and regroup before maybe going back inside to buy that painting they'd been admiring. I'd passed the sign before: GALLERY, with an arrow pointing down a grassy lane, but I'd saved my visit for another day, not wanting to squander the island's treasures.

I crossed the flagstones, sweaty and out of breath from my run. Maybe being around art for a while would center me, apply balm to my wounds. It usually did. I found the silence of an art gallery soothing and restorative, the way some people were calmed by the orderly peace and quiet of a library or a hardware store.

The gallery itself was in a converted barn, its weathered gray boards picturesque in that self-consciously artsy way prized by hip travel publications. The modest sign next to the open barn door said "Kilronan Gallery" with a logo above it that looked runic. Another sign, in the adjacent window, said, "Help wanted. Apply inside."

I paused on the threshold to let my eyes adjust to the dim interior after the bright afternoon sunshine. Track lighting threw soft spotlights on the art along the walls, augmented by light streaming down from a pair of big skylights in the roof. An open stairway led to a loft area where I assumed more art was on display.

When I stepped inside, my eyes were immediately drawn to a series of black-and-white photographs lining the wall to the right—gorgeous seascapes and island shots, the images so clear you could almost feel the texture of the rocks, the wetness of the surf. The blacks were velvety, gelatinous. Here was an artist who knew something about shadow, about negative space. I stared, entranced, almost forgetting the emotional upheaval that had brought me here.

I was alone in the main gallery, but I sensed the presence of another human nearby, the way you do when you've gone for many days without company. A slim, fortyish man appeared in a doorway at the far end of the space. In the room behind him, I glimpsed a worktable, the place where the matting and framing were done. We traded a friendly nod and I went back to studying the photos.

But he didn't go away. "Just let me know if you need any help, miss."

Miss. The quaintness of it disarmed me. A faint lilt in his voice suggested the trace of an Irish accent.

"Just looking," I said, and thanked him.

"Well, don't be shy."

Maybe he was lonely, too, starved for casual conversation.

I moved to the next photograph—a tree clinging to a surf-blasted rock, its growth stunted by the harsh climate. Like a desert, but wet. I thought of all the desert shots I'd taken back home and never gotten around to printing, how long it had been since I'd picked up my camera. I'd actually brought it with me: my old Nikon SLR, a high school graduation present from my parents. Hoping that grief would permit me the comfort of a perfectly framed shot.

I came to the last photo on the wall, a different theme—a gaggle of young children in T-shirts and shorts, squinting into the sun against a pastoral backdrop, their faces smeared with something. Chocolate ice cream? Strawberries?

I heard footsteps behind me and turned, a bit startled, to see the man approaching. He stopped by my side and looked at the photographs with me, without any awkwardness, as if seeing them for the first time himself. It was an odd thing to do and should have made me feel uncomfortable, but the truth was, it felt good to be standing close to another human, even a complete stranger.

Furtively I registered the subtle warmth coming off his skin, his quiet exhalations. His sandy hair stood up in an unruly cowlick in back, making him look appealingly young in spite of the faint lines etching his face.

I cleared my throat. "These are great photos. The use of light and shadow is amazing."

"It is that."

"Is the artist local?"

"She was. Not anymore."

Was everyone on the island as cryptic as Gar Hunt, I wondered, and left his side to take in another wall of pictures. A different artist was on display, one who worked with oils—bold splashes of color depicting beach houses and kayaks and flowers spilling out of pots. I stood still and drank in the vivid hues, studying the artist's technique but also wondering if the gallery owner, if that was who he was, would follow me.

He didn't. Instead he retreated to a counter in a back corner, where he began leafing through papers and making quick scribble marks, keeping his head down. I climbed the stairs to the loft above, where some stunning modernistic canvases with big price tags were on display. But I was more interested in the homely scene out the back window overlooking a lawn. Sheets and towels hanging on a line. It appeared the gallery owner lived next door. I returned downstairs, intending to leave.

The man looked up from his paperwork. "So are you an artist yourself?"

Could I still call myself an artist? It had been too long since I'd made art for the sheer pleasure of doing it. Even so, I nodded. "I am."

"What's your medium?" His tone was businesslike enough, but I detected a note of curiosity.

"Pastels mostly. Some photography. In my free time, that is. I do computer graphics for work."

He nodded. "What brings you to the island, then?"

"I'm renting for the summer."

"Ah."

"I live in California," I volunteered, not knowing why.

"Really now? That's a long way to come." The elusive Irish lilt again.

"I grew up in the Boston area, so I know Maine pretty well."

"It's a grand place."

I took a moment to study a nearby pen-and-ink sketch of a seagull, hoping he'd explain how he himself had washed up on its shores, but he'd gone back to his paperwork.

"That's an interesting logo," I said, nodding at the gallery sign. "It looks like a rune, but I don't think it is."

He looked up again, smiled briefly. "It's my wife's initials."

"Ah."

If I sounded a bit deflated, he didn't seem to notice. "Kerry Kilronan," he explained.

When I looked again, I saw it. The two Ks, their backs pressed against each other, facing in opposite directions.

I nodded. "Nice."

A warmer smile. "Enjoy your stay."

I was halfway home, lost in thought and hardly noticing the scenery, when my phone rang in my pocket. Jacey again. My heart jerked. "Hey."

"Look," she said, "I'll buy you some water globes for your plants."

"What?" I stopped walking.

"You know, those continuous watering thingamajigs. That way *nobody* has to water the god-damned plants."

"You don't have to water the cactuses at all."

"I know that. I mean, duh. Earth to Melissa."

I closed my eyes, grateful for the gentle gibe. Maybe, just maybe, we could get past this.

When she spoke again, her voice was gentler. "I'm worried about you, Mel. You sound like you're in trouble, and I hate it that you don't trust me enough to tell me what's wrong."

"That's not it," I said quickly. "Of course I trust you. It's just—I want to tell you what's going on, I really do, but I can't. Not yet. I'm sorry."

"Shit, Mel. Are you okay?"

"I just—" I stopped to keep my voice from breaking. "I wish you were here. You and the kids."

"Yeah, but you know what my summers are like."

I did. All those summer weddings. An event planner was lucky if she had a minute to call her own this time of year.

"Just come home soon," she said.

Chapter 24

A fork slipped through my fingers as I unloaded the dishwasher the next morning and landed tines-first on the wide-plank kitchen floor. I heard my grandmother's voice as clear as day: *There's a man coming.* Her soft chuckle when sharing a little inside joke with me.

The view out the kitchen window was the same as always, the short expanse of lawn and gravel beach and beyond it, empty ocean—gray today because it was cloudy and humid. Gar had been over, early, to cut the grass and haul off my trash, the highlight of my week as far as people contact went. The steady whine of the ride-on mower filling up the silence had comforted me for the hour or so it lasted. Now the house was quiet, as quiet as any place I'd ever lived, the random creaks and wind whispering in the eaves only intensifying the stillness.

"If you say so, Gram," I said out loud and bent to retrieve the fork. I rinsed it and dried it with a dishtowel, then plunked it in the tray with the rest of the silverware.

The back of my neck prickled as I shut the drawer. *A man coming.*

So what are you thinking here, Melissa? The intruder, if there was an intruder, didn't find anything when he broke into the El Dorado Hills house, so now he's on his way here? You're insane. You know that, don't you?

Maybe, but I jumped when my phone started buzzing on the dresser upstairs. It was Tom calling, the first time I'd heard from him since our conversation on the pier in Southwest Harbor.

"How's life in Vacationland? All quiet on the eastern front?" his genial voice quizzed me, sounding like he was just next door instead of three thousand miles away.

"Yep," I said, smiling in spite of my jumpiness, the way I always did when I heard his voice. "Very quiet."

"A nice quiet, I hope."

"You could say that."

"Glad to hear it," he said, sounding sunnier than usual himself. "Hey, I'm coming to Boston to visit my sister Eileen. It's been a few years since we've seen each other. I thought I'd swing up your way while I'm there."

"Oh." So Gram was right. A man *was* coming.

Well, at least he's not a thug.

Still, I wasn't entirely relieved. Tom as a houseguest—now there was a possibility I hadn't considered, even with all the extra beds in the house. On the one hand, the prospect of company—real company—should have made me jump for joy. On the other hand, having the investigator on my husband's murder case sleeping in the next bedroom? Sharing the same bathroom? The intimacy, though innocent, seemed too much for me in my current state.

"Are you sure?" I asked him. "It's a five-hour drive from Boston—at least. Plus a ferry ride."

"Hey, if you don't want me to come, just say so. My feelings won't be hurt."

Right. "No, um, okay. The truth is . . ." *yeah, why not?* " . . . the company would be nice."

"Good, because there's a lot I want to catch you up on. Seems like it'll be more efficient to talk to you in person."

If you consider a three-hundred-mile drive just to talk efficient.

"Besides," he went on irrepressibly, "I want to check out your set-up there. Make sure it passes muster."

"Sounds like a plan."

"Great, I'll book my motel room."

The little knot of tension in my stomach eased. "Okay, but just so you know, there are no inns on the island. You'll have to stay across the water."

"Not a problem. Looks like this place by the seawall has the best rates."

I pictured him sitting at his computer at work, clicking through the Trip Advisor site, and couldn't help smiling again despite my qualms. "So when are you coming?"

"Flying to Boston this Sunday. How does next Thursday sound?"

A wave rolled in listlessly on the shore below the house. The morning torpor continued. "Thursday sounds . . . absolutely fine."

I spotted his tall, slouched figure almost immediately among the horde of tourists piling off the ten o'clock ferry. In truth, I would have known him anywhere, even on the busiest city street. At first glance his only concessions to vacationer status were the knit pullover sport shirt and a beat-up backpack slung over his shoulder. Then the rest of his body came into view. Apparently he hadn't gotten the fashion memo about baggy Bermuda shorts and tube socks. His long, pale, skinny calves made him look oddly vulnerable—not exactly the look you want in a private investigator. But this was real life, I reminded myself, not the movies.

"Hey, kiddo," he grinned as he reached the top of the ramp. So I'd already graduated from "Melissa" to "kiddo." "Mrs. Stevenson," was a relic of the past. "You look great, I have to say. Island life must agree with you."

"It does," I said. It was easy to look happy in his friendly presence, even if I'd been too depressed to get off the couch yesterday.

Hugging would be the natural thing to do, and after an awkward pause, we did, my face jammed briefly into his shoulder. I came away from the embrace with the piney scent of his deodorant in my nostrils.

He looked around with interest, at the boats crowding the harbor, at the half-dozen red and yellow kayaks beached on the gravel shore next to the pier, at the weathered-shingled restaurant we were standing in front of—the only eatery on the island. "So how'd you find this place?"

"In a magazine, actually. It was billed as an artist's retreat."

"Well, you can't accuse anyone of false advertising."

"Nope."

We joined the column of tourists heading inland, the sun hot in a cloudless sky.

"How's your motel?" I asked.

"Basic, but comfortable. Stone quiet. Just the gulls and the roar of the surf to serenade me."

"What time did you get in?"

"Late." The last time he'd called, he'd mentioned that he'd be making a side trip on his way up to Maine—to visit a nephew, his sister Eileen's son, on Lake Winnipesaukee. "They gave me the full prodigal uncle treatment. Boat ride on the lake, barbecue, cards after dinner. It was hard to get away."

"I'm sorry," I said, feeling a twinge of misplaced guilt.

"For what?"

"It's not like they get to see you every day. Maybe you should have stayed longer."

He grinned. "And miss seeing you? Not a chance."

Okay, you fell right into that one.

The ten-minute walk to the house passed quickly, with Tom noting the schoolhouse, the defunct general store and post office, the rusting hulks of ancient cars in various yards. "A fifty-seven Olds? Look at that. And check this out, a Hudson Hornet? Holy shit. When was the last time I laid eyes on one of those? My grandparents had one when I was a kid." His excitement was infectious; I saw the boy he must have been. "This place is a time capsule. I wonder how they got them over here in the first place," he mused, "and what for? No roads, no place to go, right?"

So the PI was a car buff. "There's a museum down by the dock. Maybe they can tell you."

His wide-eyed tourist demeanor faded, though, as the houses got further apart, the surroundings lonelier. We came to the end of the dirt and sand track that I'd already come to think of as "my street." Catherine Sutton's house slumbered in the shade of the beech tree, the ocean sparkling beyond it. I turned to gauge his reaction, the proud parent showing off her firstborn.

"This it?" His gray eyes narrowed, taking in the roofline. I followed him as he strolled the perimeter of the property, checking everything out. Suddenly I was seeing it all through his eyes. The glass panes in the front door—easy to smash a fist through and unbolt, the slider opening onto the back deck (more glass), the lawn sloping down to the empty beach with no neighbors in sight.

The surf was up today, the breakers roaring dully a little ways out. We climbed the springy porch steps and went inside, into the welcoming coolness of the downstairs rooms. It felt odd to have him in my living room, the first piece of my California life to break off and find its way to my refuge. I went to the shelf by the TV and pulled out the VHS tape I'd discovered on one of my rainy day investigations of the house. A dangling black phone cord divided the faded cover like a jagged slash, separating a seductively barebacked young Jane Fonda from a suit-and-tie clad Donald Sutherland, revolver in hand, his pale face deadly serious. I didn't need to read the jacket blurb to understand that Jane's character was caught up in some serious shit, most likely from some male predator, and her only hope of rescue was the gun-wielding cop.

I handed the VHS tape to Tom.

"Klute," he said softly. "One of my favorites. Have you watched it?"

"The VCR isn't exactly functional."

"Probably just as well." He handed it back to me. "Hey, before I forget." He unzipped his backpack and rummaged inside, withdrawing a hard plastic case. I knew from experience what the case held. Against the backdrop of Catherine Sutton's cozy cottage furniture and reclining cat watercolors, it looked almost obscene. I supposed I'd almost invited it by showing him the "Klute" cover, but still it jolted me.

A Walther, I noted, as he snapped open the case and palmed the gun. Something inside me clicked. So this was the real reason for his visit.

"Whose is it?" I asked.

"It's registered in my name."

"Don't you need it?"

He shrugged. "Let's say it's a spare."

"Are you allowed to do that? Lend it to someone else, I mean?"

"The laws vary from state to state, but under the circumstances, I'm willing to take the risk."

I took it from him gingerly, the heft of it bringing back long-archived memories of my visits to the shooting range as a teenager. I could almost feel my father standing behind me now, his cheap aftershave, a whiff of beer and cigarettes on his breath as he moved closer to guide my aim. There was something repulsive about how natural the grip felt against my palm, as if my arm had sprouted a lethal extension.

Tom watched me. "I thought we might head over to a firing range this afternoon, if we have the time. Get you used to the kick."

Another unwanted piece of my California life broke off and headed at me like a flying object. I carried the gun over to the lamp table next to the easy chair and opened the drawer, dropped it inside and closed the drawer firmly. When I turned, Tom was holding a small cardboard box in his hands.

Cartridges.

His glance was almost apologetic. "It won't be much use without these."

I took the box from him and placed it in the drawer with the gun. "Do you want some iced tea?"

He covered his surprise. "Sure. Iced tea would be great."

In the kitchen, I fumbled ice cubes into two tall glasses and poured tea from the pitcher in the fridge, slopping some on the counter with my shaking hand. Tom stood in the doorway, silent. I nodded toward the deck. "Let's go outside."

We sat side by side in the two Adirondack chairs and sipped our iced tea, not talking. The sun bounced off the back of the house, brutally hot, tempered only slightly by a whisper of a southeasterly breeze coming off the water. We watched the breakers crest and roll towards shore, one after another.

"Amazing spot," Tom said at last.

His tone was carefully neutral, I noticed with a clarity bordering on resentment. "Yeah."

"Guess I shouldn't have come, huh?"

"Why not?"

"You looked happy when I got here. Now you don't."

My stomach clenched a little. I felt ungenerous, sulky, a child throwing a tantrum. "It's not like I've forgotten that Andy's dead. It's just—since I've been here, I'm remembering him the way he used to be, the way *we* used to be, before we moved to California. Before his job took over his life. Before . . . everything else."

"And I've woken you up from that dream by coming here?"

The waves collapsed on the pebble beach with sleepy regularity. I decided to voice the thoughts I'd been nursing since the California break-in that turned out to be a false alarm. "What if Andy wasn't murdered at all? What if it's just some story I've been telling myself—a weird, twisted way of holding onto him? What if he really *was* doing coke, and he really *did* die of an overdose, and he really was in trouble at work—"

And really was having an affair with that woman.

"Doesn't explain the baseball cap," Tom said quietly.

The baseball cap.

Right.

He let out a breath. "There's something I want to show you. Something that's come to light since we last talked."

Dread lodged in my chest as he disappeared into the house and came back carrying something in a zip-lock bag. "What—"

"Evidence." He handed it to me.

A Samsung Galaxy phone. Andy's.

"Jesus, where did you find it?"

"It was bugging me. The missing cell phone, the missing briefcase, the missing half-hour the night he died. I studied the floor plan of the Hyatt. The most direct route from the function room to the garage is a short corridor that goes past a block of rooms. The exit at the end of the hall leads down to the parking garage, one flight. The same level your husband's car was parked on. On a hunch I called Lost and Found at the hotel and asked if a cell phone had been turned in recently. Housekeeping turned it in a week ago. The maid found it under a bed in one of those rooms. She was doing a more thorough cleaning that day. Other maids had missed it."

"What was it doing there?"

"I don't know, but—"

"He was meeting her, wasn't he?"

He raised his hand, as if he could hold back what I was thinking. "No. Not necessarily."

"Did you check to see whose name the room was under?"

"Yeah. Andrew Stevenson."

"What the hell, Andy? What the hell?"

"It doesn't prove *anything*," Tom talked over me. "Do you hear me? *Nothing*. For all we know, he could have been meeting someone else there—a business associate. His *killers*." He stopped. "I'm sorry—"

"Oh, Tom."

He crouched next to me, gripped my shoulders. "Look, this is the biggest break we've had yet. It establishes Andy's whereabouts after he left that dinner! And by the way, what the hell was his phone doing under the bed?"

"It probably fell out of his pants pocket when they were tearing each other's clothes off!"

"Okay, yeah, maybe. Or it could have been kicked there during a struggle."

The rage inside me stilled.

"Two scenarios," Tom said. "Which one do we go with?"

"You tell me."

"Look, it's natural to want to jump to the most obvious conclusion. That's how the human brain works—the emotional brain. But we don't even know if it was your husband who booked the hotel room."

"Who else would it be?"

"Whoever made the reservation used a credit card but paid cash at check-in."

"Of course. He didn't want the charge on his credit card bill in case I saw it."

He waved me off. "I questioned the desk clerk who was on duty that night, but he couldn't give me a description. They see hundreds of people a day, especially on a busy Friday."

"But it was Andy's card, right?"

"Yeah," he said after a pause. "His Amex card. But that doesn't mean squat either. *Anybody* could have gotten access to his card number."

A disbelieving snort escaped me. "Anybody?"

"The firm issued that card to him, didn't they?"

I nodded reluctantly. "But why didn't the Hyatt call to tell me they found his phone? My name must be in his contacts."

"They *did* try to call you. But you said your reception is spotty here. The calls kept getting dropped. So they went to the next number that appeared most frequently in his call record. Reg Wolders' private line."

"Shit. Wouldn't Reg have sent someone over to pick it up?"

"That's what's crazy about it. He did. But I got there just ahead of them. When they asked me if I was from Wolders Palmer, I said yes."

I dug my elbows into my knees, my brain churning.

"Look," said Tom quietly. "I know it's a lot to take in and there's nothing that can make any of this less painful. But if a crime *was* committed, we now have a possible crime scene—the hotel room or the parking garage. The only thing we're missing is an eyewitness. I've been working my way through that list of people who may have been in the garage at the same time as your husband. One of them knows something, I think, but for whatever reason she's reluctant to talk."

I tried to listen to him, to take in what he was saying, but another question was forming in the back of my brain. "The call data. What did you find?" *Who was he calling? Who was calling him?*

"Nothing that set off alarm bells." But there was a flash of sympathy in his eyes.

"It's okay," I said. "You can tell me."

"Well, almost nothing. A lot of calls to you, of course. A few to and from what appear to be clients. Some to and from work associates, especially Wolders. Quite a few from what appears to be a disposable number. *Those* could be significant." He stopped, looking uncomfortable.

"And?"

"Several calls over a period of a couple of months that stood out because they were very brief, most of them less than a minute, and one way, meaning your husband didn't return the call, at least not on that phone."

Okay, I told myself, I'd expected the worst and now I was getting it. "When was this?"

"They stopped in April, I think."

"Do you know who made the calls?"

"Yeah, we ran down the number, along with all the others. The caller's name is Leslie Marshall. She's a paralegal at a firm in New Orleans."

I handed Andy's phone back to Tom, still in its zip-lock bag. Neither of us spoke again, Tom waiting, giving me space. Then he touched his hands to his knees and stood up. "Enough gloom. Let's get out of here. Take the ferry back to Mt. Desert. You can show me the sights."

What I wanted at that moment was to crawl back into bed and forget he'd even been here. Take Andy's phone and throw it in the ocean. Here you go, fish, scarf this down. I could barely look at Tom.

"Unless there are some sights here on the island that I haven't seen," he said with a lame smile.

"Nope," I admitted. "You've had the nickel tour."

"So come on. I'll treat you to a lobster roll."

I reminded myself that the man had driven three hundred plus miles to see me, that he was springing for a motel room on top of it, even though I had four extra beds in the house. That it wasn't his fault he'd disrupted my pathetic island idyll—he was just trying to help me. I might want to shoot the messenger, but I was not about to let him treat me to an overpriced Bar Harbor lobster roll. "If there's one thing there's no shortage of on this island, it's lobster. I made lobster salad yesterday. We can eat before we go."

He smiled. "Okay, kid, you're on."

Chapter 25

 "W here's your car?" Tom asked, as we walked off the ferry into the parking lot in Southwest Harbor.

I nodded vaguely in the direction of the Corvette, tucked into the back corner of the lot. "Over there."

"Never mind," he said, jingling his keys. "Mine's right here."

I followed his eyes to a black Kia subcompact, perfectly nondescript—the standard issue rental car. "The leg room in this beast is nonexistent," he said apologetically, as he folded himself into the driver's seat. He reached over to sweep a map, yellow legal pad, camera, and empty fast-food tray from the passenger seat so I could sit down.

"You know what," I said. "Let's take mine."

"You sure? I know you're upset—"

"I'm fine now." The ferry ride over and the good cheer of the tourists traveling with us had restored my equilibrium, at least enough to function.

I led the way across the crowded parking lot. Tom's observant gaze fastened suddenly on the far corner. "Whoa, what's that beauty over there?"

I followed his gaze, already knowing what he was seeing— a flash of LeMans blue in the shimmering heat, the sun almost hot enough to make the paint melt.

"Is that a sixty-nine?" he muttered. "Let me check this baby out." He made a beeline for the Corvette, his long strides outdistancing mine. When I caught up with him, he was passing his hand admiringly over one gleaming flank, as if the car were a supine woman. "Whoever owns this beauty should keep it covered. The hot sun is going to ruin the paint job."

I decided to look on the bright side. Hey, at least it hadn't been stolen yet.

My cool, competent private investigator took a reverent turn around the 'Vette, babbling something about the vacuum operated headlights, flow-through roof, and hidden wipers, a blind, faraway look in his eyes. "A college buddy and I used to drag race back in the day. What I wouldn't have given to race one of these thoroughbreds."

I dangled the car keys casually in front of him.

"What?" he asked, surprised.

"Wanna take it for a spin?"

He looked at me, stunned.

"It's my father's car," I said. "I thought I'd save money on a rental."

His face cracked open in a lopsided grin. "Holy Mother of God, you're kidding me."

"So, you want to try it out or not?"

"Hell, yes."

A half-hour later, with Tom at the wheel, we arrived at the turn-off leading to the Cadillac Mountain summit. For maximum effect, we'd cranked down the top before we left the parking lot. "You think the old girl has it in her?" he asked, his sparse gray hair blown back above a pair of aviator sunglasses that were looking more rakish by the minute.

I shrugged, the painful revelations of an hour ago blown to oblivion in the hot breeze blasting through the open convertible. "Let's find out." If the engine crapped out, blew a gasket, or whatever antique cars did when strained beyond their aging capacity, I was beyond caring. Let my mother yell at me from now until doomsday, let her condemn me to the special purgatory reserved for daughters who didn't sufficiently honor their dead fathers' legacy—I didn't care, because bombing around Mt. Desert Island in a 1969 Corvette with Tom was the perfect antidote to just about anything I could think of at the moment.

The breeze was delicious at the summit, a strong southerly flow that seemed to originate in a different stratum of the atmosphere. Tom and I perched on a large flat-topped boulder and dangled our legs over the edge, the town of Bar Harbor spread out below us along the blue slash of Frenchman's Bay. Off to the southeast, just visible in the heat haze, the Schoodic Peninsula stretched its skinny arm into the Atlantic.

"Have you ever been up here before?" I asked him, my words snatched away by the wind.

"Yeah, once," he yelled. "A camping trip with some high school buddies. Then I went west for college and never came back."

"Where'd you go to school?"

"Cal State. Majored in criminal justice."

"Of course." I smiled and lay back against the boulder to get out of the wind.

A few minutes later we found a more sheltered spot. Tourists roamed around us, picking their way over the rocky terrain like mountain goats. A group of teenagers linked arms and posed daringly on the downslope edge of a boulder that looked like it might be capable of teetering.

"So you wanna talk about the case some more?" Tom asked, calling an official end to our people watching.

I watched the teenagers disperse, their jokes and laughter ringing out among the rocks. For the moment, I felt pleasantly protected from whatever "the case" could throw at me. I gave Tom the nod to go ahead.

"For openers, your friend Warren Cheung hasn't been forthcoming."

"Really?" Come to think of it, the text I'd sent Warren alerting him that he'd be hearing from Tom had gone unanswered.

"He hasn't returned my calls," said Tom.

"Doesn't sound like Warren," I said, worried now.

Tom studied the horizon, his eyes narrowed. "Fortunately, this case is generating more leads than I have time to track down. Take this guy Wolders. He's made some interesting friends over the years. And one name keeps coming up."

"Who?"

"David Escondido." He read my puzzled look. "Yeah, I'm not surprised you're drawing a blank. People of his ilk keep a low profile."

I'd never heard Andy mention him either. "Who is he?"

"The Escondidos are one of the most influential families you've never heard of—that is, unless you live in Mexico or have a stake in the cocaine trade. They led one of the early drug cartels, back before the current crop of murderous thugs took over. The family, to their credit, aspired to gentility, and for the past generation or two, that's what they've been working towards. They have a big compound outside Mexico City and all the trappings of respectable wealth, if that's not an oxymoron. David, the scion, was educated in the U.S. He got his law degree from Stanford back in the early 'eighties. That's where he and Wolders crossed paths and began the bromance that's alive and well today."

A little boy wandered into our line of sight, his parents right behind him. The father swooped forward and gripped the boy's arm as he toddled determinedly toward the edge.

"David, even more than his father, appears to have a sincere desire to go legit, or at least to give that appearance," Tom went on. "He's been buying up real estate all over Sacramento County for the last twenty years. My guess, though I can't prove it yet, is that he's had ample help from his pal Wolders."

My attention was caught now. "How so?"

"Well, David wants to get clean, but he can't quite manage it. He's got all this wealth stashed in offshore accounts from the family's very profitable gambling and loan-sharking operations in Reno and Vegas. Not to mention the ongoing drug trafficking. So how does a guy like him get all that dirty money scrubbed?"

"Tell me."

"One way is to run it through assorted real estate escrow accounts. Care to guess who his favorite closing attorney might be?"

"Reg?"

"I'd bet money on it."

"But that's illegal, right?"

Tom cracked a grim smile. "You'd think so, wouldn't you? But the criminal code gets squirrelly on money laundering. Lawyers have no legal obligation to report the suspicious financial activity of their clients. This means guys like Escondido can have their offshore money wired directly into a client escrow account, make their real estate purchase, and emerge the legitimate owner of a shiny brand-new office building or apartment complex, no questions asked."

"No kidding."

"That is, after the money passes through several anonymous shell companies to wash out most of the grimy build-up."

"But you said you can't prove Reg's involvement."

"Not yet, but the signposts are there. I've got a couple of contacts in the fed who are helping me piece it together."

I realized I didn't like where this was going. "So if Reg was involved, does that mean Andy was involved too?"

"Depends on what you mean by 'involved.' When I reached a dead end with Escondido, I started looking at Wolders directly. Back in 2009, when the California real estate market was in the toilet, a company calling itself the American River Group began buying up distressed commercial properties in and around Sacramento."

Some real estate deal with the American River Group. They're a big client of Reg's.

"I've heard that name before. Warren Cheung mentioned it. When I asked him what case Andy was working on when he died."

"Bingo." Tom trained his narrow-eyed gaze on the blue horizon. "The American River Group is a Nevada corporation, making it next to impossible to find out who its directors and officers are. But, as luck would have it, the company was the subject of a federal investigation a couple of years ago. Working backwards, I was able to establish that Wolders is their legal counsel *and* one of their directors. Guess who else is a director."

"David Escondido?"

"Yep."

That would explain Andy's furtive behavior the last months of his life, the obvious stress he was under. Would he have been happy to have a drug kingpin and money launderer as a client? Not likely. As much as Andy had excelled at corporate law, his true calling was as a prosecutor. Too bad his father, a corporate attorney himself, nixed that ambition while Andy was still at BU.

"So you think Andy got caught up in all this and threatened to blow the whistle?"

A fugitive gleam lit Tom's eyes. "It's looking that way, isn't it?"

I let the implications sink in. "But it's so simple. It seems too . . ."

"Obvious? Sometimes the simplest explanations are the right ones. And if our supposition is correct, we have a motive."

The rest of the sentence hung between us, unsaid. Motive indeed.

"There's something I still don't get," I said later, as Tom and I walked along the beach at Seal Cove, a pristine stretch of sand and pebbles I'd visited a couple of times since arriving.

By then the adrenaline rush from our nail-biting drive down Cadillac Mountain—wondering with each hairpin turn if the Corvette's old brakes would give out and send us hurtling off into oblivion—had long since dissipated. By tacit agreement we'd called a moratorium on discussing the case to do the tourist thing for a couple of hours, driving the Park Loop and stopping at Thunder Hole and all the other natural attractions along the way. Just a couple of vacationers, a father and daughter perhaps, enjoying the radiant July afternoon.

"What don't you get?" asked Tom.

"If Reg wasn't doing anything illegal, then why would he risk . . ."

"Murder?"

I nodded, hating the word.

He picked up a flat rock, took aim, and skipped it expertly over the water. "I didn't say it wasn't illegal. For an attorney to be a party to money laundering carries a prison sentence. It's just hard as the devil to nail somebody on it. Lawyers who traffic in that kind of clientele are notoriously slippery themselves."

"But why would someone like Reg—rich and successful, a name partner with plenty of legitimate clients to pay the bills—get involved with criminals at all? So involved that he has to kill one of his own employees to protect himself?"

How naïve my question sounded as I remembered my last encounter with Reg, that day in his office, the ugliness lurking beneath his paternal exterior.

Tom wiped his wet hands on his shorts. "It boggles the mind, doesn't it? But never underestimate the power of greed. In my experience, it's hard-wired. Maybe acting as David Escondido's water carrier was how he *got* successful. Maybe the legitimate business of the firm is just . . . window-dressing."

"That's a horrible thought."

"Yeah, it is, but ugly people make an ugly world."

We stood ankle deep in the placid cove water, our eyes on the opposite shore. "Though I admit, I don't quite get it either," he said at last. "Not entirely. How much of a zealot was your husband?"

"What do you mean?"

"If he uncovered wrongdoing at the firm, why didn't he just resign? Why confront the boss and put his career—hell, his life

—at risk? Let's face it. Lawyers represent unsavory types every day of the week. Wolders could have given him the spiel—this is the way it is at a big firm like this. If you're not cut out for it, you're free to go. Instead . . ." He skipped another rock, but his wrist action was off this time. It sank after the first skip. "There's gotta be more to it, something Wolders wanted to keep hidden at all cost."

Regular ferry service to Mizzen Island stopped at six p.m., but I didn't have the heart to deny Tom a dinner together in town. In the morning, he'd be driving back to Boston for one last evening with Eileen and then flying home to Sacramento on Saturday. It was as good an occasion as any to try the after-hours water taxi.

The sun was low in the sky by the time we were seated at an outdoor table at the restaurant in Southwest Harbor. We'd stopped first at Tom's motel to freshen up, Tom remaining outside with the car while I washed my face and combed out my tangled hair in the little motel bathroom.

Tom ordered a beer and I ordered a glass of wine, my first in many weeks. Whether exhausted by the heat of the day or the content of our conversations, we sat without speaking, content to be quiet for a few minutes as the restaurant filled up around us. The bar, situated in a quaint lean-to shed along the side of the building was drawing a raucous crowd. My depression seeped back in as the loud, oblivious conversations crowded in on us. In a couple of hours, I'd be returning to the island alone, carrying with me the knowledge that my husband almost certainly spent the last hours of his life in the company of either murderers or another woman.

The waiter came back to the table to take our orders. Tom ordered the fisherman's platter and I ordered the baked sole. The waiter picked up our menus and breezed away, but soon returned to light the candle on our table with a flourish, as if we were some romantic couple. All around the restaurant, individual flames danced at individual tables in the soft twilight. "Can I get you another wine?" the waiter asked before he left us.

My limbic system said yes, but I shook my head.

"So what made you decide to go into business on our own?" I asked Tom.

"As a PI? I was furloughed during the '09 budget crisis. I never got reinstated." He caught my inquiring look. "Let's just say I have a habit of ruffling people's tail feathers. The wrong people."

"So do I."

We both smiled, but his had a wistful edge. "I miss the force sometimes. PI work looks glamorous on TV, but the interesting cases are few and far between. I spend most of my time tailing unfaithful spouses."

No wonder he was so eager to take on my case. "So why don't you go back to police work?"

"Maybe I will some day. At the time I had child support to pay. Couldn't afford to sit around waiting to get reinstated."

"So you've been married?"

He looked away. "Oh, yeah."

"What went wrong?"

"She got tired of my long hours and left me for another man."

"Ouch. I'm sorry."

He shrugged. "Hey, it goes with the territory. But it wasn't all bad. I have a daughter. Grown up, of course. She lives up in Oregon. Corvallis."

"How often do you see her?"

"Not as much as I'd like. Her mother poisoned the well pretty good. But you know how that goes."

"Any grandkids?"

"She's pregnant now. Her first." He gave me a shy look. "You remind me of her. Defiant, but . . . vulnerable." His fingers worked at the label on his beer, peeling it away a little piece at a time. "Sorry. That was a dumb thing to say."

I wanted to tell him that it wasn't dumb at all, that I wished more than anything that he had been my father instead of the father I had. But it seemed too intimate a thing to say, so I stayed silent. Our food arrived, saving us from further conversation.

Later, standing on the pier in the black, breezy night waiting for the water taxi to arrive, I told him the one thing I'd withheld during our long day of conversations. "They broke into my house, you know. Well, somebody did. Maybe. My neighbor said the alarm was off when she went in to water my plants. And one of the kitchen drawers was open."

"Did she call the police?"

"I did. But there was no sign of forced entry. Maybe Jacey was having a senior moment."

"How old is she?"

"Thirty-five."

He gave a soft snort.

"I know," I said, "ridiculous, right? But nothing was stolen."

He thought for a minute. "Maybe they didn't find what they were looking for."

I suppose I would have thought more about his words, but I was tired from the long day and the wine at dinner and the water taxi was arriving. It was a much older boat than the daytime ferry, with two sofas in the stern instead of built-in benches, like something out of the Arabian nights. The mate hopped down onto the pier to help me aboard, his face almost too dark to see.

Tom and I hugged good-bye, a proper hug this time, his chin resting on the top of my head for just a second before he pulled away. He stayed on the pier watching me leave as the water taxi cut a splashing arc toward open water. A sense of foreboding grew in me as the we cleared the no-wake zone and picked up speed, a sense that I was being willful and foolish in going back to the island instead of returning to California with my private investigator. But eventually the white speck that was Tom disappeared, and the lights of Southwest Harbor and their reflection in the black water disappeared too, and the feeling passed.

Chapter 26

As reluctant as I'd been to have Tom visit, I missed him acutely when he was gone. The spell the island had cast over me was broken. Vanished was the therapeutic value of sitting in the surf in my Adirondack chair, replaced by the taunting image of Andy's phone lying on the floor in that hotel room and the torment of doubts it raised. Which was the worse scenario: that my husband had gone there to meet a woman or to meet his killers?

Whichever one was true, I lived in a self-created hell that even my daily swims in the icy Maine water failed to shock me out of. It was almost enough to persuade me to call off the investigation.

To distract myself, I took the ferry to Southwest Harbor for much-needed groceries and stopped at the post office to collect my forwarded mail. Sitting in the Corvette, I leafed through the stack of bills and sympathy cards to the official-looking letter from the life insurance company. I tore open the envelope and scanned the cold prose. As expected, Andy's claim had been rejected. The reason given was his failure to disclose his cocaine use that led to his fatal heart attack. I tossed the letter on top of the pile of unopened mail on the passenger seat.

Seeking refuge from the bad news, I left the Corvette and crossed the street to the public library. At first I perused the stacks in their quaint alcoves with unseeing eyes, but then I discovered a section dedicated to French language editions, coyly hiding on a high shelf. As much as I'd enjoyed learning French in high school and college, I hadn't picked up a French novel since then. What better antidote to my wretched state of mind than to puzzle my way through Balzac's *Eugénie Grandet* and Malraux's poetry in the original language. I took both volumes to the circulation desk and was surprised when the librarian permitted me to check them out just by showing my driver's license and giving my address—Splendid Isolation, Mizzen Island.

But reading French was not the panacea I hoped it would be. Curled up on the couch, I stared at the pages, unable to comprehend the simplest words in the onslaught of images my brain kept generating. Andy burying his face in Leslie Marshall's brunette mane, his discarded clothes littering the cheap hotel carpeting. Or Tom's alternate scenario—Andy wrestling with unknown assailants, the phone knocked out of his hand and kicked under the bed.

Giving up on Balzac, I opened the drawer of the lamp table next to the sofa, where Tom's Walther lay untouched. Gingerly I lifted the handgun out and checked to make sure the chamber was empty, then sat cradling its cold metal heft in my lap. Eventually I removed the magazine and loaded it, pinching my fingertips as I jammed in one round after another. I put the gun back in the drawer without replacing the magazine.

A few days later, my loneliness weighing on me like winter clothes, I went back to the gallery. How could I not, when the gallery owner's smile was the only warmth I'd known since arriving on the island? When I strolled into the barn, though, I got a surprise. A dumpy elderly woman was installed at the counter, and her first glance in my direction was not welcoming at all.

I turned away, crushed. It was then that I noticed a girl of five or six sitting at a kids' table tucked away in a corner, absorbed as only young children can be in the business of crayons and paper. Her brown-gold hair was curly, a bit unruly, a telltale cowlick sticking up in back. I smiled, but she didn't smile back, so I turned to study the art on the nearest wall, respecting her space. A row of watercolors, quite beautiful, was in front of me. They hadn't been there the last time I visited. After a few minutes, the little girl stopped coloring to watch me curiously, her gray eyes the color of beach rocks. Encouraged, I sidled over to her table. If conversation was what I wanted, a child was as good as a man.

"That's a pretty drawing," I said, nodding at her paper. A stick figure little girl and man stood in the foreground holding hands, while a third figure with a pink triangle for a skirt floated in the sky between a puffy cloud and a bright, spoked sun. I pointed to the child figure with yellow hair. "Is that you?"

She nodded solemnly.

"Is that your daddy holding your hand?"

She nodded again. "But he's not here right now."

"He isn't, huh?" I said.

There was a cough over at the counter. "Esme, let the lady look at the paintings," the elderly woman said.

"It's okay," I told her, but she frowned and went back to whatever she was doing.

Esme ignored the mild reprimand. "He went on the ferry with a painting," she said.

"I see." Whatever that meant.

She studied me curiously. "Do you know my dad?"

"No. But I talked to him the last time I was here." I pointed at the stick figure floating in the sky. "Who's that?"

"Mommy."

"Ah," I smiled, "your mom can fly."

Her brow puckered and she looked away.

"Esme," the elderly woman interrupted us again. "It's time for lunch now. Pick up your things, and we'll go over to the house."

If there was a stronger note of disapproval in her voice this time, it was directed at me and not the little girl. I stepped away from the table.

"It was nice to meet you, Esme."

But Esme was already turning toward the older woman. "Mabel, are we having macaroni and cheese?"

"We are," said the woman.

"Yay!" Esme said, and dutifully began putting her crayons back in the box.

I'd been on the island long enough to know that Gar Hunt was married to a Mabel, a bit of trivia made interesting, titillating even, by boredom and isolation. The woman who might be Mrs. Gar looked at me directly. "The gallery will be closing in five minutes. If you want to speak to Mr. Kilronan himself, he'll be back at two o'clock."

Mr. Kilronan. Her voice fairly dripped with disapproval as she said it. Or maybe I was being wildly oversensitive, given my state of mind. I remembered the Help Wanted sign I'd seen on my first visit to the gallery, tacked up next to the barn door. Was it still there? I hadn't noticed it on my way in, but I hoped it was. "Actually," I blurted, "I'm here to apply for the job."

Suspicion glinted in Mabel's eyes. "Indeed. As I said, Mr. Kilronan will be back at two."

My nerve was already beginning to fail me as I groped in my bag for a pen. "Maybe you could have him call me. I mean, when it's convenient for him." Leave it up to fate, I thought. Either he would or he wouldn't. Without waiting for her to respond, I picked a business card out of the holder on the counter and scribbled my name and phone number on the back.

She took the card with a grudging nod. "I'll see that he gets it."

I hurried away from the gallery, breathless and off-kilter. What the hell was I doing? Barely three weeks on the island and already so lonely, I was applying for a job? If being alone was this unbearable, how on earth was I going to manage being single again?

I'd almost managed to forget the whole embarrassing encounter when my phone rang late that afternoon. The New York City area code made me curious enough to answer the call.

"Melissa?" a man's voice said.

"Yes, speaking."

"Jack Kilronan."

"Oh."

"You inquired this morning about the job?"

"Um, yes. I did."

"Have we met? Your voice sounds familiar."

"We have, actually. I came into the gallery about a week ago. We talked about the photographs—"

"The graphic artist from California. I remember."

"Right," I said, surprised.

"I thought you were here on vacation."

"Not exactly a vacation. More just a, um, change of scene."

"You've come to the right place for that."

There was a small silence between us.

"So, let me tell you about the job," he went on. "It isn't much, I'm afraid. It's been a busy summer for me, being the jack-of-all-trades at the gallery. I'm basically looking for someone to run paintings over to the mainland for shipment on an as-needed basis. Believe it or not, it's more economical than having UPS or Fed Ex come out here. I can't pay much, but you'll have a free ferry ride to Southwest Harbor once or twice a week. Takes some of the sting out of the grocery runs."

"Sounds great. When can I start?"

"As I recall, you have an honest face, but I wouldn't be much of a businessman if I didn't check your references."

"Oh right. Of course."

"We're just about to close for the day. Can you come in tomorrow morning and fill out an application?"

Jack Kilronan proved to be an easy man to work for, perhaps because I hardly saw him, except when I came to the gallery to pick up pieces for shipment. When he wasn't on the gallery floor talking to a customer or standing behind the counter doing paperwork, I found him in the back workroom, matting or framing or taking care of some other mundane task. Sometimes, he wasn't at the gallery at all and I had to deal with Mabel instead, who had yet to warm to my charms.

Still, my new sense of purpose, the tenuous link I'd formed with another adult on the island, and my semi-weekly rides across the water to Southwest Harbor began to lift my mood. On my second trip over with a couple of framed canvases in crates, I found myself wedged in next to another local on the crowded noon ferry.

"You must be working for Jack," he said, by way of introducing himself. He didn't have to identify himself as an artist. The gray hair straggling out from under a faded Red Sox cap, the paint-spattered jeans, and the bits of colored oil pigment under his fingernails said it for him.

"Yeah," I said, "I just started."

"I heard he hired someone."

I smiled. "I'm only here for the summer."

He shrugged. "Good enough. The gallery closes after Labor Day. Sometimes Jack keeps it open into October, but not usually. The tourists are mostly gone by then."

I nodded and turned my face back to the cool breeze coming off the water. It was one of those jewel-like July days that defies darkness to linger in the spirit.

"Jack's a very quiet guy," my seatmate went on suddenly. "He's been pretty closed off since Kerry died."

I stared.

"His wife," he said.

I remembered Esme's drawing—the stick figure with the pink triangle skirt floating in the sky. How could it not have occurred to me? It explained the strange vibe I'd picked up from Jack—warmth, but distance too. I wondered what blindness had kept me from recognizing a fellow sufferer.

"I'm sorry to hear that," I said.

"He does his best with Esme, and he's active in the community," the man went on, "but we keep expecting him to pick up stakes and go back to New York one of these days."

It felt weirdly voyeuristic to be having an unsolicited conversation with a complete stranger about my new, very circumspect boss. But I couldn't help taking the bait. "New York?"

"That's where he and Kerry met. She was the artist. She inherited the gallery from her aunt."

"Oh," I said, wishing there was room to move to another seat, but I was wedged in on either side, and even if I could get up, I'd have to stumble over the coolers and backpacks at everyone's feet. "You sound like you're a close friend of his," I said, hoping to jog his conscience.

"I'd better be," he laughed. "He exhibits most of my work." Then, seeming to detect my discomfort, he said, "No, we're great friends actually. I'm just happy he's hired someone and not trying to do it all himself, like he usually does. Pig-headed Irishman. But then I shouldn't talk with a name like O'Brien." He held out his hand. "Richard."

His palm was sandpaper rough, his knuckles split and weathered. Turpentine hands, I thought, recognizing one of the hazards of the trade. "Melissa," I muttered in return.

I turned away from him after that, to enjoy the rocking motion of the ferry in the chop from a brisk northwest breeze. The low, green Manset shoreline slid past on the approach to Southwest Harbor, punctuated by imposing shingled vacation homes and the boat works famous for its luxury yachts. Richard soon started a conversation with the woman on his other side, and I saw his indiscretion in a different light. Maybe he was starved for human contact, just like me.

Tom called a few days later, city noises in the background.

"Where are you?" I asked, sitting on my beach with *Eugenie Grandet* open on my lap.

"Downtown Reno."

"What's in Reno?"

"I'm in the parking garage where that black SUV was stolen—the one that followed your husband's car out of the Hyatt garage. I'm on the third level in the exact spot where it was jacked. Guess what the view across the street is."

"Tell me," I said, making an effort to focus. The heat and sun and my uphill battle with French were making me dopey.

"The Baja Wind Casino. Owned by take a wild guess—David Escondido."

"No shit."

"Here's the thing," Tom began, but the sound of a car engine and protesting brakes drowned out his next words.

"Sorry, I didn't catch that. Say again."

"I was saying the accountant who owns the SUV and reported it stolen is an employee at Escondido's casino. Odd coincidence, don't you think?"

"Yeah."

"Not. I don't believe in coincidences, remember?"

"Right. So are you saying Escondido had something to do with Andy's death?"

"If Escondido is implicated, Wolders is, too. If anything, this strengthens our case against him."

I wanted to feel as excited as my private investigator obviously was. "Great work, Tom," I said, hoping my words alone could fool him.

For once, his almost preternatural ability to read me was disengaged. He scoffed. "The sheriff's office could have found out that much if they were doing their job. It'll be a good day's work if I can actually get this bean counter to talk to me. He lives in some upscale development out in the desert. I'm heading over there now to stake him out."

That woke me up. "What for? I don't get it."

"I want to see his face when I ask him why he waited twenty-four hours to report his vehicle stolen."

"Won't you be blowing your cover?"

"No, I'm the friendly insurance adjuster, stopping by to dot the *i*'s and cross the *t*'s."

"What if he already talked to the insurance adjuster?"

"Hey, kid, you think of everything. Don't worry, I'll improvise."

"Be careful, okay?"

His reply was snatched away by another car squealing around a corner in the garage. But the excitement in his voice lingered like an afterimage as I ended the call. I pictured a cartoon bloodhound, wrinkled muzzle to the ground, tail wagging furiously, and smiled.

It was only later, when I was in the kitchen throwing together a simple dinner and Tom hadn't yet reported back, that it occurred to me to feel anxious for him. Here I was, spending the day lounging in my beach chair with my head up my butt while he was running around putting his life on the line to find out what happened to my husband. Be careful, I'd said almost blithely, knowing how quickly conditions could change from seemingly innocent to deadly. If it could happen to Andy—nope, not going there.

He called at eleven-fifteen, just as I was climbing into bed.

"Hope this isn't too late, kid."

"No, I'm glad you called." The tight knot of anxiety in my throat dissolved for the first time in four hours. "What did you find out? Did you talk to the guy?"

"Yeah, we talked." From his dejected tone, I figured the news was not positive.

"And?"

"Claimed he was at an accountants' wingding up in Vegas the day his SUV was stolen. Rode up there with another guy from work and left his car in the parking garage back in Reno overnight."

"Wasn't that in the police report?"

"Yeah. But I wanted to hear it from him. No matter, his story checks out. So then I asked him if he was aware his car might have been involved in a crime in Sacramento that night. Either he's got the best poker face on the strip or the guy knows nothing."

"So now what?"

"It's really a matter for the SaCo sheriff's office at this point. They need to see the security footage of this guy's stolen SUV leaving the Hyatt behind your husband's car, and then showing up again on the county road where he died."

"So why not talk to them? What's stopping you?"

There was a tiny pause. "You."

"Me?" I asked, startled.

"Your husband's death should have been classified as suspicious from the get-go. I see that now. But it wasn't. Why not? In my opinion, somebody is protecting Wolders. Until I know who that is, I'm reluctant to open a can of worms. Especially with you on that island up in Maine."

It didn't take a degree in Tom-speak to connect the dots. A clammy breeze came through the open bedroom window and I pulled the covers up over my shoulders. "Do you want me to come home?"

In the few seconds before he answered, I heard soft piano music in the background, muted laughter. "No, I'll hold off on the big reveal, see what else comes to light in the meantime."

"I'm sorry I'm holding up the investigation."

"Hey, you needed a rest."

Ice tinkled in a glass.

"So where are you?" I asked.

"Having a celebratory drink. Don't feel like going home just yet."

Odd. The news he'd just given me didn't seem like much to celebrate about.

"My grandson was born today," he said.

"Tom, that's wonderful news! Congratulations."

"Thanks."

"Mom and baby doing well?"

"Yep, doing great. I'm heading up there tomorrow to visit them. My daughter actually invited me this time."

"What's the baby's name?"

I heard him take a swallow of his drink. "Andrew."

"Oh."

"Yeah."

My throat ached.

"Don't be sad, kid, it's a great name. Strong and honest and true." He snorted softly. "Listen to me. I sound like I've had a snootful. Time to say good night."

"Good night, Tom."

"Good night, Mrs. Stevenson."

Chapter 27

A sweltering spell settled over Mizzen Island the first week in August, the air hardly moving and the humidity intense. I'd always assumed an island guaranteed free air-conditioning in the summer. Wrong. I managed to stay cool by regular swims in the still chilly ocean, but my swims didn't stop the afternoons from being oppressive. On the third day of the heat wave, I took a walk to the harbor, thinking there might be a cooling westerly breeze there, but the air was as dead calm as the sea, the docks baking in the sun like a New York City street.

I stopped by the gallery on the way back to see if I'd be needed the next day and found Jack at his worktable, the air-conditioning blasting from the wall unit across the room. An artist who spent every August on the island had handed over a large number of oil canvases for an exhibit that was scheduled to run through Labor Day, and Jack was hustling to get the pieces ready to show.

"I could help with that, you know," I said.

He glanced up, considering.

"I worked in a gallery in college," I reminded him.

I was about to add that the workroom was cooler than being at home, but it seemed like an unnecessary admission. The truth was, I would have offered to help even if the workroom was a hundred degrees.

"All right then," he said, "grab a knife."

I'd barely had time to clear a space on the cluttered table when Esme came running in from the house. She ran straight to Jack, hardly noticing me. "Daddy, when are we going on the boat?"

"Later, Ez. When I'm finished working. Remember?"

She stamped her feet in her purple Crocs and sighed extravagantly. "When?"

He glanced at the clock over the door. "In about three hours."

"Three hours? Is that a long time?"

"You know what will make it go by fast? Going for a swim down at the cove. Ask Mabel."

"We already did that."

"Then give your dolls a tea party."

She groaned and flounced out of the workroom.

Jack and I worked side by side after Esme left, not talking much except to ask each other's opinion on the color of a mat or the kind of frame that would look best with a particular picture. I'd worked at a Boston graphic design firm in my early years with Andy, but mostly solo in a cubicle. Once I got over the awkwardness of working next to Jack in near silence, I found his proximity strangely restful. My romantic nature attributed it to the fact that we'd both lost mates and were therefore kindred spirits, even as I felt a bit guilty about the underhanded way I'd learned this information about him.

By three o'clock the sun had swung around to the windows on the west side of the workroom, prompting Jack to cross the room and pull the blinds shut. Still, the temperature in the room crept up. Sweat trickled from my scalp and my underarms, but I was too engrossed in the task at hand to care how wilted I looked.

"Arrgh," I muttered, as my knife hung up for about the tenth time on a thick sheet of matting. Even with a dehumidifier working in tandem with the AC to suck the moisture out of the air, the mat felt limp, almost spongy. The pile of discards was growing on the floor next to me.

"Change your blade," Jack said.

"I just did two mats ago."

"Change it again. Can't be helped. The weather isn't our friend today."

I grabbed a towel and wiped the sweat off my hands before changing the blade. "I thought islands were supposed to be cool in the summer."

Jack laughed. "If you don't like it now, wait six months."

"Cold?"

"Shattering. Not always, but enough of the time."

"What do you do here in the winter?"

"A smidge of this, smidge of that. A bit of carpentry—there's always work to do to get the rentals ready for next season. When I'm not doing that, I substitute teach at the grammar school. That can be a full-time job at times."

I'd passed the one-story schoolhouse many times on the walk from the harbor to Catherine Sutton's place, but even with the colorful jungle gym out in front, I'd never quite believed the little building was more than a movie prop.

"How many students?" I asked.

"Twenty-seven, at last count."

I whistled. "That many?"

"There are more year-round residents every year," he said with a tinge of regret.

"You must love it here."

"I do." He held up the canvas he was framing, businesslike again. "So what do you think?"

Esme came and went throughout the afternoon, increasingly restless. At four-thirty, she arrived holding her doll by one arm and plunked herself down near our feet.

"Just a little while longer, Ez," Jack told her. "Is Gemma coming with us?"

She frowned at the doll on her lap. "Maybe."

"I don't see her bathing suit."

She ignored her father's attempt at teasing. Instead, I felt the beach-rock-colored eyes studying me. "How do you make your hair like that?" she asked finally.

"Like what?" I asked, utility knife poised for a cut.

"Crinkly."

"That's just the way it is."

"Ez," Jack laughed, "leave Melissa alone."

A little while later, I felt her eyes on me again. "Did you make your hair a different color?"

Jack's gray eyes were bright with embarrassed amusement. "I'm sorry," he said, "she has a mind of her own."

"It's okay," I said and turned to Esme. "You mean, do I use hair color? Nope. I mean, well, yeah, I suppose I do a little bit." I recalled the long sessions in the hair salon, my wavy, naturally dark blond hair rigged up in enough bits of foil to transmit radio signals. "I put streaks in it," I told Esme.

"Why?" she asked gravely.

"So I look like I've been outside in the sun."

"Why don't you just go outside?"

"Well, it's kind of hot where I live—I mean, *really* hot in the summer. So I don't go outside that much."

"Why do you live there then?"

"Esme," Jack cut in, laughing. "Why does anybody live anywhere?"

Her eyes still on me, she went to her father's side and tugged impatiently on his arm. He bent down and she whispered in his ear, her hand cupped over her mouth so I couldn't hear.

"I don't know," Jack said. "Why don't you ask her?"

"Can you come on the boat with us?" Esme said to me.

Caught off guard, I tried to read Jack's expression. He busied himself gathering up his tools.

"Sure, I guess so," I said. "If your dad thinks it's okay."

"It's just a little skiff," Jack said. "But it'll be cool on the water."

The water was oily calm, the wind nonexistent as we motored out into the sound from the mooring behind the gallery. Rounding the point toward the harbor, though, we came up against a southwest breeze that was cool enough to make me regret not bringing a sweatshirt. I wrapped a faded beach towel around me instead.

"Help yourself to a beer," Jack said from the tiller, nodding at the cooler near my feet.

"I'm good for now," I said. A beer would have been a welcome thirst quencher, but not at the expense of having to jump overboard to take a pee. I could just picture hauling myself back into the precariously rocking boat like a drowned rat, my shorts and tank top stuck revealingly to my skin.

Ten minutes later we passed the harbor mouth, deep swells rocking the skiff as we cut across the wakes of larger boats on their way in. A hearty voice called over from an incoming lobster boat. "Not hauling traps tonight, Jack?" A big bearded guy in rubber overalls leaned his elbows on the portside rail, grinning.

"Not tonight. Enjoying a bit of family time," Jack called back.

The lobsterman laughed. "So, Jack, is that your sister?"

"Daft brute," Jack muttered.

"Wait," I said, wanting to change the subject. "You fish for lobster in your spare time?"

"Ah, well. Not strictly speaking. A mate hurt his back a few months ago. I've been pulling his traps for him while he recovers."

The harbor quickly receded behind us as we motored toward Mizzen's larger sister island to the west. Jack slowed the skiff as lobster buoys bobbed all around us.

"Can we see the lobsters, Daddy?" Esme asked, leaning far over the side to stare down into the murky water. I slid closer to her, ready to catch her by her bright blue life vest if she tumbled in.

"Have you gone out on the big lobster boat before?" I asked her.

"Uh-huh. Lots of times."

Jack laughed. "Once. It's slow, filthy work, not much fun for a kid."

"Can we see the lobsters, Daddy?"

He tried to talk her out of it, but eventually, with the boundless energy of the very young, she wore him down. "All right, we'll pull up one of Dan's traps, just to show Melissa, okay? Look for a red and yellow buoy with a white stripe in the middle."

"Over there!"

He steered the skiff alongside the one Esme was pointing at and idled the engine. "Help me pull it up, Ez." Wet coils of blue nylon warp filled the bottom of the boat as Jack pulled hand over hand with Esme pressed up against his leg supervising. The trap emerged from the depths, dripping water and seaweed. A green-black lobster was inside, its antennae moving.

"Brilliant," Jack said, "we're in luck, Ez."

I watched them together from my side of the boat, my insides aching for what might have been with Andy, but happy, too—happy in a way I hadn't expected to be for a very long time.

Jack rested the dripping trap on the rail and gave me a quick lesson in its intricacies. "If you're going to be an honorary lobsterman—or rather lobsterwoman—you have to know the proper terms. This is the head," he said, pointing at the opening to the trap, "and these two compartments are the kitchen and the parlor."

"Quaint," I remarked.

"Indeed," he said wryly. "Now the vents on each end, see? They're there to let the babies escape."

"Interesting," I mused. "Come to think of it, I've never seen a baby lobster."

"That's because they look more like bugs than crustaceans."

"What are those bricks for?" I asked, just to hear him talk. The need for the bricks seemed pretty obvious.

His smile telegraphed that he was onto my ruse. "To make sure the trap lands right-side-up, of course, when it's thrown in the water. And to minimize drifting."

Esme pressed her face close to the trap, making eye contact with the inmate.

"Not too close, Ez," Jack said. "They're not pets."

"But he's cute," she said, undeterred.

Jack smiled at me and shrugged. Behind him, the setting sun flamed the western sky, turning the water into a rippling mass of pinks, purples, and grays. To the north, Cadillac Mountain, a deep violet silhouette, rose from the horizon like the extinct volcano it was.

"Can we keep him?" Esme pressed.

"Not this time. This lucky devil will live to tell the tale, at least for another week or or two." He extricated the lobster from the trap and plopped it back in the water.

A temporary reprieve from the lobster pound and some overfed tourist's stomach, I thought. The empty trap hit the water with a splash and disappeared, the nylon warp playing out from the bottom of the skiff as it sank.

"I'm hungry," Esme announced, the lobster drama already forgotten. She pried at the cooler lid with her small hands and I leaned over to help her. Someone—not Jack—had found the time to pack us a light dinner of sandwiches and potato salad. Mabel went up a notch in my estimation. I handed out the sandwiches, wrapped meticulously in wax paper and tinfoil, wondering which one was poisoned.

"Ham salad," Esme noted approvingly. "Ooh."

"Mabel's specialty," Jack said.

"Yum," I said, thrilled that it wasn't lobster. I'd had my fill since arriving on the island. I passed a beer to Jack and took one for myself, figuring it wouldn't be long now before we headed back to shore and toilets.

Later, our bellies replete with Mabel's feast, and Jack and I finishing our beers, Esme yawned and crawled onto her father's lap. Jack asked me to cover her with a blanket from one of the lockers, making no move to get the engine started. Now that the sun was below the horizon, the air was even cooler.

"What brought you to the U.S.?" I asked, acknowledging aloud what he hadn't volunteered yet—that obviously he was from Ireland.

"I came over one summer during college to work on Cape Cod. Kitchen staff at one of the resorts. My first chance to see the world. I liked it so much I came back after graduation, but not to work in a hotel. I joined a construction crew in Brooklyn."

"Doing what?"

"Renovating brownstones. Cheap Irish labor. There were a lot of us back in the nineties."

His braided wedding ring caught the fiery sunset as his hand absently stroked Esme's hair. I wondered again how I'd missed it the first time.

"It's where I met my wife," he said casually.

"Brooklyn?" I asked, casual too.

"Yeah. She was just out of college, doing the big city thing. Photographing all the city life like mad."

Esme's eyes were open, listening.

"Was she American?" I realized I'd slipped.

Jack ran his hand up and down Esme's blanketed arm. "Past tense. How'd you know?"

"I sat next to a very chatty friend of yours on the ferry."

"Let me guess. Richard."

"Right."

"The man gossips more than an old nanny goat."

Esme sighed and burrowed deeper into her father's arms. Soon her eyelids drooped and her body relaxed.

"Is she asleep?" Jack asked.

I nodded. Not knowing how to fill up the silence, I said, "I'm so sorry."

"She's been gone three years. And yeah, she was American."

I spoke carefully. "I know how it is. My husband—"

An odd look crossed his face. "Well, this is awkward."

"What?

"Richard isn't the only nanny goat on the island."

"Gar?"

He nodded. "Gar told Mabel, and Mabel told me. How long has it been?"

"Two months."

"Jesus." *Jaysus.* "They didn't tell me that. What are you doing here?"

"I had to get away from our house in California. Too many memories."

He squinted at the horizon, the indistinct line where the pearl gray sky met the deeper gray of the water. "Funny how memories work. It's the memories that keep me here."

Jacey was stunned into silence on the other end of the line. I'd called her as soon as I got home, floating on the sweetness of the walk from the shore to Jack's house in the moonlight, Esme riding sleepily on her father's shoulders, our whispered good-byes.

"Jace, are you there?"

"Yeah, I'm here."

"Good. I thought I lost you." Catherine Sutton's house still held the heat from the day, but the breeze on the attic balcony was delicious. The moon, about to set, was orange and caved in on one side liked a smashed pumpkin, the black ocean shot through with the reflected light of it.

"So you met *a guy*?" Jacey asked, not bothering to hide her shock.

"Not *a guy*," I said. "A *friend*. I hope. Maybe."

I could see how this was playing with her. I couldn't blame her for being skeptical.

"Okay, so you're *not* interested in dating him."

"That's a loaded question."

"Is it?"

"I'm not interested in dating him *now*. I'm not interested in dating anybody. But down the road—"

"But he lives in Maine and you live in California."

I told myself she was just trying to protect me. While Andy and I were leading our happy married life, she was out in the dating trenches, trying to overcome her negative programming about men after a nasty divorce. She couldn't help being a she-bear in my defense, or maybe she was even a little envious.

"Will you stop? I met someone here that I can actually talk to, somebody I actually *like*. What's wrong with that?"

"You're right. There's nothing wrong with it. It's none of my business."

"Besides," I said, clearly not getting the memo to quit while I was ahead. "Who says he's even interested in me? He's got his own stuff to deal with."

"What stuff?"

"His wife died three years ago. He has a six-year-old daughter."

More silence. I could almost hear what she was thinking. Clearly the guy was looking for a mother for his child.

"Mel, I just worry that you're not thinking straight. How many guys did you date before you met Andy?"

"You know how many. A couple. Neither one serious."

"How old were you when you met Andy?"

"Twenty."

"Mel, you haven't dated anyone else since Andy. In dating years, that means you're still *twenty years old*."

"That's a scary thought. Twenty-year-old Melissa loose in the dating world."

"Okay. Now you're mad."

"I'm not mad," I lied. "Just surprised. Give me a little credit, you know?"

The truth was, I felt more like my twenty-year-old self than I cared to admit—anxious and edgy, in danger of flying away if I didn't have something, or someone, to anchor me to earth. And it did feel like dating, the best kind. I was smart enough to know that it was probably just my grief taking a new tack, but what harm did it do? Wasn't it healthier to daydream about a possible future romance than to destroy my sanity thinking about Andy's phone under a hotel room bed?

But Jacey had a point, as much as I hated to admit it, even as I hated her a little for bursting my bubble. Jack and I had had an unexpectedly fun evening, that was all, over a couple of beers and Mabel's ham-salad sandwiches. And even if he sort of liked me, I knew in my bones he wasn't the kind of man to make a move on a woman whose husband had just died. So we'd said good-night and that was that. No "What are you doing this weekend?" which, of course, would have been entirely inappropriate. Instead, as I'd started to walk away after saying good-bye, he'd called after me:

"Will I see you on Monday? I may need you to watch the counter for a couple of hours. Mabel has a doctor's appointment on the mainland."

"Sure," I'd said. "Sounds good."

"Grand," he'd smiled. "Enjoy the weekend."

"You, too," I'd said, and pointed myself towards home, already looking forward to Monday.

Chapter 28

The late afternoon sun came slanting across the treetops, already noticeably lower in the sky for this time of day than when I'd arrived six weeks ago. I leaned against the attic balcony railing and drank in the quiet island scene, savoring my last moments of peace before I tapped on my mother's number. We'd talked only once since I arrived on the island, and guilt told me I owed her a call.

Off in the direction of the harbor, a motorized hum signaled the departure of the ferry. So it was no surprise initially when I glimpsed, through the screen of leaves, a flash of white on the road below the house. A moment later, a man emerged through a gap in the trees. It was unusual for a tourist to hike all the way out to this side of the island, but not unheard of. He must have walked quickly if he'd arrived on the five o'clock ferry and had already come this far.

Curious, I kept my eyes on the striding man as my mother's landline began to ring. Dark-haired and deeply tanned, I noted—and young, judging by his purposeful strides. Like most visitors to the island, he had a backpack slung over one shoulder. Still, his clothes looked oddly businesslike for a tourist's—a white button-up shirt rolled up at the wrists and khaki trousers.

My mother's landline rang four, five, six times. Just a couple of more rings and voicemail would pick up, releasing me from my obligation to talk to her. She owned a cell phone but stubbornly kept it in her purse turned off, to be used only if her car broke down.

The stranger below kept walking. There was one house left before the road stopped at the beach. Mine. An odd familiarity about his gait, the way he held his body, made me lean out over the railing and squint to bring his face into focus. My mother's voicemail came on, but I barely heard her voice. The phone was slick in my hand.

The man coming toward my house was Ralph Gutierrez.

And I hadn't even dropped a fork.

I could run down the stairs and duck out the back door, skulk along the shoreline to the next property, but the tide was up and it would be heavy going along the rocks and through the seaweed. Even if I succeeded in escaping without Ralph spotting me, what would I do then? Hide until nightfall? Hope he left the island without seeing me? Not likely, considering he'd come all the way from California.

I climbed back through the window into the attic and tiptoed down the narrow stairs to the second floor landing. His feet hit the porch floorboards with soft thuds, followed an agonizing couple of seconds later by the soft rap of knuckles on glass. I inched down the second flight of stairs until the front door came into view. Behind the wavy glass, a blurred form waited.

Another burst of rapping. "Melissa?" The voice was muffled by the door, but Ralph's, no question about it. He sounded hoarse, as if he'd walked across a desert without water to find me.

I shrank back against the wall. *Damn you, Ralph. Damn you for showing up here. What gives you the right—*

"Melissa! Are you in there?"

—to track me down like an animal!

The doorknob turned.

Jesus frigging Christ. Just walk right in, you son of a bitch.

In a minute he'd be standing in the hallway looking up at me. But, no, the door was bolted, thank God, but only because I hadn't left the house that day, except through the slider onto the back deck.

I crept to the bottom of the stairs and stopped again, my breath frozen in my chest. His blurred outline behind the glass shifted, as if maybe he was about to give up and leave. But no, he rapped again, his knuckles shaking the glass.

Behind me in the living room Tom's Walther lay in the drawer. I crossed quickly to the lamp table and retrieved it, shoving the magazine in with a loud click even as another, calmer voice kicked in—the voice of reason, or so I told myself. This was Ralph at the door, just Ralph, Andy's archrival at work and Reg's left-hand man, yes, but still Ralph, a guy I'd known for four years even though I'd never liked him very much. How insane would I look if I opened the door waving a gun in his face? I put the Walther back in the drawer.

And then it happened the way it always happened for me. When given the choice of fight or flight, I chose fight. Every time. I yanked open the door.

He stepped back, surprised.

"What are you doing here, Ralph?"

"Nice welcome. I could ask you the same thing."

"What does it look like? I'm on vacation."

His upper lip twitched in a tiny smirk. "The grieving widow."

Bastard. "How did you find me?"

His gaze slid to the plaque on the wall next to the door. "Splendid Isolation," he mused. "Catchy name."

I saw it then. The ad in *The Artist* magazine, circled in pencil, the page lying open on my worktable at home. No high-tech surveillance necessary to track me down, just an unknown intruder walking from room to room until he found something that gave me away. Could it be?

"Look, it wasn't that hard, believe me," he said, as if reading my thoughts. "Your mother was happy to help us out."

"You called my mother?"

"Take it easy. I was polite."

"But I didn't tell my mother where I am."

"So you're hiding from her too?"

I didn't laugh.

"She gave us your general location," he said. "The WP investigator pinged your cell phone." He glanced over my head, into the house. "Can we sit down and talk?"

I tightened my grip on the front door. There should have been a chain on it, but of course there wasn't. The island was a safe place. No would-be home invaders here. "No, you can't sit down. You have to go. Now."

"Not gonna work. Not until we've talked."

"You could have called. You have my number, right? You *pinged* it to find me."

"I called you about twenty times today. The calls kept getting dropped."

Shit. "What do you want?" I asked, anger starting to creep in. Good. Anything was better than feeling weak and scared.

"Reg sent me."

"What for?"

"He wants to help you."

I laughed. "Really? After I threatened him with a lawsuit?"

"Hey, he's the forgiving type. He knows you got fucked over by the insurance company."

"And how does he know that?"

"Great cross, Melissa. You should have been a lawyer. But can we continue this inside? Or do you want your neighbors to know all your business?"

"Right. What neighbors?"

He flicked a glance behind him. "Yeah. What neighbors."

I cursed myself for my careless words. But then again, he didn't need me to point out the isolation of the house. My fingernails dug deeper into the peeling paint on the edge of the door. "Sorry, Ralph. You've come a long way for nothing."

His chest hair showed dark through the damp places on the front of his shirt. A drop of sweat appeared at his hairline and rolled down his forehead. "Yeah, that may be true, but I'm here."

The sudden weariness in his voice put me off guard. He didn't sound threatening, only resigned, as if he wasn't any happier about being sent on this errand than I was about having him here.

"There's a restaurant down by the docks," I said, relenting. "It's the only restaurant on the island. I can meet you there."

"When?"

"Half an hour."

He stared at me hard. "You gonna show up? You're not blowing me off? Because I'll be back if you are."

"No, I'll be there." I shut the door in his face and threw the bolt, then hurried to the other side of the house to lock the slider. I grabbed Tom's Walther from the lamp table drawer on my way upstairs to change.

My hand shook as I brushed the tangles out of my hair in front of the bedroom mirror, strands of hair ripping away from my scalp. I showered quickly to wash off the day's worth of salt and sand, then threw on my least wrinkled sleeveless cotton dress. A pair of turquoise earrings and my favorite shell necklace felt necessary to complete the outfit, and a couple of silver bracelets, too. I wanted to appear strong in front of Ralph, and making the most of my looks was the only way I knew how. I left the house a few minutes later with my bag slung over my shoulder, the Walther nestled heavily in the bottom.

The holes in my makeshift plan were immediately obvious. It was a long walk past the dense pinewoods just to get to the nearest neighbor's house—a neighbor whom I'd never met and who gave no evidence of even being in residence except for the dog barking inside the ramshackle cottage. I could call Jack and ask him to accompany me to the restaurant, but how would I explain my sudden need for a bodyguard? I decided to take my chances in the pinewoods.

It was the beginning of a beautiful evening, the southeast breeze soft and salt-laden as the punishing heat of the day abated. I walked the whole way to the restaurant with my hand inside my shoulder bag clutching the loaded gun, but the only thing that attacked me on the way was the usual cloud of mosquitoes among the pines. I relaxed as I reached the more settled part of the island, even though there were few people around. The dock was busy, though, a larger than normal crowd of tourists waiting to catch the last ferry of the day.

Shit, I thought, stopping dead. The last ferry. The last effing ferry.

I found him sitting on a rock outside the restaurant. He smiled when he saw me.

"I hope you're a good swimmer, buddy," I called.

"Why?"

"Because the last ferry is about to pull away from the dock."

He laughed, looking like a different man than the Ralph I knew. "You look great."

I ignored the compliment. "So what are doing out here?"

"So happens there's a wait. Not to worry though. I've got it covered." He reached into his backpack and showed me the slender neck of a wine bottle, beaded with moisture inside a paper bag.

"Where'd you get that?" There were no package stores on the island.

"Picked it up before I came over," he grinned. "Always thinking ahead."

"It can't be very cold after the long ferry ride."

"You want everything, huh? Hold on. Be right back." He disappeared into the restaurant. I took a seat on the rock he'd just vacated and waited for him to return, willing myself to focus on the beauty of the evening. A few fishermen were still on the docks, but mostly it was quiet, the water oily calm, the sun flaming the western sky. Noise carried out into the harbor from the open windows of the restaurant—loud, convivial conversation, dishes clattering in the kitchen. I wondered if Jack had gone out fishing today and was now inside the restaurant having a beer with his buds. I hoped not.

Ralph rounded the corner from the restaurant entrance carrying two hard plastic cups filled with ice. He squeezed onto the rock next to me and handed me the two cups to hold while he pulled the bottle of wine from his backpack. It was a New Zealand Sauvignon blanc, my drink of choice back when I was confident I could stop after a glass or two with dinner.

"Gotta love these screw tops," he said, opening the bottle with a quick turn of his hairy wrist.

I watched the straw-colored liquid spill over the ice.

"Stop," I said. "That's enough."

He filled his cup and touched it to mine. "Chin chin."

It was the first wine I'd had since Tom's visit. Maybe it was the tension of having him next to me, but that first citrusy swallow tasted dangerously good going down. "I didn't have you pegged as a white wine drinker," I said.

He took a sip and grimaced. "I'm not. I'm more a single malt kind of guy."

So he'd bought the wine for me, hoping to get me drunk. Well, that wasn't going to happen. Just the same, the wine tasted even better as it got colder and a little watered down. "It's not true, you know," I said, determined to stay on the offensive.

"What isn't?"

"The insurance company didn't screw me over. Andy died of a drug overdose and it voided the policy. He broke the rules. Or do you know something different?"

"Melissa, are you always this much of a hard-ass when somebody's trying to help you?" He nudged my arm playfully. "Come on, relax. You're on vacation, right?"

His courtroom voice, I told myself, the one he used when he wanted to cajole the jury instead of hitting them over the head with his argument. Still, my body loosened a little in spite of itself.

The hostess appeared at the corner of the restaurant and waved us inside. The place was packed, the booths along the walls all taken. Lobstermen and women, just off their boats, pressed up against the bar, knocking back beers and whiskies and talking over the soccer match on the overhead TV. Jack wasn't among them, I was relieved to see.

The din pressed on my ears as the hostess led us through the crowd to a table in the middle of the room. Ralph pulled out a chair for me and then took the seat catty-corner to mine. A menu appeared in my hands and the hostess left.

Ralph opened his menu. "Let's order some more drinks."

"You go ahead. I'm fine with iced tea."

He chuckled at my obstinacy. "Okay, be that way. But it's a night out. For both of us. How many of those have you had recently?"

What harm could one more glass of wine do? If I had to endure his company for the next hour or so, I might as well be a tiny bit anesthetized. I shrugged my capitulation.

A black-aproned server appeared to take our drink order, strands of hair escaping from her blond ponytail. I ordered another glass of Sauvignon blanc and Ralph a Glenlivet on the rocks.

The wine, when it came, was much better than I expected it to be in a downscale island hangout. A couple of swallows slid down my throat, almost without volition.

A raucous cry went up from the bar as one of the teams scored a goal. I looked toward the sound, my nerves jangling.

Ralph's fingertips on the back of my hand made me turn back. He smiled innocently. "Hey, somebody's having a good time, right?"

I took my hand away and reached for my wine again.

He sipped his scotch, watching me, his gaze an odd mixture of appreciation and something else I couldn't read. Or didn't want to. His irises were so black they merged with his pupils. "Look, I'm sorry if I was a dick back there at the house. I didn't come here to scare you. I work for an asshole, what can I say?"

"You mean Reg?" I stared, unable to cover my surprise.

"Yeah, Reg."

"Why would an asshole want to help me?"

"I don't know. Because he feels guilty?"

"About what exactly?"

"That he didn't see how sick Andy was. That he didn't do anything to stop him from wrecking his life. And yours, too."

It rang hollow after his first statement, which sounded truthful, unguarded, an unexpected glimpse into the cipher that was Ralph.

He swirled the ice in his glass. "It's a good offer, you know. How does a half mil strike you?'

The exact amount of the forfeited life insurance payout. Still, I wasn't about to cave to Reg's apparent goodwill gesture. Not yet. "What does he want in return?"

"No civil suit. No more adverse publicity."

Another surprise. No mention of the missing thumb drive.

"I'll think about it," I said.

"Hard-ass," he muttered, openly teasing now, and looked away, feigning interest in the soccer game on TV.

I remembered the Ralph who kept staring at me at Andy's wake, the Ralph who could barely choke out a word of condolence. Was it possible I'd read him completely wrong? That the sullen edge he projected on the world was just an act, the armor he threw up to get by in the ultra-competitive environment of Wolders Palmer?

A soccer player head-butted the ball halfway down the field, prompting more cheering at the bar.

"You ready for another?" Ralph called over the noise. His glass was empty but I still had a swallow or two left in mine.

"Nope, I'm good," I hadn't had much to eat that day and my brain was definitely buzzing.

"Suit yourself," he said and signaled the server. He ordered the pan-fried scallops and, when I couldn't decide, ordered the same for me. "And an IPA for me," he added, handing the server our menus.

"So what made you want to be a lawyer?" I asked, as a commercial came on TV and the soccer crowd quieted down.

"My dad got Parkinson's when I was sixteen, they think from all the pesticides he came in contact with. He was a farmer up in Fresno. I wanted to be an environmental lawyer, take on the Monsantos of the world."

"So why didn't you?"

"Too many debts from law school. I took the job that offered the biggest money instead. I ended up defending the corporate criminals, not bringing them to justice."

I reflected on what I knew about Ralph's life—the Porsche, the cute little house in tony Rosedale, the parade of strikingly attractive, if not beautiful, girlfriends. Not exactly the stuff of self-pity.

"We all make compromises," I said. "It's called being an adult."

"Right. How many compromises did Andy make?"

"Some."

"Like?"

"He wanted to be a prosecutor, work in the DA's office. His father wanted him to go into corporate law."

"That so."

"It's okay to admit it, Ralph. I know you never liked him."

"Not true. I liked Andy fine. The only beef I had with Andy was that he had you and I didn't."

My fingers froze on the stem of my now empty wine glass. I didn't know what I'd expected him to say, but it wasn't that. His words wormed their way into me despite my effort to keep them out. One of the hardest things about Andy's death was the loss of his admiration. The kind of admiration only a sexual partner can give. Here, at least, was a guy who had no problem telling me he found me attractive—unlike, well, Jack Kilronan.

It occurred to me to care that there might be people in the restaurant who were taking note of my intimate conversation with Ralph, gossipy islanders like Richard who might be only too eager to report to Jack. But my concern soon melted away, crowded out by a sudden need to be desired, to feel alive again, if only for a couple of hours on a summer Friday night.

The server dropped off Ralph's IPA and he took a couple of swallows. We sat without speaking, our eyes glancing off each other's. Something inside me was thawing, opening up, something beyond the reach of judgment and inhibition. What I really wanted to do, I realized, was to fix the bad feelings between Andy and Ralph. Then everyone could be happy, even Andy. Even though he was dead.

"So, what was it, Ralph? What was it really? This big rivalry you and Andy had."

He laughed. "Oh, so you're my shrink now?"

"Just a friend." My words came out gentler than I intended.

He hid his surprise behind another slow swallow of IPA. "Oh, maybe getting it rammed down my throat for the thousandth time that I wasn't a Harvard or Stanford grad."

"Andy wasn't a Harvard grad. He went to B.U."

"Hey, same difference. Isn't that what they say in Massachusetts?"

"Did Andy treat you that way?"

"Not him. Reg."

"Reg?"

"You don't understand what life is like at WP. All this one big happy family bullshit is just that, total fucking b.s. Reg does everything he can to foster a cage fight mentality. He thinks he gets more work out of his associates that way."

"Well, it worked, didn't it?"

"Yeah, it worked. You have no idea how well."

I ignored the bitter edge in his voice. "But you and Andy —"

"Let's not talk about Andy anymore. He's not here. We are." He ran his little finger over my knuckles. "You and me."

I studied the fine black hairs on his tanned wrist before I pulled my hand away. "I thought you were here on business."

"Our business is on hold. You're trying to decide whether you have room in your bank account for a half-million dollars."

"Wise-ass," I said. My limbs felt warm and liquid suddenly, a beguiling sensation. *No,* a voice whispered inside my head, *don't do this.* I blinked and stood up. "Excuse me." I floated toward the ladies room like a gull riding the thermals. When I returned, Ralph had his phone pressed to his ear. He said good-bye quickly when he spotted me. Our dinner had arrived while I was gone, two steaming plates and another glass of wine for me.

I looked down at the scallops glistening on a bed of angel hair and wondered how I was going to eat it. I wasn't remotely hungry, too nervous at first and now too buzzed. It didn't matter that I'd only had two glasses of wine. I was no longer thinking straight. I took several gulps of water, ignoring the glass of Sauvignon blanc. I pushed the scallops around on my plate and sipped water, while Ralph washed his dinner down with swigs of beer, unimpaired. I was relieved when the server came to clear and Ralph took out his credit card to pay the bill.

Outside, in the cool quiet twilight, away from the din and distractions of the restaurant, I had to face the obvious—that technically I might not be drunk, but I'd let him get to me, anyway. Even worse, instead of saying good-bye and heading off into the night, Ralph walked with me in the direction of Splendid Isolation.

"You should have eaten your dinner," he scolded gently. "You're gonna be hungry later."

The urge to lean against him was almost overpowering but I kept some space between us, determined not to give in. We walked on a few paces, the twilight heavy with the sound of crickets. Children's voices drifted out of one of the houses we passed.

Just two nights ago I'd said good night to Jack in the twilight. How different that had felt. Then I'd felt lighthearted, hopeful even—that grief might be finite, that new life was waiting for me at the end of it. But tonight my brain and body were at war with each other, and the sick feeling in the pit of my stomach told me which one had the upper hand.

I tripped over a rock in the dark and he grabbed me, throwing his arm around me. He pulled away abruptly. "Jesus, what have you got in there? A brick?"

I looked down to see my bag wedged between us. I'd completely forgotten about Tom's gun. "Hey, you can't be too careful," I said, shifting my bag to my other shoulder.

"Guess not," he said and made another attempt to drape his arm around me.

"You can't stay at my house tonight," I said.

He laughed and took his arm away. "Hey, I'm here on WP business. Just walkin' you home."

From feeling put-upon to feeling rejected was a short hop for me these days. Jesus, Melissa, get a grip, I told myself. "I'm sorry."

"Don't worry about me. I'll just go and sleep on a rock somewhere. Catch the first ferry in the morning."

"Ralph!"

"Unless you're offering your guest room."

But I didn't want him in the guest room bed, separated from me by a flimsy wall. I knew that by now. There was only one bed in the house I wanted him in. "There's a water taxi," I said.

He nodded. "I already called them."

"You did? When?"

"When you were in the ladies' room."

"Oh." So taking advantage of the vulnerable widow wasn't part of his plan. Now I felt absurdly grateful. And a little impressed, I had to admit.

Ahead of us the house loomed dark, the gabled roof black against the sky. I'd left in full daylight, so I hadn't thought to turn on any lights.

Crickets sawed noisily in the bushes next to the porch steps as we turned to face each other.

"So, you gonna accept Reg's offer?" he asked.

Reg's offer. Right. "I'll think about it."

Our faces were inches apart. I waited for him to close the distance, for his lips to find mine, my first non-Andy kiss in twelve years. Instead he hugged me quickly and stepped back. "Good night."

Ralph the gentleman.

He was walking away before I recovered enough to call "Good night" back.

He wheeled to face me, a ghost in a white shirt walking backwards into the night. "I'm here till Sunday. Can I call you tomorrow?"

"Um, yeah. Maybe."

He laughed. "Major hard-ass."

And then he was gone.

Chapter 29

I woke the next morning with a borderline migraine and the firm conviction that I'd dodged a bullet the night before. It was already past ten and there were no messages on my phone—proof, I told myself, that he had no intention of calling me, that he'd realized, like me, what a bad idea it would be to take advantage of the situation.

His text arrived as I was shaking two Excedrin out of the bottle in the medicine cabinet. *S'up? I could catch the next ferry.*

I downed the aspirin and swallowed some water, checked the time and did a quick calculation. The turmoil in my stomach was back, but my fingers ignored it. *I'll come over there instead,* I texted.

No response.

I texted him again. *More to do over there.* More people around, and safer, too. Though by then it was glaringly clear who I needed protection from.

You're the boss. What time? he texted back.

If I motivated, I could catch the noon ferry. *1:00. Meet you outside the bakery?*

Fab, he texted back. *Bring some raingear. Could get stormy later.*

I spotted him standing beneath the bakery's blue-striped awning as I walked up from the dock and crossed to his side of the street. He was dressed casually today, board shorts, a faded t-shirt under a black cotton hoodie, killer shades. "You're rockin' it, dude," I said.

"You like?" he said, looking pleased, and took my arm like we were some dating couple.

"So what are you thinking?" I asked. The fact that he hadn't tried to sleep with me the night before made me feel relaxed in his company. More relaxed, I told myself, than I had any right to be.

"Hungry?" he asked.

"Not especially. I had a big breakfast." My minor hangover combined with my skipped dinner the night before had left me with an unreal appetite that morning. I'd eaten through half a week's supplies at one meal.

"Yeah, me too."

"So, what . . ."

He smiled his little Ralph half-smile. "Let's take a ride up Cadillac Mountain. Get high the natural way."

I laughed, remembering Tom's visit. "Hey, I've got just the ride for that."

But when I showed him the Corvette, his eyes didn't pop with boyish admiration the way Tom's had. If anything, he looked uncomfortable. "Extra," he remarked. "Your old man a flamboyant type?"

"Nope. Just a weekend car guy like a lot of guys used to be." I held out the keys. "Wanna drive?"

"Nah, you drive," he said, surprising me. "I wanna check out the scenery."

We started out with the top down, taking the road out of Southwest Harbor a shade too fast, but were soon slowed by the heavy Saturday traffic backing up into Somesville. I downshifted and then downshifted again, the Corvette's predatory growl mingling with the first rumbles of thunder overhead. By the time we reached the turnoff to the mountain summit, fat raindrops were pelting the windshield and our heads. Ralph flipped up his hoodie without commenting.

"Too bad," I remarked and pulled into the first scenic overlook so we could put the top back up. Apparently familiar with vintage convertibles despite his lack of enthusiasm, Ralph expertly snapped the ragtop to the windshield frame, then climbed back in, his hoodie splotched with raindrops. The musky scent of his aftershave pressed on me in the suddenly enclosed space. He folded his arms across his chest and looked out at the rain as we started off again.

The long silver arm of Eagle Lake played hide and seek below us as we wound our way up the mountain, but the scenic vistas soon faded in the intensifying rain. By the time we reached the top, a steady stream of cars and RVs was heading down the mountain, the remaining ambushed tourists running to their cars and tour buses. Within minutes the parking lot was utterly deserted, not another vehicle in sight. Improbably, we were the only two people at the island's biggest tourist attraction on an August afternoon just because of a little cloudburst.

Ralph studied the rain streaking the windshield. "Let's get out."

I stared at him. "In this? Are you nuts?"

Thunder clapped almost on top of us, and a fork of lightning lit up Frenchman's Bay. The rain was hitting the pavement so hard it bounced, but Ralph was already opening his door.

"Come on!" he called, laughing.

He grabbed my hand as I joined him, and we ran toward the edge. The rain lashed us, startlingly cold, plastering our clothes to our skin. He dropped my hand and opened his arms wide, threw back his head and let his mouth fall open, as if to slake an unquenchable thirst. It struck me then that he was suffering from the same desert sickness that had brought me here. When was the last time it rained like this in Sacramento?

I laughed, too, despite the lightning flashing all around us, despite the driving rain, despite our exposed position on a large, slick boulder jutting out over the void.

He glanced at me—for approval, I thought—his wet head sleek as an otter's.

"You nut!" I yelled against the wind, because it was windy, too, the way it always was on top of a mountain.

But his smile was gone, his eyes black under his rain-soaked hair. He hopped down to the next boulder and held out his hand to me. I gripped his fingers and stepped down gingerly, but my foot slipped in my soaked sandal and Ralph's hand slipped out of mine and I felt my balance going. For a split second my mind floated free of my body and I saw what the next moments held for me—a long, bouncing, ragdoll drop over cascading rocks and bushes to the bottom. Then his arm snaked around me and he pulled me tight against him. "Careful!" he said in my ear. He steered me up the steep couple of steps back to safety, not letting go as shock took hold of me and I began to tremble uncontrollably.

"Let's get you in the car," he said.

Inside the Corvette I kept shivering as the rain drummed without stopping on the ragtop. "You're frickin' soaked," he laughed. "You got a towel anywhere?"

"There might be one in the trunk," I said through chattering teeth.

He ducked back out into the rain and around to the back of the car, returning with a threadbare tartan blanket. It was the one my father used to throw on the seat for our old cocker spaniel. I hadn't spared a thought for poor Bitsy in years, but seeing the red and green plaid called up memories of her awful canine breath from her decaying teeth. I let Ralph wrap it around me, dog hair and all.

"Better?" he asked, even as I continued to shake.

"A little."

"You need to get those clothes off."

"Nice try."

"Just sayin'."

He rubbed my arms some more through the blanket, letting his scratchy cheek brush mine. I smelled the rain on his skin, the tang of his sweat mingled with his musky aftershave, and gave in to it, letting my chin rest against his muscular shoulder. He hugged me tight through the blanket, his breath warm on my face. My teeth stopped chattering long enough for me to notice the change in his breathing, the hard-on straining the saturated fabric of his shorts. His glance followed mine. When his lips grazed my cheek, I groaned.

Our embrace turned awkward in the Corvette's cramped interior. Suddenly we were both looking around, wondering if we could act on what was undeniably there in the car with us, if such a feat was even possible. Ralph decided for both of us, angling his hips up in the passenger seat and pulling down his surfer shorts to release his erection. My body answered before my brain could even catch up, a slow, hot tidal wave swamping any thought except what we were about to do. "Climb on top of me," he whispered in my ear. "We can do this."

I wriggled out of my own shorts and straddled him. His groan as he entered me sounded closer to agony than ecstasy.

I'd forgotten how right it felt, the fundamental rightness of sex. It had been so long since I'd felt anything approaching this good. I pulled him against me, his hard, muscled body, his wet, salty skin. I bit his shoulder, grabbed his wet hair, let my head bang against the roof of the Corvette as his body reared up against mine, again and again. Our teeth glanced off each other's and I felt a stinging pain. Blood, salty and pungent, welled in my mouth. "You're so beautiful," he whispered, "you're so hot."

He cried out when he came, as if he'd been stabbed in the back. Seconds later I came too, a sweet clenching ripple that left me whimpering against him.

The rain drummed down on our cocoon, the windows completely fogged over. When at last I summoned the energy to lift my hand and wipe away the condensation to look out, the surrounding terrain looked as forlorn as November. If anyone had witnessed our lovemaking, they hadn't stuck around for the cuddling part.

Ralph held me tight. "Christ. That was amazing."

I waited until his arms relaxed and then eased my body off his, climbing awkwardly over the gearshift to my side of the car. We didn't speak or touch. The rain slowed in its intensity and then stopped. Steam swirled up from the pavement as the sun broke through. Far too soon a new invasion of cars and RVs began, intrepid tourists piling out to go stand on the edge and wait for the inevitable rainbow. It came, spanning the gray-blue vault of sky with its crayon box colors. I thought of Esme for an instant, then Jack, and finally Andy. I reached for my wet shorts, my heart twisting in on itself.

It was then that I saw the dent in the Corvette's dashboard, the clear imprint of a heel, made by Ralph, or me, as we'd slammed against each other. "Shit."

He followed my eyes. "Rut rho. Looks like we broke Daddy's car."

"It's not funny. My mother is going to kill me."

"You can get it fixed, right?"

"Yeah, when? Where?"

He ran his fingertips down my arm. "Hey, come on. Don't spoil it."

Awhile later, dressed again, Ralph took the wheel. "Where to now?"

We drove back down the mountain and turned toward Southwest Harbor, stopping at his inn long enough for him pick up his overnight bag. We caught the next ferry out to Mizzen Island.

We were barely through the door of the cottage before he was inside me again, carrying me to the kitchen, my legs straddling his hips, and plopping me down on the counter. He pulled out long enough to get my shorts off and kick out of his. In the noise and fury of slamming into each other, I worried briefly that the drawer front below us would break where his knees banged against it, that I'd have to explain the damage to Catherine Sutton, just like I'd have to explain the damage to the Corvette to my mother. But of course I wouldn't have to do either. I'd get the drawer fixed before my summer rental was over, just as I'd get the 'Vette's dashboard fixed before I returned my father's car. And just then Ralph carried me to the living room and laid me on the rag rug to finish screwing me properly.

Later, coming downstairs after a shower, I found him out on the deck in his boxers, his bare shoulders almost black from the sun. He was typing rapidly on his laptop.

"You're working?" I said, surprised.

I reminded myself that he was a lawyer, after all. And lawyers worked—most of the time, from my experience. In fact, it was a miracle he'd taken the afternoon off to fuck me to oblivion and back.

"Email," he said. "Reg wants to know how you're doing and whether you've responded to his offer."

I stood at the slider and didn't answer.

"I told him you've accepted," he said, and closed his laptop. He sauntered over to me, the look in his eyes clearly saying what he had in mind for the rest of the afternoon and night. And that's when I felt it, my foolishness in letting him come back to the island with me. The madness that had driven me into his arms was spent. All that was left was the cold, hard need to be alone again.

It was approaching five o'clock, not too late to send him back to Southwest Harbor. But he'd already checked out of the inn, planning to spend the night with me. The magnitude of my transgression against Andy hit me, making me almost physically ill. How was I going to climb into bed with Ralph that night? Of all the acts lovers shared, sleep was the most intimate. But then I saw Andy doing to Leslie Marshall the same thing I'd just been doing with Ralph, the heat and ferocity of it, and I didn't know whether to cry or be sick. If I had to be honest, there were other reasons for regret. Foolishly, sleeping with Ralph felt like a betrayal of Jack, or at least the promise of Jack, even as Andy had betrayed me.

Ralph touched a knuckle to my forehead. "What's going on up there?"

I crossed the kitchen and flung open the refrigerator. "Nothing. I'm just hungry."

He came up behind me as I surveyed the mostly empty shelves. My head was beginning to ache again. "Looks like we're going to have to eat out again," I said. "It's slim pickings here."

"I'll pass. I'm not really hungry."

"You're not, huh?"

He hugged me from behind. "I practice intermittent fasting at home. Keeps me lean and hard."

I pulled away from his embrace.

For the first time, he looked surprised at my lack of enthusiasm. "Hey, I'll take you out if it means that much to you."

Don't bother, I wanted to say. "It's fine," I said.

I could just about make a meal out of crackers and cheese, an apple, and the last container of yogurt. There was a frozen chicken breast in the freezer, but I didn't have the energy to cook it. I sat on the deck devouring my improvised meal while Ralph retreated to the living room with his laptop.

The evening was cool, but my body temperature seesawed between cold and hot. I supposed it was the lingering effect of my morning hangover, the emotional turmoil of the day. I went inside and told Ralph I was going swimming.

"Now?" he asked, surprised. "It's almost dark."

"Yeah." I left the house and walked across the lawn to the beach, stripped off my shorts and T-shirt, and waded in. The water had its usual icy edge, but my skin felt curiously numb. I swam out past the breaking surf and stopped to tread water, enjoying the gentle push-pull of the waves, the faint afterglow of the sun on the horizon. A loud splash near the shore made me whip my head around. I squinted through the dusk to see what had caused it. Ralph's wet head bobbed up next to me, a sea creature emerging from the deep.

"Jesus," I said. "You scared me."

We treaded water, nose to nose, breathing.

His black hair was plastered over his eyes, his head otter sleek, the way it had been on Cadillac Mountain. The memory jolted me. All over again, I felt my sandal slipping, my balance going, his hand suddenly not there. Almost as if he'd pulled it away.

The icy water gripped me, making it hard to breathe. I kicked away from him and swam toward shore.

"Hey, where you going?" he called.

"I'm cold. I'm going in."

"You mean I got wet for nothing?"

"Sorry."

I took another shower as soon as I got inside, the hot water nearly scalding, but the ocean cold inside me refused to leave. He was in bed waiting for me when I came out of the bathroom with my towel wrapped around me. A breeze, deliciously cool, puffed back the curtains next to the bed, the humidity of the morning swept out by the day's thunderstorms. A perfect night for sleeping under other circumstances, but tonight I'd be denied that luxury. I took my time drying off, so long that he pulled my towel away and dragged me onto the bed.

I groaned and tried to wriggle free. "Ralph, please, I'm going to be walking bowlegged for a week."

He laughed, bear-hugging me. "I want you walking bowlegged. I don't want you leaving this bed."

I wondered how he could still be so tone deaf to my change in mood. I twisted in his arms to look at him. "So what happened that night? At the Hyatt?"

If I was desperate for something to create distance between us, this was it. But it was also a question I'd long wanted to ask him, and I might not have another chance.

His arms went slack.

"Ralph?"

"Do you really want to go down this road?"

"You were there. Maybe you saw something nobody else did."

"Christ, Melissa, what good will it do at this point?"

"He was my husband, Ralph. How can you ask that question?"

He sighed. "Okay, but don't say I didn't warn you. Andy was coked out when he showed up at the dinner. Reg was pissed. He pulled Andy aside and told him to go home."

"Did Reg tell the police this?"

"I don't know what Reg told the police."

"What did *you* tell the police?"

"I ran into Andy in the men's room, before the dessert course. He was pretty messed up. I offered to drive him home, but he laughed, said he wasn't going home."

It hurt, of course, as I supposed it was intended to hurt. Like a knife slipped between my ribs. How many times was I going to be ambushed like this?

He watched me intently. "I'm sorry. I didn't want to be the one to tell you."

"But Warren said Andy was fine the night of the dinner."

He snorted. "Warren."

We were both silent, at an impasse.

He reached for my hand. "Everyone wanted to protect you from the truth, Melissa."

The offended look was gone from his eyes, replaced by what? A tiny glint of triumph? Gotcha back. I rolled over to my side of the bed, switched off the bedside lamp, and pressed my face into my pillow. After a while, he touched my shoulder.

"No, don't." I had let him share my most intimate parts, but I was not going to let him share my silent tears.

"Wow," he said. "That's cold."

Anger surged up inside me. It was all I could do not to round on him. *Look, bud, don't go turning manipulative on me. My husband is dead, so you're just going to have to give me some space. Who are you, anyway, and what are you doing here, really? Why the hell don't you just go back to where you came from?*

At a minimum, I wanted to tell him to go sleep in the other room, but something stopped me. A niggling fear of how he'd react. Because, despite our intimacies of the past several hours, my radar told me to be afraid of him, afraid of his latent physical power, of what he might be capable of doing if I provoked him enough. So I said nothing, ignoring him.

"Hey, s'okay, I get it. The widow isn't horny anymore," he muttered, and retreated to his own side of the bed.

I lay there not sleeping, my heart racing, my mouth dry, as he sighed and tossed restlessly and then became still and finally began to snore softly, the cares of his day forgotten.

Chapter 30

The bed was empty next to me when I opened my eyes, the smell of percolating coffee drifting up from the kitchen. Sometime after two, in desperation, I'd taken a sleeping pill and fallen into a drugged sleep. I had a vague memory of being prodded awake at dawn, his lips on my neck and his fingers trying to arouse me, but I'd rolled to the edge of the bed and lapsed back into unconsciousness.

Now, exhausted from too little sleep, I got up and sleep-walked to the bathroom. His voice came to me through the open bathroom window as I splashed water on my face. A few seconds of eavesdropping told me it was not a friendly conversation. I pressed the towel to my face and watched him pace back and forth where the lawn dipped down to the beach. Reg, I thought. Who else would it be?

My hair was a mare's nest despite my efforts to comb it out. Giving up, I pulled on a tank top and a pair of shorts and went downstairs. His overnight bag was open on the couch, his clothes neatly packed. He was catching a commuter flight from Ellsworth at noon and flying to Portland. From Portland he'd fly to Chicago and then on to Sacramento, arriving at eleven p.m. Pacific time, two a.m. tomorrow East Coast time. The sheer inconvenience of the trip underlined my importance in whatever scheme was going down at Reg's direction.

Out on the lawn, he stopped pacing and pocketed his phone. He hesitated when he spotted me standing at the slider, then walked up to meet me, his face a mask.

"You're up," he said tonelessly.

"Who was that?"

"Who do you think?"

"I'm going to have some coffee." I turned away, but he put his arm out.

"Wait."

I stopped, turned slowly.

"Where is it?" he asked softly.

So it was going to come to this after all.

"Where's what?"

"The documents Andy lifted off the server at WP—the thumb drive. You know what I'm talking about."

"No, I don't. I don't know anything about it. I told Reg that."

"Well, he doesn't believe you."

"So this isn't about the insurance," I said, unable to keep the bitterness out of my voice.

"That too. If you cooperate."

"Cooperate. I see." I turned away again, my head starting to pound.

His fingers closed over my arm. "Come on, baby, don't make this hard on yourself. Just tell me where it is."

Baby. I felt the first glimmer of anger. I twisted to face him. "No. You don't get to call me baby. Andy called me baby. You don't get to."

A look, almost of disgust, crossed his face. "You mean the guy who cheated on you? The guy who got himself killed?"

The house was very quiet, just the kitchen clock ticking faintly on the wall, the refrigerator humming. "What do you mean, got himself killed?"

He pressed his thumb and forefinger to the bridge of his nose. "Melissa, be reasonable. I don't have much time here. Just tell me. Where. It. Is."

"I said I don't have it."

"That detective you hired. Did you give it to him?"

So he knew about Tom. Of course he did. I didn't answer.

He pounded the kitchen counter in frustration. "Come on, Melissa! Just tell me the truth, and we can get this thing over with. Did you give him the thumb drive?"

"How could I give him something I don't have?"

He stepped toward me, touched his knuckles to the cabinet next to my head.

I took a step back. "How do I know Andy didn't put it in some safe deposit box somewhere? How do I know it even exists?"

His desperate look stilled. "What safe deposit box?"

I turned away again. "Just go, Ralph."

There was a sharp pain in my shoulder, my arm yanked viciously from behind. I wheeled on him, every murderous impulse I'd ever felt rising up inside me. I shoved him hard with both hands, but it was like shoving a wall.

He caught my wrists and gripped. There was anger in his eyes, but something else, too. "I don't think you get it. I can't go back there empty-handed."

"Well, that's not my problem, is it?"

It was amazing how fast the floor came up to meet me. My right cheekbone smacked the floorboards just as the left side of my head exploded in pain.

He stood over me, panting. There was a moment of shocked stillness, filled only by his hoarse breathing. "I don't believe this," he muttered. "I don't fucking believe this."

I crawled to my feet, pain hammering through my skull, and ran for the living room. He strode after me. I flung open the lamp table drawer, but Tom's Walther wasn't in it. "Shit!"

"This what you're looking for?" His hand was inside my bag, left carelessly on the newel post at the foot of the stairs. He pulled out the gun.

I crouched and hugged my knees to hide my shaking. Instinct told me to curl up in a ball, but I had too much pride. Still.

"A brick, huh?" he said softly.

"Ralph, please," my voice said, "you don't want to do this."

"Do what?"

"Whatever it is," I choked, "you're about to do."

"How do you know what I'm about to do?" Out of the corner of my good eye I watched his fingers play over the gun barrel. Weighing the situation. His breath was ragged, the way it sounded when he was on top of me in bed. "What am I going to do with you, Melissa? Huh?"

I pressed my forehead to my knees, on the edge of sobbing.

"Fuck," he muttered and turned away, yanked open the front door. The gun sailed into the bushes next to the porch. I squeezed my eyes shut again and curled up tighter, waiting for what was coming next. The thing that was worse than a bullet in the brain.

Below the sound of his breathing was the faint jingle of his belt being unbuckled. My head snapped up.

"I really don't have time for this," he said, "but what the hell."

"Ralph, no."

I tried to get up but he gripped my shoulders and pushed me back down.

"Ralph, stop."

"What's this?" he said softly. "You don't like me anymore? You were hot for me yesterday. Weren't you? Huh?" Darkness covered me, blocking the light. He was on top of me now, his shoulder banging into my jaw as he pushed himself inside me. "Oh, you're gonna fight, huh? What's the matter? Don't I do it as good as your little Asian boy toy?

His stubble raking my cheek, his salty skin. I slammed my fist into the side of his head.

"Oh, you like it rough? Well, so do I. Go ahead, Melissa, hit me. Oh yeah, that feels good. Do it again, baby, hit me hard. Oh, you're gonna scream? Go ahead and scream. Who's gonna hear you? We're at the end of a dirt road in the middle of fucking nowhere."

I suppose I floated out of my body and drifted off, a damned soul looking down at what was proceeding on the living room floor. Until suddenly the darkness was in me, that woman on the floor, every part of her screaming in need, crying to be filled up again and made whole. "That's it," he whispered in her ear. "Yeah." And he came with a cry that sounded like surprise and an almost childlike whimper.

We lay together, gasping. The curtain behind the sofa stirred and a warm puff of breeze reached us. It brought the smell of the ocean with it, until the cloying odor of Ralph's aftershave blocked it out.

He turned his head and brushed my throbbing cheek with his lips.

I jerked my head away. "No."

He laughed. "Okay, if you say so." The weight of his body left me, the cool air rushing in where his warmth had been. He stood over me for interminable seconds and then left. His footsteps receded down the hallway to the kitchen. I heard the slider open and, a second later, the sound of his urine drumming the dirt below the deck. The slider slid shut and the water came on in the sink, followed by vigorous splashing. Cleansing himself of the morning's deeds. He grunted and blew his nose. An ice tray cracked open. Then he was back, pressing cold onto my swollen cheek, ice cubes wrapped in a dishtowel.

"Look at me," he said softly.

I opened one eye, the eye that wasn't smashed.

His face was in shadow. "I tore this place apart and didn't find anything."

I imagined it—shattered dishes littering the floor, chairs overturned, Cat Sutton's husband's British history books heaped in a twisted pile, spines broken, the bookshelves empty.

Behind him the room was untouched. Did I read remorse in his eyes? My vision was too blurry to tell. He touched the scratch on his cheek, his bruised lip. "And if anybody asks, we had consensual sex that got a little rough. Because that's the kind of people we are."

"Fu' you."

He shook his head, disbelieving. "You still don't get it, do you, Melissa? I'm trying to save your ass here. If you know where that thumb drive is, you need to tell me now. 'Cause the next guys who show up here aren't gonna play nice. There's a great big lonely ocean on your doorstep, and they won't think twice about dumping you in it."

A tear leaked out of the swollen eye and ran down my throbbing cheek.

"Just go," I whispered.

Chapter 31

J ack began texting the next morning, wondering why I hadn't shown up at the gallery. That afternoon, he showed up on my porch, rapping on the door and calling my name. I lay frozen on the couch, swaddled in my afghan, barely breathing until he went away. My face was a purple mess, the skin over my left cheekbone split and leaking ooze. Worried that he'd call the police if he didn't hear from me, I sent him a cryptic text. *Called out of town unexpectedly. So sorry for the inconvenience.*

That night, I woke with a jerk at one-thirty and felt Andy standing over me. He was weeping. I swallowed the last of my emergency sleeping pills and tunneled back into oblivion.

The next night, unable to sleep without pills, I paced the house until dawn and exhaustion drove me back to bed. The sheets still smelled of Ralph, his pungent sweat, his sickening aftershave. I stripped the bed and went downstairs to sleep on the couch.

I thought about going to Jack and telling him what had happened. But what would he say? What could he say? *You have to report this.* And how would he look at me afterwards? A rape victim? Worse, a willing participant in my own rape? I could see the disgust on his face. And even if I omitted the rape from the retelling, how could I even begin to explain why a lawyer from my dead husband's firm had come three thousand miles to beat me up? The only explanation that made any sense at all was the truth. And I wasn't close to being ready to admit that. Apart from everything else, I didn't want to drag any more innocent people into my mess.

On the fourth day I woke to abdominal cramps and blood on my underpants. So at least I wasn't pregnant, I thought, and reached for the box of tampons. The news brought relief, but only a very little.

By the fifth day, the cupboards were bare. I was down to eating peanut butter sandwiches and bowls of white rice and drinking water instead of milk. The cat food ran out, too, and Juju prowled the house restlessly, making sleep impossible, until I opened the back door in surrender and let him out into the night to fend for himself.

My face went from deep eggplant purple to hideous blue and yellow swirls. I was still too bruised to go out in public. By the sixth afternoon, late, as the sun was setting, I covered my wounds with make up, put on my sunglasses and my trusty baseball cap, and went down to the harbor to buy six lobsters off of one of the fishing boats. I worried that I would run into Jack, but by then I was too hungry to care.

I brought the lobsters home and cooked four of them immediately, tossing them without remorse into boiling water and standing numb as they struggled against the pot lid. I fed the meat of an entire lobster to Juju and ate the other three myself, sucking the meat and juice from the legs and licking my fingers until I was almost sick.

On the eighth day, I took the ferry over to Southwest Harbor.

I knew I was in the right place as soon as I turned off the highway because of the Ford F-150 bumping along in front of me. The dirt road wound through scrub pine to an outdoor shooting range, the nearest one I could locate in my Web search. I could hear the reports of different firearms as I got closer, the sharp cracks of a hunting rifle, the obscene *thunk-thunks* of a handgun. Tom's Walther lay in its plastic case on the passenger seat next to me, along with the ammo I'd stopped at Walmart to buy because Ralph, who must have searched the house while I was in the shower or lying knocked out from my sleeping pill, had taken the box of cartridges. I'd also picked up a pair of noise-canceling earmuffs.

Raising my firing arm and taking aim, I soon realized I'd forgotten nothing from my days at the shooting range with my father. The bullets ripped across the paper target, shredding the midsection of the human form superimposed on it as spent casings chinged all around me. I lowered the Walther and broke my stance, the jolt of the recoil making my arm ache.

I reached for the open box of ammo and reloaded, the stiff action of the magazine pinching my fingertips as I pushed the cartridges in. I raised my arm again and sighted along the barrel, then emptied the gun into the target in one go, thinking only of Ralph and my own stupidity. Dirt devils puffed up from the earthen backstop as four or five shots missed their mark.

The two guys at the next target over, a father and son duo by the look of it, hooted like they were watching some brain-dead action movie.

"Whoa, take your time there, sweetheart. He's not goin' anywhere," the son, a lank-haired dude in a camouflage cap, drawled.

"That piece is too big for you," the gray-mustached father observed. "Why don't you try this one?" He held up a pearl-handled revolver, comically dainty compared to Tom's Walther. "Belongs to my wife."

My murderous desire for revenge on Ralph vied with an obligation to be polite, even to a couple of gun enthusiasts I was never going to see again. I took the pistol from the older guy and squinted down the line of sight at the ripped-up target.

"That baby is smooth," he purred. "Just squeeze the trigger real gentle."

I did as he instructed, and the bullet glided down the barrel and out to the target. Bulls-eye.

The man's eyes crinkled with pride. "See what I mean?"

"Nice," I said, and handed the revolver back to him.

I loaded the Walther again, my fingertips getting sorer with each round I jammed into the magazine. The two men observed with their arms crossed as I plinked the target three times in a row.

"Better," the father said, my new cheering section.

"You know what helps me," his son pitched in with a sneaky little chuckle. He held up a paper target with a familiar head and shoulders superimposed on it, chin tilted up and eyes gazing nobly into the distance.

Racist creeps, I thought, using our African-American president for target practice. I was tempted to turn the Walther on the pair of doofuses and kneecap them both, but I told myself it was just their way of being friendly. Instead, I raised my firing arm and emptied the gun into the target in front of me, a surprising number of rounds hitting the bulls-eye mean and clean. My anger at Ralph stilled after that. A few minutes later I packed up and left.

I thought about cutting my losses and going home—I would have been a fool not to—but I dreaded the barrage of questions I'd surely get from my mother if I arrived back in New Hampshire a week ahead of schedule. Besides, I needed to wait until my face was completely healed. My mother may have been a full-on narcissist, but I trusted she had enough maternal feeling to sense something monstrous like her daughter being raped. At least I hoped so. So I stayed on at the cottage, locking the doors and downstairs windows at night, pushing the dresser in front of my bedroom door, and sleeping with the Walther under my pillow. Juju protested loudly at being shut out of the bedroom, yowling to be let in as only a Siamese can yowl, but when I relented and let him into the room, he was soon scratching at the barricaded door to get back out.

A toxic soup of fear, anger, and exhaustion poisoned my days and nights, but a stubbornness I didn't know I had asserted itself the more I suffered. I was determined not to let Ralph's threats drive me off the island until I was ready. Besides, I had some unfinished business to take care of before I left.

I found Jack in the workroom at the gallery, tapping a frame into place in his quiet, methodical way. Esme wasn't with him — a good thing, because I needed some uninterrupted time to explain myself. I must have looked worse than my reflection in the bathroom mirror was telling me, because the smile dropped off his face when he saw me.

"Jesus, what happened?"

I froze in mid-step, at a loss for words.

I'd covered what was left of my bruise with make-up, but my hand went to it automatically. Perhaps it showed through in the strong light coming from the west-facing windows. "I, um, tripped over the cat. In the dark."

He stared at me, unconvinced.

"Look, I just wanted to apologize—" I began.

"No need to. You're on vacation. Things come up."

There was a studied carelessness in his words, as if they hid a wound. I glanced around the workroom, the place I'd felt happiest, the most like myself, since coming to the island. "I'm ready to come back to work. If you'll have me."

He put the hammer down, looking distinctly uncomfortable. "I'd like nothing better, but . . . "

I waited, holding my breath.

He sighed. "It's like this. We're a small operation here, but I do need someone I can depend on. When are you going home?"

"End of August." Or I could leave tomorrow. Maybe this was just the push I needed.

"Barely a fortnight. Wouldn't it be best to just get on with it, enjoy what's left of your time here without worrying about the gallery?"

The rejection stung me, made worse by his kind tone. "What you really mean is I've let you down."

"Well, you have done that, but not in a big way."

I felt my face coloring, the smarting sting of tears held back.

"Mother of God," he muttered, and came out from behind the worktable. He raised his arms, as if to hug me, but I took a step back and his arms dropped to his sides. I didn't think I could bear to feel a man's arms around me. Not yet. Not even Jack's.

He watched me helplessly. "I'm sorry. I know what it's like to have your life blown to smithereens."

I nodded, choking it all back. "Thanks for understanding."

"I owe you your wages," he said, and stepped over to the cash drawer.

"No, please. Keep them. I'm sorry I wasn't more reliable." Time to get the hell out of there.

"Melissa," he called after me.

I stopped, almost through the door.

"Don't leave without saying good-bye. Esme and I can cook you a meal."

My remaining time on the island ticked away, the days perversely beautiful. It stayed very hot, unusual for that time of year. Back when Andy and I had lived in Boston, the second half of August typically featured the best weather of the summer—warm days but cool nights, a harbinger of fall. But now another heat wave rolled in, bringing with it mercilessly clear skies that felt more like San Diego than New England.

I didn't go back to the gallery, not even to say hello, my pride keeping me away. But the abrupt end of my friendship with Jack and Esme felt almost as unbearable as losing Andy. A bruise on top of a bruise. Perhaps it was my overburdened psyche's way of deflecting all the grief I'd yet to work through surrounding Andy's death, or even a defense mechanism against the much more disturbing prospect of being dumped in the ocean by faceless men. But it didn't lessen the aching emptiness of this fresh loss. By the twenty-ninth, I was packing to leave, fully aware of the ludicrousness of coming to Maine to escape the memories of California, only to flee home to California to escape the memories of Maine.

Two evenings before my departure date, as Juju sashayed around my legs meowing to be fed, I made the dreaded discovery that I was opening my last can of cat foot. I'd made an effort to dwindle my remaining food down to nothing so I wouldn't have to transport it home or throw it away, but running out of cat food was a nonnegotiable, especially after asking Juju to starve a couple of weeks before. I'd have to take the ferry over to Southwest Harbor the next day—an expensive trip just to buy cat food, but I could defray the cost by doing the other errands I'd planned to do the day after that on my way out of town.

As soon as the ferry docked the next morning, I walked up the street to the market. After buying cat food, I dropped Balzac and Malraux at the library and then stopped by the post office to end my forwarding order and pick up any last mail. Back in the car, I reached for my padded camera bag and unzipped it. As an afterthought, on my way out of the house that morning, I'd grabbed it off the top shelf of my closet and brought it along. In the eight weeks I'd been in Maine, I hadn't taken a single photograph as a visual memory of my visit.

My old Nikon felt reassuringly heavy as I cradled it in my hands, a tool I knew how to use. So what if I wasn't so great at holding down a job at the local gallery—I was good at photography. I pressed the lever to open the back of the camera and reached into a side pocket of the camera bag for a fresh roll of film. But when I popped the lid off the plastic film canister, a plastic Hello Kitty figure dropped into my palm instead, the size of a truncated ring finger.

Sadness stabbed my chest. So the game was continuing from beyond the grave. A game my once playful husband had invented to make me smile, as a way to keep me close, because even in the early days of our relationship, my unfulfilled inner artist had a habit of drifting off into bouts of unhappiness. As endearing as Andy's hiding places were—inside a bag of walnuts in the freezer or peeking at me from a potted cactus on the kitchen windowsill or inside a sock in my sock drawer—the sheer variety of the cat figurines he found to hide seemed even more a proof of his love. Until the game stopped, like so much else. For an unbearable moment the pain of losing him was as devastating as it had been on the morning of June sixth.

I squeezed the pink-bowed little cat in my hand for comfort, kissed it softly. It was a long clueless moment before I realized. Hello Kitty had a top and a bottom part, a glimpse of metal peeking through where her head and body joined. It was a thumb drive.

I walked quickly back to the library and went straight to the bank of aging PCs along one wall. There were three folders on the top level of the thumb drive, each titled with an opaque acronym. I moved the cursor over the first folder and clicked. Its contents made enough sense to get my heart racing and my palms sweating. I clicked the files open, one after another, fast and furtive, the information flashing across the screen in a dizzying barrage—columns of data, dollar figures with impossible numbers of zeroes, bank account numbers, addresses in Cyprus, Malta, the Grand Caymans. The second folder contained mostly scanned legal documents, some dated as far back as 1987. The names David Escondido and Reginald S. Wolders jumped out from the legalese again and again.

I hunched closer to the screen as a library patron passed behind me on the way to the restroom. When I closed the second folder and opened the third, it was instantly clear I'd made a mistake. The computer screen went blank for a heart-stopping moment, and then code began filling the screen, line after line of ominous white letters on blue.

It had been a long time since I'd used a PC, but I recognized the blue screen of death. Shit. I pressed Control-Alt-Delete, but nothing happened. The escape key didn't work either. I knew that yanking the thumb drive from the USB port could damage its contents but there was no way to safely eject it. Across the whisper quiet room, the gray-haired librarian was shelving books, serenely unaware of my sweating panic. I turned off the computer and pulled the thumb drive from the USB port, hoping for the best. I walked away without turning the machine back on.

The wind was blowing when I left the library, storefront awnings snapping and bits of trash sailing down the street. It had been breezy on the ferry coming over, but nothing like this. The college kids who worked at the ice cream parlor a few doors down were taking in the outdoor tables and chairs. There was no thunder, but clearly a storm was coming. Slate-colored clouds piled up in the sky to the north.

The return ferry to Mizzen Island rocked at its mooring, the waves churning even in the harbor. I took refuge in the cabin as soon as I boarded, wedging myself between two passengers on an already crowded bench. More people crowded in, exchanging pleasantries about the abrupt change in the weather.

I rested my head against the clammy bulkhead as the ferry chugged slowly out of the harbor. Swells rolled in from the open water, jostling us in our seats. A few adventure seekers planted themselves on the open stern deck, eager to experience the elements, but soon scrambled for cover when a burst of spray exploded over the starboard rail. The cabin was standing room only now. One drenched man stood over me, his glasses fogged with salt water, his windbreaker dripping cold water on my sandaled feet.

I angled my body away from the man and took my phone out, intending to text Tom that I'd found the thumb drive. But my phone vibrated in my hand before I began to type. Swiping down the screen, I saw a number I didn't recognize and a one-line text.

We know you have it.

Chapter 32

I walked off the ferry oblivious to the waves splashing over the floating dock, the wind shrieking in the rigging of the nearby boats. All I wanted was to get back on land and away from the other disembarking passengers so I could think. Since the day Ralph left me cowering on the living room floor, I'd done my best to discount his parting warning about the fate that awaited me if I didn't cooperate, but there was no way I could ignore it now.

Leaves skittered through the air and trees swayed all around me as I headed inland, thinking about how long it would take me to pack up my things and make my escape. The rain still held off, but the temperature was dropping, a giant unseen hand pulling in gusts of chill North Atlantic air. So this was what the island must be like in the fall, I thought, when all the tourists were gone—cold wind blowing, fallen leaves piled high, bleak sky.

My phone, still clutched in my hand, vibrated again. My heart slammed against my ribs as I thumbed down the screen, bracing for whatever new threat awaited me.

But it was a text from Tom. *How soon will you be home? We need to catch up.*

I pocketed my phone without texting back. I hurried through the pinewoods, the mosquitoes blown away by the coming storm. Catherine Sutton's house came into view up ahead, stalwart against the elements. The wind was even stronger on this, the northeast, side of the island, with nothing to block it as it blew in off the ocean. In the front yard, the beech tree's elephant's trunk branches creaked, the leaves shivering copper to silver and back again.

Splendid Isolation. This house I'd loved so much on first sight had stopped feeling like a refuge the day I let Ralph in, but it was still my home on the island, if only for the next couple of hours.

I crossed the leaf-strewn yard wondering what was different about the house from when I'd left that morning. Something. Before leaving to catch the ferry, I'd locked up carefully, my only real concession to fear since Ralph's visit. I distinctly remembered pulling the swollen front door shut and turning the key in the lock. So why was it wide open now?

Gaping darkness confronted me where the locked door should have been. It took only a moment for the implication to sink in. I turned and walked briskly away, back through the pinewoods, past the grammar school and derelict general store and post office, past the church. I turned right at the Gallery sign and jogged the hundred yards or so to the gallery, where I came to a standstill in the courtyard, met by another unexpected sight. The barn door was rolled shut, a Closed sign hung in the window.

A child's voice, high and clear, carried in my direction on the wind—Esme, asking a question, as always. Jack's voice answered her, sounding amused even in the din. Their voices drifted from an open window in the house next door.

I crossed a strip of lawn to the side entrance and banged on the wood-framed screen door. Jack opened the inside door with a dishtowel slung over his shoulder.

"Melissa," he said, startled. His eyes went to the seething sky behind me. "You can't be here to say good-bye."

The look on my face was enough.

"Jesus, what's wrong? Come in."

I stepped onto the braided rug just inside the door. There was a welter of shoes next to it, Jack's and Esme's jumbled together. A weather radio played in the room down the hall I assumed was the kitchen. The announcer's voice managed to sound monotonous and dire at the same time.

I faced Jack, hoping I didn't look and sound totally insane. "I think somebody broke into my house. I took the ferry over to Southwest Harbor and when I came back, the front door was wide open."

Jack frowned. "Maybe the wind blew it open."

"No. The door sticks on the bottom. I remember pulling it shut and locking it. I'm—," I cleared my throat, "afraid to go in the house."

Esme appeared at Jack's side, her eyes going round at the sight of me, my hair made Medusa-like by the wind. I reached up to smooth it down.

Jack slipped his arm around his daughter's shoulders. "Seems unlikely you've had a break-in. The crime rate on the island is less than zero. Ez and I will walk over with you, get it sorted."

"No," I said, a bit too emphatically. How to explain the image that flashed through my brain, the three of us shot dead on the floor of Catherine Sutton's cozy living room. "I—don't want Esme to go."

Jack turned to Esme, covering his surprise. "Have you finished your grilled cheese?"

She nodded.

"Okay," he said calmly. "Melissa and I will take you over to Mabel's for a bit. We'll be back soon." He took her purple raincoat off the peg next to the door and helped her put it on. His glance took in my thin sweatshirt and shorts, my exposed skin bluish and goose-pimpled, and handed me the man's raincoat on the adjacent peg.

"What will you wear?" I asked.

"Don't worry about me. I'll be fine."

The three of us left the house huddled together, holding hands in a daisy chain with Esme in the middle. A fine mist was coming off the water now, creeping among the trees. Jack led the way along the grassy track to Mabel and Gar's place, a few doors away. A once proud Victorian, the house looked forlorn and ramshackle in the swirling mist. Piles of lobster traps, buoys, and snarled-up pot warp crowded the front yard, along with the battered hulls of a couple of abandoned skiffs, contributing to an air of utter desolation.

"That's Gar," Jack remarked as we approached the front door. "Never met a piece of junk he didn't want to hang onto for dear life."

Mabel answered Jack's knock in a flowered apron over a cotton dress, like some nineteen-fifties housewife—an almost comforting sight given the circumstances.

"Hiya, Mabel," Jack greeted her, as if the three of us were out for a casual stroll. "Filthy weather to be sure, but can you watch Esme for a bit? Melissa's had some trouble at her place and we're going over there to sort it out."

Mabel's eyes, a murky brown behind her reading glasses, strayed in my direction. "What kind of trouble, Jack?"

"Possibly a break-in."

"A break—"

"Is Gar here? Maybe he'd like to come along."

"Gar!" she called over her shoulder, into the dark interior of the house. "He's out in back seeing to the generator."

"Go with Mabel," Jack whispered to Esme.

Esme stepped reluctantly over the threshold, where Mabel drew her to her plump side with a pointed look in my direction.

"So it's a fair bet we'll lose power, wouldn't you say?" Jack said conversationally to Mabel as we waited for Gar.

"You've lived here too long, Jack Kilronan, to be asking that question," Mabel retorted, a surprising hint of flirtatiousness piercing her battle-axe demeanor.

Gar appeared behind his wife in his Tattersall shirt, a greasy rag in one hand. As many Tuesdays as he'd come to my place to cut the grass and collect my trash, we'd never exchanged more than the barest minimum of words. Now he gave me a curt nod and turned to Jack.

"Sorry to disrupt your Saturday, Gar," Jack said pleasantly, "but as I've telling Mabel—"

"A break-in over at the Sutton place," Mabel cut in, disbelief tinged with suspicion. Or was it scorn?

I shrank back a little, feeling ashamed. I'd brought trouble to the island.

"When? Today?" Gar asked Jack. He snorted. "I was just over there myself not two hours ago. Nothing out of order that I could see."

Jack exchanged a glance with me. "You were over there this morning?"

"Furnace guy came over from the mainland to write his job order. He's starting work next week."

"Did you lock up when he left?"

Gar's gnomish face colored a bit. "I told *him* to."

"You didn't stay?"

He snorted again. "Didn't think I needed to. Fellow's honest. Besides, Mabel was on me to get back here and get the generator working."

Mabel muttered something, clearly not happy with her husband's attempt to shift the blame.

"What's all this folderol?" Gar asked Jack, ignoring her.

"The front door was open when Melissa got home from Southwest."

I spoke up. "It sticks when you shut it. Sometimes you think it's locked and it's not."

Gar sniffed. "Since when have folks locked their doors on Mizzen, anyway?"

Jack laid his hand lightly on my arm. "Well, thanks, mate," he said to Gar. "I'll let you get back to it. Stay safe in the storm, yeah? Come on, Ez."

We walked away as quickly as we'd come, Jack and I exchanging an amused look over Esme's head. But dread crept back in at the thought of saying good-bye to my only friends on the island and returning to the Sutton place alone. I silently reviewed what I needed to do when I got there—finish packing my clothes and toiletries, clean out the nearly empty refrigerator, take out the trash, feed Juju then get him into his carrier. From Southwest Harbor, it was a four-hour drive to my mother's. If the storm made driving too difficult, I could stay at a motel on the way. I stopped suddenly, bringing Jack and Esme up short.

"What is it?" Jack asked.

"I can't stay there tonight. I want to leave today. Will you come back with me while I pack?"

He looked puzzled. "You're still afraid?"

I nodded. "I'm sorry. I can't explain it."

"The thing is, the ferry has stopped running. I heard it on the radio a while ago."

I stood there at a loss, unable to think a coherent thought, and as I did, the rain started, a big wet blowing sheet of it, much colder than anything I'd felt in my two months on the island.

"Daddy, I don't like it," Esme said plaintively from inside her hood. "I want to go home."

"Come to our place," Jack said to me, the rain already dripping down his face. "You can stay with us tonight."

But the furnace man had failed to lock the door at my place, and unless the wind had blown it shut, it was still standing wide open to everything the storm wanted to throw at the house. We would have to walk over there and shut the door before we took shelter at Jack's, and I was still afraid to bring Esme with us. So we marched her back to Mabel and Gar's, where Mabel brought Jack a towel to dry his already soaked body and fished an oilskin of Gar's from the crowded hall closet to lend him while continuing to ignore me completely.

Jack thanked her and we headed back across the island, just the two of us, leaning into the driving rain and dodging bits of branches turned projectiles.

The front door gaped open and the wide-plank floor of the entrance hall was awash in rainwater when we reached the house. Jack got busy mopping up the water while I ran upstairs to close all the windows I'd left open that morning, which now seemed like at least a century ago. In the master bedroom, the rain had swept in through the window next to the bed and soaked the bedspread and pillows, but there was no time to deal with that now. I grabbed an empty tote bag and threw in the things I'd need to get me through the night at Jack's.

There was no sign that anyone had been in the house and also no sign of Juju. That stopped me cold. It seemed unlikely he'd run out into the teeth of the storm, but if he'd escaped before the rain started, he probably would have taken refuge under one of the porches and wouldn't reappear until the rain stopped. Damn Gar and his carelessness.

Jack was stowing the bucket back in the utility closet when I came downstairs.

"The cat's missing," I told him, too defeated to hide my dismay.

"Do you want to look for him?"

It would be a supreme f-you from the universe, I thought, if after losing my husband and my entire married life, I would now be asked to lose my beloved cat, too. But I couldn't ask Jack to hang around waiting for a cat who most likely wouldn't show up until he was good and ready. I reminded myself of the night I ran out of cat food and threw Juju outside to hunt a meal in the wild. He came back then and he would come back this time, I told myself.

"He'll be fine," I said half-heartedly, and went to open one of the just-purchased cans of cat food to leave on the back deck in case he showed up while I was gone.

Jack followed me to the kitchen and watched me scoop the food into a dish. "Let's have a look around," he said. "It's better than worrying all night, don't you think?"

"You sure?" A rush of gratitude melted some of my anxiety.

"You check his hiding places inside. I'll check outside."

I started to protest, but he pulled the hood of Gar's oilskin over his head and left the house through the kitchen slider. I was in one of the bedrooms checking under the twin beds when my phone chirped and another text from Tom appeared. *Haven't heard from you in a while. Everything ok?*

A movement outside the window caught my eye—Jack, half-obscured by a curtain of rain, coming across the back lawn with a sodden bundle in his arms.

Juju.

I let Tom's text go unanswered.

I met them at the slider. "Oh my God, you found him. Juju! My poor baby. What happened to you?" I looked up at Jack. "Where was he?"

"Hiding in the woodpile, under the tarp. Smart kitty."

"Thank you so much. Thank you for finding him." I took Juju's trembling body from Jack's arms. His fur was wet but not as soaked as his rescuer. Even as I hugged Juju against me, I wanted to reach up and brush the wet hair out of Jack's eyes. Instead I said, "I feel like I've caused you so much trouble."

He grinned. "Aye, but isn't that the main event in life? Trouble?"

Whether it was a firmly held belief of his or not, he looked decidedly untroubled at the moment. And if I hadn't been hugging Juju, I'm pretty sure I would have hugged him for it.

Chapter 33

"**O**kay, what do you want me to draw now?"

Sketches lay strewn around us on the living room rug: a turtle, an owl, a lobster.

"A fox!" Esme said.

"A fox? Hmm . . . " My hand moved quickly over the drawing paper, sketching in the alert ears, the pointy nose, the bushy tail, while Esme hunkered down on elbows and knees watching the animal take form.

"That's not a fox," she declared. "It's a cat."

"A cat? A cat with a pointy nose?"

Esme giggled. "It's a dog."

"A dog? Since when does a dog have a bushy tail like this?"

"No, it's a raccoon!"

"Okay, now you're just being silly."

Almost as soon as he'd escorted Esme and me back to his house, Jack had gone back out in the rain to the harbor to check on his buddy's lobster boat and to see if anyone else needed help securing theirs. The weather radio, still on in the kitchen, gave terse, static-filled updates to the empty room about the rare August nor'easter crawling over us.

A gust of wind moaned in the eaves and fresh bursts of rain lashed the big picture window with its view of the cove below the house. The living room lamp flickered and went out.

"Uh oh," Esme said and looked at me.

There was still plenty of natural light to see by, but the storm sky, weirdly greenish, cast gloom over the room. "Where do you keep your candles?" I asked.

She jumped up and led me to the dining room. A heavy mahogany dining room set and lace curtains dominated the decor, not at all how I'd imagined Jack's house to look. I supposed I'd been expecting a domestic version of the gallery next-door—white walls, Shaker-style furniture, lots of light. Then I remembered that Jack's wife, Kerry, had inherited the house from her aunt, and most likely the dark, old-fashioned furniture with it.

Esme pointed to the top drawer of the curved front sideboard. "In here."

Sure enough, nestled among folded tablecloths and placemats was a good supply of long tapers, some of them partially used as if stored after dinner parties. My fingers closed over the candles, but my eyes were drawn to the framed family photos arranged on the sideboard. A dark-haired, pixie-faced woman with a wide, generous smile looked at me from several of them. In one, a younger Jack had his arm around her as she held baby Esme in her arms, their blissful smiles leaving no doubt of their contentment as a family unit. I was still studying the photo when the side door burst open and Jack came in, bringing the wind and rain with him. Esme ran out to the hall to meet him. "Daddy, did you fall in the ocean?"

"Might as well have, Ez."

He was bending over to take off his rubber boots, his raincoat dark and dripping, when I joined them. He glanced up at me and then at the candles in my hand.

"The power just went out," I said.

"It's a miracle it didn't happen sooner. The wind is screeching like a banshee."

"I thought I'd light these, unless you're thinking of turning on the generator."

"Not just yet. It's a noisy beast. Be nice to enjoy the sounds of the storm for a bit, don't you think?"

So the man's a romantic, I thought.

"What do you say, Ez?" he asked his daughter. "Do you like listening to the storm?"

She nodded. "Except when it's scary."

"Is it scary now?"

"Not too scary."

Jack and I both laughed.

"Come on, you," I said to Esme. "Let's finish drawing Mister Fox."

"How do you know it's *Mister* Fox?" she asked as she followed me back to the living room.

"What do you mean?"

"Maybe it's Missus Fox."

I put my arm around her for the first time. "I wouldn't be surprised if it is."

We feasted by candlelight on American chop suey made by Mabel and warmed up on the Aga, and all I could think, as I sat at the kitchen table with Jack at one elbow and Esme at the other, was *I don't want to go back to California. I want to stay here for the rest of my life.* The terror of the morning—the threatening text and the wide open door—were forgotten, or at least consigned to the back of my mind. My phone lay on the guest room bed upstairs, turned off, because the last thing I wanted was to receive another missive from an unknown sender. But I felt no urgency to talk to Tom either. I didn't care about the thumb drive and its implications for the case, not in that moment. And even if I had, the thought of going up against whoever was behind that threatening text sent a preemptive chill through me.

The truth was I'd stopped caring about the case, period, even as I recognized that my wish to stay on the island with Jack and Esme was impossible. When I left the next morning my appealing domestic fantasy would be over, and in all likelihood I'd never see my new friends again. In a few days time I'd be three thousand miles away, dealing with the mess my life had become while my friends remained here, safe in their island idyll, a warm but inevitably fading memory.

So I munched on bibb lettuce picked fresh from the garden that morning, before the storm, and sipped red wine, and tried to focus on the gratitude I felt for the smidgeon of normalcy this unexpected evening afforded me. Esme and Jack's back-and-forth chatter eased the knots in my stomach and telegraphed to me that I was home. As close to home as I would likely come for the foreseeable future.

After cookies and milk for dessert, Esme went off to play with her dolls, leaving Jack and me alone for the first time that evening. I ran my forefinger along the rim of my wineglass to make it sing, suddenly shy of meeting his gaze. I felt his eyes on me, studying me quietly.

"What is it?" he asked.

"Why do Mabel and Gar hate me so much?" I said it casually, as if earning the crusty old couple's approval was my only care in the world.

He laughed. "They don't really. They're islanders born and bred, and you're a stranger. They didn't like me much either when I washed up here, but they tolerated me because of Kerry. Her aunt was an islander, too."

It surprised me in a good way to hear him say his wife's name out loud. I hoped it was a sign that he was beginning to trust me—as if that mattered at all considering the circumstances.

"Well, you've won over Mabel," I teased him.

"Aye, but that came later," he said with a rueful smile. "And it was only because I needed help with Esme."

Later. There was an entire world in that word.

He poured a splash more wine into each of our glasses.

"I'll do the dishes," I volunteered.

"They can wait till morning. No sense using the water."

He'd informed me of that awhile earlier. Without the generator, the well would stop pumping water and the faucets would eventually go dry. "Which means the loo won't flush either," he'd said, glancing at me for a reaction. "But I filled some buckets earlier. Do you mind?"

"Not at all," I'd replied blithely. "I can rough it with the best of them."

But the look he was giving me now seemed far from plumbing concerns. "So, what was all that about today?" he asked carefully. "You were so . . ."

"Spooked?" I didn't pretend to not know what he was talking about.

"Yeah."

Since Andy's death, I'd had multiple opportunities to be honest—with Jacey, with Liz, with my mother—and each time the best I'd been able to deliver was half-truths and distortions. The only person I trusted enough to be completely honest with was Tom. But I was tired of lying, even my lies of omission. I realized that I trusted Jack the same way I trusted Tom, and maybe that was a good enough place to start.

I swirled the wine in my glass, working up the courage to begin. "My husband didn't just die of a heart attack, although that's what they thought at first. There's a pretty good chance he was murdered."

He had a mobile, expressive face, and I saw the shock ripple over it. "Wow."

It was still raining outside, but the wind had gone quiet for the moment. I traced the gray-veined pattern on the 1950's-era Formica tabletop with my fingertips. The next bit was going to be harder. I took a deep breath to dispel the weight of it. "So I had a visit . . . here . . . from somebody who may have been involved in my husband's death. They were lawyers together at the same firm. This guy came on firm business, but later," I swallowed, "he, um, threatened me and roughed me up."

"He struck you?" His eyes searched my face for traces of the bruise.

I nodded.

"Did you go to the police?"

"No."

"For the love of God, why not?" He said it gently, without condemnation, but I colored despite his kindness.

"I guess I was too ashamed to."

"Ashamed?" That gave it away. He was wondering if I'd been raped.

Yes, I was raped, I wanted to say, but it was *after* I gave myself willingly to that scumbag. What are your thoughts about that?

"I shouldn't have trusted him," I said, forcing myself to meet his eyes. "I should have known better. My face was such a mess. I looked like one of those battered women."

"Where is he now, this . . . cretin?"

"He went back to California."

"And you're leaving tomorrow to go back there?"

I nodded again.

He was quiet, puzzling it out. "You'll go to the police when you get there?"

I thought of Darla Roussekoff, the coroner—all the people who seemed determined to toss aside the unanswered questions about Andy's death instead of helping me. How could I explain any of it to Jack?

"I've hired a private investigator to get some answers. He's looking out for me."

"Daddy," Esme's voice interrupted, calling down the stairs. "I'm sleepy. Can you read me a story?"

Jack had drawn leaned closer to me while we were talking, but now he sat back in his chair. "I'll be up in a minute, Ez."

I tried to smile. "A kid who asks to be put to bed. That's a novelty."

He shrugged in mock wonder, acknowledging the truth of it. Many more words hung in the air between us, too many to be said. Their weight pressed down on us for a long moment, then he left the kitchen to go to Esme.

I teetered on a boulder in the pouring rain, a dizzying void below me. Ralph stood above me on the next boulder, his wet hair plastered to his skull, his eyes onyx black. He smiled as I reached for him, then pushed me hard. I woke with a cry in a single bed in a strange room, falling. It took me a minute to remember that I was at Jack's house, in the guest room at the end of the hall. I'd woken once already, earlier in the night just after I nodded off, to Esme's cries, her bare feet running to Jack's room. The unsettled night was giving all of us nightmares.

Now I lay in bed listening to the storm over the thudding of my heart. The wind had picked up again, shaking the house with each gust. A deafening bang rent the night. Coming on its heels was an eerie shrieking noise, as if the clapboards were peeling off the house in one long, continuous sheet. Something racketed across the yard below the bedroom window and was swept away.

Storm noises, nothing more, I told myself. Except something was wrong. My nightmare lingered, jumbling my thoughts. I felt Ralph's presence, as if he were right in the room with me. Maybe he hadn't left the island at all. Maybe he'd been hiding somewhere nearby the whole time, biding his time until I felt safe and protected, until I let my guard down.

I sat up in bed, fear driving my thoughts. By being here in Jack's house, I was putting Jack and Esme in danger. I had to get out of here fast, go back to the Sutton place. I couldn't save myself, but I could save my friends if I left now.

I slipped out of bed, phone in hand, and opened the bedroom door. The phone's flashlight beam was way too bright in the blackness of the power outage. It bounced over Esme's room across the hall, her empty bed, her jumbled assortment of stuffed animals. The old floorboards creaked as I crept past the bathroom towards Jack's open bedroom door. In the shielded light from my phone, I could just make out the sleeping forms of father and daughter. I stopped a couple of feet from the door, not knowing what to do next.

The covers rustled and Jack sat up, an indistinct form. "What is it?"

"That noise," I whispered. "It woke me up."

"It woke me too. Probably a shutter getting blown off the house."

"I have to go home," I said.

He got out of bed instantly and came to me in his pajama bottoms and T-shirt. "You mean, home to California? Tomorrow?"

"No. Now. To Splendid Isolation."

"You can't be serious. It's not safe outside."

"But I have to. I can't—"

He clasped my shoulders lightly. "Can't what?"

"Can't—" I stopped, unable to say it.

"Melissa, are you asleep?"

"I'm afraid," I whispered. "I'm so fucking afraid."

"Of what?" he whispered back.

The words wouldn't come.

"Come on," he said, "let's go downstairs. I'll make us some tea."

I followed him down to the kitchen, watched him strike a match to light a candle. The kitchen was very warm, the Aga still throwing heat. The water in the kettle on top of the stove had stayed hot, sending up a cloud of steam as Jack poured it into our cups. We carried our tea to the living room and sat next to each other on the couch in the dark. The cushion caved under me, sending a splash of hot tea onto my lap.

"Sorry," Jack said, "The springs are gone. That's what happens when you let a six-year-old use it as a trampoline."

We sat with a couple of inches between us, sipping our tea and listening to the wind and rain. Jack yawned and rubbed his eyes.

I yawned too. "Sorry I woke you," I said.

"You didn't wake me. The storm did."

"Will Esme stay asleep without you there?"

He chuckled. "We'll see."

A strong gust rattled the picture window next to the couch, pushing in a draft of cold air. I set my cup down on the coffee table and pulled my knees up to my chest.

"Cold?" Jack asked.

"A little."

He retrieved a quilt from the armchair across the room. "Here," he said, and tucked it over me. Ralph came uninvited into my mind, wrapping Bitsy's tartan blanket around me in the car on Cadillac Mountain. I must have stiffened because Jack let go of the quilt and moved back to his side of the couch.

"Sorry," I said, "I guess I'm still a little jumpy."

"Right," he said. I couldn't read his expression in the dark.

"It's okay if you want to go back to bed. I just need to stay up for a while." Being on the ground floor felt safer, somehow, than being upstairs in the guest room. If an intruder forced his way in, at least I'd hear him.

Jack's mug was empty, but he didn't get up. "How do I know you won't try to go home?"

"I won't. I promise."

He leaned back against the couch cushion, his breathing slow and even. "It's nice, the quiet. I'm not usually up this time of night."

"Me neither," I said, a true enough statement—though only because I'd drugged myself with sleeping pills most nights since Andy's death.

"I'm awake now. I'll stay until you fall asleep, if you like."

The father comforting the child. He'd had plenty of practice with his own motherless child. How could I say no? And why would I want to?

"Thanks," I murmured. "That would be . . . nice." I rested my head against the back of the couch and closed my eyes. The chance of falling asleep was almost nil, I thought, but I didn't care. Any awkwardness that had been between us was gone. Eventually, as my body relaxed and my thoughts began to drift, I felt him adjust his position next to me, stretch his legs out on the coffee table. In my drowsiness, I moved closer, let my head rest against his shoulder. After a while, his arm slipped around me, a half-embrace so natural I relaxed into it. His skin, through his T-shirt, smelled of sleep and laundry soap. I felt his heart beating, the rise and fall of his breath.

He pulled the old quilt, homely and domestic, up over both of us, and I let him hold me, not thinking about my physical violation by another man or of anything else but the warm place our two bodies, Jack's and mine, made in the space between us. Until, impossibly, I drifted back to sleep.

I woke an hour or two later, in the first light of dawn, to a feeling I hadn't experienced in what seemed like forever. The safety and comfort that only the warmth of another human can provide. I must have moved because he stirred too, and for a tiny moment, still more asleep than awake, his arms tightened around me and he pressed his face into my hair. Then he raised his head and gave an embarrassed cough. He extricated himself gently from our embrace. "Sorry. I fell asleep."

I wanted to take his hand, to tell him there was no need to apologize, that he'd helped me more than he knew, but he was already on his feet. "Time to get back to my own bed. Esme will be waking soon."

Outside the picture window, it was quiet, the wind gone, taking with it the shrieking chaos of the night.

I became aware of how much I needed to pee. Time to put the flush bucket to good use. "Bathroom," I murmured and followed him up the stairs.

When I woke again, in the guest room bed, weak sun was poking through the clouds and the bedside clock was flashing yesterday's time. A patter of feet in the hallway stopped at my half-open door. I peaked over the edge of the blanket. "Well, good morning, Miss Esme."

The doll, Gemma, was dangling at her side by one arm. "Do you want to play dolls with me?" she whispered.

"Ez!" Jack called from downstairs.

"It's breakfast!" she announced and left my room, skipping back down the hall.

In the kitchen, the weather radio was on again. Jack stood at the Aga, pushing bacon around in an iron skillet. The table was set with plates and flatware and orange juice. Toast popped up in the toaster as I leaned against the doorjamb in my T-shirt and flannel boxers. "I'll butter that," I said, and moved forward to help.

The three of us ate the eggs and toast and bacon Jack served up, as if it were just one day out of many in our life together on the island. But the weather radio broke in, announcing that the Mizzen ferry would start running again at noon.

"You know, you're welcome to stay a few more days," Jack said, surprising me. His gray eyes held a look I hadn't seen in them before. Hope, and what usually came with hope—vulnerability.

Esme nodded. "Stay, stay, stay!"

My heart danced a little Irish jig in my chest. Sure. Why not? But my nightmare of the night before lurked at the edges of my consciousness, an insidious poison. *We know you have it.* How long would it take them, the men who were coming to dump me in the ocean, to figure out that I was still on the island? How long would it take them to track me down at Jack's house?

"I'd like that," I said, unable to meet either pair of expectant eyes. "I'd like that so much . . ."

They waited.

"It's just—I told my clients I'd be back by the third. I'm lucky they haven't abandoned me already."

Esme's face fell. "Daddy," she whined.

Jack went back to eating. "Melissa has to go home, Ez. She has to work." A few minutes later he got up to clear our plates. "Finished with your eggs, Ez?"

She nodded, scooped Gemma into her arms, and left us, but not before throwing me another disappointed look. Jack kept his back to me at the sink.

I stayed at the table, feeling like a skunk at a picnic, while Jack washed up the plates. "I'm sorry to disappoint her. I just don't think it's a good idea."

He dried his hands on a dishtowel, looking thoughtful. "What were you so afraid of?"

I stared.

"Last night. When you woke up. You said you were afraid."

I wanted to brush it off, to say it was nothing, but his gaze was so searching, I couldn't. Jacey's voice, the awful accusing note in it, invaded my thoughts. *You mean I was in danger and you didn't tell me?*

"I had a nightmare. I dreamed he came back. Not just came back, but was in the house. With the three of us."

"Who? The brute who roughed you up?"

"Yes."

He hung the dishtowel carefully over the back of Esme's vacated chair and sat down in his own chair. "Don't take this the wrong way. But as a substitute teacher, I was required to take some training in recognizing trauma. I think you need to talk to someone."

If only it were so simple, I thought. He was trying to help me, I knew, trying to be kind. And to tell him the stark, ugly truth —that talking to someone wouldn't make me any safer, maybe even the opposite—would only alarm him, possibly even frighten him for his own and Esme's safety. And I wasn't about to do that. The only thing I could do at this moment would be to thank him for his kindness—for taking me in during the storm— and to remove myself as far away from Esme and him as possible.

So I said, "You're right. I do need to see someone."

After breakfast, they walked me back to the Sutton place to finish my packing. A fresh, cool breeze blew in off the water, promising a return to fair weather. The only real evidence of the storm was some downed branches and a thick carpet of green leaves, wrenched off the trees by the previous day's wind. They rustled like autumn leaves as we walked through them.

Catherine Sutton's house was undamaged by the storm, I was relieved to see. I watched Esme run across the front yard and hurl herself at the lowest branch of the beech tree before I turned to Jack. "I really do wish I could stay. You have no idea how much. But my life is so complicated right now."

"You don't have to explain," he said and went off to grab Esme, hanging upside down from a branch and swinging recklessly back and forth. "We'll come down to the harbor to see you off," he called before they headed towards home.

I finished packing quickly and went through the kitchen throwing out all the mostly empty packages and condiment bottles. Another text from Tom came through as I sprayed cleaner on the stovetop and counters and wiped them down. *Hey, I'm getting worried. Please let me know you're okay.*

I knew I couldn't ignore him this time. *I'm fine,* I texted back. *Sorry I haven't been in touch. Just getting ready to leave the island.*

He answered immediately. *Safe journey home. Call me when you're ready to talk.*

Will do, I texted back and pocketed my home.

Gar picked me up in the golf cart in time to catch the noon ferry. I sat with Juju on my lap in his carrier, my luggage piled in back, the way I had when I arrived. The cart bumped over broken branches, jostling us. The harbor itself had survived the storm intact except for a sailboat that had slipped its mooring and was jammed up against the boat in the next slip.

True to his word, Jack was waiting at the pier with Esme to say good-bye. I hugged them both, Esme first and then Jack, a hug that lingered a few extra seconds.

"For God's sake, take care of yourself," he said, his face taut with fatigue, his eyes bruised-looking.

I tried to smile. "Thank you for your kind—"

"Daddy," Esme cut in. "I don't like saying good-bye. It's too sad."

"I don't either," Jack said. "But Melissa has to go home."

"Is Melissa coming back?"

"I hope so."

"I will," I said to Esme. "I promise."

I was wheeling my suitcase down the ramp to the ferry when I heard Esme ask Jack, her small, clear voice carrying across the distance between us, "Daddy, can we ride on the golf cart on the way back?"

I swallowed my tears until I was on board, then turned my face to the open water and let them fall.

Chapter 34

"You don't look like you've had much of a rest," my mother said, suspicion and reproach at war on her face when I showed up at her condo five hours later. Nor was she happy with the damage to the Corvette's dashboard, which she soon discovered. I was forced to eat crow, kicking myself that I hadn't found the time to get it fixed before I returned the car, for breaking that promise to myself. In an attempt to placate her, I apologized for not inviting her to spend a few weeks with me on the island during the two months I was there. "You wouldn't have liked it though, Mom," I couldn't resist adding. "Way too many bugs."

Aside from driving the Corvette to a local vintage car dealer to be repaired, I spent most of my short visit in my bedroom in a deeper funk than when I'd visited at the end of June, before I left for the island. No text from Jack asking me if I'd arrived safely —that surprised me a little—but another one from Tom, clearly sensing that something had changed. *Some new developments I know you'll want to hear about. Hope you're not thinking of pulling the plug.*

I wanted to call him, of course I did, but every time I thought about doing it, I wondered how I could possibly tell him what I'd learned from Ralph without admitting to my fling with him. Worse than the shame that overwhelmed me was the sickening fear that, even if we had a case against Reg, I'd compromised it by letting Ralph—his loyal lieutenant—into my bed. I was increasingly paranoid, too. I'd watched enough episodes of *The Good Wife* to know that cell phones were not secure, that anyone could be listening in on your calls, that nothing was beyond the reach of the investigators the top law firms routinely employed to get dirt on the opposing side. As soon as I talked to Tom, *they* would know it, and my lurid imagination was only too happy to contemplate what they'd do to shut me up.

So I stared at the text bubble from the one person who could help me, and let it go unanswered.

And then, the last night I spent at my mother's, just before bed in my time-capsule room with John Cusack's brooding gaze watching over me, another text arrived that wasn't from Tom or Jack.

We need to talk.

It wasn't a number I recognized, but somehow I just knew.

I willed myself to stay cool, to not react. *Seriously?* I texted back.

Yeah seriously.

About? I typed.

I think you know.

Oh right, the thumb drive. *We know you have it.* That was why he was getting in touch. My anger, uneasy in its shallow grave, exploded out through my fingertips. *How dare you contact me? You're lucky I haven't pressed charges.*

It took him longer to respond this time. *Melissa, you need to be smart here.*

Maybe so, but my hothead self was back, the one who didn't think through the angles, who just reacted, consequences be damned. *It's gone. I threw it off the ferry.*

Seconds passed. Our conversation bubbles shimmered on the phone screen in the dark bedroom. Seconds turned to minutes and no other bubble popped up. At last I powered down my phone. He'd disappeared back into the ether from where he'd come.

Part III:
A Well-Constructed Lie

Chapter 35

Jacey and I ran into each other's arms at the Sacramento airport like sisters separated at birth. "My God, you're so thin," she murmured, her arms tight around me. There was so much I wanted to tell her, but so little I had the courage to say. If we could just settle back into the daily rhythm of our friendship, I'd be the happiest person alive.

Smoke veiled Route 50 on the forty-minute ride home, swirling in the slipstream of the passing cars like fog on the Maine coast. It had been a dry summer even by California standards, the third year of one of the worst droughts on record. The smoke was even thicker as we arrived on our cul-de-sac, a brush fire burning visibly on a distant ridge. It had been burning for days, barely contained, Jacey said. In other words, welcome home.

But the threat of an engulfing natural disaster barely registered against the welter of emotions crowding in as we pulled into my driveway. I'd tried to sleep on the first leg of the flight home, to lose myself in the movie playing on the tiny screen on the seat-back in front of me, but thoughts of Jack kept intruding, of possibilities cut short, of all the words held back in the final minutes before we parted. He still hadn't called or texted, a silence that was unexpected but understandable. I cringed when I pictured myself showing up on his doorstep—wild-eyed, my hair in tangles, blurting my irrational fears. I was the woman who slept with a gun under my pillow, who took two, sometimes, three showers a day, because I still smelled Ralph on me. Clearly, I was in no shape to enter into any kind of romantic liaison, I realized, as the plane flew over the endless, flat rectangular fields of the Midwest. So I didn't text him either, even though I badly wanted to.

Perhaps it was even possible that all my obsessing about Jack was, at bottom, a distraction. The truth was I dreaded going home, dreaded the moment when I would cross the threshold into the house I'd shared with Andy for the last four years and my million memories of him would come flooding back, the painful everyday reminders of the life we'd lived together, the life that would never be ours again.

That moment was upon me now.

"You're awfully quiet," said Jacey, as she switched off the engine. "This must be difficult for you."

The house was dark behind the overgrown shrubs, the terraced steps leading up to the front door unlit. A tiny shiver of fear insinuated itself into my sorrow. "I'm fine," I lied. "Just tired. Exhausted actually. It's been a long day, hasn't it, Juje?"

After enduring two flights and a two-hour layover in Phoenix without food or litter box privileges, my long-suffering feline was restless in his carrier, eager to be on familiar turf again. One of us was glad to be home, at least.

"Do you want me to stay for a few minutes while you get settled?" Jacey asked as we unloaded my luggage from the back of her SUV.

I shook my head. "It's late. Go home and feed the kids. They must be hungry."

We deposited my bags just inside the front door and then hugged again. I thanked her, my voice a bit unsteady now, for picking me up at the airport and still being part of my life. I watched her back out of the driveway and turn toward her own house further down the cul-de-sac before I stepped inside and closed the door.

It struck me as I moved from room to room switching on the lights—how little of Andy's spirit seemed contained within those four walls. Or mine, for that matter. My plants were green and thriving thanks to Jacey's water globes, but everything else about the rooms felt lifeless and alien. What had made me think we'd ever been happy here? In our bungalow in Folsom, we'd been happy together. In this house, we'd drifted apart.

I stayed long enough to hug and feed Juju, to change out of my grimy travel clothes and shower, then fled down the cul-de-sac to Jacey's, where I reconnected with her and her kids over Tex-Mex salads and iced tea. I entertained them with descriptions of the beauty of Mizzen Island, the shocking cold of the Atlantic even in July, and how Juju had dined on lobster when the cat food ran out. The kids giggled, but Jacey's smile turned puzzled at my Juju story and I looked away, afraid she'd read the truth in my eyes. I could only imagine what her reaction would be if I confessed my torrid weekend turned violent with Ralph or admitted I'd come dangerously close to falling in love with Jack. When the kids went outside to shoot baskets in the driveway, I got up to leave too.

"Are you okay? I mean, really?" she asked as she walked me to the door. "I was hoping you'd come home . . . refreshed."

I feigned a laugh. "Right? Like that meditation book. Wherever you go, there you are."

"Oh, Mel. You're going to get past this. You know that, don't you? Eventually."

"Hopefully before I'm eighty."

Out on the driveway, eight-year-old Brian dribbled around his eleven-year-old sister in the smoky dusk and shot a perfect basket.

"Swish!" Jacey called. "Way to go, Bri!"

"He's a natural, isn't he?"

"Getting there. Cassie used to kill him but not anymore. He's upped his game since basketball camp." She turned back to me. "So how did you leave things with gallery guy?"

Gallery guy.

"We said good-bye. We were friends, that's all." Did she hear the catch in my voice? "Besides, his six-year-old daughter was the one I was really in love with."

The house smelled of smoke when I got home, even though all the windows were closed tight and filtered air whispered out of the central air vents throughout the house. The back of my throat felt scratchy and my eyes stung a little, but the sealed-up quiet bothered me more. I wanted to throw open my bedroom window, to be comforted by the dull roar of the surf at the edge of the lawn, to drift off to sleep knowing that Jack and Esme slept a quarter mile away.

Instead, I undressed in the bedroom where my marriage to Andy had played out—the king-size bed where we'd never managed to conceive a child, the closet full of Andy's lifeless clothes. I lay down, weary but sleepless, Andy's side of the bed stretching away from me like an empty field. Just seventy-two hours ago, I'd drifted off to sleep in the curve of Jack's warm body, but that memory already seemed impossibly distant. My eyes flicked open repeatedly to the unfamiliar patterns playing across the ceiling from the streetlights on the cul-de-sac, the random cars passing by.

My thoughts drifted to Tom, wondering how long I could resist his questions. Being back in California without his protection felt foreign, even dangerous. I tried to comfort myself with the thought of him lying awake in his own bed, the bloodhound in him still trying to piece together Reg's role in Andy's death. But any comfort was short-lived. My wide-awake brain churned up all the other things I was determined not to think about: a faceless intruder roaming the house, this bedroom. Hands in surgical gloves rifling through my underwear drawer, Andy's desk upstairs. The uselessness of our expensive alarm system. Ralph standing over me fingering the Walther, deciding whether or not to pull the trigger.

I got out of bed and lifted the blind. Three houses away, Jacey's bedroom light was still on. I picked up my phone and called her. "Can I sleep at your house tonight?"

"Sure," she said, as if she'd been expecting my call. "The guest room is all made up. The sheets might smell a little musty, but—"

"I don't care. I just can't stay here."

"Then come on over. I'll give you one of Cassie's teddy bears, if it'll help."

I laughed. "Thanks. Just—no questions, okay?"

A small silence. "Hey, of course. No questions."

I called the security company the next morning to upgrade our home alarm system. It was probably foolish to think even the most high tech system could keep out an intruder who was determined to get in, but I knew it was important to take back some semblance of control.

The truth was I was scared, even more scared than I'd been during my last two weeks in Maine when I went to bed every night wondering if that would the night the men would come to deep-six me. My options were painfully limited, though. Turn the thumb drive over to Ralph or turn it over to Tom. Ralph or Tom. Tom or Ralph. One night, too restless to settle down, I stood Hello Kitty on the kitchen counter and studied her like a totem from a primitive culture, praying for guidance. Ralph or Tom? She didn't answer, of course, so I walked away and left her there, hoping that if somebody broke in while I was sleeping, they'd scoop her up and go in peace.

In the meantime, until an answer became clear, I tried to get on with my life, emailing clients to reestablish contact and drum up some work, because without a distraction, I feared the uncertainty of my situation would break me in two. I spent most evenings at Jacey's, whether she was home or not. When she worked late at an event, I put dinner on the table for the kids, supervised homework, and saw them off to bed. My own nights were a battle with worsening insomnia, and I was soon at the pharmacy drive-thru window picking up a refill of my sleeping pills, even though I hated the idea of knocking myself comatose when I needed to be semi-alert even as I slept.

For the first week or so, Tom continued to reach out by text.

Hey, please keep in touch. I'm ready to press the reset button at any time.

Then a couple of days later: *Trust you got back from Maine okay. At least let me know you're all right.*

Each attempt to contact me spurred another wave of guilt and just plain sadness, because I'd lost not only a private investigator but also a friend. *I'm okay,* I texted back finally. *Just trust me on this. Please.*

Soon afterwards, his final bill arrived in the mail. I stared at the seriously low amount due and thought it couldn't possibly represent the number of hours he'd actually spent on the case. That same afternoon, I wrote a check to pay the bill and added an extra thousand dollars to help defray the costs I was sure he'd incurred even if they weren't spelled out on the invoice.

It was time to focus on something positive, the one truly hopeful thing on my calendar at the moment. Warren's wedding to Bernice was set for the third Saturday in October. The invitation arrived the week I got home, putting to rest my uneasiness about Warren's peculiar silence during the months I'd been away. The four of us had been close friends, after all, and Andy would have been Warren's best man. Riding on the strength of our past friendship, I picked up the phone to call Warren one evening and was surprised when Bernice answered.

"Melissa," she said. "So great to hear from you." But underneath the warmth of her greeting was an edgy, worried note.

"Bernice, is everything okay? You sound—"

"Warren is in the hospital. He got in a bike accident yesterday."

"Oh no, Bernice. Is it serious?"

"He's going to be okay," she said quickly. "He's just really banged up. Just a broken collarbone and a separated shoulder, thankfully. And some broken ribs."

"Yikes, that is serious. But—how did it happen?"

"Some rider out at Prairie City forced him off the trail and he went down a ravine."

"Jesus," I whispered.

"The creep didn't even stop to see if he was okay," Bernice said, angry now. "He just took off."

I knew I could very well be overreacting—in fact, I probably was—but all I could think of was the patrolmen in my living room at three o'clock in the morning, the baby-faced officer's look of pity. Not again. Not someone else.

"Can I visit him?" I asked.

"Sure. He'll be home in a couple of days. We'd love to see you."

"What about the wedding? Will you have to postpone?"

She laughed then, sounding more like the Bernice I knew. "Not on your life. That dude will be at the altar waiting for me on the twenty-fourth, even if he's in a body cast."

I laughed, too, but I wasn't laughing later as I roamed the house, unable to settle. The buzzing, unreal feeling was back.

Warren's loft condo was in an upscale neighborhood just east of midtown Sacramento, in the shadow of the state capitol. As I turned onto the lushly landscaped grounds and parked in front of the balconied stucco building, it occurred to me it was the kind of high-end property David Escondido might own through one of his shell companies.

"Melissa!" Bernice greeted me with a hug at the front door and led me up a short flight of stairs into the open-concept living/ dining area. Officially she still lived with her mother in Carmichael, but the arrangement was more or less for appearances' sake. While Warren's taste in interior decoration ran to the sleek minimalist, his fiancé's softening influence was evident everywhere: in the potted herb garden in the sunny kitchen window, the Peruvian flat weave rugs covering the gleaming hardwood floors, and the colorful throw pillows on the pristine dove gray wraparound sofa, where Warren himself was ensconced in his bathrobe, his right shoulder in a cast and his upper torso swathed in bandages. His face was pale and his jaw shadowed with unfamiliar black stubble, but no one expected him to be his usual immaculately groomed self under the circumstances.

"Dude, seriously?" I said, walking over to him.

"Pretty lame, right?" he said, attempting a grin.

"Don't get up," I joked as I leaned down to hug him.

"Ha ha. Funny. It's great to see you."

"So how are you feeling?"

"Better. Not so sore today. It'll be a while before I hit the trails again, though."

"I should say."

Bernice sat down next to Warren and rested her head on his shoulder, a rare display of open affection for the usually reserved couple. It hurt a little to see their happiness, to be in their company without Andy, but it felt good to be part of normal life again, too—if witnessing the extent of my husband's best friend's injuries after a bike trail hit-and-run could be considered normal.

A moment later, Bernice left us to go to the kitchen and breezed back in carrying a tray with three glasses, a pitcher of iced tea, and a platter of lettuce wraps and sushi.

"That looks absolutely delish," I said, realizing how empty my stomach was. "I hope you didn't go to too much trouble."

"There's an Asian grocer a couple of blocks from here," Bernice said. "It's the best thing about this neighborhood, right, Warren?"

She fixed a plate for her fiancé and we all sat on the sofa as we ate. Our first topic of conversation, not surprisingly, was the accident.

"I can't believe the guy didn't even stop," I said, outraged for both of them.

"Right?" Bernice said.

Warren merely shrugged, oddly unfazed. "Maybe it freaked him out so bad, he just had to get out of there."

"Is there any way you could report him?"

"I know most of the people who ride out there, but I never saw this guy before. Hey, I'm just lucky somebody else came along and helped me. It was getting dark and my phone was halfway up the ravine with my bike."

His laconic words conjured a disturbing image: Warren thrown off his bike and tumbling through underbrush down the steep slope. I'd been to Prairie City a few times to watch the bike races and knew how treacherous the terrain was. Bernice and I exchanged a horrified look.

"It could have been worse," he pointed out, reading our expressions. "At least I was able to do a tuck and roll. If I'd landed on my neck—"

Bernice groaned, pressing her hands over her ears. "Okay, okay. Time for some happier talk. Melissa, I'm *sure* you want to hear about the wedding, right?"

"Of course," I said, relieved to switch gears. "Tell me everything."

And that's what Bernice did, visibly relaxing the more she talked—who was invited, what the bridesmaids would wear, what the dinner menu would be. The wedding would be held in San Francisco, where many of Warren's and Bernice's family members still lived. She brandished her phone to show me the photos of the elegant hotel venue and I oohed and aahed, enjoying the girl talk. If there was anything positive about the circumstances of my visit, it was that Andy's death was no longer the elephant in the room. She and Warren spoke normally, not in the hushed tones everyone had used at Andy's memorial party. There was a tacit understanding that life had moved on just enough that it was now okay to talk about something joyous and hopeful in front of me.

When we'd exhausted the wedding talk, we talked about my summer in Maine. The good parts, that is. What we didn't talk about was the investigation into Andy's death. Neither of them asked me how that was progressing.

When Bernice stood to clear our lunch dishes from the coffee table, I offered to help but she waved me off. "No, stay and talk to Warren. He's going bat crazy not being able to get around."

"I'm sorry I didn't answer your texts when you were in Maine," he began, looking a bit shamefaced, when it was just the two of us facing each other.

"Hey, I understand," I said quickly, anxious to put him at ease. Based on the misery in his eyes, I sensed it wasn't really an opening to talk about Andy's case.

"So, you must be working from home while you're recuperating," I said, trying for a less freighted subject.

If it was possible, he looked even more uncomfortable. "It's kind of hard to teach a class from the living room sofa."

"Teach a class? What are you talking about?"

"I'm at UC Davis law school now, teaching intellectual property law."

"Warren, whoa. Back the truck up."

"I resigned from WP at the end of the July."

I stared, too shocked to speak. "Why?" I managed at last.

He puffed out a small sigh, his face going a shade paler. "Let's just say it was made clear I had no future there."

"Because you were Andy's friend?"

He didn't answer. But he didn't have to.

"Oh, Warren."

"I don't plan on teaching for long," he assured me. "I thought I had a job with Valparaiso and Breem locked up before I left WP, but they pulled the offer at the last minute. That was a surprise."

"I bet."

I felt sad for Warren, and angry too, because I saw Reg's fingerprints all over the loss of the job offer. Reg, the maker and breaker of men. My outrage was building again, but I sensed that it would be wrong to show it, that Warren just wanted to shut the subject down.

He winced and shifted his position on the sofa.

Amid the clatter of dishes being rinsed and loaded into the dishwasher, Bernice called from the kitchen, apparently telepathic. "Do you need another pain pill, *bae*?"

"Nope, *bae*, I'm good for now," he called back. He reached up to his encased shoulder with his good hand, but let it fall back to his side with a grimace.

"Is it an itch?"

He nodded. "Feels like fire ants crawling around under there." A rueful smile. "Sorry, no complaining."

The awkwardness was back between us, big time. There was a new elephant in the room—the price Warren was apparently paying for being Andy's friend.

"For what it's worth," I said at last, "I think you did the right thing by resigning. If only Andy had—"

"You can't go there, Melissa. What good will it do?"

I knew I should keep quiet, that Warren was doing his best to politely telegraph his unwillingness to talk about it. But Tom's credo was doing mischief in my head. *I don't believe in coincidences.* I glanced toward the kitchen, where the dishwasher had started to hum and Bernice was wiping the counters.

"Hey, Warren?" I said.

He looked up sharply. "Yeah?"

"That guy forcing you off the trail at Prairie City. Is it possible it wasn't an accident?"

A complicated emotion worked its way over his features, revealing the toll the experience had taken on him. "Melissa, just stop, okay? I know you're not happy with the coroner's ruling about Andy's death. And I'm not either. But I just . . . can't be involved in all that right now. I'm sorry. I have to keep my head down and get on with my life."

I barely had time to feel hurt by his rebuff before Bernice appeared in the kitchen doorway, a mischievous smile on her face. "Are you guys ready for a truly decadent dessert?"

The landline was ringing when I arrived home later that afternoon, thoughts of Warren's sinister accident crowding out other worries. I answered the call absently, barely registering the unfamiliar number, but the voice of the caller was unmistakable.

"Mrs. Stevenson."

My body stiffened. "Detective Roussekoff."

"I'll cut right to the chase," the detective went on in her curt, impersonal way. "We've recovered your husband's briefcase."

"You—really?"

"A rancher turned it in. He found it on his property in a dry wash that runs under County Road."

"How do you know it's Andy's?"

"Your husband's briefcase was monogrammed, correct? AMS?"

"Of course," I murmured, feeling like an idiot.

"It was empty, but fingerprint analysis also confirmed it's your husband's."

"That's good news."

"That said, we'd like you to come in and ID the briefcase."

"Were there any other prints on it?"

"None we've been able to identify."

Hunh.

"But how did it get there—I mean, by the side of the road?"

"We can't be certain, but it's possible it was thrown from a passing car."

Andy flinging his briefcase out his car window on the way home from work? I tried to picture it, but couldn't. Not in any universe I belonged in. "Okay," I said slowly, "but why would my husband do that?"

I should have known from my earlier conversations with Detective Roussekoff that it was the wrong question to ask.

"People under the influence of drugs sometimes do strange things," she said with a maddening matter-of-factness.

I bit down on a hostile response, hope turning to bitter disappointment. Jesus Christ, not this again.

"That said," she went on.

"Yes?"

"Here at the sheriff's office, we're asking ourselves the same question."

In the kitchen after we'd hung up, I popped open a Diet Coke and studied Hello Kitty, perched on the kitchen countertop where I left her, one white paw saluting me. In my brief conversation with Darla Roussekoff, I could have disclosed that I was in possession of a thumb drive that contained tangible proof of a motive for Andy's murder. But I still didn't trust her. She'd tamped down the investigation once. I hated to think what she'd do with this new, more damning evidence. The truth was, there was only one person I trusted with that evidence.

And another truth—I was never going to get my life back until this was settled.

I could have sworn Hello Kitty was smiling, even though she had no mouth. My oracle had spoken.

Chapter 36

M y handwritten letter disappeared into the mailbox outside Safeway.

I need to talk to you. But don't call or text me at the usual number. Meet me at the Eldorado National Forest trailhead on Route 50 at 10 AM this Saturday. It was the trail Andy and I used to frequent on weekend hikes. If anyone tried to follow me there, it would be hard for them to escape notice on the winding, sparsely traveled two-lane road up into the Sierra Nevada range. At the bottom of the note, I scrawled the number of the disposable phone I'd picked off a rack at the mall. I signed it "M."

His terse reply came by post a couple of days later: "See you there."

The highway spooled out behind me in the razor sharp October sunlight as I drove east on Route 50 the following Saturday morning. I kept my eyes trained on the rearview mirror, but the nearest vehicle was a good distance back. When I pulled into a turnout, the Ford sedan drove past at a leisurely speed. I noted the Utah plate and the elderly couple inside, and relaxed.

There was one other vehicle parked at the trailhead when I arrived—a black pickup with a dirt bike in the truck bed and a "Jesus votes Republican" bumper sticker on the tailgate. His truck? Unlikely. I was a few minutes early, so I locked my car and climbed the stepped trail to the granite boulder in the copse of scrub pine where I'd taken shelter, hungover and nauseous, the day I went AWOL after Andy's memorial service. Already four months ago.

A soft breeze rose from the valley floor, bringing with it the smell of juniper and pine needles toasting in the sun. Car doors closed in the parking lot below, intruding on the ambient quiet. Less than a minute later, a young couple in hiking gear appeared on the trail, walking fast. I watched their backs recede into the wilderness and checked the time on my phone. Five minutes past our rendezvous time. What if he'd decided not to come after all? What if—

I looked up at the sound of a throat being cleared on the trail below. His familiar form, lanky and long of stride, in a plain white T-shirt and baggy shorts, bobbed toward me through a screen of tinder-dry brush, his balding head bare to the sun.

Tom. Thank God.

He caught sight of me and stopped, then flashed a crooked grin that melted away my anxiety. "Mrs. Stevenson."

I smiled too. "Hey, Tom." I glanced behind him.

"Don't worry, I wasn't followed," he said easily, and ambled over to sit beside me. He spent a few long seconds just taking me in, his eyes searching my face. "Well, you look like you're okay, so that's one worry off my plate. Why the secrecy? Has something happened?"

"Lots, actually." I felt myself blushing, but more from the comfort and relief of his sudden physical proximity than from embarrassment.

"Tell me."

I hesitated.

"As a friend," he said. "Doesn't mean you have to reopen the case."

I looked away, my nerve starting to fail me. "The truth is, I don't know where to begin."

"Let me help you out. You found the thumb drive and then you dropped the case. How come?"

Here goes, I thought. "Ten minutes after I opened the thumb drive, I got this cryptic text. *We know you have it.*"

"From?"

"Some number I didn't recognize."

"But you took it as a threat?"

"Wouldn't you?"

"You're scared now, I can see that."

I nodded.

"Did something else happen?"

Damn Tom and his uncanny ability to read me. I picked up a broken piece of scrub pine and started picking the needles off it. "A few weeks before I found the thumb drive, Ralph Gutierrez tracked me down on the island."

His body went taut beside me. "And?"

"He gave me some bullshit story about Reg sending him there to offer me money as compensation for Andy's voided life insurance policy. He tried to get me to invite him inside, but I wouldn't, so I agreed to meet him for dinner at the restaurant down by the docks. I didn't know how else to get rid of him." The little pine branch was bare of needles now. I ran it between my thumb and forefinger, wishing there was some way I could avoid saying what had to come next. "I never liked him, and I sure as hell didn't trust him showing up like that, but, I don't know, I guess I was lonely. Maybe I just miscalculated how hard being alone on that island was going to be. Anyway, he was acting like my new best friend and I was *stupid* enough to be taken in by it." If a magnitude seven quake had struck at that moment, I would have welcomed it. "I . . . let him spend the weekend with me."

Tom's gray eyes gave nothing away. Being Tom, I assumed he was judging me and trying to hide it.

I had to swallow a couple of times to get my tongue unstuck from the roof of my mouth. "I feel so ashamed."

"Hey," Tom said gently. "You did nothing wrong. You're a consenting adult."

Until I wasn't, I thought, thankful that he would never know that part. "You mean you're not going to slut-shame me?"

His tone turned harsh, almost angry. "For God's sake, be kind to yourself. How else are you going to get through this?"

"I just feel so dirty."

"Destroying people is their stock and trade," he said, his voice gentle again. "You don't have to play along."

"It's not just about *that*, though that's bad enough. It's that I walked right into it—"

"He was there for the thumb drive, wasn't he?"

"The morning he left to go back to California, he had an argument with Reg on his phone. As soon as he hung up, he confronted me. I kept telling him I didn't have the thumb drive, but he didn't believe me. He told me he couldn't go back empty-handed. I was stupid. I should have gotten the hell out of there, but I pushed him and he—.

"Christ," Tom muttered, a rare profanity for him.

"I ran for the gun, but he got there ahead of me. For a minute I thought he was going to kill me."

Tom's face turned to stone. "What stopped him?"

"Conscience? Some shred of decency? Fear of blood?"

The warm breeze sifted through the stunted pines along the trail. A motorcycle passed on Route 50 below us with a fading whine. I remembered the last time Tom and I had sat on a boulder together, that day on top of Cadillac Mountain when he'd told me about Reg's longstanding connection to David Escondido, the reluctant drug kingpin.

Tom blinked a couple of times, as if coming out of a trance. "You want some iced coffee? I have a thermos in my car."

"Yeah, sure."

I followed him back down the trail to the parking area, where he pointed his key fob to unlock a faded green Subaru wagon without bumper stickers. The car unlocked itself with a chirp. Tom's stomach gave an audible growl. "Sorry. Early morning stakeout. Beef jerky can only go so far."

In the muddled world I'd inhabited since Andy's death, I'd come to think of myself as his sole client. The news that I wasn't almost made me jealous.

He reached inside his car for the thermos tucked into the center console, then came out empty-handed. "What the hell," he said, "let's drive back down the road to Placerville and have lunch. I know a little café there that's got a righteous apple-rhubarb pie."

Righteous. I smiled in spite of myself at the innocence of the proposal, so at odds with everything I'd just told him. "You think it's safe for us to be seen together?"

He shook his head in disgust. "Those bozos have been terrorizing you long enough. It's time to start fighting back."

Chapter 37

A ragtag line of forty-niners with long beards and pickaxes gave us a gaunt collective stare from a black-and-white photo on the pine-paneled wall next to our booth. Tom cocked his head at it. "Attractive bunch, weren't they?"

I laughed and put down my menu, deciding on the avocado BLT. "The sheriff's office has Andy's briefcase. A rancher turned it in."

"Yeah, I heard," he said, surprising me. His glance turned sheepish. "I have a contact in the sheriff's office. He's been keeping an eye open for any, erm, developments." He watched the server approach our back corner to pour coffee and take our order.

"Speaking of developments," I said, as she walked away with our menus. "Before I came home, you texted that you had something to tell me."

It was only eleven-thirty, a bit early for the lunch rush—if sleepy Placerville even had one—but Tom gave the restaurant with its cheery gingham curtains and retro lunch counter a surreptitious once-over before leaning closer. "Right. Our eyewitness in the Hyatt garage finally agreed to talk to me. She's been reluctant to come forward because the man she was out to dinner with that night isn't her husband."

"Figures," I muttered.

"Anyhow, they were exiting the garage in their car when they passed three men who appeared to be helping a fourth man

—who appeared to be drunk or otherwise incapacitated—to his car."

I took a swallow of the hot, bitter coffee. "What did the fourth man look like?"

"She didn't get a good look because his head was down and the other men were blocking her view. The only reason she remembers the encounter at all is because she's a part-time EMT and she asked her companion—not her husband—to stop the car so she could see if they needed help."

"So they stopped?"

He shook his head. "It was getting late and they'd both been drinking, and her companion didn't want to risk it. Apparently he was more interested in getting home to his wife."

Adulterers everywhere, I thought, and might have allowed another wave of bitterness to sidetrack me if the scene the woman had witnessed weren't so potentially important. "What about the three men who were 'helping' the other guy? Did she get a good look at them?"

"Unfortunately, no. Keep in mind that she saw them for literally ten, fifteen seconds tops as they drove by. What she remembers—at least the detail that stayed with her—was that two of the men were dressed casually, but the third guy was in business attire—and carrying a briefcase. It seemed like an odd detail to her."

"Casually how?"

"Jeans, hoodies, she thinks. Dark clothes—she was specific about that."

"Baseball caps?"

He smiled faintly. "You ask all the right questions, kid. Maybe. She wasn't sure."

"What about the guy in business attire? What did he look like?"

"Again, her memory is fuzzy. Dark-haired, maybe. Young. Younger than the other two guys, she thought. You know what the lighting in that garage is like."

"Huh."

He studied me, his fingers toying with a packet of raw sugar. "So what are you thinking? I see the gears turning."

"I'm thinking the guy in business attire was Ralph."

Excitement sparked in his eyes, quickly tamped down. "Say more."

Reluctantly I told Tom what I'd pried out of Ralph the night he shared my bed—that Andy had arrived at the Hyatt dinner high on coke and a pissed-off Reg had ordered him to go home. And Ralph's feigned reluctance as he delivered the coup de grace. *I ran into Andy in the men's room before the dessert course. He was pretty messed up. I offered to drive him home, but he laughed, said he wasn't going home.*

Tom's eyes grew bright as I repeated Ralph's statement word for word. "You realize what this means, don't you? That Warren Cheung wasn't the last person your husband talked to that night. The men's room encounter was after the dinner."

And then I remembered Warren's words at Andy's memorial, how they'd penetrated my drunken fog. *He just got up and left. I thought he was going to the men's room, but he never came back.* It stunned me, the obviousness of it. How could I have missed it?

"Ralph's story contradicts Warren's by a lot," Tom said, watching me. "Which one do you believe?"

Sitting in a tiny café in a rural town three thousand miles from where my bedroom drama with Ralph had played out, I didn't have to think twice.

"Warren," I said. "Hands down."

Tom leaned closer across the table. "So consider this. Why would Gutierrez lie to you about what happened that night?"

"Because he was involved. Because he was in the garage that night with Andy."

We broke apart, startled, as two plates of food were put down in front of us. "Anything else for you folks?" the server asked.

"Not right now," Tom muttered. "Thanks."

The aroma of bacon wafting up from my plate made my salivary glands ache. I realized how hungry I was, hungrier than I'd been in months. But I wasn't ready to start eating yet. "I'm right, aren't I?" I whispered as the server moved on to another table. "You know I'm right."

Tom took a healthy bite of his turkey club and chewed thoughtfully for a few seconds. "Knowing something isn't the same as proving it."

I groaned in frustration.

He held up a hand. "Yeah, I know you get tired of all the cornpone wisdom I dispense—"

It was just the kind of Tom remark I needed to break the tension. I snorted with laughter, loud enough to cause the biker-looking guy at the counter to look over at me. I didn't care. How had I gone so long without Tom in my life?

My private investigator flashed a gratified grin. "So let's go back over what we know about the night your husband died," he said, as we both ate. "First scenario. Your husband was a busy man that night. He showed up at the company dinner high, quarreled with the boss, was told to get lost, left the dinner but somehow had time to stop off in a hotel room long enough to lose his phone and maybe have a romantic assignation. Then a half hour later he was out on County Road throwing his briefcase off a bridge. Does that sound plausible to you?"

"No. It doesn't sound like Andy at all."

"A good defense attorney—and you know Wolders will hire the best if he's ever charged," Tom went on, "could make it hang together, mostly, except for the time frame. So let's look at the counter-arguments, the case for the prosecution. Second scenario. Your husband called you before the dinner, sober, and told you he wouldn't be late that night. His friend Warren said he was drinking club soda all night and left the dinner perfectly fine —early, in fact, like he promised, because they had a plan to go mountain biking the next morning. Your husband left the dinner at nine-forty-five, but his car wasn't picked up on video leaving the parking garage until ten-twenty. That's the crucial thirty-five minutes that's still unaccounted for.

"What we do know is that an eyewitness leaving the garage at the same time as your husband saw three men helping a fourth man to his car. That the driver of your husband's car left the parking garage wearing a baseball cap that never turned up in the deceased's possessions. That your husband's car was followed out of the garage by a stolen vehicle that just happens to be owned by an employee at one of David Escondido's casinos, which ties him indirectly to Wolders."

He dragged the last of his fries through the smear of ketchup remaining on his plate. "And now we're learning that your husband's briefcase turned up in a dry wash on a rancher's property a mile down the road from where he was found in his car—possibly the briefcase the unidentified man in business attire was carrying in the garage—and that there's a plausible alternative to your husband throwing his own briefcase off that bridge. That in all likelihood it was somebody else driving his car, and it was this other man—let's call him Mr. Baseball Cap— who disposed of the briefcase after emptying it of its contents. So what's going on here? In my experience, there's usually not much daylight between the truth and a well-constructed lie, but there's always some, and in this case the daylight is beginning to stream through."

"What about Andy's phone being found in that hotel room?"

"That's a sticking point all right. But what does it really mean? Did he in fact stop by the hotel room on his way to the garage and, if so, why? Or was his phone planted there later? Again, why? Was he meeting a romantic partner, or was he killed there? That's why it's imperative that we nail down what happened during those missing thirty-five minutes. Without it, all we really have is circumstantial evidence that points to foul play."

"So what's our next move?

"For now, the safest option for you is to give Gutierrez what he wants."

"Excuse me?" I almost choked on my last mouthful of bacon and avocado.

His response was deadpan. "The thumb drive."

"Seriously?"

"If it means getting them off your back so you can return to some semblance of normal life, yes."

"But I told Ralph I threw it in the ocean."

"So you lied."

"But . . . are we just going to give up? Let them win?"

"Not at all. The obvious next step is to see what's on that thumb drive. I've got my data expert on standby, ready to look at it."

"But you told me not to open it."

"Yeah, I did, and I'm sorry I didn't warn you about that earlier. The truth is I didn't think it would turn up. One of the files your husband uploaded was probably booby-trapped, but there are ways around that, trust me, and the data expert we use is one of the best. "

"And then what?"

"Depends on what's on it. My guess is that whatever it is is pretty damning.   If there's enough to support a racketeering charge, it automatically becomes an FBI matter." He wiped his mouth with his napkin. "I hope you brought it with you."

"You bet." I fished in my bag and placed Hello Kitty on the table between us.

Tom's perplexed look dissolved into an appreciative smile. "Your husband had a sense of humor."

"He did," I said. "It's one of the things I loved most about him."

Chapter 38

Early the next evening, much sooner than I expected, Tom called on my disposable phone to tell me he'd turned over the documents on the thumb drive to the FBI. "There's enough evidence to support a RICO charge all right," he reported. "Against Escondido *and* Wolders. But here's the shocker. The Bureau has already opened an investigation into Wolders. He's been under surveillance since June. Turns out Hello Kitty, ahem, is just a copy. Which, if you think about it, makes sense. Your husband handed the files over to the feds a few days before he died."

For several long seconds I was speechless.

"You still there?" Tom asked.

"I—it just explains so much." Andy's tense behavior in the last days of his life. His secretiveness. It wasn't because he was having an affair. It was because he was about to betray his boss to the FBI. "No wonder Reg wanted Andy dead."

"As a motive, it cuts both ways," said Tom. "Strains credulity to think Wolders would have the balls to order a murder if he suspected he was the subject of an active investigation. On the other hand, if he was trying head off an investigation by having Andy killed before he turned over evidence—well, the motive for murder just got a lot stronger."

I stayed silent, struggling between immense relief that Andy's actions were finally beginning to make sense and horror that Reg almost certainly was behind his murder.

"So we did it, right?" I said at last. "We've nailed Reg."

"It certainly explains why they're leaving you alone. Two suspicious deaths would be a lot harder to explain away."

"You say it like there's some bad news."

He didn't answer right away. "There's one big question hanging out there. I've been in the biz long enough to know how these investigations can play out. Will you be satisfied if Wolders gets put away for his criminal dealings with Escondido but walks for Andy's murder?"

"Could that happen?"

"If the feds think they can use Wolders to get to Escondido, chances are they'll be open to a plea bargain."

A door that had creaked open to emit a tiny sliver of light slammed shut again. "Of course," I said bitterly. "Why wouldn't they?"

"Sorry, kid," said Tom. "Welcome to the criminal justice system. There's a lot of evidence pointing to murder, but as I said, it's all circumstantial. What we really need at this point is a confession."

In other words, I thought, we're screwed.

I hung up and went back to my computer screen and the brochure I was working on for a new client, a medical devices start-up with enough graphic design work to potentially keep me busy through the end of the year. It would be a much-needed slug of income while I figured out whether I could afford to stay in California without Andy's life insurance payout, and I didn't want to screw it up by turning in my first job late. But thoughts of my conversation with Tom kept intruding on my progress.

It came to me while I was fiddling with a microscopically small Illustrator adjustment on my iMac screen. An answer to our problems.

I picked up my disposable phone and texted Tom. *I have an idea, but I don't think you're going to like it.*

He called immediately, despite the late hour. "Okay. I'm listening."

The silence on the line said it all as I told him what I was thinking. I waited for him to weigh in.

"You're right. I don't like it much. It's risky. You have no idea how much could wrong in a situation like that."

"But I think it could work," I pushed, undaunted.

What made me so sure? Because Ralph could have shoved me off Cadillac Mountain during the thunderstorm, or drowned me during our evening swim, or shot me with Tom's Walther while I was cowering on the floor of the cottage. But he didn't. Here I was, sitting in my study at home in El Dorado Hills, still alive.

Why?

Even if I was too ashamed to spell it out for Tom, I was pretty sure I knew the reason. Because Ralph wanted me more than he wanted the thumb drive.

"It won't be admissible in court," Tom went on, his tone as icily wary as I'd ever heard it. "And it's hard to fool a lawyer. You'll have to be damn persuasive."

"I know," I said, excited and terrified at the same time.

He sighed, relenting. "But maybe, just maybe, you can shake something loose that we can use."

Chapter 39

I spotted his Porsche parked down the cul-de-sac a half-hour before our agreed-upon meeting time, but he stayed in the car, watching the house. No doubt wondering if he was walking into a trap. I didn't blame him. I would have been suspicious, too, given the circumstances. But his wariness didn't help to calm my nerves. *You can do this*, I pep-talked myself, going from the bedroom window to the bathroom mirror to check my appearance and back to the window at least five times before he pulled into the driveway at eight o'clock sharp and got out carrying something.

A large bunch of yellow roses bobbed toward the front door in the blue-black twilight.

Roses.

He'd brought me roses.

The evening had barely started and already I was losing my nerve.

Did he think when I'd texted him that I was asking for a date?

Get a grip, I answered myself. If that's what he thinks, so much the better.

I almost felt sorry for him—the way the bouquet quivered in his hand as he approached the steps.

"Roses," I said as I opened the door. "They're . . . beautiful."

"The least I could do." His eyes grazed mine, the irises black. Did I read shame there, or was it just wishful thinking?

He was dressed casually this evening—a black T-shirt, black jeans, the same black cotton hoodie he'd worn on our "date" on the top of Cadillac Mountain. An intruder's outfit. My insides clenched as the familiar musky scent of his aftershave floated in on the evening air.

"Come in," I murmured.

He stepped over the threshold and bent his head toward mine, throwing me off balance again. I took a step back then yielded reluctantly, allowing his lips to graze my cheek. He was freshly shaved, but I could already feel the stubble wanting to push through his skin.

We separated.

"I thought you hated me," he said, relief in his voice.

I do hate you. I just can't hate you tonight.

"You look great, by the way," he went on.

What I was noticing, in the recessed lighting of the front hall, was how not great he looked. Beneath the sickly fragrance of his aftershave, a sour smell came off him in little whiffs and his eyes were bloodshot, as if he hadn't slept in weeks. I'd seen that hunted look before—Andy arriving home from work in the last months of his life.

His black eyes darted around, taking in the surroundings. "You alone?"

"Of course. Why wouldn't I be?"

The ghost of the old Ralph smile made an appearance, here and then gone. "Right. Why wouldn't you be?"

I could see, in the way his jaw clenched as he swallowed, his shoulders squared defensively, that he was as nervous as I was, maybe more. He handed me the bouquet, the paper wrapper damp from his sweaty grip. "Mind if I have a look around?"

"Knock yourself out."

I trailed behind him as he made the circuit, through the dining room to the kitchen to the back hall, poking his head in the laundry room and powder room before moving on to the study, and then back around to the front of the house. He stopped on the threshold of the master bedroom, looking.

Hands in latex gloves pawing through my underwear drawer, searching.

Maybe it was the king-size bed that threw him, neatly made but suggestive of the beating heart of my marriage to Andy. Or perhaps it was the more homely reminders of our life together — the jar of loose change on my husband's dresser, untouched since his death, the framed photo of me next to it. He turned away without entering.

"Don't you want to check the closets?" I asked, still holding his bunch of roses. Stop, Melissa, I chided myself. This isn't the way you want this to roll.

His eyes flicked to the stairs instead.

"Go ahead, I'll wait here," I invited, praying the basement wouldn't be next.

But he backed off with a shrug. "Feels a little weird being here, if you want the truth."

I'll bet. Returning to the scene of the crime. One of them, at least.

"How about a drink?" I said.

"If you're having one."

He followed me to the kitchen. I deposited the roses next to the sink, resisting the urge to throw them in the garbage instead. I brought out a bottle of Glenlivet and a short glass for him, a bottle of Sauvignon blanc and a wine glass for me.

He planted himself on the other side of the island, watching me. "You don't know how much I've missed you."

I poured the scotch into his glass without answering. Glug glug.

"And how shitty I feel about what happened," he went on. "You have to believe me about that."

Outside the kitchen windows, the ground lights illuminated the terrace and pool, the surrounding tangle of shrubbery. It was another warm night, too beautiful a night for this, the task at hand. But there were so many beautiful nights in the California desert.

"Ice?" I asked.

"Please."

He came up behind me as I opened the freezer, his body hard against mine. "I'll make it up to you, I promise," he whispered into my hair.

I whirled on him before I could stop myself. "Don't. Please."

He stepped back, surprised.

Don't blow it, I told myself. For God's sake, don't blow it. I dropped some cubes into his glass and handed it to him, then reached for the bottle of wine. I poured a splash into my glass, hoping he wouldn't notice how much my hand was shaking.

"Sorry," I said. "I'm just, you know . . . after what happened."

"Yeah."

"Before I forget." I reached into the kitchen drawer and placed Hello Kitty on the counter between us.

His stare was blank. "What's this?"

"The thumb drive?"

He picked it up almost disinterestedly. "Hello fucking Kitty? Andy was one sick fuck."

Something felt wrong. Where was his triumphant smirk?

He dropped Hello Kitty back on the counter. "So you didn't throw it off the ferry?"

"No. I told you. I lied. Sorry."

Stop saying you're sorry.

"So why are you giving it to me now?"

A cold trickle of perspiration sprang from my armpit. "I want it to be over. I just want to get on with my life." I'd prepared myself for the question, but how lame it sounded spoken out loud.

"Right," he said softly. "Turn Ralph in and get on with your life."

Shit.

"Excuse me?" I managed.

"A federal agent paid me a visit the other day. He was interested in how much I know about Reg's business dealings."

"Wow."

"Surprised? I wish I could believe you."

"Why would I do that? Even if I wanted to, what makes you think they'd listen to me?"

"Maybe you have a story they want to hear."

I took a careful sip of wine. "There are worse things than cooperating. If you know something—"

He scooped Hello Kitty back into his palm. "They know too much. Things they couldn't *possibly* know unless they had what's on this."

"I didn't, Ralph."

"Don't lie to me, Melissa. Please. Don't lie." He said it softly, almost seductively, but that only chilled me more.

Tom, I thought. *Tom.*

I stepped back instinctively, out of reach. "If you hit me again—"

It startled him, my change of tone. His olive skin went pale and sweat beaded on his forehead. I wondered if he was about to be sick.

He pocketed Hello Kitty and reached for his drink. "I won't," he muttered. "I promise. Never again."

"You want to sit down? We could go into the living room."

He nodded and followed me without speaking, bringing his drink and the bottle of Glenlivet with him. We passed through the unlighted dining room to the living room, where the lamps at either end of the sofa cast a soft light.

Outside the windows the streetlights glowed peacefully along the cul-de-sac. I sat down in an armchair with my glass of wine. Ralph set his glass on the coffee table, then still holding the scotch bottle, crossed the room to peer out the front windows. He yanked one blind shut and then the other before taking a seat across from me on the sofa. He was silent, his elbows on his knees, his head down.

"Ralph?"

"Sometimes I see him," he said, his voice almost a whisper. "When I'm in the men's room taking a piss. In the parking garage when I'm leaving work. At night when I'm lying awake. He's there. "

I held my breath at the admission.

"You want to know the real reason I came here?" He raked a hand through his short black hair, made stiffer with product. I tried not to think about how it had slipped through my fingers when I'd grabbed onto it in bed. Like an animal pelt. "Because you're the only person . . ."

"The only person who what?"

"Who can possibly know what I'm going through." His bleary eyes met mine. "Look, I know what I did was unforgivable, but you can't begin to appreciate how much pressure I was under when I came to visit you in Maine."

Visit you. Just another summer guest. "Tell me."

"Reg," he started, then stopped.

"Reg what?"

"You don't know what a shitshow my life at WP has become. The Mexican-American homeboy. Give *him* all the dirty jobs. The jobs nobody else wants to touch."

"What kind of dirty jobs?"

"The jobs Reg wants done."

"What are we talking about here?"

It was hard not to read his tortured look as guilt.

"Ralph," I said gently. "Are we talking about Andy?"

He laughed, swiped his hand over the sweat beaded on his upper lip.

"Do you know how Andy died?"

No answer.

"Were you there when he died?"

Another head shake.

"Did you kill him, Ralph?"

He looked up sharply. "No."

"Okay," I said gently.

"How can you even ask me that? You think *I'm* so bad? You think I'm a killer? You want to thank somebody for the fact that you're still alive? Thank me."

"Okay."

"Okay? That's all you can say?" He took another gulp of scotch. "Reg was pissed off that you hired a private investigator. He thought you were going to make trouble for the firm. It doesn't take much to make major clients bail. They smell blood in the water, they're gone. He was about to send some, let's call them emissaries, up to that island of yours to rough you up, scare you so you really got the message . . ."

"Rough me up? Or kill me?" *His hand slipping out of mine on Cadillac Mountain.*

He studied what was left of his drink. "I talked him into sending me instead."

Right. Better to be killed by someone you know.

"Why would Reg want me 'roughed up' unless he had something really awful to hide?"

"You know I can't answer that question."

"Come on, Ralph. Why are you protecting him? You said he treats you like shit. What has he done to deserve your loyalty?"

"He pays my father's medical bills, for one."

"Well, good on him. Is that worth going to prison for? Or worse? Where would your father be then?"

"You think I haven't thought about that?"

"So leave. Resign. Walk away. The way Warren did. The way Andy should have."

"It's way too late for that."

"So talk to the FBI. Tell them what you know."

"Right. Spend the rest of my life in witness protection in some shitty North Dakota prairie town? No thanks. The whole thing's a joke anyway. They'd kill me first."

"Who?" I asked. "The feds?"

No answer.

"The Escondidos?"

He snorted. "You know about them? Why am I not surprised?" He tipped two more fingers of scotch into his glass. "How? Andy?"

"No. My God. Do you think Andy would have put me in danger by telling me something like that?"

"That private detective then?"

"Maybe."

"Shit. Where is he, by the way? The WP investigator says he disappeared off the radar."

"I don't know. I dropped the case awhile back."

"Come on, Melissa, don't bullshit me."

"I'm not."

"So why?"

"I just got tired. I couldn't get past the fact that Andy cheated on me."

"Right. Andy the cheater."

"What's so funny?"

"Andy the Eagle Scout, cheating on *you*? Melissa, get real. I thought you were smarter than that."

For a few long seconds I forgot to breathe. "What are you saying?"

"I'm saying it was all a set-up, standard operating procedure. A woman approaches you at the bar, gets you to buy her a drink, slips something into it when you're not looking. Suddenly you're woozy and she's leaning over you saying, 'Are you all right? Let me help you to your room.' Maybe she even gets somebody from the bar to help, too, because your legs are wobbly like you're stupid drunk. Except she doesn't take you to your room, she takes you to *her* room, where you pass out cold on the bed. Then she leaves—but not before she sprinkles perfume on the sheets, maybe leave a pair of panties behind. The next thing you know it's morning and you're waking up in her bed, alone, thinking how in shit did I get here."

I stared at him, horrified. "Were you part of this? Was this part of your job description?"

Another swig of scotch. "What did I tell you? I get the dirty jobs." For a moment, contrition, or maybe just more self-pity, won out over cynicism. "But no, I wasn't involved in that one. Reg set it up. Personally."

I leaned forward in my chair. "Why, Ralph? Why? Why would Reg do that to Andy?"

"Because Andy wasn't smart. Maybe he was this brilliant lawyer, maybe he was Reg's idea of the son he never had, but he just didn't know how to play the game. Reg handed him the most lucrative cases in the firm and he wasn't happy. He took a moral stand, refused to be part of it. Reg tried to send him a warning, hoping he'd come around. But he just got more self-righteous, like he was asking to be—" He stopped.

"Asking to be what?"

Silence.

"What, Ralph? Killed?"

He wouldn't look at me.

"Ralph? Was Andy asking to be killed?"

He looked up slowly. "Are you recording this?"

My heart dropped in my chest. *Not now*, I prayed, *not now when we're so close.*

"No," I said, "I'm not."

"Where's your phone?"

"In the kitchen."

"Show it to me."

I brought it to him. He scrolled through it suspiciously and then powered it off. But that wasn't enough to reassure him. I sensed him pulling away from me. In a minute the gulf between us would be too wide to pull him back. I leaned even closer to him, across the coffee table. "Ralph. You say no more lies. Well, I say no more lies too. If you care so much for me, then tell me. Please. Tell me who killed Andy."

"I can't."

"Why not?"

Anger flared in his eyes, mixing with desperation. "Because they'll kill me, too." He shifted in his seat, looked over his shoulder as if he expected Andy's ghost to appear. "You still don't get it, do you? Every time I go into that parking garage, I think this is it, the night I get a bullet in the back of my head."

"Would Reg let that happen to you?"

"I committed the cardinal sin. I came back from Maine without getting the job done."

"You mean finding the thumb drive?"

"No. He wanted you dead, Melissa."

"He *said* that?"

"Not in so many words, but he didn't have to."

It would be hard to imagine my blood running any colder.

"He didn't trust me anymore. He accused me of being more interested in protecting you than in finishing the job."

"I suppose I should thank you for that, at least."

He looked up, pathetically hopeful. "Yeah, you should." He seized my hand. "Melissa, come on. Let's blow this joint. Let's get the hell out of here. You think you're any safer than I am? You should have taken that half mil when Reg offered it. My uncle has a ranch down near Oaxaca. It's a nice spread. Cartel country, but we'd be safe there. You know how places like that work. He's got his own private army."

I freed my hand from his. "If I find out Reg murdered Andy, the only place I'm going is to the police."

His body went slack, the fight draining out of him. Or maybe it was the scotch taking effect. Finally. He slumped on the sofa like a cowed animal.

"Ralph, what happened the night of the dinner? You told me you saw Andy in the men's room before the dessert course. Just before he left, it turns out."

"Yeah?"

"Was he high on coke?"

He shook his head, childlike now. "No."

"So what really happened?"

A thin rope of snot dripped out of his nose. He wiped it away with the back of his hand. "I can't tell you. I want to tell you, but I can't."

"Yes, you can." I reached across and took his hand, the snot-free one. "Ralph, please. I need to hear the truth from . . . *someone*."

His eyes were two black holes when he finally spoke. "I followed Andy out of the function room when he left the dinner. I told him I needed to talk to him about a case we were trying to settle. He followed me down the corridor to where the rooms started. The guys Reg hired were waiting for him there. They walked by and grabbed him, took him into one of the rooms." His voice was a monotone, lifeless. "I went into the room with them, because that's what Reg ordered me to do. One of them had Andy in a hammerlock. The other was forcing coke up his nose. He had his hand over Andy's mouth so he couldn't breathe."

My sorrow for Andy was too much for me. I could barely keep my focus as Ralph went on.

"Then the other one gave him an injection."

"Injection?" I whispered.

"I didn't know about any of this going in. Potassium chloride. It mimics a heart attack. Undetectable. He died within a couple of minutes."

"You watched him die? Why didn't you do something?"

"Melissa, I swear to God, it happened so fast—"

"You could have fought those guys. You could have stopped it."

"You weren't there. You don't know."

"You could have come to his defense! You're a body builder, for Christ's sake."

"You think I don't know that now? You don't think if I had it to do over again—"

You wouldn't have done exactly the same thing?

"So what happened then? Those murderers dragged Andy's dead body down to the parking garage? How did they manage that?"

"I don't know. Honestly I don't. I went into the bathroom and puked and then I went back to the dinner."

I knew that wasn't true, that he'd gone with them, the guy with the briefcase supervising the thugs, making sure they got the job done, but I was not about to challenge him on it. I felt like vomiting too. "Ralph, you *murdered* my husband."

"No. I was an accomplice. Not that it makes much difference under California law. I'm looking at twenty-five to life. That is, if I'm lucky enough to serve any of it. I'm a dead man walking, Melissa. Just like Andy was."

I wasn't thinking about Tom and the plan we rehearsed. I wasn't thinking about protecting myself because Ralph was in no way threatening me. I was thinking of Andy and what he suffered in the last minutes of his life—how desperately he must have struggled. How futile his struggle must have been against two professional killers and the guy from work whose envy knew no bounds. I should have waited for Tom, but in that moment I understood completely what murder was all about, the need that could drive an otherwise sane, compassionate person to kill another human being. My hand slid down the side of the chair next to the cushion and closed around cold metal. A new nine millimeter handgun—lightweight, compact, the perfect sidearm for a woman—bought a couple of weeks ago to replace the unwieldy Walther and registered in my name. Tom had instructed me to plant it there for self-defense, in case things got rough, in the likely event Ralph turned on me to save himself.

I raised it slowly, amazed to see I wasn't shaking at all.

Ralph laughed out loud. "Oh, great. Oh, perfect. What's this? Vigilante justice? You've been watching too many movies, Melissa."

I clicked off the safety, let my finger rest on the trigger.

He was on his feet now, sizing up the situation. He touched the center of his chest. "You know what, baby? Go ahead. Right here. Aim straight. Steady arm. You'll be doing me a favor."

I sighted down the barrel. He stood on the other side of the coffee table, just a couple of strides away, his body ready to spring.

"What are you waiting for?" he taunted. "Shoot me. Just do it and get it over with."

My finger closed on the trigger, but froze, unable to squeeze it. The sane part of me woke up. *Shit. Where was Tom?*

"I didn't think so," Ralph said softly. "You don't have the killer instinct. Neither did your loser husband." His body remained still, all the coiled energy in his brain now. I could read it in his eyes. Calculating what to do next. "Okay, you know what? I'm outta here. I'm going. You can shoot me in the back if you want." He spun on his heels and made for the front door.

A metallic double click split the quiet, Tom racking the slide on the Walther. "I'd rethink that, pal," his disembodied voice said. He advanced slowly from the shadows of the dining room in a shooter's stance, the Walther trained on Ralph.

Ralph stopped and raised his arms slowly, his back to both of us.

"On the floor, pal," Tom said. "Face down."

"Bitch," Ralph said and spun around. The next instant he was on top of me, grabbing for my gun. An explosion filled the room. Smoke and the smell of cordite. Ralph's body crumpled and writhing on the floor, a stain blooming on the front of his black jeans, blacker than black. His groans and curses muffled by my ringing ears.

Tom stood over me, his mouth moving. *You okay?*

I nodded.

His free hand reaching down to gently pry the gun from my fingers. "Nice work, kid. He's lucky you didn't aim any higher."

My ears kept ringing. "Huh?"

"You shot him, not me."

Ralph gasped through gritted teeth, "I'm bleeding out here. You gonna call an ambulance?"

"You'll be fine. She barely grazed you."

"How the fuck do you know?"

"The bullet's in the wall behind you." Tom picked up his phone just the same.

I sat there catatonic, only now aware of the jolt radiating up my firing arm.

"This is total fucking entrapment here," sputtered Ralph.

"A subject you perps know something about," said Tom, and turned away to speak into his phone. " . . . Self-defense shooting . . . 15233 Ledgewood Circle . . . adult male down with a thigh wound, non-life-threatening."

Ralph trained a look of pure hatred on me, and something else too. Hurt. Betrayal. Blood oozed out between his fingers as he pressed down on his wound. "You're a bitch, Melissa. A stone-cold bitch."

I wanted to tell him I was sorry, because in a way I couldn't even begin to understand, I was. But the room was full of smoke and my ears kept ringing. "Yeah," I said. "And don't you forget it.

Chapter 40

The fall rains started a few weeks later, putting out the last of the brush fires in the surrounding hills. Our cul-de-sac was saved for another year from an engulfing conflagration. I wandered the house in my fleece, shivering, because our too-spacious El Dorado Hills home was not cozy that time of year.

For a while after Ralph's arrest everything was quiet, as if the whole ordeal had been some fever dream. But slowly the details of the scandal Andy's murder was meant to conceal began trickling out. First came the stunning news of Reg Wolders' indictment for real estate fraud as a principal of the American River Group, a scheme involving the misappropriation of hundreds of thousands of dollars of investor money in a luxury retirement community that never got built. The limited liability company was now in receivership, with Reg facing serious jail time and his beloved Napa vacation property seized.

Days later, a more subdued item appeared in the Sacramento Bee, as shocking in its own way as the story that preceded it. It announced the dissolution of Wolders Palmer the law firm. With one of its name partners under federal indictment and the other long deceased, the future of the firm had become untenable. As usually happened in these situations, several of the remaining partners had banded together to form a new partnership, hoping to retain the majority of the client base under a new, untainted firm name.

I tried to ignore the media coverage, sickened that the crime that had cost Andy his life was being used as clickbait, but the downfall of one of Sacramento's leading attorneys, with ties to the statehouse, had sent the local news outlets into a feeding frenzy that was almost impossible to avoid. As much as I resented the in-your-face coverage, I resented even more that a big piece of the story—the heart of it for me—was going unreported. So far, as Tom had predicted, there was no mention of Reg being charged with murder. That, apparently, was the carrot the feds were dangling to get him to flip on his long-time friend and partner in crime, Escondido.

Until one night in late November. I'd spent the day cleaning out closets because I'd just put the house on the market and there was a lot of stuff I wouldn't be able to take with me, wherever I ended up. Collapsing into bed wearily, I reached for my laptop out of habit, only to open my web browser to the lurid headline. *Accident or murder? Wolders implicated in death of law associate.*

"Oh my God," I muttered, my fingers madly scrolling, "oh my God."

Past the ads and filler, the flashing attempts to make me jump to another page, I came face-to-face with a photo I'd never seen before: three men in black tie at an unnamed San Francisco event. Two older men—silver-haired, paternal, aging gracefully —flanking a much younger man, fair-haired and attractive, his smile framed by familiar ditches in his cheeks.

Andy.

The man to his left was Reg. I didn't recognize the man to his right, but knew instinctively, by a prickling on the back of my neck, that it must be David Escondido. Dark-eyed and handsome in a spare, genteel sort of way, there was nothing about him that said drug capo. If anything, he looked more like a college professor in his retro wire-rimmed glasses. But the haughtiness in his bearing gave it away, and the caption confirmed my suspicion: *Wolders, Stevenson and Escondido at San Francisco charity event.*

I had no memory of attending such an event with Andy, and certainly no memory of ever meeting Escondido. But there was my husband, standing between Reg and Escondido as if caught.

I picked up my phone to call Tom, as I usually did when a fresh story broke, seeking the comfort of hearing his wry take on the latest revelation. But it was much later than I realized—almost midnight—so I put down the phone and started reading. The accompanying story, an investigative piece, was explosive, delivering a new twist on Reg's ignominious end.

His crime, at bottom, was more desperate than Tom or I could have imagined. It wasn't about helping Escondido launder drug money through a limited liability company under the guise of building a luxury retirement community, although that was part of it. It wasn't even about embezzling investor funds for personal gain. It was about the betrayal of a friend by a friend.

For Reg, as an equal partner in the American River Group—ironically one of Escondido's legitimate business ventures—had betrayed Escondido's trust by skimming from their joint venture to pursue his own dream, a vacation home in Napa with a winery attached.

"What was Reg thinking?" I asked Tom the next morning, scarcely able to believe it. "Getting crosswise with Escondido and the cartel?"

"I think it's safe to say the bromance is dead," he replied, terse to the end. And doubtful, he added drily, that Reg would survive prison very long before retribution found him.

The motive, the investigative piece pointed out, remained murky. All those years watching Escondido run his criminal enterprise, with no consequences. Did the temptation to emulate his friend, to get away with his own crime, just prove too strong? After years of being in the toilet, the California real estate market was finally red hot again. Plenty of time, Wolders must have told himself, to replace the funds he was siphoning off. The one thing he hadn't planned on was Andrew Stevenson, his trusted associate, the man he was grooming to be his successor at Wolders Palmer, blowing the whistle on him.

"So Reg didn't have Andy killed to protect Escondido," I mused, the missing piece of the puzzle clicking into place. "He did it to save his own skin."

"Looks that way, doesn't it?" Tom said.

I would have years to try to make sense of what drove Reg, already a wealthy man, to murder my husband for the sake of getting even richer. But right at that moment, there was something else I needed to understand. If I had any hope of getting past Andy's death.

It was something Tom said, the day he'd visited me on the island and we'd stood ankle deep in the water of Seal Cove. The questions he asked: *How much of a zealot was your husband? Instead of putting his life at risk, why didn't he just resign? Does that make sense to you?*

Sitting in bed with my laptop, the night the story broke, I surrendered myself to what was right in front of me, as painful as it was—the photo of my husband gazing out at me, handsome in black tie, the familiar ditches in his cheeks. How could you have put yourself in such danger? I asked him silently. How, when you had everything to live for? Why couldn't you just walk away? Hang out your shingle in Genoa and let us live happily ever after? Was justice so important to you? Or was it more personal than that? Did you feel betrayed by Reg, the father you wished you'd had, for letting you down so badly?

I tried to read his expression, wanting desperately to understand, as he stood there frozen in time, caught between Reg and Escondido. But his black-and-white image yielded no answer, nothing to explain his fatal decision. Just a wistful smile that didn't quite make it to his eyes.

Chapter 41

*T*hree *months later.*

The snow was coming down hard when I left the office building, icy flakes slanting through the iron-gray air. It was already piling up in the gutters and crosswalks along Boylston Street, where pedestrians' tromping feet turned it to slush. It was the first blizzard of the winter, at least the first one I was getting to experience since my return to a northern climate.

It was only two-thirty in the afternoon, but the sidewalks were crowded with people leaving work early to get home ahead of the storm. I walked quickly with the flow toward the Arlington T-stop, the icy flakes peppering my wool hat and new winter jacket and dripping their metallic taste into my mouth. Water coalesced around particles of pollution, that's all a snowflake really was, I reminded myself, but I was as thrilled as an eight-year-old with a sled that the city around me was slowly turning white.

Inside my coat pocket, the faint chirp of an incoming text reached my ears over the stalled traffic noises. I was tempted to ignore it, but curiosity won out over my desire to get home, so I ducked into the Au Bon Pain I was passing and dug out my phone, hoping it was Jacey or Tom, the two friends I missed most from California.

The message bubble appeared on the screen. *Esme says hi.*

And then a couple of seconds later, *Jack says hi too.*

In the time it took me to breathe in and out, my legs turned to jelly and my phone almost slipped through my fingers. I stood just inside the doorway and stared slack-jawed at the screen like some idiotic Millennial, which, of course, technically I was. My pride told me to pocket the phone and just go back out on the street in the snow. Did he really think he could text me to say hi and everything would be chill after all this time? But I stayed where I was, half-blocking the entrance. I pulled off my right glove with my teeth and tapped the keyboard tentatively.

Hi back.

His reply came seconds later. *Thinking of you in warm California. It's cold as a witch's well you know what up here in baltic Maine. Just wondering how you are.*

I studied his message long and hard, like an Egyptologist in front of a just unearthed hieroglyphic. A guy in an even puffier jacket than mine jostled my arm as he exited the restaurant, trailing the aroma of steaming coffee from the paper cup clutched in his gloved hand.

Jack again. *Of course feel free to ignore this feeble text. Wouldn't blame you at all . . .*

I sat down at the nearest empty table and typed. *Not in California anymore. Moved to Boston.*

A swift reply. *That's big. Can I call you??*

Oh, God, I breathed. *On my way home from a job interview. About to get on the T.* My fingers stopped and then plunged on. *I'll text you when I get home.*

Brilliant, he texted back. *Will be great to talk to you.*

The entire way home, on one lurching, screeching, jam-packed subway car to Park Street and then another to Cambridge, and finally on the too hot, standing-room-only bus from Kendall Square to my stop on Huron, I warned myself not to expect too much, that it would probably be just a friendly call prompted by cabin fever, which I imagined must be rampant on Mizzen by this point in the winter. But excitement buzzed through me as I burst through the door and kicked off my boots, slung my dripping jacket over a kitchen chair, and shed my damp clothes in a pile on the bedroom floor. I changed into my warmest fleece pajamas, lit the gas fireplace, and made cocoa, drawing out the moment before I texted Jack to tell him I was home, because anticipation is half the thrill of anything.

It was getting on for late afternoon and gray, snowy light filled the apartment, the corners in shadow as I carried my phone and steaming mug of cocoa to the sofa. I'd lucked out on the rental, the whole second floor of a Craftsman-style two-family on a quiet tree-lined street off Huron Ave. in Cambridge—a two-bedroom with hardwood floors, glass-fronted cabinets in the kitchen, and an enclosed sun porch off the living room. The rent should have been staggering, but the elderly owners who lived downstairs were more interested in having a reliable tenant than charging a sky-high rent. The truth was I could have afforded something a lot more upscale now that I had Andy's insurance money and the proceeds from the sale of the El Dorado Hills house, but I had a taste these days for a modest life in modest surroundings.

He called me as soon as I texted him. "It's good of you to take my call," he said, his faint Irish lilt thawing my frozen extremities more effectively than my warm pajamas, roaring gas fire, and hot cocoa combined. "You've probably got me down as a tosser, not getting in touch all this time."

I laughed. "Not at all. I was such a mess when I showed up at your house that day. I was sure I scared you off. But I'll never forget your kindness."

"So how are things? Better, I hope. What's brought you to Boston?"

The need to feel close to Andy, I could have said, the Andy I knew before we moved to California. Instead I talked about the murder case, telling him everything—well, nearly everything— over the next hour, as the winter light faded from the windows. He listened, mostly without commenting, as I related that my husband *was* murdered, that the name partner in the firm had been indicted for investment fraud and, thanks in part to my private investigator's work on the case, was now awaiting trial for Andy's murder. I didn't tell Jack of my own involvement in the case—how I'd tricked my former attacker, who was also an accomplice in the murder, into a confession that ended with him lying shot on my living room floor. Or how, after the shooting, I'd been subjected to a tense few interviews with the El Dorado Hills police myself, even though I'd shot Ralph in self-defense.

"Wow," said Jack after a stunned silence, "that's a lot to go through. I knew you were in trouble last summer, but Jesus . . ." *Jaysus*. "So it's behind you now?"

"Yes, thank God." I crossed my fingers as I spoke.

"New start on the East Coast?"

"Yup."

I didn't ask him what prompted him to finally get in touch with me, but I thought I detected it between the lines of his breezily delivered account of life on Mizzen since the previous summer. The loneliness of a long, hard winter on an isolated island, the regret that maybe he'd let something promising slip away. He was telling me about pipes freezing in houses all over the island during a frigid Valentine's Day weekend when Esme's chirpy voice interrupted him. I could almost see her hanging on her father's arm, trying to get his attention about some picture she'd drawn.

"How *is* Esme?" I asked.

"Her irrepressible self, as usual. What do you say, Ez? Do you want to say hi to Melissa?"

An enthusiastic shout. A soft explosion of breath came through my phone and then a giggle.

"Esme, how are you? I've missed you!"

Silence. Suddenly shy. Then, her small voice, "Are you coming to visit us?"

"Yes, I'd love to."

"When?"

"You'll have to ask your dad."

"I don't want you to go home next time."

"Enough, Ez," Jack said, taking the phone back before I could answer. He was laughing, most likely to cover his embarrassment. "Esme, unfiltered. No one can accuse my daughter of not putting it out there."

I laughed too, but my heart was pounding in anticipation.

"But it's funny you're in Boston now," he went on. "I'm bringing Esme down for a wee visit for spring vacation. We do it every year. Just to get away from the island for a bit. Stay in a swank hotel, visit the museums, take a ride on a Duck boat."

"Go ice skating!" Esme said in the background.

"And what else, Ez?"

"Swimming!"

"Swimming?" I asked, picturing the L Street Brownies plunging into Boston Harbor on New Year's Day.

"The hotel we stay in has an indoor pool."

"Oh, of course." *Duh.* I was about to suggest that maybe they would like to stay with me, but the indoor pool nixed that idea.

"You could come over for a swim," Jack said, apparently reading my mind. "We'll take you out for a fancy dinner."

"I'd love to."

He turned away from the phone. "Ez, would you like Melissa to come swimming with us when we're in Boston?"

From the jerky way she shouted "Yes!" I could tell she was jumping up and down.

"That settles it, then," Jack said. "It appears you're going to be stuck with us."

Neither Reg nor Ralph had yet to stand trial during my first months in Boston, but time had a way of hurtling forward regardless of the circumstances. Already in the rear-view mirror was Warren and Bernice's October wedding in San Francisco, a joyous occasion for all, followed by my exhausting but hopeful move to the East Coast. I landed the contract job at the Boylston Street publishing house where I'd interviewed the day of the snowstorm, and with work to structure my days around, and Jack and Esme's April visit to look forward to, there were days when life actually felt bearable again.

I would never truly finish saying good-bye to my husband —would never wish to—but the part of me that was slowly healing recognized the need for some sort of closure on the past year's tragedy. In early March, I made the two-and-a-half hour drive to Wilton, Connecticut, where Andy's ashes lay at rest in the churchyard adjoining the Episcopal church. It was a still day, not a hint of a breeze, a bright crust of snow on the ground, the sky powder blue and cloudless. Robins chirped in the bare branches overhead as I stood in front of the plain granite marker. Andrew MacLeod Stevenson, Beloved Son and Brother, 1981–2015.

Beloved husband, too, I thought, stung by the omission. But really, what could I expect after my shameful behavior leading up to the funeral? I'd sent Liz a long email after the case was concluded, telling her of Tom's work as an investigator, letting her know that Andy was neither a coke addict nor an adulterer, and apologizing for letting my anger and doubt override my grief.

I received a guarded reply thanking me for my honesty, but nothing more. I'd learned through Warren, who still had friends from his time at Wolders Palmer, that the Stevenson family had filed a wrongful death suit against the dissolved firm. Winning a civil suit was a flimsy sort of justice, I knew, but I hoped it would bring them a measure of solace.

As for me, I stood at Andy's grave and for the moment was genuinely grateful for the warmth of the sun on my face, the quiet of the churchyard, the fine person my husband had been, and the twelve years we had together.

I dreaded the first anniversary of his death, imagining when the day came I'd relive every painful moment of it, but I'd relived it so many times already that the day itself was not much worse than any other. It arrived with beautiful late spring weather, the sun hot but tempered by a mild breeze. The kind of day New Englanders restlessly waited for each year, a signal that the long, cold spring typical of coastal Massachusetts was at an end. Rollerbladers glided past me and sailboats tacked on the brilliant blue Charles as I found the bench on the Esplanade where Andy and I had first met. I closed my eyes and pictured him on his rollerblades reaching out his hand to me after I'd fallen, his faded Life is Good T-shirt, his ragged smile as he assured me it was easier than it looked, that all I had to do was find my center.

All at once I was sure in a way I hadn't been until now that he'd forgiven me for my recent transgressions—not only my fling with Ralph but for ever doubting him in the first place. For my part, I'd try to forgive him for dying prematurely and taking the best part of my life with him.

As I walked slowly back to my car in the dry, bone-warming heat, I reminded myself, as I often did, how much there was to look forward to. In a few weeks Tom would be making his annual trip to Boston to visit Eileen, and I'd finally get to meet the sister I'd heard so much about. Jacey had promised to visit with her kids in August, and I already had a plane ticket to visit her and Tom in California in October. Maybe best of all, Jack and I had fallen into the habit of daily texts since his April visit with Esme.

Lights out. Thinking of you, he'd text as I lay in bed reading before going to sleep.

Thinking of you, too, I'd text back. *Did you have a good day?*

That our relationship remained undefined was understandable, I told myself—it was early days, after all. Still, it provided much fodder for my tendency to dwell on things. There seemed no doubt that his interest in me was romantic, but then again maybe it was just a warm friendship. So far, he appeared content to leave things long-distance and noncommittal. In the absence of a clear answer, I fed on the details of his April visit with Esme, in particular the night I'd invited them to dinner at my place and we'd stayed up talking on the enclosed porch off the living room. Esme had nodded off on Jack's lap, exhausted by our afternoon of swimming in the hotel pool, and she lay draped across both of us, her pink-socked feet in my lap, abandoned to sleep the way only young children can be.

Jack took my hand and rubbed his thumb over my mine as I tried to make sense of my vague unhappiness in my last year with Andy. "I stopped growing," I said. "I was living in his shadow. I was living in reaction to who he was."

"Isn't that what married couples do?"

I held Esme's warm little foot with my free hand as I talked. "It's not like we wouldn't have gotten past it. We would have stayed together, I'm sure of it."

His eyes, full of kindness, found mine in the April dusk. "I'm sure you would have, too."

A streetlight lit up the branches of the tree in front of the house, black and bare. The warmish spring evening was cooling fast and I let go of Esme's foot to reach for the afghan draped over the back of the loveseat.

"Cold?" Jack asked and slid his arm around my shoulders, the way he had the night of the storm. He let it rest there, lightly.

"I admire you for taking the time to sit with your grief," I told him, made bold by his closeness, the companionable darkness. "I didn't want to sit with my grief last summer. I wanted it to be over, so I could move on."

"And what about now?"

His proximity was making me lightheaded. "I don't know."

"Be gentle with yourself. There's no timetable for grief. When Kerry died . . ." he stopped as if it still hurt him to say the words. "I had to stay positive for Esme, but I was dead inside, an emptied-out shell. For a very long time."

"When did you come back to life?"

He laughed softly. "That beast of a hot day when you and I were doing the framing for the exhibit. You scared the bejesus out of me. That's when I knew I was still alive."

Our faces drifted closer and our lips touched, but Esme twisted in his arms and whimpered, "Daddy, you're squishing me."

They left a few minutes later, Jack carrying his sleepy daughter to the car. He held me for a moment after he'd helped Esme with her seatbelt, and promised to call me when they arrived back on the island, since they were leaving the next morning.

Two months and many texts later, the beach weather arrived, and I did what Andy and I used to do, except alone—packed up the car for the day and spent it on one Cape Ann beach or another, dragging my chair into the surf and falling into the kind of reverie that only sun, salt air, and lapping waves can induce. Often, as I sat there, I gazed northeast over the ocean toward Mizzen Island. Did I feel guilty about desiring another man so soon after my husband's death? Yes, every day. But I was thirty-three now and my experiences of the past year had taught me there were few guarantees of a long and happy life.

At last came the text I'd been waiting for. *Come up. I'll be here.*

When? I texted back.

Surprise me.

It was odd. The first time he'd said *I*, not *we*. *Me*, not *us*.

Are you turning spontaneous on me? I texted.

Hey, I'm a work in progress.

Taking extra time off over the July fourth weekend, I packed my car and headed north, my thoughts full of my last journey to the island, almost a year ago to the day in my father's Corvette with Juju. Then I'd been so desperate to get away from my grief and pain, I didn't care what lay at the end of the road. Now I knew what did, and I knew that I wanted it. But being the work in progress I was, I lost my nerve as I pulled into Southwest Harbor and texted Jack a warning, giving him a chance to still change his mind.

I'm here in SWH. Just about to get on the ferry.

!!!! We'll be waiting at the dock. A string of fireworks emoticons followed his words.

The sun was bright on the water, the breeze fresh and salt-filled out of the southeast as the ferry pulled closer and their tiny figures got larger, Jack in his shorts and T-shirt, his sandy hair tousled, Esme dancing a little tattoo as she waited. Jack's arm shot up in an enthusiastic wave when he spotted me on deck, and I waved back. Then he leaned down to point me out to Esme and together they waved again, Esme springing up and down in excitement. The ferry docked and the passengers lined up to disembark and my body was so light with excitement and gratitude, I wanted to jump up and down, too.

At last my turn came to step over the gunwale onto the floating dock. And then I was inching up the metal ramp behind the others, steep because it was low tide, my single suitcase well in hand. In a minute I'd be on land and I'd walk into their arms, Jack's and Esme's, my island friends. I wondered how losing the person I loved most in the world could have brought me here, to this moment in this place. But it had. So I kept moving forward.

The End

About the Author

Lucinda O'Neill knew she wanted to be a novelist at an early age. Her first story was a chapter book. As a teenager, she wrote several novels (still in a carton on the top shelf of a closet) and dreamed of having a runaway bestseller. She is the author of the indy novel ALMOST RIGHT WITH THE WORLD, a contemporary story of love, friendship, and second chances. Her mystery suspense novel, SPLENDID ISOLATION, was published in 2022. She lives in Massachusetts, north of Boston.